UNDERLAND

UNDERLAND

✧ BOOK 1 ✧

MAXIME J. DURAND

aka Void Herald

Podium

Podium

UNDERLAND

1

BENEATH THE EARTH

Valdemar was raising the dead in the basement of the barn when the knights broke down the door. He knew they were knights because of their metal footsteps above his head and because his protective wards hadn't alerted him to their approach. This implied the presence of at least one magician, and local militias couldn't employ spellcasters. The Dark Lords would never allow it. Just as they didn't allow Valdemar to practice magic in peace.

Unfortunately, though he was no stranger to escaping from the law, the necromancer didn't have time to flee these imperial lap dogs. He had already started the ritual and wouldn't back down. Valdemar had invested too much in this project to stop *now*. He had spent years of his life fruitlessly trying to decode his grandfather's journal, consorting with criminals to get his hands on banned occult texts, studying derro technology to fill the gaps in his spell . . . He knew it would work, if only people would just let him *work in peace*!

An otherworldly crimson light illuminated the dark basement, as the young warlock's blood circle radiated with necromantic energy. A pyramidal, ox-size machine of Valdemar's design stood at its center, a pedestal of metal plates and pipes holding a conical glass container. His late grandfather's old, black journal rested inside it, working as a focus to summon what remained of the owner's essence.

Or at least, that was the idea, but the spell demanded more. More power, more *life*.

So Valdemar, who had already lightly cut his thumb open to draw the circle, dragged an athame dagger from under his black robes and slashed his left palm open. Blood poured down his pale skin, and he applied it to the circle. The magical symbol hungrily drank his life fluid, while the machine's pipes let out crimson steam. The knights had moved to right above his head, the wooden planks creaking below their feet as they moved toward the basement's trapdoor.

"Stop this foul sorcery at once!" one of them called from above.

A translucent, greenish ectoplasm had started to form inside the flask. The ghostly matter rushed through multiple shapes as it gained strength, its surface so smooth and polished that Valdemar could see his own gaunt reflection in it. His short, messy white hair bristled from the ambient magic, and his ghost-gray eyes had turned bloodred.

"I was right!" Valdemar grinned, as the ectoplasm coalesced into the shape of a skull. "My ritual works!"

Every illegal spellcaster Valdemar had met had told him that it was impossible, and yet here he had proven them all wrong! He had pushed beyond the boundaries of magic!

The trapdoor suddenly splintered behind him, and he looked over his shoulder as lanterns cast additional light into the basement. A warrior in plate armor took a step down the stairs, the conical shape of his helmet and the golden links around his neck identifying him as a Knight of the Chain. He carried a blue lantern in his left hand and a sword in the right.

"Valdemar Verney," the knight bellowed. "Cease this spell at once!"

"Don't come down the stairs!" Valdemar warned him. "I trapped them! If you trigger my spell, I can't stop—"

The inquisitor continued, ignoring the warning, and activated the summoning array beneath the steps. A flash of violet light erupted from beneath the stairs, and green tentacles surged from beneath them. They caught the knight's legs and slammed the warrior against the wall. His lantern shattered on the ground, the ghostly fire within extinguished.

"You fool!" Valdemar scolded the knights. "I can't control it after it's summoned!"

The writhing mass of tentacles, sharp-toothed mouths open, sought the flesh beneath the armor.

"A Gnawer!" the captive knight shouted, before letting out a scream.

A tentacle had twisted his sword arm, and another violently struck his helmet. Gnawers were the weakest and stupidest of the Qlippoth extra-dimensional entities but still far stronger than any normal human. Unfortunately, these monsters only sought to feed after being called to the material world. The best Valdemar could do was to exclude himself from the menu when he set the summoning array.

"Release him!" Valdemar ordered just in case, but his summoned attack dog summarily ignored the command. *Oh well, I tried.*

He could always interrupt his ritual and magically dismiss the Qlippoth back to its home dimension, but that meant a quick arrest and the destruction of his machine. Valdemar didn't wish to add the maiming or death of a knight to his already existing list of crimes . . . but his work was too important.

Besides, he was already bound for prison, what was one more crime? In the end, his success would excuse everything.

While the knight struggled against the Qlippoth, the ectoplasmic skull beneath the glass started to grow ethereal skin and hair. At long last, Valdemar recognized the old, wizened face of his maternal grandfather.

"Grandpa, it's me, Val," the warlock whispered. "Come back to us . . ."

Two more knights jumped into the basement to help their struggling comrade: another Knight of the Chain and a figure wearing the purple pointy hat and cloak of the Knights of the Tome over their armor. The latter didn't carry either a weapon or a lantern—and didn't need them.

"Begone, monster!" the Knight of the Tome shouted at the Gnawer in a high-pitched female voice, her hands shining with a crimson light. The flash forced the eldritch monster to release its prey, allowing the two Knights of the Chain to hack its tentacles with their sharp blades. *"Begone!"*

To Valdemar's horror, the light of her spell started interfering with his ritual as well. His grandfather's ectoplasm flickered; the machine's pipes thrummed like a beating metal heart.

"Stop!" he shouted, as the ectoplasmic face beneath the glass started degrading back into a skull. "Your spell is messing with mine!"

As his blood fueled the circle, Valdemar raised his dagger at the Knight of the Tome. He sensed her magical defenses flaring to life as he attempted to establish a mental connection with the blood flowing beneath her skin. Fortunately, she was a middling spellcaster and too busy focusing on her own spell.

"You are strong in the Blood, Verney, but you cannot hope—" The Knight of the Tome never finished her sentence, as Valdemar telekinetically slammed her against a wall. This disrupted her magic but not quickly enough to save the Gnawer from a sword strike to the eye. The monster dissipated into eldritch smoke, and the remaining knights immediately charged at Valdemar. They tackled him against his machine before he could retaliate with a spell and forced his bloody hand away from the summoning circle. The necromancer's shoulder hit a metal pipe, while his magical symbol shrank into nothingness. The absence of a blood source disrupted the spell.

"My ecto-catcher!" Valdemar panicked, despairing as one of the knights twisted his dagger out of his hand and another slammed his face against the machinery. "No!"

But the damage was done. The glass container cracked and the ectoplasmic skull within screeched, its ghostly substance evaporating. Within seconds, the blood circle vanished, and the ectoplasm dissipated into green smoke.

Years of effort and sacrifice, wasted!

Valdemar let out a roar of despair and fury as a Knight of the Chain placed fanged shackles around his hands. The warlock sensed sharp teeth digging into his flesh and sucking his blood like leeches. He tried to telekinetically toss his attackers backward, but as more of his already depleted life fluid abandoned him, so did his magical might.

"Fucking cultist," one of the Knights of the Chain said while hauling Valdemar away from his device. "When will your kind learn?"

"I'm not a cultist, you judgmental moron," Valdemar protested. In response, the knight pointed at his black robes and the bloody dagger on the floor, to the warlock's annoyance.

"I was so close to bringing him *back*! You ruined everything!"

The Knight of the Tome had recovered her bearings by then, her eyes peering at the prisoner from beneath her helmet. "Valdemar Verney, you are under arrest for the importation of derro technology, unlicensed necromancy, Qlippoth summoning, grave robbing, worshipping the Strangers, possession of forbidden texts, wounding a member of the Knightly Orders, resisting arrest, and forgery. What do you plead?"

"I don't worship the Strangers!" Valdemar protested. First rule of summoning: never summon something stronger than you. "And I didn't rob any graves!"

"You illegally reanimated the Hermitage family's patriarch as a Mindless," the Knight of the Tome replied.

Was that how they had tracked him down? "I received authorization from the Hermitage family to animate their patriarch as a zombie, so he could keep working on their mushroom farm!"

"An honest family, whom you deceived when you pretended to have a necromancer license," said the armored witch. "You'll go straight to Spellbane for this."

"And the book?" one of her Knight of the Chain comrades asked, glancing at the journal. "Probably some forbidden magical text. We better burn it."

Valdemar's eyes almost bulged out of his skull. "It's my grandfather's journal!" the warlock shouted, his voice heavy with panic. "You mustn't destroy it! There's nothing magical about it, and the knowledge inside—"

One of his captors backhanded Valdemar in the face before he could finish, his left cheek and jaw smarting from the blow. The necromancer's vision whited out for a second, and he could hear his own heartbeat slow down to a crawl.

"I will ship this document to Paraplex for study," the Knight of the Tome replied as she smashed the glass container with her gauntlet and seized the journal inside. "Along with your device and whatever notes we find in that rat's nest of yours."

"You don't know what you're do—" The Knight of the Tome raised her hand and Valdemar's lips snapped shut. Then the Knights hauled him out of the barn like a sack of flour, Valdemar's vision blurring as his eyes set upon the Hermitage farm. Rows of tall blue mushroom trees stood around them, surrounded by green moss. The place looked so quiet, so peaceful, that the warlock almost considered going to sleep. The blood loss had exhausted him.

The black guard hounds protecting the barn watched Valdemar in silence, their will suppressed by a spell. The undead Roger Hermitage, a cadaverous corpse raised and animated by the necromancer himself, cut a purple mushroom without paying any attention to the group. His scythe was sharp, his eyes white and soulless. He would work tirelessly in death as he had in life, cutting crops to feed the living.

Valdemar's eyes looked up to the dark rock ceiling three hundred meters above his head. Strains of luminescent lichen covered the stone, providing a dim light for the cavern's inhabitants. This roof was the Empire of Azlant's sky, the frontier of their civilization.

Only a frozen wasteland and endless night awaited them on the surface, condemning mankind to eternal darkness.

I just wanted to see the sun, Valdemar thought darkly.

Valdemar spent the next few days in a daze.

Or were they weeks? Years? He couldn't tell. The knights had strapped their naked prisoner to a wheel-shaped device inside a lightless cell, unable to move, unable to sleep. An iron mask covered his jaw, preventing him from speaking a word. Metal tubes implanted into his veins and linked to the machine drained his blood, replacing it with nutrients and chemicals. The potions kept the necromancer awake but too weak to do anything except think. Smart. For all the knights knew, Valdemar might have been an oneiromancer too, more dangerous asleep than awake.

But the wait drove him mad. The prisoner tried to kill time by imagining new rituals or pondering ways to escape, but he struggled to focus for long. The chilling cold didn't help either, and the silence . . .

Sometimes Valdemar could hear the sound of crashing waves beyond the cell's barred window. The prison of Spellbane had been built in the middle of a lake inside the vast Domain of Alogi. When the seven Dark Lords had wrested control of the empire, they carved out its vast caverns between themselves and called them Domains. Alogi's ruler Ophiel was by far the most unstable of these godly sorcerers, an immortal body snatcher. She raised a new fortress every few years in an attempt to create the perfect palace but never felt satisfied with the end result. Spellbane had been one of her many abandoned projects, repurposed into a prison for spellcasters.

Valdemar knew his stay would be temporary. The knights would torture the necromancer until they learned everything he knew, and then they would either execute or condemn him to the mines. In either case, they would reanimate his rotting corpse for labor. The Empire of Azlant didn't waste resources.

Valdemar's eyelids slowly rose as he noticed a glow in the dark. Metallic footsteps echoed in the corridor leading to his cell. Finally . . . By now the promise of a sharp questioning sounded almost like a relief. Anything but the *wait*.

The cell door opened, and a Knight of the Chain with a torch walked into the dark, wet chamber. The multiple chains around his neck, each forged from a different metal, identified him as the prison's warden.

Valdemar had learned that the hard way when the man had strapped him to the wheel. A Knight of the Tome followed him, and a slender woman closed the march. She didn't look like a knight. She wore a conservative outfit: dark red, leather trench coat, black shirt underneath it, pants, and boots. Her face was the fairest Valdemar had ever seen, with pale blue eyes, chiseled cheekbones, and short pale blonde hair. Her expression was as blank and unreadable as any mask. A rapier and a pistol hung from her belt.

Her visage looked familiar to the sorcerer but he couldn't put a name on her.

"That's barbaric," the woman said with a hint of reproach, her voice sounding as clear as water. By the Light, Valdemar would kill for a drink. "You're killing him."

"I wish, Milady," the warden replied. "Never seen someone with a metabolism like his. We had to triple the usual doses to keep him docile, and he's already building up a tolerance."

"He's probably a mutant of some kind," the Knight of the Tome added. Valdemar recognized her voice. She was the same witch who had caught him at the barn. "Maybe even a biomancer who modified his own body."

The blonde woman examined Valdemar with a quizzical look. The warlock held her gaze, his gray eyes cold and hateful.

"What can you tell me about his abilities?" the woman asked the inquisitors. If she could order them around, she was probably an agent of the Dark Lords or maybe the Church of the Light. Both spelled bad news. Besides, the fact the knights called her "Milady" also meant she was a noble of the Oldblood . . . and thus probably a spellcaster.

"He has very little training, Milady," the Knight of the Tome said. "When he psychically struck me, he was all strength without precision. But the fact he could maintain his ritual *and* attack me implies a tremendous natural talent. We didn't take any risks."

"So he's an autodidact?" the noblewoman asked.

The warden nodded in response. "Any surviving Verney was banned from practicing magic after Her Imperial Majesty ordered their purge, per the anticultist protocols. This degenerate probably taught himself from whatever wretched grimoires he could find."

That wasn't entirely true. The downfall of Valdemar's paternal family had barred him from practicing magic *unless* he joined the Church of the Light or the Knights of the Shroud. In the first case, he would have spent the rest of his life in a monastery, forbidden from delving into the higher mysteries of the cosmic; in the latter, he would have been ritually slain, raised as an undead warrior, and sent to perish again against the derro kingdom's golem armies. Obviously, neither option had sat well with Valdemar. He had inherited his grandfather's dream and sworn to fulfill it no matter the cost. Even if it meant violating imperial law.

"Why was he spared?" the noblewoman asked with clear curiosity.

"He's a bastard. Only the main Verney line was wiped out," the warden said. "Other branches had their assets confiscated and were subjected to heavy restrictions. We hoped to *question* him and learn more about his occult contacts or have the Knights of the Mind open his skull." The prospect of torturing Valdemar further certainly seemed to excite the inquisitor.

The noblewoman's lips twisted in clear distaste. "I will have no torture on my watch," she said. "Remove the mask."

The Knight of the Tome slipped a key into the device, allowing Valdemar to move his jaw. He breathed through his mouth for the first time in what felt like years.

The woman observed him for a few seconds, before politely introducing herself. "I am Marianne Reynard. I represent Lord Och, the Dark Lord of Paraplex."

Lord Och. The oldest magician in the Empire, the third most powerful, and the supreme master of the Knights of the Tome. Wonderful. Valdemar wondered if this woman had come to order his execution in person on behalf of her dark master or to send him to the mines.

"How did you . . ." Valdemar's throat felt sore, and he struggled to articulate words. The chemicals in his body made him tired, so very tired. "Catch me?"

The warden snorted. "We're the ones asking the questions here, mongrel."

"How did you catch him?" "Lady" Marianne asked softly, to the knights' puzzlement.

"We caught his derro tech supplier, Armand of Mantebois," the warden said with a shrug. "He sold out all his customers for a lighter sentence."

"Did you kill him?" the prisoner rasped. The knight shook his head in response. Good—Valdemar could murder that traitor himself if he ever managed to get out of here. If Armand's betrayed associates didn't get to him first.

"I have questions for you, Mr. Verney," said Lady Marianne.

"You already took everything from me . . . even my notes." Even his grandpa's journal. "What more do you need?"

"Clarification," the woman replied, moving her gloved hands behind her back. "Our researchers have studied your device, and from what they gathered, you were trying to revive a lost soul using a ritual of your own creation. What bothers our spellcasters, however, is that your spell contains no sign of necromantic magic," she said. "You used conjuration instead. A summoning circle. It is well known that all attempts at summoning souls from the afterlife have ended in disastrous failure and yet . . . witnesses affirm that you successfully called an ectoplasm of some kind."

"I wasn't trying to summon my grandfather's soul." Valdemar's own experimentations had shown that if there was a way to break the Veil between Underland and the afterlife, it would need far more blood and resources than he would ever get his hands on. "I was trying to create an . . . echo."

His interrogator frowned in confusion. "An echo?"

Valdemar was sorely tempted to stay quiet and let her figure it out by herself, before deciding otherwise. If these people truly wanted an answer, they would have the Knights of the Mind steal it from his brain. Besides, maybe a far-sighted mage could use the knowledge to pick up where Valdemar left off. The prisoner doubted it, but hope was all he had left at this point.

"Souls leave a psychic imprint wherever they go . . . especially in their most precious earthly possessions," he explained. The journal had been his grandfather's lifework, his constant companion since he mysteriously landed in Underland. "My plan was to gather that . . . that remnant of psychic energy into an artificial ectoplasmic body . . . the way some extra-dimensional creatures manifest one to interact with our reality."

"So you tried to create an artificial ghost?" Lady Marianne asked. The captive warlock nodded. To her credit, she seemed to grasp the concept. "I see. You used your own blood as its anchor to the material plane, since you were the deceased's last living relative."

"Yes. My ecto-catcher device would have prevented the specter from . . . dissipating." Valdemar would have crafted a golem to house his grandsire's replica if he could, but the material had proven too expensive. "I knew the construct wouldn't have been my grandfather's soul but an echo . . . Still, I hoped that he would remember some things from his past life."

"For what purpose?"

Because I wanted to see my family again, what else? Valdemar thought. *And because I couldn't fully decode the journal on my own.* "I had . . . questions about his home."

The more he spoke, the deeper Lady Marianne's frown became. "His home?"

Valdemar sneered. "You won't believe me . . . you'll call me mad." Nobody believed him. At best, open-minded people entertained the truth without truly accepting it. At worst, they laughed or accused him of being a cultist. By now, Valdemar knew better than to open his mouth.

"I can't believe your words if I don't hear them first," Lady Marianne argued. Valdemar couldn't figure her out for the life of him. "I will not judge."

She would. But in the end . . . what did Valdemar have to lose? He was already doomed.

"My grandfather is not of this world. He came from another place. Another world that still has a sun in the skies." And he had spent the rest of his life trying to go home, without ever succeeding. On his deathbed, Valdemar had promised to pick up where he had left. "I wanted more information about it. To open a portal."

Lady Marianne's expression remained a blank, unreadable mask, while the knights behind her exchanged a glance.

"What was that world's name?" the warden asked.

"Earth," Valdemar replied.

A short silence followed.

And then the knights burst out laughing, to Valdemar's silent rage. Only Lady Marianne remained serious, her gaze thoughtful.

"Earth, like the dirt?" the warden asked with a mocking chuckle. "You cultists couldn't find a better name for your pipe paradise?"

"Earth exists, you close-minded moron," Valdemar said angrily when he couldn't take the laughter anymore. Somehow the rage made him stronger, dissipating the chemical-induced haze. "And one day I will find it. A land with a clear blue sky and where the sun—"

"Still shines, yes, I've heard those words before," the warden cut him off dismissively. "You'll prove nothing, you madman. If you're lucky, you'll spend the rest of your life and undeath toiling in the mines. Or maybe we'll burn you. It's been a while since we put oil on the pyre, and the kids love the fireworks."

"No," Lady Marianne said softly. "Release him."

The knights stopped chuckling. Valdemar blinked in surprise. "Milady?" the warden asked in confusion.

"Release him," Lady Marianne ordered, this time firmly. "He's going to the Domain of Paraplex with me."

"Milady, you cannot be serious?" The warden didn't bother to hide his displeasure. "He's a cultist's spawn, a bastard brood, and a criminal. You heard him, he's deluded."

"These are Lord Och's orders," Lady Marianne replied, her words sending chills down Valdemar's spine. "The Dark Lord wants to interrogate him personally."

He has read the journal, the prisoner realized, half with hope and half with dread. *And if he believed even half of it . . .*

Maybe Valdemar would get to see the sun one day after all . . .

2

THE DARK LORD

The ebony carriage rode through the tunnels, pulled by a giant cave beetle. The coachman hadn't spoken a word since they left the prison, and Lady Marianne had proven to be no chattier. She had spent hours looking through the window, at the ghostly lanterns illuminating the road.

At least she gave me food and clothing, if not a conversation, Valdemar thought, his teeth sinking into a piece of fungus bread. The carriage was large enough to house a small table, allowing the prisoner to feast on a plate of mole cheese, badger steak, and spicy mushrooms. A simple linen tunic covered the wounds made by the knights' blood-draining wheel, though they had already started to heal. He had noticed that Lady Marianne paid a lot of interest to his bruises when she wasn't looking through the window.

She shifted on her leather seat and eventually couldn't suppress her curiosity. "Are you a biomancer?" she asked Valdemar.

"No, I am not," the prisoner replied. Valdemar had made forays into the field of biomancy but had decided to focus on necromancy and summoning. "Not yet."

"A mutant then?"

"Maybe. I do not know." Whenever he had asked the same question of his family, his poor mother answered with tears and his grandfather with silence. "I've always healed fast, and it's possible that my father experimented on me while I was in the womb. I heard the Verneys did that to their children, to make them healthier."

"Did you know him?" Marianne asked. Valdemar couldn't tell if she was being sincerely curious or just interrogating him. "Your father?"

"No." The Verney purge had happened while he was a child learning to walk. All Valdemar had was a name, Isaac Verney, and whatever tidbits of information that he had managed to piece together. "Why these questions?"

"I am curious," she admitted. "A normal human would have died from all the blood loss and the treatment you suffered, but one meal and your health is already improving."

"Shouldn't that concern you? I am almost back at full strength." The Blood was tied to willpower and health, as it was the very essence of life and death. Valdemar had sensed his power returning as he recovered from the blood loss and drugs.

Lady Marianne responded with a soft, amused smile.

"You think you can take me on alone, if needed," Valdemar said. He had wondered why the carriage traveled without an escort and why she didn't put shackles on him.

"I do not think that I *can*," Lady Marianne corrected him. "I know that I *will* defeat you if I have to."

Truthfully, Valdemar believed her. She directly answered to a Dark Lord and thus probably wielded great power of her own.

"Will you try to escape?" Lady Marianne asked with a raised eyebrow.

"Spellbane's warden took samples of my blood during my capture. The knights can track me down anywhere," Valdemar replied with a shrug, as he finished his plate. "Besides, at least *you* aren't strapping me to a torture device."

She scowled in genuine disgust. "That kind of treatment is unbecoming of true knights," the noblewoman said. "We become no better than the derros by sinking to this level of inhumanity."

Valdemar observed her, and to his surprise, she seemed to earnestly believe her own words. She struck the sorcerer as strangely candid. "You are a noblewoman of the Oldblood, no?" he asked.

"I am," Lady Marianne confirmed, before looking away. "I was."

"Disgraced?" Valdemar asked, highly curious. He had heard Oldblood rivalries and feuds could get quite lethal.

"Yes." She responded with an embarrassed smile. "It's a long story. Perhaps I will tell you one day."

Valdemar took the hint and didn't press the matter further.

The carriage approached one of the Earthmouth portals linking the Dark Lords' domains together. The construction appeared at the end of the tunnel, a foreboding archway of pulsating flesh and hungry jaws whose gullet led inside a crimson fog. This device had been a human being once, a martyr who willingly sacrificed his life for the sake of knitting the empire's lands together.

A group of Knights of the Gate protected the pathway, their armor black as night with the white eye of the empress painted on their chest and shoulders. They checked the coachman's documentation and let them pass through the crimson mist. The world turned red for a moment as the coach crossed the portal, Valdemar's body shuddering as it traveled from one point in space to another.

What should have taken months of harrowing travel through caves and tunnels lasted only an instant. The carriage emerged through another Earthmouth Gate, one that led into the quiet streets of Pleroma, Paraplex's only city.

Valdemar had already visited it, back when he still held on to the dream he could pursue a career in sorcery. He had likened it to a maze of stone, its labyrinthine alleys threatening to devour the unwary or hiding the unsavory from sight.

Pleroma had been built on a plateau overseeing the toxic marshes that made up most of the cavern, and the lack of space had forced architects to raise ever-higher buildings to accommodate the growing population. Lanterns illuminated narrow streets trapped between looming rows of brick houses as tall as watchtowers, penned in by colossal bladed walls.

Some buildings were in the process of being demolished to raise taller structures in their place, while others had their facade repaired by tireless undead workers. Only a third of the houses showed a light at this hour, making the streets appear empty and gloomy. If not for the veins of shining, purple crystal growing on the cavern's ceiling and the pyres of the Church of the Light's cathedrals, Pleroma would have been cast in darkness.

The carriage passed by fewer than twenty people as it started ascending on steep, lonely road toward the Dark Lord's seat of power. Valdemar had never visited this part of the city, largely because he could never get past the numerous patrols of undead warriors and gatekeepers. On one side of the road, he could see the purple bogs and marshes surrounding the city; on the other, a gargantuan fortress of black oily stone. Monstrous gargoyles oversaw its walls, while its watchtowers looked like the fangs of some wicked beast. Dark knights patrolled the skies on the back of mighty dragobats, those black-scaled giant bats which biomancers created from the blood of subterranean dragons.

A black pillar stood at the fortress's center, covered in arcane symbols and connected to the cavern's ceiling. This was the abode of the Dark Lord Och, the supreme master of the entire cavern.

Valdemar remained silent as the carriage crossed the only bridge linking Pleroma to the fortress, a narrow passage more than three hundred meters long. Below the bridge was a rift so deep that nobody could see the bottom. The warlock could only marvel at this wonder of engineering.

"Why didn't you try to join the Pleroma Institute?" Lady Marianne asked upon noticing Valdemar's awed silence. "Lord Och is not as . . . *rigid* as the other Dark Lords."

"I did try to join, twice. Once under my own name, and another time under a false one." It had been the first time he forged official documents—but not the last. "I sent hundreds of letters to Lord Och to plead my case, but I never received an answer."

Lady Marianne nodded. "I suppose that makes sense. Lord Och's staff is very mindful about security. Your letters probably never reached him. If they had, he would have granted you a fair hearing."

"What is he like?" Valdemar asked, trying to suppress his anxiety. Lord Och was the most elusive of the Dark Lords, and extremely mindful of his privacy. Valdemar knew only a few things for certain about this man: that he had trained two other Dark Lords, the fearsome Valar Bethor and Phaleg the Binder, the latter of whom became his bitter rival; that he only left his fortress to attend the yearly Sabbath with his corulers; and that he was an undead necromancer of tremendous power.

"Wise. And patient," Lady Marianne replied. "He is older than the empire, and as such his approach to time differs from ours. He cares more about memories than life. The latter always ends, but the former can last forever."

"That does not reassure me." Valdemar would rather avoid ending up as a brain in a jar or bound to a soulstone, compelled to answer a necromancer's questions for all eternity.

"I believe you will find common ground. Lord Och was very interested in your notes."

The carriage reached the end of the bridge and passed beneath a gate-house. Valdemar immediately shuddered as he sensed an invisible force weighing down on his soul.

There are spells woven in these old stones, the sorcerer thought as the carriage stopped.

"We are here, Milady," said the coachman, his voice coarse and dry. The man moved to open the carriage's door, his pale, predatory gray eyes gazing at Valdemar with suspicion. The prisoner sensed a psychic force probing him, ready to strike at the first sign of hostility.

He's a sorcerer too, Valdemar thought, as he examined the coachman. He looked unassuming with his short black hair and leather coat, but the way he stood reminded the prisoner of a cave lion. *They're all sorcerers within these walls.*

"Thank you, Bertrand," Lady Marianne said, as the coachman helped her out of the carriage. Valdemar didn't receive any such courtesy and had to make his way outside on his own. "Mr. Verney, welcome to the Pleroma Institute of Sorcery."

Valdemar took a deep breath and looked around. The carriage had parked in a colossal courtyard shielded by the black, oily curtain walls and watchtowers. All the guards manning them either belonged to the Knights of the Tome sworn to Lord Och, or were well-preserved undead. The latter's shining eyes betrayed the presence of a soul animating the remains. The Black Pillar occupied the center of the fortress, a stone sun around which everything revolved. To Valdemar's puzzlement, it had stained-glass windows shaped like eyes but no doors.

The more Valdemar's gaze wandered, the more amazed he grew at the complex's true size. Everywhere he could see the shadows of barracks and stone halls, even the shining flames of a cathedral of the Light. Not everything was made from stone, however. The locals had raised vast and beautiful gardens of mushrooms and alien plants, catered to by steel golems and animated statues. The Institute even had a hedge maze, made of strange thorny black plants and blooming crimson flowers.

What his eyes couldn't see, the Blood did. Valdemar closed his eyes and let his arcane senses expand. This place was unbelievably ancient, and the pillar more so. It was here when the humans descended into Under-land, to flee the chilling cold. The new inhabitants had raised quarters and gardens over the ruins of a far older civilization. He sensed the pres-ence of life below ground, an ant farm of humans toiling in underground vaults. And the deeper he looked, the more Valdemar trembled. A dark force slept far beneath the stone, stirring in its slumber. This place was *thin* . . . The very fabric of space and time had been weakened, one spell at a time. The wall between realities had turned from strong stone to soft mud, making it easier for the planes of existence to align.

The Pleroma Institute was the foremost center of knowledge in all of Azlant, even more famous than the Academy of Saklas, where nobles sent their whelps to study . . . But it was also far more secretive and restrictive. Only scholars handpicked by Och himself could enter its halls. And clearly they had called upon forces that would make imperial citizens shudder in their sleep.

"You can wander around the fortress for now, but neither leave it nor access restricted areas." Lady Marianne's voice returned Valdemar to reality and his eyes snapped open. "I must bid you goodbye for now. Other duties await me."

"You will not escort me to Och?" Valdemar asked.

"*Lord* Och will summon you soon," she replied. "I can tell he is already watching." The noblewoman left after giving her "guest" a respectful nod, the coachman following her shadow. Only then did Valdemar notice that Lady Marianne made no sound when she walked.

After waiting a moment to confirm that yes, he had been left to his own devices, Valdemar started carefully exploring the Institute. Knights of the Tome observed him from afar and moved in front of the barracks' doors when the warlock approached. It appeared he was restricted to the outside areas until the Dark Lord granted him an audience.

Valdemar noticed stairs leading underground and animal life inhabiting the shadows. The sorcerer sensed rats crawling inside the walls, flocks of vampire bats resting beneath roofs, and pet badgers running around. A large stable housed giant beetle mounts, dragobats, and other mutated warbeasts best left undisturbed. At one point, Valdemar walked by a hooded man near the gardens, only to see a swarm of flies and maggots underneath the tattered rags. And the walls . . . Some walls had human faces carved into the stone, their lifeless eyes following him as he walked.

Everywhere, *someone* or *something* was watching Valdemar.

The only part of the complex which he found halfway comforting was a thorny cathedral dedicated to the Light, resting on a stone platform threatening to fall into the rift around the fortress. Pyres burned on its roof and beacon tower, their glows warm and soothing.

A part of Valdemar wanted to examine the Black Pillar in detail, but he let his arcane sight guide him southeast of the complex instead. Having trained half his life in the field of summoning, the warlock was highly attuned to the fabric of space, and he had noticed an anomaly. His quest led him to a deep, circular pool of clear water, located right outside a vast greenhouse heated by steam machinery. Valdemar approached the banks and peered into the liquid. The water reservoir was so deep that the warlock couldn't see the bottom with his human eyes. His arcane sight, however, wandered into its depths, sensing the rift at the bottom. A wound into the very fabric of space.

This is how they produce the water needed for the gardens, Valdemar thought. He couldn't help but respect the sheer beauty of this magical wonder. *Crafty.*

"Interesting," a voice said.

Valdemar almost jumped back, as an old man appeared to his left, gazing at the pond with curious blue eyes. He had appeared out of thin air, and Valdemar hadn't even *sensed* him.

"Usually visitors pay more attention to the Black Tower than the well," the man said with a kind fatherly voice. His face was wrinkled by age and wisdom, his hair white as milk. He looked unassuming, and he wore modest brown robes. "The former was there long before we raised the fortress and the latter is relatively recent."

"I find this well a more impressive display of magic," Valdemar said as he gazed at the bottom. He tried to suppress his uneasiness. "It is a permanent portal to the Elemental Plane of Water, isn't it?"

"Not quite." The old man put his hands behind his back, his gaze as blue and clear as the pond. "Paraplex is poor in drinkable water, and most wells ran out long ago. But extradimensional water extracted directly from the source of all sources? How could this well ever dry up? Unfortunately, we haven't yet figured out a way to create a truly stable portal to another plane, so one of our scholars, young Poingcarré, suggested a new solution. Do you know how an Earthmouth works?"

Valdemar instantly caught on. "You tried to turn a summoned water elemental into a portal?"

"That was the plan, but it didn't work as expected. The elemental instead kept summoning water into our reality, and the experience drove it mad. We bound it at the bottom of the pool, where it kindly solves our agricultural problem. I often shed a tear at its silent suffering, but such is the cost of scientific progress."

He sounded almost sincere, but Valdemar knew better. His sadness was a mask, just like the face and the flesh.

"What's the matter?" the old man asked with false concern, clearly delighting in Valdemar's uneasiness. "Am I scaring you?"

"A little," Valdemar admitted, clearing his throat. He had to choose his words carefully. "You are Lord Och, aren't you?"

"What makes you think so?" the mysterious individual's lips smiled, but his eyes remained cold and unblinking.

"Your magical defenses are too perfect," Valdemar replied, having psychically probed them.

The Knight of the Tome's magical protection had been a wall, but this man's was a deep, impenetrable fog. There was nothing to grasp, no hint about what sinister thing hid beneath the mist. You could break a shield, or bypass it, but how did you fight a fog?

"Oh?" The Dark Lord chuckled. "And here I thought I cloaked my armor behind a veil of harmlessness."

"You can hide your smell from a bloodhound with a great amount of perfume," Valdemar said, "but he will find it suspicious in itself."

"Do you consider yourself a hound? You seem more like a caterpillar to me. Bound to the earth at your young age, but with the potential to fly when you grow old."

"Am I a moth or a butterfly?"

"A moth. They always strive to reach the candle's flame, even when it burns them."

Valdemar hesitated before asking his question, wondering what game the Dark Lord was playing. "And *what* are you?"

"Why, what else but an old man?"

For a moment, the old man's illusion vanished to reveal a ghastly black skull beneath the kind face, its eyes twin blue stars shining in the dark. Two blue abysses calling Valdemar's soul, telling him to sleep forever. The younger warlock instinctively strengthened his defenses to protect himself, but they could have been made of paper. Chilly ghostly fingers shattered his psychic shield and grabbed his soul with surgical precision, threatening to extract it the same way a dentist would a tooth. Valdemar's blood became as cold as ice, his breath a white mist. The moment passed and the undead put his mask of life back on. The Dark Lord let Valdemar's soul go, and the young warlock fell to his knees, gasping for air.

For a brief instant, he had peered at Lord Och's true form, an ancient horror beyond the reach of death and time. A lich.

"You built a wooden house on strong foundations, young man," Lord Och said, before offering his hand to Valdemar. "One that can resist the wind, but which will fall to flames and fold before a battering ram."

Valdemar glanced at the hand with fear. The fingers looked so weak, and yet they hid savage claws.

"I can snuff your life out with a thought," the Dark Lord said, "why would I need a hand?"

Valdemar clenched his teeth and accepted the help. Lord Och's fingers felt warm to the touch, the glamour so perfect that it fooled all of the weaker warlock's senses. And yet this creature had shed his humanity long ago. The Dark Lord could kill Valdemar in a heartbeat, and he wouldn't feel anything about it.

"You never practiced with another sorcerer," Lord Och observed, "Not for long anyway. Or else you would have better defenses."

"No, Your Dark Majesty." Valdemar could never find an official mentor, and illegal sorcerers frequenting black markets demanded high payments for training—especially on combat-related matters.

"Majesty? I do not call myself an emperor, unlike a certain arrogant colleague of mine. Lord Och will do for now, young Valdemar." The old man searched for something beneath his robes and brought out a black, blank book. "This is yours, I believe."

The book's pages were yellowed by age and dust, its cover made of simple leather. It looked like any diary, and yet Valdemar could recognize it anywhere. Suppressing his urge to grab it, the young warlock glanced at a smiling Och and then carefully took his heirloom out of the undead's hands. How good it felt for his fingers to brush against the old leather. Valdemar checked the pages, gazing at walls of texts handwritten in a foreign tongue no one in Underland could speak, at the drawings of a pointy tower of steel and of flying balloons crossing an endless sea.

"I did not recognize the main language used when I read this book, which drew my curiosity," Lord Och admitted. "I thought it was a code at first, but I know enough about linguistics to recognize a foreign tongue. Thankfully, you added notes in the common tongue."

"My grandfather called it French," Valdemar said, clearing his throat. "His homeland's language. He taught it to me."

Lord Och raised an eyebrow. "I thought his homeland was called Earth?" He had clearly done his research.

"Earth was his homeworld," Valdemar explained. "France his country."

"Here at Plemora, we research interdimensional travel too. Partly out of intellectual curiosity, partly because of the potential applications of this magic . . . and mostly for the purpose of future colonization. It may have been centuries since we retreated here underground, but our people will never stop dreaming of seeing the sun again."

"How far are you into these research efforts?" Valdemar couldn't help but ask. If they already had succeeded in creating interdimensional portals . . .

"We are early pioneers, I'm afraid, and our efforts are fraught with failures and dangers. But perhaps your help will prove a decisive push in the right direction."

Valdemar's fingers clenched around the journal as hope filled his heart. "You believe me?"

"I do not believe, I think," Lord Och replied. "The paper used for this journal is unlike anything I have seen in Underland, and this does add credibility to your tale. However, if your grandsire taught you his native tongue, why would you need his postmortem guidance?"

"Some parts of the journal were written in a second tongue that I couldn't identify," Valdemar admitted. His grandfather had clearly feared that some people would read his innermost secrets and encrypted them. "I've tried for years to decode it and failed."

"And you found it easier to create an artificial ghost than to translate a few chapters? Then again, I've met very few youngsters capable of binding a Gnawer at your age."

Valdemar's chest swelled with pride. "I can summon more than a Gnawer, Lord Och."

"Oh? We shall put that boast to the test soon." The lich swept some dust off his robes. "There are thousands of tales like your grandfather's, though most are simply the result of feverish imagination or madness. Hence, while I heard rumors about your family, I disregarded them. It may have been a mistake on my part, but there is time to correct it."

Valdemar cleared his throat, unsure what to make of this ancient archmage's words. "What do you want with me, Lord Och?"

"I want the same thing as you, young Valdemar. I want to confirm whether or not this 'Earth' plane exists, and if it does, how to reach it."

"Earth exists," Valdemar insisted, his faith unshakable.

"Maybe your grandfather was mad or maybe he came from another world. We will check and see which option is true."

We? Valdemar closed the journal and held it close to his chest. "And what will you do with me, my Lord?"

"You are a criminal and as such forbidden to leave Pleroma without my express authorization," Lord Och replied. "If you try, I will eat your soul, spit it out, and throw your hollowed body into the abyss outside my walls. Consider your stay here . . . a chance at rehabilitation."

He said that with the same passion as someone discussing the daily humidity.

This did not sit well with Valdemar. *He just needs me to translate the journal*, the warlock thought. *He will kill me right afterward.*

"I could easily extract that knowledge from your mind, mortal," the lich said. "But why would I? People are like plants. For them to become beautiful, you must water them and let them grow. I would rather add a flower to my garden than eat a seed."

Could he read Valdemar's mind? "So I traded one cell for another?"

"A cell?" The Dark Lord let out a cavernous laugh. "Would you consider a workshop and a furnished lab a cell? You wanted to join our Institute once, and you shall. You will only have limited resources until I have ascertained the true depths of your magical talent, but I shall reward loyalty and hard work. You will also run errands for me on occasions." Lord Och's smile turned predatory. "On *any* occasion I choose," he said, his voice as sharp and delicate as an assassin's knife.

Valdemar squinted, trying to think this through carefully. "I may keep the journal and work in peace?" he asked.

"Yes," the Dark Lord answered.

"And I don't have the option to refuse, I suppose?"

"I can send you back to Spellbane, if you prefer," Lord Och said with false kindness. "From what I heard, the warden kept your cell intact. He misses you greatly and believes you will come back soon."

"Alright, alright," Valdemar sighed. He had no desire to get strapped on a wheel again and although doing research under a Dark Lord's thumb made him uneasy it still beat the alternative.

"Do not make that face, young Valdemar," Lord Och replied with a chuckle. "We will complete your magical education, and maybe one day I will grant you an official pardon. Do you have a hobby? I personally like to go fishing, but if you have another passion, I can accommodate it."

"I paint," Valdemar admitted. "And draw."

"Oh, you will get along with young Hermann then. I will be sure to introduce the two of you, but for now . . ."

The lich put a hand on Valdemar's shoulder, his fingers turning into claws of black bone.

"Let us see what you can do," Lord Och said with a wicked grin.

3

MARIANNE

The longsword lunged for Marianne's head, and she unsheathed her rapier. The blades clashed, the song of their steel echoing through the room. Fighting with her left hand behind her back, Marianne adopted a defensive fighting style and focused on dodging her training partner's swings. Her retainer was a powerful foe, though he favored a longsword over a rapier. Bertrand's bladed thrusts were as powerful as Marianne's were quick, and unlike her, he never tired nor needed to catch his breath. Each blow was as powerful as the first. Only the living could suffer from exhaustion. His first blow would have probably shattered Marianne's rapier if it hadn't been a soulbound weapon. The founder of the Reynard line, Lucien, had been a famed swordsman. Only the strongest of magics could destroy this weapon, and Marianne often felt her ancestor's spirit stir whenever the blade tasted blood.

Bertrand's pale eyes turned red, his movements quickened, and she couldn't find any flaw in his offense. He unleashed a swing so swift that Marianne barely saw it coming.

Parrying again would end with her thrown against a wall at best. Marianne called upon the power of the Blood to help her. She strengthened her legs and jumped before Bertrand's steel could cut her wide open. She leaped over her retainer and thrust her rapier in midair above his shoulder. Bertrand responded by turning into a pale mist. Under normal circumstances, Marianne's soulbound rapier should have hurt him even in this form, but Bertrand used his natural malleability to swirl out of the blade's reach.

No matter. Marianne landed gracefully on her feet and prepared for the counterattack.

She didn't have to wait long. Bertrand reformed on her flank and lunged at her with his blade, his canines sharp as daggers and his nails had turned to claws. He moved swifter than a cave lion, too fast for Marianne to dodge.

So she didn't. Finally deciding to use her left hand, Marianne used a spell to cover her palm and fingers with a layer of bone as strong as steel. She used it to catch Bertrand's blade by surprise. The steel longsword cut through Marianne's glove, but her bones stopped his weapon. At the same time, the noblewoman's rapier aimed for her retainer's throat.

Marianne struggled to stop the sheer strength behind Bertrand's blow, but her magic empowered her body with superhuman might. The flooring creaked beneath her feet. Bertrand had put everything behind his attack; he had nothing left to stop her counterattack.

Marianne stopped before she could inflict a fatal blow, her rapier's tip within an inch of her retainer's carotid. "That will be all for today," Marianne said as she released her retainer's sword and sheathed her rapier.

"Milady might prefer another training partner," Bertrand suggested while putting his sword on the wall's display of weapons, next to halberds and axes. As befitting her status, Marianne's apartment included a small training hall, one that she had decorated with weapons and coats of arms belonging to Oldblood families. The Reynard family's white fox banner stood next to wolves and other extinct surface creatures, while will-o'-the-wisps imprisoned inside lamps illuminated the chamber. "You have long surpassed me in the arts of war."

"You are the best swordsman in all of Paraplex." Very few fighters could leave Marianne winded after a session, and Bertrand ranked highly among that number. "Short of myself, of course."

"Milady is too kind, but the point remains. I do not think our sessions will improve your skills any further." Bertrand put his hands behind his back, his fangs and eyes returning to normal. "May I suggest contacting someone like Lord Bethor? He is the best warrior in the empire."

"A Dark Lord has better things to do than practice with me." Especially Lord Bethor, who coordinated the empire's armies and safeguarded the border with the derro kingdom. Marianne had come very close to joining his court rather than Lord Och's. Sometimes, she wondered how her life would have gone if she had been dispatched to the border, fighting the empire's external enemies instead of the internal ones. *I would probably have become an undead by now,* Marianne mused. *Maybe one day, when my living body has grown old and sick.* "These matches don't teach me anything, Bertrand, but they prevent me from getting rusty. Hence we shall continue them."

Marianne was weak in the Blood, the magic of life and death that had brought the empire prosperity. She was efficient, using barely any energy to fuel her spells, but greater displays of sorcery like summoning were beyond her. Marianne favored a more practical approach to fighting. She used the Blood to boost her physical abilities and supplement her skills. Her body was as much a weapon as her rapier.

A shame she couldn't practice her gunmanship. Bullets cost almost nothing, but gunpowder a fortune. The government restricted its use, and even though Lord Och provided her with a sizable salary, Marianne didn't believe in wasting money. She had struggled financially for a brief time after her family had all but exiled her, and preferred to keep her own funds in case of an emergency.

"As Milady wishes," Bertrand said with a curt bow. "Does Milady desire tea for her morning brew?"

"If you would be so kind. Bring the news too."

I will need to sew this glove again, Marianne thought as she examined her left hand, her bone armor receding beneath her skin. Bertrand's blade had left a deep cut in the velvet glove. By now, repairing such damage was almost second nature to the noblewoman.

Marianne retreated to her bedroom, a beautiful place with intricate swirling patterns carved in the marble paneling. A stained-glass window gave her an impeccable view of the hedge maze outside, which she found more beautiful than any painting. A pile of novels had accumulated on her bedside table, with *The Clockstopper's Dilemma* and *The Leaden Moon* sitting on top. She had been halfway through reading the latter before Lord Och sent her on her latest errand.

"What would I do without you, Bertrand?" Marianne asked, as she sat next to her tea table and started sewing her velvet glove back into shape. Her mother would have scolded her, saying that such labor was beneath her. Marianne missed her family sometimes, even if she was glad to live her life as she wished far away from noble etiquette and petty intrigues. Only Bertrand remained of her old existence. The vampire had served the Reynard family for centuries and never faltered in his loyalty. When Marianne fled the imperial capital in disgrace and found refuge in Lord Och's court, her retainer had dutifully followed her.

"Milady would probably ruin herself in tea shops," Bertrand replied as he brought her the day's newspaper. Trees and paper were rare, while parchment was expensive. Newspapers were issued in a more common artificial paper substitute created by alchemists from giant fungi, and the substance barely lasted more than two weeks before rotting away.

Marianne read the titles while Bertrand poured her a delicious, fruity mushroom tea.

"Inauguration of the Underland Express planned for next month."

"Sixty-four people died in a cave-in near the Domain of Ariouth."

"The Church of the Light will plead for the reconquest of the surface at the Dark Lords' newest assembly."

"Derro troops noticed near the border: is a new war inevitable?"

A reconquest of the surface? Though Marianne believed in the Light, she couldn't help but see the idea of reconquering the surface as a doomed effort. The world above had been cold and dark since the Whitemoon arrived to blot out the sun, with monsters roaming the icy ruins humankind left behind. The Institute's idea of colonizing other worlds sounded more feasible to her.

Marianne paid more attention to the derro article. She considered a conflict with these degenerate dwarves inevitable. As the noblewoman had expected, the press only reported an increased presence of enemy golems and quakes in the tunnels near the empire's borders, alongside grisly tales about derro king Otto's cruelty.

The Knights of the Chain maintained a tight grip on the empire's cultural policies and carefully controlled what newspapers printed. Marianne found it harder and harder to distinguish the propaganda from the truth, to her dismay. She understood why the Knights of the Chain believed that some information had to be buried or destroyed for the sake of preventing social unrest. When the body was strong, a cunning enemy targeted the mind—and in the empire's case, those of its citizens. Cults of the Strangers always lurked in the darkness, waiting to exploit times of unrest and fear to recruit people in the service of their vile eldritch patrons.

But by destroying all knowledge contradicting the imperial orthodoxy, the Knights of the Chain left the citizens unprepared and ignorant.

How could the empire fight its enemies if it didn't understand them? The Pleroma Institute had been a breath of fresh air on that front, and Marianne had found it good to discuss freely without looking over her shoulder.

People don't call you Otto the Demented for being a kind and stable ruler though, she thought, sipping her tea. The new derro king was as frighteningly mad as he was maniacally competent.

"Lord Och asked for your presence in the Hall of Rituals," Bertrand informed his mistress.

"For what purpose?"

"To observe our new acquaintance's trial by fire," the retainer said with a sneer.

"You don't like Valdemar?" Marianne herself felt rather neutral about the newcomer. Valdemar struck her as too clever by half, and hiding a tinge of darkness, but otherwise a reasonable fellow. He hadn't deserved being strapped to a wheel like an animal. "Then again, you dislike everyone at first glance."

"It's the smell, Milady."

Marianne raised an eyebrow. "What does that mean?"

"Milady cannot smell it, for she is still a mortal," Bertrand replied. "But a hideous stench follows this man. The Institute's animals have sensed it too and avoid him."

"What does he smell like?" his mistress asked with a chuckle, amused by the idea of her retainer twitching his nose every time he crossed Valdemar's path.

But Bertrand remained entirely serious. "That is what worries me, Milady. He doesn't smell like any scent I recognize. He smells of the unknown; that's what disturbs the animals."

Oh? Could it be related to his grandfather's otherworldliness? Marianne thought. She didn't fully believe Valdemar's tale, but she was open-minded. Lord Och at least seemed to believe it possible and the lich was rarely wrong.

"No matter," Marianne replied, as she emptied her cup. "Lord Och will handle him if he tries anything dangerous."

"Of that, I have no doubt."

After finishing her breakfast, Marianne left her quarters and Bertrand behind for the Hall of Rituals. Located at the northern point of the Pleroma Institute, this underground chamber served as a secure, warded location where magicians could run dangerous rituals without threatening the rest of the facility. Marianne made her way down the long, spiraling staircase, whose top was guarded by two undead warriors in heavy armor. A black, looming stone archway waited at the bottom and generated a blue magical barrier. Marianne crossed it without any problem and entered the Hall of Rituals.

Created by the ancient civilization that had once inhabited the cavern, the underground dome was supported by twelve columns of the same black, oily stones as the pillar at the fortress's center. The ceiling reached ten meters at its highest point. Ancient mosaics and murals covered the walls. All of them represented enormous, cyclopean beings engaged in acts of worship around sinister monoliths. The scholars believed them to be the extinct Pleromians, the first inhabitants of the Domain of Paraplex.

Lord Och awaited her between two pillars, next to a pile of books and paintings topped by an old, tiny music box. Marianne recognized them as Valdemar's belongings, collected by the inquisitors after his arrest. Valdemar himself was trapped inside a vast cube of red energy in the middle of the dome. He wasn't alone inside. An insectoid warbeast shared the man's cell and furiously attempted to devour him. The result of biomancers' experimentations, the chimera reached almost three meters in height. Its legs belonged to a spider and the upper body to a cave crab, with an elongated neck, four eyes, and a fanged lamprey maw. Marianne didn't dare imagine how many animals had perished before the monster's maker could create a functional fusion. The Blood sympathetically bound the living and the dead together, like the cells of a singular organism. It was the invisible essence of life itself, and no creature could fully escape its grasp. But magicians did their best to give warbeasts resistance against common spells, and this creature was no exception. Instead of telekinetically crushing its head, Valdemar was forced to run circles around the angry creature to avoid its pincers. Worse, he had been given no weapon and was reduced to grabbing stone pebbles laying on the ground. The Dark Lord liked his skill tests hard and deadly.

"Ah, young Marianne," Lord Och greeted her, "you've arrived just in time for the good part."

The noblewoman silently joined her master to watch Valdemar's struggle, though her attention remained mostly focused on her patron. Lord Och wore his old man disguise, as he usually did, and most importantly, he was *smiling*.

Och has been dead far longer than he has been alive, one of the Institute's scholars, Edwin the Crow, had informed Marianne on her first day. *Undeath sucked the warmth out of him centuries ago. He's only going through the motions of life so as not to creep us out . . . but it's all theater to him, a game you play with a pet. None of it is genuine. Always remember that.*

Marianne highly respected the Dark Lord, and he had always treated her nicely since she had entered his employ. But she knew better than to relax in his presence.

"Is this really necessary, my lord?" Marianne asked, trying to vouch for the poor imprisoned sorcerer as politely as she could. She couldn't protest to her patron's face the way she did the Knights of the Chain, but the idea of watching a man die for nothing didn't sit well with her. "You might kill him."

"Death is fine, I can raise him again," Lord Och replied without any care in the world. "But that will not be necessary."

Valdemar bit his thumb, spraying a stone pebble with his blood. This excited the warbeast's hunger, and it rushed at the human in a frenzy. Valdemar threw the stone into the monster's mouth while running as fast as he could toward the crimson barrier.

The pebble flew down the warbeast's throat almost unnoticed and Marianne sensed magic at work. A second later, the beast's neck violently exploded, spraying the arena with blood and guts. The monster's head flew against the crimson barrier, right in front of an unblinking Och, and shattered on impact. As for the body, it collapsed on the ground, a smaller humanoid of pure stone and dirt rolling out of the beheading wound. The creature lingered only for a few seconds before vanishing into dust and returning to its home plane.

Valdemar had summoned a minor earth elemental *inside* the warbeast.

"The stone," Marianne guessed, astonished. "But how?"

"He altered his blood to form a miniature summoning array," Lord Och answered while Valdemar regained his breath. The trapped sorcerer didn't notice the people discussing outside the barrier, as the energy prevented him from seeing or hearing anything.

"In seconds, my Lord?" A summoning ritual usually took hours of preparation.

"Young Valdemar is an unpolished diamond." Lord Och looked very happy with the results of the cage match. Marianne felt some pity for

Valdemar. A Dark Lord's attention was a double-edged sword. "He possesses incredible natural talent, especially in the fields of summoning and necromancy. I dare say I haven't seen such an untapped well of power since my last apprentice."

"Since Lord Bethor?" Marianne asked, utterly shocked. Some said he rivaled the empress herself in sheer magical power.

"Rivaled?" Lord Och chuckled, having read Marianne's mind. "Some say that, yes . . . Such a waste that young Valdemar never received an education worthy of his capabilities. Better late than never, I suppose. The iron hasn't yet rusted and can still be refined into true steel."

Marianne observed Valdemar. The young sorcerer, his clothes covered in the warbeast's body fluids, had regained his composure, and awaited the next challenge. Marianne wondered how many he had suffered through so far. "Will you take him under your wing, my lord?"

"Mayhap. But something bothers me about young Valdemar." A blue glow briefly appeared in the lich's eyes, his true undead nature shining through. "I analyzed his blood sample and noticed details that eluded our inquisitors. His body overflows with Orgone, an energy usually generated by summoned creatures, in a concentration I would expect from a high-level Qlippoth instead of a human being."

"So he was telling the truth?" Marianne asked. "He descends from a summoned human?"

"Perhaps . . . or perhaps the true explanation is even stranger. I have a theory."

"Which is, my lord?"

"That is not for you to know yet, young Marianne," Lord Och replied dismissively. "You shall investigate the Verney case on my behalf and get to the bottom of this."

"As you wish, my lord."

Since her arrival in Paraplex, Lord Och had made Marianne a private agent of sorts, trusting her to do his bidding and giving her a large amount of leeway. It hadn't taken long for her to understand why. Lord Och trusted Marianne because she was entirely reliant on him. As a disgraced noble completely unwilling to return to her old life, she needed a powerful patron to protect her from the imperial court's intrigues and let her live as she wished. But she could still use her noble name to present a good front and open some doors; even though she had been disgraced, the Reynard name still carried weight. Marianne was a velvet glove, suitable for diplomatic and investigative missions. And if she died, the lich wouldn't lose much.

Marianne knew that Lord Och had other protégés dedicated to other tasks. Like that strange boy Iren and his mutant bodyguard, whom the Dark Lord used to further criminal enterprises he couldn't officially be connected with. As for the Knights of the Tome, they were loyal to the Dark Lord but followed a strict hierarchy and protocols. The other Dark Lords, always eager to sabotage their rivals, regularly tried to infiltrate Lord Och's court through bribery, blackmail, or insidious schemes. The Knights of the Tome were specialized in dealing with illegal sorcerers or supporting other chivalric orders on magical matters. They weren't investigators, and the Dark Lord understood the value of specialists like Marianne.

"I want to know where this young man truly comes from," the lich said.

"I haven't found much so far," Marianne admitted. She had already done cursory research on her way to Spellbane and quickly faced obstruction.

She knew that the Knights of the Road, who specialized in finding escaped criminals or missing people, had supervised the Verney case. The Knights of the Chain, in charge of protecting the Azlant Empire's cultural uniformity, and the Church of the Light had cooperated on the purge, as they usually did when Cults of the Strangers were involved. The worship of these eldritch entities was strictly prohibited by the Dark Lords, and for good reasons. The Strangers only craved one commodity, the souls of mortals.

Marianne hadn't found out much about the Verneys' beliefs, since the inquisitors had destroyed every text and executed every cultist they could find. All she had learned was that the family had led a cult called the "Seekers of the Grail," but she couldn't find anything about their grail's nature or purpose.

"You are resourceful and quick-witted. I have no doubt you will deliver." Lord Och snapped his fingers, collapsing the barrier and allowing Valdemar to see the two. "Congratulations, young man. Few mortals have met my expectations, and fewer exceeded them."

"Thank you, Lord Och," Valdemar said, before bowing. "Lady Marianne."

"I will let you rest a little for today," the lich said. "Young Marianne will show you to your room and help you check on your belongings. I hope we recovered everything, but feel free to inform me if anything is missing."

The Dark Lord vanished without a sound, space collapsing around him until nothing remained.

"Teleportation?" Valdemar asked Marianne, amazed by this casual yet awe-inspiring display of magic.

"Lord Och is a master of all fields of magic," Marianne said, before observing him closely. The necromancer looked in good shape for someone who had just killed a monster out for his blood. "You impressed him."

"I hope so. It's the fifth creature I had to kill today," Valdemar replied, glaring at the warbeast's remains. "Is this going to be a recurring thing?"

"Lord Och is a harsh but fair overseer," Marianne reassured him. "You may face other tests in the future, but he will reward you in turn."

"By giving me back my stuff?" Valdemar asked, as he checked his belongings. His eyes immediately softened upon seeing the music box. The device was a box made of carved amber full of strange machinery Marianne didn't understand. Valdemar pulled a smaller lever on the box's side, and a beautiful, slow-paced lullaby came out. It sounded both happy and sad to the ear.

"It belonged to my mother," Valdemar admitted, his voice breaking, his gaze faltering. "It was the only thing that soothed her in her last days."

"It's a beautiful song," Marianne said, finding the sound peaceful. She wondered if Valdemar's mother resembled her own. "How was she? Your mother?"

"She . . . was not well," the sorcerer confessed as he paused the music box. "I don't want to talk about it."

"I'm . . . I'm sorry for opening an old wound," Marianne apologized. "Is she . . ."

"She's dead. Grandpa and I didn't have the funds to buy a Soulstone, so her soul passed on."

Soulstones were designed to catch their wearer's soul upon death, allowing a necromancer to revive them as an intelligent undead or sentient golem after their body's demise. Marianne kept one in a pendant around her neck, hidden below her coat.

"Do you have any other family members?" she asked. "Maybe a survivor of the Verney purge?"

"As far as I know, I'm the last of them." He squinted at her. "You were asked to investigate me."

"I was," Marianne replied. He had the right to know.

"Can't blame you. I do look suspicious." Valdemar frowned. "I had nothing to do with the Verney family, besides sharing a name. I was a child when the purge happened."

"I know," Marianne replied. "I don't hold your name against you, if that's what worries you. It's your acts which determine your worth, not your name."

"I wish the Knights could think like you." Valdemar crossed his arms, his face thoughtful. "What do you need to know?"

He won't open his heart to me anytime soon, but he's willing to cooperate at least, Marianne thought. "I know you were a child when they were purged, but is there anything you can tell me about the Verneys? How did you become recognized as a bastard?"

The necromancer shrugged. "I was supposed to receive an inheritance. My paternal grandfather, Baron Aleksander Verney, recognized me as his son Isaac's brood in his testament. I was supposed to inherit the family's estate if my father died without official issue, along with their occult and religious texts collection."

"They wanted you to carry on with their cultist activities," Marianne guessed.

"Probably. But the inquisitors burned everything anyway, and the Verneys were extinguished. I wasn't allowed to get anything, except a stay from execution."

A hard life creates hard men, Marianne thought with sympathy. She could see that a part of Valdemar still felt sore over the whole matter. *If he had inherited some of the Verneys' money, he could have bought a Soulstone for his mother.*

"I tried to learn more about my paternal line, but the Knights stymied my efforts and prevented me from accessing the Verneys' old lands," Valdemar explained. "Grandpa told me nothing good would come out of my search and that I would catch the inquisitors' deadly attention if I persevered."

He didn't know much, but Marianne could work with it. If there had been a testament, then there was a paper trail. "Thank you for your answers," she said. "If I learn anything, I will tell you."

"Really?" The necromancer seemed skeptical. "Shouldn't you keep everything for yourself?"

"I am not a knight bound to secrecy," Marianne replied. "I believe you are entitled to learn about your origins. If I keep information from you, it will be because Lord Och ordered me to."

Valdemar sounded pleased by that and gave her a respectful nod. "Thank you."

"You'll find that the Institute's denizens are more open-minded than the knights," Marianne said with a smile. "Most of the scholars are very nice people."

"Most?"

"Most," Marianne admitted.

"I will take what I can get," the necromancer said. "Speaking of names, I don't remember hearing of a 'Reynard' Oldblood family."

"That doesn't surprise me," Marianne replied. Since he had answered her questions about his family, she didn't see why she would keep her own origins from him. "We are a secondary line of a cadet branch of Empress Aratra's family. We're very far away from better known families."

Valdemar's eyes widened in surprise. "You descend from the empress herself?"

"I'm only a distant cousin. A very distant cousin." Marianne had only ever met Empress Aratra herself twice in her entire life, with the second audience ending with her banishment from her court. Her Majesty was very selective about who she invited to her balls and parties. "It's not as important as you think."

Empress Aratra officially ruled the Azlant Empire, but she was only one Dark Lord out of seven, the first among equals. She acted as the nation's figurehead and maintained the Bloodstream circuit of portals across human territories, but her influence was limited to her Domain of Saklas and the imperial capital. Though Her Majesty usually cut out the tongue of anyone who pointed it out.

"We can talk while transporting your belongings," Marianne suggested.

"Good point." Valdemar sighed.

"Lord Och has already set up a workshop for you in the second underground level, with the other apprentices." The first level was reserved for the Knights of the Tome, the third for the Masters, and nobody but the Dark Lord knew what the fourth level was for. "Let me help you carry your belongings."

"You're sure?" he asked her with an amused smile. "Shouldn't a noble watch me, the poor half-breed, do the work and stick to command?"

"Now that's unkind," Marianne replied with a smile. "But I can leave you to do it alone, if you prefer."

"No, it's alright, just joking. Thanks for the help."

And so Marianne helped the Institute's newest scholar carry his books to his new home. After talking with Valdemar, she had come to agree with Lord Och's assessment.

Why would a cultist baron bequeath everything to a bastard? Marianne thought, her eyes peering at Valdemar. *Something doesn't add up there.*

There was more to this man than met the eye.

4

APPRENTICE

He dreamed of the well again. His hands scratched the stone wall, while he heard the rats crawling above his head. The hole above him shone with a soothing crimson glow; the light of freedom. But it was so far away, and he was trapped at the bottom deep below the earth. The rats tossed him a half-eaten bone, one that joined their pile of treasure at the bottom. The well's bottom was covered with the remains of animals and humans unlucky enough to fall down, but he wouldn't waste away like them.

He would escape. He would be free.

Once again his nails sank into the stone, as he began his perilous ascent toward the light above. One meter. Two meters. Three meters . . .

Strange symbols carved into the stone shone with a yellow light, one that burned and blinded him and made the rats scamper off. He fell back to the bottom, howling his frustration and despair. The walls of the well trembled, and the dream collapsed into nothingness.

Valdemar fell off his mattress and woke up facing the cold stone floor. He had rolled out of his bed in his sleep, and someone furiously knocked on his workshop's door. "Hello?" a woman's voice echoed past it. "Is someone there?"

Valdemar mistook it for Marianne's voice for a moment, before realizing that it was different, higher-pitched. A lifetime of fearing inquisitors kicked in, and his psychic sight expanded beyond his door. The sorcerer didn't recognize the presence on the other side. He could tell it was a woman, one who hadn't prepared proper magical defenses.

That dream will never let me go, Valdemar thought with annoyance as his hands fumbled in the dark, seeking an oil lamp. Weeks or months often passed between two episodes, but the nightmares always returned. Once in his childhood, he had asked his grandfather about them, and he said Valdemar had fallen down a well when he was too young to remember. He had been lucky to survive long enough to be rescued.

Perhaps his mind did its best to suppress the memory, but the dreaming world left the door open for it to haunt Valdemar. Or perhaps his subconscious expressed its frustration with his lack of progress on his goal to reach Earth in an allegorical way.

Whatever the cause, Valdemar had strongly considered contacting an oneiromancer to deal with this nightmare. It always left him exhausted and troubled in the morning, and though good dream-manipulators were expensive, he would rather pay to enjoy quiet nights.

"Who is it?" Valdemar asked, as he finally found a lamp and lit his workshop. True to his word, Lord Och had afforded his newest recruit a laboratory far superior to anything the summoner had ever enjoyed in the past. His collection of grimoires and his music box had found a new home in shelves next to a writing desk, while tools, alchemical reagents, and magical concoctions covered tables of chiseled stone. He had received a magical, smokeless forge, with the remnants of the broken ecto-catcher resting on the anvil. Stairs led to his bedroom above, and a locked door to the outside.

The solar upstairs wouldn't see much use. Valdemar had put the mattress downstairs so as not to waste time going up and down the stairs each day; nor did he use the shower above unless he had to clean himself up to go outside.

"Liliane!" the woman replied, clearly overjoyed to receive an answer. Valdemar wondered how long she had knocked on his door before she managed to wake him up. "Liliane de Vane! I'm in the workshop right next to yours! I'm bringing you your new clothes!"

With a name like that, she had to belong to the Oldblood. Valdemar wondered how many nobles had made the Institute their nest. "I don't need any," he replied, still wearing yesterday's clothes.

"It's really important! Unless I'm interrupting something?" Valdemar sensed an undercurrent of fear and panic in her voice. "Oh, I'm so sorry, I didn't want to bother you! I can pass by later if you want!"

"It's alright," Valdemar said, suppressing a groan as he rose to his feet. Truth be told, he was always a bit cranky upon waking up, but that girl sounded too nice to complain about. "Take a step away from the door, I warded it."

"Oh, with what kind of warding spell?" she asked with curiosity.

"The hungry kind." Valdemar unlocked the door, removed the magical wards, and welcomed his guest.

His visitor was a pretty little thing no older than nineteen, with shoulder-length red hair, kind blue eyes, and freckles all over her cheeks. She was surprisingly small, barely reaching Valdemar's nose, but radiated some kind of hyperactive energy. She wore a blue and orange variant of the Institute's standard magical robes and carried a pile of clothes in her hands.

"Hi!" She introduced herself with a bright smile. "Sorry, did I just wake you up?"

"It's fine, waking up was long overdue." Valdemar took the clothes off her hands. They included a black and gray hooded coat, with a purple shirt and pants underneath. A pair of black leather boots tastefully completed the set. "The fabric seems a bit different from your own robes."

"Lord Och thought you might want something more practical, so he asked the acolytes to make adjustments," Liliane replied with a grin. "They're woven with protective spells too. You would need a very sharp sword to cut through them."

Nice, though Valdemar would examine these clothes later. He suspected they included tracking spells or similar measures. "Do you want to come inside?" Valdemar asked his visitor. "You came all the way, the least I can do is offer you a cup of tea."

"Oh, it's alright, I already had breakfast with my mentor," she replied with a slight blush. Did she believe he was making a pass at her? "But sure, I can take a look. Do you need help moving in? I heard you arrived yesterday."

"No, it's fine." Marianne had already helped with that, before leaving the Institute on her master's behalf. Valdemar didn't ask her about which mission, but he suspected she had gone to investigate his family. She would probably find nothing, as he did.

Valdemar led Liliane inside his workshop and her eyes immediately wandered to his paintings. The sorcerer liked to paint real world sights.

The pictures included a cute mole rat peeking through its hiding hole, his grandfather's crumbling old shack, and mushroom farmers hard at work. Valdemar had sold some of his artwork to fund his activities in the past, though he had never fully committed to a career.

Liliane looked at the paintings with admiration, before freezing before the most beautiful of them all. "Oh, who is this?" she asked, pointing at the portrait enthroned above the forge.

"My late mother," Valdemar replied, before putting the clothes on a table next to his potions. He had been so focused on repairing the ecto-catcher that he hadn't cleaned up the rest of the workshop. Unfortunately, the knights had damaged the device to the point it would take weeks to repair it. "Her name was Sarah."

"She's beautiful," Liliane said, mesmerized by the painting. And she was. Valdemar's mother had been a raven-haired beauty, with her son's pale gray eyes, and looked graceful in a blue dress. She hadn't yet gone mad when her child had painted her portrait. "But she seems so sorrowful."

Indeed. Valdemar's mother always had a sad expression, and only the music box could make her smile for a reason that always escaped her son. Whenever he had pushed the subject, she always burst out in tears. "I don't think it was in my mother's nature to be happy," he admitted.

"It's strange though," Liliane said. "Her hair is black and yours is white. Isn't raven hair dominant?"

"It's not unusual." Now that mankind had lived centuries underground, more and more people were born without hair, eye, or skin pigmentation. Sometimes all at once. Valdemar was fortunate enough to only have whitened hair, rather than look like an albino. No way people wouldn't have mistaken him for an undead otherwise. "You said you live in the workshop next to mine?"

"Yes, though I spend most of my time in the greenhouse. I'm studying alchemy and petalmancy under Lady Mathilde."

Lady Mathilde, Lady Mathilde . . . Valdemar tried to remember where he had heard the name, his eyes wandering to his potion cookbooks. "Mathilde de Valnoir?" he asked, astonished. She had written over a third of the alchemy recipes he had memorized. "The inventor of the Elixir of Life?"

This horribly expensive potion reversed the drinker's aging, returning them to the peak of their life. Though immortality in various forms was common among those of the upper classes who could afford it, most rich nobles preferred remaining young forever to becoming an intelligent undead or having their soul transferred into a golem. Since the elixir's recipe was known only to its creator and no one had managed to reverse-engineer it yet, Oldblood members paid fortunes for a dose . . . and criminals like the Midnight Market's members stopped at nothing to steal the potion.

"Herself. She is a Master at the Institute, and my mentor." Liliane raised an eyebrow upon noticing his confusion. "No way, you don't know what a Master is?"

"No, but I have the feeling you will tell me."

"And you thought right," she replied with a grin. "The Institute follows a strict hierarchy. At the bottom, you have the Acolytes, who aren't Scholars but assist us. They're the cooks, suppliers, guards . . . Do you know Iren? You'll like Iren, he can get you anything you need."

"Are the Knights of the Tome considered acolytes?" The thought of being higher in the hierarchy than the people who imprisoned him amused Valdemar to no end.

"Technically, but don't try to give them orders," Liliane replied with a giggle. "They only answer to Lord Och and the Masters, to a lesser extent. Now, you have Scholars like us, the researchers. We each have a workshop, a limited budget, and we can access the libraries except the forbidden stuff. And above you have the Masters, who answer only to Lord Och. They're the elite of the elite, sorcerers who have achieved immortality and mastered a magical field. They have unlimited resources and they can access all kinds of restricted knowledge. Each Scholar must answer to a Master, who serves as their mentor."

"Really?" Marianne hadn't informed Valdemar of that part. "So I have to find a teacher?" Valdemar wasn't going to spit on a sorcerer's mentorship, but the idea of a higher authority looking over his shoulder bothered him. Lord Och's attention was already more than enough.

"Yes, but no rush, you just arrived." An idea seemed to cross Liliane's mind. "Oh, you could ask Lady Mathilde to be your mentor! She's so warm, and she's also in charge of the local cathedral of the Light. You'll learn a lot of things with her, and we could help each other!"

Valdemar wasn't sure how to answer. A part of him wondered if Liliane's niceness was genuine, but he prided himself in being a good judge of character and sensed no falseness in her. She was just *that* friendly.

"Thanks for the offer," he said, "but I would prefer a teacher specialized in dimensional magic."

His answer clearly worried her. "Dimensional magic? It's dangerous stuff. You know, the last adventurer who tried to teleport to another world was cut in half. His torso ended up in another dimension, while the legs stayed at the Institute, so we couldn't raise him back. We had a funeral and everything."

"Well, it means half of him reached the intended destination," Valdemar replied. Personally, he would consider dismemberment a small price to pay if he could reach Earth. "Though I wonder what you put on the eulogy. 'Here rest his legs, because he could never run fast enough'?"

Liliane chuckled at his dark joke. "You're cruel," she said. "We shouldn't laugh about it."

"What plane was that scholar trying to access?"

"I think it was the elemental plane of fire," the witch replied, though she didn't sound so sure of herself. "The Dark Lord Bethor funded that project for military purposes. Something about opening a gate in the middle of the derro kingdom's border fortresses and incinerating them. But I think Master Poingcarré and Hermann could tell you more. Oh, did you meet Hermann?"

"I'm afraid not, though Lord Och said I should meet him. He's a painter too from what I heard?"

"Wait, you painted these?" Liliane whistled while glancing at the paintings. "Then you *must* meet Hermann, and Frigga too! She really wants to commission a portrait of herself, but she doesn't like Hermann's style. Why don't I show you around?"

"Uh, thanks, but I must work on my ecto-catcher—"

But Liliane wouldn't hear any of his protests. "It will take twenty minutes tops, in and out."

"I'm sorry, but I really must work." His grandfather's ghost wouldn't return to this world on its own.

"But I came all the way to help," she said, her blue, innocent eyes looking at Valdemar as if he had just beaten a helpless mole rat to death. "You . . . you don't want to return the favor?"

Valdemar squinted. "Are you trying to make me feel guilty?"

"Is . . ." She looked almost ready to cry now. "Is it working?"

Valdemar sighed, as her painful stare became unbearable. "Yes," he said with a sigh. She had brought him his clothes and given him some info, he could spare twenty minutes.

"Awesome!" Liliane said, her chirpy mood returning. Valdemar couldn't help but find the change of demeanor a bit jarring. "But first you need to wash yourself. You look as if you haven't gone out in days."

Ugh, what had he gotten into?

A few minutes and a shower later, Valdemar emerged from his workshop in his new clothes. He had to admit they felt rather comfy, though he couldn't recognize the texture. Linen? Silk? The magic inside the fibers soaked him like water.

The Scholars' workshops were located on the third level of the Institute, with the first floor used for common facilities and the second floor mostly belonging to the Knights of the Tome. The third floor took the shape of a long tunnel almost two hundred meters long whose stone walls and floor had been polished to the point of becoming smooth as a mirror's surface. Workshops and individual facilities were honeycombed around the cavern, while crystals in the ceiling produced glimmers of light. The most beautiful structure in the layer was a giant clock around which the spiraling stairs leading to the upper and lower levels were coiled. Powerful engines fueled by bound earth elementals allowed the device's crystal needles to turn, and the whole cavern trembled whenever the clock struck.

Liliane indeed occupied the workshop to the left of Valdemar's, while Hermann occupied the one on the right. The sorcerer wondered whether his own location had been selected at random or as part of some gambit.

Liliane proved a charming conversationalist, quizzing him about his origins and regaling him with tales about her arrival to the Institute.

"Let me get this straight, you arrived here because of a flower?" Valdemar asked his neighbor.

"I did," Liliane replied with a grin. She seemed quite proud of it. "My parents wanted me to join the Saklas School of Sorcery in the capital, but it's full of stuck-up jerks who prefer partying over studying. Still, I was preparing to attend it when the Church of the Light asked for flower contributions as part of their foundation's anniversary. I sent flowers I had created myself and alchemically modified to produce glows of different colors. Lady Mathilde liked them so much that she visited me, and she offered me a scholarship."

"I remember that competition," Valdemar said, though he hadn't witnessed it. He had been hiding from the authorities back then and followed the event through the newspapers. "It was only open to Oldblood families."

He couldn't hide the envy in his voice, and Liliane noticed. "I'm sorry," she apologized. "I'm sure you would have done well."

"You don't need to apologize, it wasn't your decision. Besides, you earned your stay here." Creating a new species of plant with alchemy took incredible skill, especially at her age. "I would have been more resentful if you had bought your scholarship."

"The Institute doesn't work that way, thankfully. The Masters recommend a new Scholar, and Lord Och has to give his assent." Liliane sighed. "Truthfully, I don't think I will return to the capital after I finish my studies. I would prefer to become a Master and keep working, rather than spend my days going to balls and fending off marriage proposals."

"Marriage proposals? Are you an heiress or something?"

"I'm the only daughter of Count de Vane, from the De Vane Armories."

Valdemar recognized the name as one of the imperial armies' main suppliers of metalwork. Dear Liliane was set to inherit a sizable fortune if her father ever decided to retire. Considering his wealth, he had probably purchased immortality by now.

Liliane cleared her throat. "It's not going to be a problem?"

"Forgive my language, Milady," Valdemar said while locking eyes with her. "But frankly, I don't give a fuck." Valdemar had never licked nobles' boots, and he wasn't going to start now. If he befriended Liliane, it would be because he liked her, not for her money or connections.

Thankfully, the witch sounded quietly relieved. "Great," she said. "You know, it's nice to talk with people who aren't after my money or a favor."

That explained her chattiness. She probably felt lonely. Valdemar could sympathize, having had a solitary homeschooled childhood with few friends to speak of. He made a note to get to know Liliane better, if it didn't interfere with his own research.

The duo waited at the entrance of Hermann's workshop, a single door built into the smooth wall of the tunnel. "Hermann," Liliane knocked on the door. "It's me, Lily! I'm bringing you a new painter friend."

Valdemar took a moment to examine the door, as he waited for his neighbor to open it. He didn't recognize the wards used to lock it, though he could tell the workshop was overflowing with magical energies. What kind of sorcerer inhabited these halls?

Valdemar had his answer when the door opened and milky reptilian eyes faced him. As it turned out, Hermann had white scales instead of skin, horns instead of ears, and black claws for nails. The humanoid lizard was almost two meters tall, covering his body with heavy black robes and a hood. His tail anxiously wavered behind him, and a pair of glasses glittered on his nose. A troglodyte.

"Hello," the reptile said shyly as he faced Valdemar, his voice sounding like a serpent's hiss. His robes were covered in fresh paint, and he carried a brush in his right hand. "Nice . . . to meet you."

"N-nice to meet you too. I'm Valdemar," the sorcerer introduced himself, taken aback. "Sorry, I, uh . . . I didn't expect a troglodyte researcher."

"It's alright . . ." Hermann replied, though he clearly struggled to speak the words. Valdemar suspected that troglodyte throats weren't properly equipped to use the human tongue. "It happens . . . often."

Though they could use the Blood, troglodytes lived in primitive tribes. The Empire of Azlant had all but driven them away from their home caverns; they had remained fierce foes of mankind ever since. Valdemar had never expected to see one in a Dark Lord's retinue.

"The Institute does not discriminate between species," Liliane said, amused by Valdemar's reaction. "We have a sentient swarm and a dokkar."

"You have dark elves?" Valdemar all but choked. How could they convince one of those sadists to behave? "Don't tell me you have derros too?"

"Don't be silly, Val, derros can't use the Blood." Liliane giggled. "Can I call you Val? Valou? Valdy?"

To his dismay, Hermann started to sniff Valdemar as if he were a piece of ham. "You smell strange," he rasped. "It's . . . an odd smell."

"Valdy, you said you would take a shower!" Liliane complained.

"I did!" he protested.

"It's fine," Hermann replied, before inviting them inside his workshop. Studio might have been a better term. The troglodyte's home was as large as his fellow Scholar's but lacked anything one would expect from a magician's laboratory, such as grimoires or potions. Hermann had traded his forge and shelves for a cabinet full of painting supplies and large canvas, even using his walls as murals.

The troglodyte favored a stranger style than Valdemar's realistic one, transforming common objects into abstract form. A portrait of an ashen-skinned woman had transformed into a collection of cubes and rectangles, while a representation of the hedge maze on the first floor became a strange, but recognizable, amalgamation of geometric shapes. The murals presented strange symbols, each written in a different color, with titles such as *Morose Blue* or *Furious Red* written underneath. When Valdemar blinked, the symbols shifted as if alive. The strangest painting, however, was a canvas so tall that it reached the ceiling. The surreal work represented an abyss of multiple colors, of yellow eyes, red veins, and blue chains surrounding a bright magenta rift at the picture's center; this crack pulsated as if alive, growing and shrinking around a single black spot like a beating heart.

Valdemar frowned, as he sensed something watching him. He approached this eerie masterpiece, gazing in the magenta rift and the black hole at its center. His eyes lost themselves in the black pigment, trying to distinguish—

There. A painted figure sat on a throne of thorns at the center of the abyss, watching back. A hooded figure covered in green robes, with colored shrouds for eyes and swirling tentacles for a beard. It silently called to Valdemar like a flame to a moth, telling him to fall into the void and join it inside this black sun. Yet when the sorcerer touched the canvas, his fingers only brushed against lifeless pigments.

"You're seeing him too . . ." Hermann rasped, as Valdemar pulled back. "You have . . . good eyes."

"Seeing him?" Liliane peeked into the black hole. "I distinguish a form, but . . ."

"This thing, it's alive," Valdemar said, using his psychic senses to try and analyze the painting. He could tell that the troglodyte had woven spells into his work—in all his paintings in fact—but he received no feedback from the creature looking from inside the ghastly masterpiece. And yet, the necromancer was convinced that this . . . this entity was watching them. "This is no ordinary painting."

"No . . . it is not," Hermann confirmed. "I am a pictomancer. I weave my spells . . . with pigments. Some pictomancers can create . . . pocket dimensions. Small . . . private worlds."

Valdemar instantly caught on. "And if powerful pictomancers can create artificial worlds, then maybe they can create pathways through space. You're trying to open a door. But a door to where?" The summoner cleared his throat, a chill going down his spine as he glanced at the black hole. "To what?"

Though his reptilian expression didn't change, Hermann's fingers fidgeted and his tail stopped moving. It reminded Valdemar of a prey animal freezing in place, as if preparing to run any moment. Even Liliane bit her lower lip, clearly knowing something but refusing to elaborate.

"It's something fishy, isn't it?" Valdemar surmised.

"Of course not," a voice whispered into his ear. "There is nothing fishy inside my fortress."

Valdemar froze as a chilling cold invaded the studio and the Dark Lord's shadow rose behind him. Liliane's face lost all color, while Hermann quickly lowered his head to avoid his newest visitor's gaze.

How does he do that? Valdemar thought as he turned to face the smiling lich, unsettled by his sudden appearance. Did he teleport without a sound, or use invisibility? "Lord Och . . . when did you arrive?"

"I was always here, young Valdemar. You only notice now because I wanted you to. Your psychic defenses have improved since our last meeting, but they remain painfully easy to disable." The Dark Lord glanced at the other Scholars. "The same goes for the both of you."

"I'm . . . I'm sorry, Lord Och." Liliane bowed so low that Valdemar thought she might hit the ground with her forehead. "I . . . I didn't expect it."

"Few expect an attack or a trick, so you must always be on your guard. But I am glad you youngsters have started to bond. I can see the beginning of a fruitful study group." Lord Och chuckled to himself, as if laughing at a joke only he could comprehend. "And to answer your question, Young Valdemar . . . you may see things here that the Church of the Light would find questionable. Heretical even. But you will not care. What happens within my walls stays there." The lich looked at Valdemar, his eyes briefly glowing blue for an instant. "Do you *understand*?" the ancient undead asked, his words cold as ice and the threat as heavy as gravity.

"Yes." Valdemar gulped, while Liliane held her breath. "Yes, Lord Och."

"Good," Lord Och said with a jovial voice, his eyes returning to normal. "Here in Pleroma, no path to knowledge is forbidden so long as proper safety protocols are respected, and young Hermann is very mindful of them. Perhaps you could even help him. You both approach art so differently, I delight to imagine what new idea will spring from your brushes."

Hermann nodded slowly. "I will not say no to help . . . I am struggling with an obstacle."

"Truly?" Liliane turned toward the reptilian researcher. "Anything I can help with?"

"Maybe," the troglodyte replied before scratching the back of his head with a claw. "I need to think . . ."

"I will let you bounce ideas," Lord Och said, his gaze focusing on Valdemar alone. "Young man, come entertain an old undead on his morning stroll." The Dark Lord didn't wait for an answer as he walked out of Hermann's studio. Valdemar exchanged a worried glance with his fellow scholars, before walking after the lich. The workshop's door closed behind him on its own.

Lord Och walked toward the entrance of Valdemar's own lair, where they had a better view of the clock. "What do you see?" the lich asked as he stopped to look at the device.

"A clock," Valdemar replied after some thoughtful consideration. "An imitation of derro technology."

This must have been the wrong answer, because the lich shook his head with a look of sadness. "You can't see them yet."

"Them?" Valdemar asked.

"You felt it when you arrived, and you still do," Lord Och replied. "That sensation of being watched."

Valdemar's eyes widened. "There's something invisible in this room," he guessed. "Something I can't perceive but that can see me."

"Human brains do not perceive the true reality that surrounds us. Our eyes are blinded by the light and the darkness, unable to see behind the veil. Sometimes it is a blessing, for kindness is only found in lies; but a true sorcerer must aspire for the truth, no matter how horrifying." The Dark Lord adopted his favorite pose, putting his hands behind his back. "The point, young Valdemar, is that your psychic sight is powerful but limited. There are things right before your nose that you cannot perceive, and unless you learn to remove the veil covering your eyes, you will remain blind to the true nature of our world. And if you do not understand this world, how can you hope to reach another?"

Wounded pride was a bad advisor, but Valdemar accepted the challenge. "How does one acquire this true sight?"

"Training and potions, for a start. You will have to make the latter yourself, I'm afraid. Truth is not for the unfit."

Valdemar made a note to research the subject, if only to improve his own summoning. If he couldn't perceive invisible things right before him, it might impact his own research in the future. "May I ask you a question, Lord Och?"

"Asking questions is a sign of intelligence."

Valdemar took it as a yes. "I've been told that as a Scholar, I must study under a Master and mentor. Can I pick my teacher, or will one be assigned to me?"

"You can change mentors if you like," the lich replied, "but I wonder who caught your eye."

Valdemar frowned. "Change mentors? Has one already been selected?"

The lich's eyes squinted in amusement, as if he were looking at a fool. No way . . . "Lord Och, what are you implying?"

"I imply nothing," the ancient archmage said before glancing back at the clock. "I would not be so bold as to call myself a master, for there is always more to learn. But I have many things to teach you, if you desire my knowledge."

Valdemar still couldn't believe it. It had to be a joke or something. "But why me?" he asked. "Thousands of experienced sorcerers would murder their own family to serve you."

"Why not?" Lord Och shrugged. "Truth be told, I have high expectations for what we may achieve together, young Valdemar. I will have to kill you if you fail to meet them, but hopefully, it should prove a temporary punishment in your case."

Valdemar didn't miss the ominous way he said "hopefully." "Does it have something to do with whatever force slumbers in your basement?"

"A sharp insight," the lich replied. "And a correct guess."

"Did you bind a Nahemoth?" Valdemar asked. Nahemoths were the most powerful of the Qlippoths, demigods so powerful that their presence warped reality itself. Each attempt at summoning one ended in disaster, but Lord Och could have done it. Since Valdemar had a certain talent for binding these creatures, it would make sense that the lich would use him for such a purpose.

"Who tells you the source of this disturbance is a living being?" Lord Och's smile turned almost predatory. "I will reveal to you what my fortress is sleeping on in due time, when you are ready. It may even prove the solution to your quest. But first, you must get stronger and develop the True Sight. Only then will I show you my . . . little secret."

Valdemar wasn't blind to the manipulation attempt at work. The Dark Lord dangled the promise of supernatural insight and the answer to an intriguing mystery, but only if the younger sorcerer would follow the path laid before him. The necromancer still had some reservations at serving under such a ruthless being, especially since his "entrance exam" had consisted of battles to the death with warbeasts. An apprenticeship under Lord Och would prove even deadlier.

But for all his ruthlessness and cruelty, Lord Och was the most powerful mage Valdemar had ever met; one that terrified the inquisitors themselves into obedience. The lich was older than the empire, and learning from his boundless knowledge would help Valdemar achieve his goal.

In the end, one did not say *no* to a Dark Lord.

"So how do we do this…" Valdemar cleared his throat. "Apprenticeship?"

Behind Lord Och's smile, there were fangs.

"I am a very busy undead, *apprentice*," the undead said, "and so I will only spare you one day at the beginning of each week. Otherwise, I expect you to learn and experiment on your own. This fortress is full of experts in all fields of magic. Learn from them, even if this seems a waste of time. Innovation comes to the open-minded, and inspiration often takes circuitous turns. What did you intend to work on this week?"

"Repair my ecto-catcher, and repeat the experiment that landed me in jail." But this time, successfully.

"Good," Lord Och replied with a pleased tone. "You are free to continue with your experiment, but you will also assist young Hermann in his ambition. Our scaled friend has engaged in a quest that some would find a source of concern, but I foresee you will both learn a great deal from it. The humble art of pictomancy might appear unusual to you, even useless, but it will help you on your journey."

Could I paint a portal to Earth? Valdemar wondered. What did it even look like? He had his grandfather's notes to fall back on, but they were secondhand accounts. The summoner had a picture of Earth in his mind, but he wasn't certain that it fit reality.

Lord Och immediately laid down the homework. "In parallel, you will refine your senses and strengthen your body. You heal quickly, young Valdemar, but you are alive and thus limited by your flesh; the healthier you are, the stronger you will be in the Blood. I will teach you refinement exercises so you may purify your body from the waste that obstructs your full potential, and you shall feed on potions to enhance your senses. I will give you the names, but you will have to research and make them on your own."

"This way will be slower, but earned?" Valdemar surmised.

The undead archmage nodded. "Apprentice?"

Valdemar held his tongue.

"All I offer is the truth," Lord Och said, his deep voice devoid of false playfulness. "But it is true what fools say. Ignorance is bliss, and the path we walk is not a happy one. Power, real power, demands *sacrifices*."

"I understand."

"No, you do not." The lich looked at the clock with a distant gaze. "But you will."

5

THE PAINTED KING

The world was painted in crimson when Valdemar reached the Institute's first floor.

The Potion of Insight he had drunk was meant to prepare his body for a genuine Elixir of True Sight by enhancing his sensitivity to magic. Valdemar had read that the effects could get stronger with some people, but he hadn't expected *this*. He noticed vibrant crimson lines coursing through the Institute's walls and floor, like the veins of a living body. He suspected that these lines represented the wards set around the Dark Lord's citadel and the complex network of spells meant to protect it from intruders. Valdemar would have considered the ability to see them without focusing on his psychic sight a boon, if it wasn't so distracting. He suffered from headaches, and he found himself distracted whenever one of the illusory stone veins glowed with magical energy. It would take him days to get used to it.

As he had suspected, most of the bloody leylines gathered into the Black Pillar at the fortress's center, but other areas showed a great concentration of these veins: the cathedral of the Light; the water well; the Hall of Rituals where that sadist of a lich had made Valdemar fight multiple monsters in a row; and the greenhouse.

Speaking of the Institute's greenhouse, Valdemar had to admit that it was the most well-stocked he had seen in his life. The scents of a hundred different plants reached his nose the moment he took a step past the glass doors, as miraculous herbs and subtle poisonous flowers both grew on trellises. Unique flowers infested isolated alcoves illuminated by magical crystals, and Valdemar couldn't recognize half of them. Vines and squirming foliage grew on the glass walls, tended by golem gardeners. Valdemar even noticed a few farming plots allocated to crops and mushrooms. Come to think of it, the place was much, much larger on the inside than the outside. Valdemar wondered if the red lines were the cause. They probably fueled space-alteration spells to increase the interior size. He promised himself to learn more once he had finished his current projects.

As she had told him yesterday, Liliane indeed managed the greenhouse on behalf of the Institute. Valdemar found her drying herbs on racks in the middle of the building in the company of a handsome gentleman of her own age. Or was it a gentlewoman? Valdemar had to admit he struggled to identify the person's gender. Their face was graceful and androgynous, with long silver hair falling down on their shoulders and they had beautiful purple eyes. Valdemar immediately recognized the coloration as a weak illusion spell, the purple blurring to reveal green irises underneath.

"Valdy!" Liliane greeted him with a smile, while the gentleperson examined the newcomer from head to toe. They dressed quite like a rogue, with a black coat and travel cloak. "Iren, Valdy."

"Hi, sweetheart," Iren said with a masculine, baritone voice. "So you're the new one? I heard of you, but you're more dashing than I imagined."

"Uh, thanks," Valdemar replied, not sure how he should take the compliment. "So you're the famous Iren. Liliane mentioned you."

"In a bad way, I hope," he replied with a chuckle. "I do have a reputation to keep up. I prefer to be known as mad and dangerous to know. It's better for my line of business."

"Pff, right," Liliane rolled her eyes. "Don't listen to him, Valdy. He's adorable and he'll get you anything."

Valdemar started to regret allowing her to give him nicknames. "Anything?" the sorcerer asked with a raised eyebrow.

"Well, if you're asking for a dragon's egg, I'll tell you to fetch it yourself," Iren replied. "But otherwise, just tell me what you need and I'll see what I can do. You fancy something in particular?"

"I came here to find some ingredients for a potion," Valdemar admitted. "But if you're really that talented, I'll need rare mechanical pieces. I'm also looking for Hermann, if you know where he is."

Valdemar had knocked on the troglodyte's workshop, only to be met with silence. Lord Och had all but ordered his new apprentice to help the reptilian scholar on his secret project, and even though Valdemar would rather focus entirely on his work, he wasn't mad enough to disobey the lich.

"You'll find Hermann in the greenhouse's back," Liliane said. "He has been painting a tree for a while now. As for ingredients, you've knocked on the right door!"

"Potion-making is more of dear Lily's expertise," Iren said with a raised eyebrow. "As for your other request, I'll need more info on these pieces."

"They're derro technology," Valdemar warned. "You'll need to have contacts in the Midnight Market to get them." To his frustration, Valdemar faced some hurdles in trying to rebuild his ecto-catcher. A few components had been made with derro steel, a special alloy created through a metalworking process that the derros kept secret. Azlantean alchemists had tried and failed for years to reverse-engineer it. Valdemar had heard rumors that the production method needed specific crystals only found in a very specific location in Underland, but he could never confirm them.

"Not a problem," Iren replied, confirming Valdemar's suspicions. "Truthfully, the market's head honchos asked me to keep an eye on you. You and a few other clients ended up arrested, but you're the only one who got out. It's suspicious."

"It's my former supplier, Armand de Mantebois, who sold out everyone for a lighter sentence," Valdemar replied. "My jailers said as much and Marianne will confirm it. I didn't betray the Market's secrets."

Iren shrugged. "I won't bother Lady Reynard, and I will take you at your word. Even if you were behind the leak, you're under a Dark Lord's protection now and out of reach. As for Armand, the Market put a bounty on his head. We'll get to him."

"Midnight Market?" Liliane asked, completely sold. "What are you talking about?"

"The Midnight Market is a, shall we say, *secret association* of underground merchants, fencers, and smugglers specialized in distributing illegal goods," Valdemar explained. "Especially forbidden derro technology or foreign magical items. Sometimes you'll find fenced goods too."

"What?" Liliane choked, before glaring at Iren. "Don't tell me some of the ingredients you gave me were stolen?"

"I don't ask my suppliers where they get their stuff," Iren replied with a laugh, causing Liliane to punch him in the arm. "Besides, it's not illegal if a Dark Lord does it. Lord Och and the Midnight Market have something of an agreement. They don't cause problems in his Domain and let me purchase stuff from them, and in exchange, he looks the other way."

Valdemar had figured as much. His new lich teacher didn't seem particularly concerned about imperial regulations. "How much would your service cost?" he asked Iren.

"Since it's your first time, I'll do it for free if the pieces aren't too expensive," Iren replied, smiling. "Next time we'll see. If you're up for it, you could also pay me with work. I have a bounty hunting business on the side, and I need tough guys who can keep their mouths shut."

"I'm forbidden to leave the Institute for now," Valdemar replied, though he wouldn't have accepted even if he could. Hunting people down for money didn't interest him. "And Lord Och gave me enough work on top of my own research."

"Is it true then?" Liliane asked with wide, sparkly eyes. "That Lord Och took you as his apprentice?"

Valdemar blushed. Who told her that? "It doesn't really matter."

"Are you kidding?" Iren asked with a chuckle. "The last two people who survived his tutoring became Dark Lords in their own right."

Valdemar squinted. "Those who *survived*?"

Iren responded with a wink, while Liliane looked happy enough for the two of them. "He's pulling your leg, Valdy," she reassured him. "I never heard of Lord Och killing any apprentice. In fact, I think he only took Lord Bethor and Lord Phaleg under his wing, no one else."

"That's because he erases any information about those who disappointed him," Iren said mirthfully.

"Pff, you're just trying to frighten Valdy."

"Honestly, it wouldn't surprise me," Valdemar admitted. He still shuddered upon remembering his "entrance exam." "Lord Och is as ruthless as you would expect a Dark Lord to be."

"But no more than he has to," Liliane countered with optimism. "Lord Och is just putting up a front so he doesn't look weak before the other Dark Lords, but he's not as bad as you think."

Valdemar raised an eyebrow in skepticism. "Do you try to think the best of everyone?"

"Would you rather think the worst?" Liliane replied with a kind smile.

"At least I wouldn't feel disappointed."

And Iren agreed with him. "Spoken like a wise man," the rogue praised him. "Forgive Liliane, she arrived only a short while before you did and under the kindest mentor of the lot. Give her a few months and she'll see the big lich upstairs doesn't have a single good bone in his body."

He probably had a point. Liliane had only seen the smiling old man disguise so far, not the cruel lich underneath. Valdemar hoped that she would take the truth well enough.

"Anyway, that apprenticeship opportunity is amazing!" Liliane said, trying to change the subject. "You're going to do great things, I just know it! Oh, and is that potion a secret project on behalf of the Dark Lord himself? You can tell me anything, you know that? I'll never tell anyone else."

That didn't inspire confidence. "I'm just looking for dreamshade leaves, fleshroot powder, a bottle of elemental flux, and some night fruit for a potion," Valdemar replied. "Nothing unusual."

Liliane's joy turned to worry. "Valdy, what potion are you making?"

"An Elixir of True Sight."

"What?" Liliane all but choked. "Are you mad? Do you know how dangerous that stuff is?"

"Isn't that the potion that drives half the spellcasters who drink it mad?" Iren asked, recognizing the elixir's name.

"Because they didn't prepare properly," Valdemar replied, having done his research. "One must first acclimate their brains to the higher truths of the world. I had to brew a Potion of Insight this morning to strengthen my mind, and Lord Och gave me multiple exercises."

Well, to be precise, the lich had given his new protégé a scroll full of exercises and expected him to master them on his own. According to the text, the essence of the Blood coursed through seven "locks" or "chakras" inside a human's body. Bodily wastes and emotional debris clogged them, greatly restricting a magician's full potential unless cleaned.

Valdemar had heard of the theory, but it served as a fertile ground for all kinds of hocus-pocus "magical enhancement rituals," frauds, or sometimes just as a front to promote questionable dietary regimes. Lord Och's scroll, however, limited itself to breathing exercises and using the Blood to cycle magical energy through his body to eliminate the accumulated wastes. Nothing too hard, though Valdemar had to practice every day.

"I don't believe you about the potion part," Liliane said with a frown. "If you had really taken that stuff, you would be sick in bed right now."

Valdemar shrugged. Truthfully, he had expected something like this to happen. "My body filters out that kind of stuff quicker than most. I can't even get drunk."

"A fair warning, pal," Iren said. "If you take that elixir, don't drink it without supervision. I heard the first hours are harrowing. I know a guy who knew a guy who ended up walking through his window thinking it was a door to another world."

"Did he reach it?" Valdemar asked, curious. "The other world?"

"If you consider the afterlife as another dimension, then, yes, he did."

Liliane sighed. "You're really set on taking that potion, Valdy?"

"I have to, Lord Och ordered it," the sorcerer replied. "Besides, it will help improve my spellcasting."

"Fine, I'll give you the ingredients . . . but you have to brew and drink the potion under my care. I'm not letting you hurt yourself."

"You'll drink potions alone with a boy in his workshop?" Iren raised an eyebrow in a way that Valdemar found obscene. "Of course. Nothing suspicious about this, nothing at all." An annoyed Liliane tried to punch Iren in the forearm, but the rogue had good reflexes and dodged.

Afterward, Valdemar gave Iren his shopping list, and the young man replied he would come back next week with the pieces. The summoner would have preferred to get them earlier, but it wasn't like he could go buy the devices himself. He also took the opportunity to ask Liliane what she had asked Iren to fetch her, but as it turned out, they had been negotiating a deal before he arrived. The young alchemist would provide her roguish friend with potions, which he would sell to shops in exchange for a cut.

"Why do you need more funds?" Valdemar asked Liliane. "I know our monthly budget isn't all that high, but certainly your father can provide all the money you need."

"Dad says that I have to learn that money doesn't magically appear out of nowhere," Liliane answered with a sigh. "He isn't going to trust me with the family fortune until I prove I can manage my own funds."

Huh. Wise. Valdemar had heard many horror stories about children squandering their parents' fortune when left to their own devices, and from what he had gathered, Count De Vane had no intention of dying anytime soon. Even if he did, he would probably have his soul transferred into an undead, go into quiet retirement, and keep a voice on his company's board.

His business with the two done, Valdemar bade them goodbye and went on a troglodyte hunt. As Liliane had told him, he found Hermann painting in an isolated area of the greenhouse. The pictomancer had chosen a majestic plant as his model, a three-meters-tall life-form with armor made of strong black bark, green leaves basking in a crystal lamp's light, and strong roots digging into the dirt. It was a tree. A true *tree*, not a giant mushroom.

"It's the first time I've seen one," Valdemar admitted as he approached the troglodyte. Most trees had gone extinct when the sun vanished, as they needed light and heat to survive. The few that survived underground either grew in special forests fueled by luminescent crystals, or had been alchemically modified to thrive underground. "What is it called?"

"An oak," Hermann replied, still carrying a brush. Valdemar noticed that he had brought two canvases along with his painter tools: the one he was working on and a blank. The troglodyte used a pile of books as support to sit on. "The species . . . is long extinct . . . but Master Malherbe recreated it with biomancy. She's . . . working on birds now."

"I hope to see them with my own eyes." Valdemar glanced at the troglodyte's canvas. To his surprise, Hermann had copied the tree in a realistic style rather than in the strange geometric one he used in his workshop. The summoner also noticed traces of Blood magic in the pigments. "You mixed some of your blood with the paint."

"Along with . . . the tree's bark." Hermann pushed his paintbrush against a black pigment. "Look." As swiftly as a serpent striking its prey, the troglodyte slashed his own painting, targeting the extremity of a branch. To Valdemar's surprise, one of the oak's branches fell on the ground.

"This is the simplest use . . . of pictomancy," Hermann explained while Valdemar examined the fallen branch. The cut was clean, as if an impossibly sharp blade had cut through the bark without resistance. "By using my own blood . . . and that of a target . . . I capture the essence and shape of a living being . . . to alter from afar."

"It's impressive," his fellow scholar admitted. "But any spellcaster could have achieved a similar result with a telekinesis spell."

"Yes . . . but you would have needed to be close. Once a painting perfectly captures . . . a creature's essence . . . distance becomes an illusion. I could cut that tree . . . from the other side of the world."

Valdemar admitted that it changed everything indeed. The Blood worked by establishing a sympathetic connection between multiple creatures, allowing one to influence the other; even spatial magic or item-related spells usually worked by mixing blood and souls with inanimate objects or patches of land. Valdemar suspected that Lord Och's teleportation spell used the crimson ley lines across his fortress as a way to travel between two points, the same way two Earthmouths worked to create a gate.

But the greater the distance separating a sorcerer from the target, the weaker the magic. That was why summoning was an extremely difficult art. Creating a bond with an entity from another world needed a lot of magical support to work, from specific geometric arrays to intimate knowledge of the target. And even then, it was only possible because most summoned entities used the sorcerer's magical energies to create a temporary body.

If pictomancy worked by using a painting as an intermediary to bypass the physical distance, then a pictomancer could hit a target with a spell's full power from any place. Though considering it wasn't known as an assassination method, Valdemar guessed that pictomancy had to face severe limitations. The portrait probably needed to be a nearly perfect representation of the target and couldn't bypass their magical defenses.

Hermann gave his brush to Valdemar, who slashed another branch of the painting. This time the real tree didn't suffer any damage. "I see," the summoner said. "The spell only works with the pictomancer who mixed their blood with the pigments. Do you also need the target's blood for the painting?"

"No . . . but it makes it considerably easier. Pictomancy can do many other things . . . capture a soul . . . imprison a spirit . . . create a pocket dimension . . . influence a person from afar . . . and even imbue an image with the gift of life." Hermann coughed and cleared his throat. "Sorry."

"You struggle with our language?"

"Yes," Hermann admitted. "We troglodytes use . . . smell and visual information . . . to communicate. Our vocal cords are underdeveloped, and . . . I'm still learning your language. I know the correct sound, but my mind struggles to . . . to associate it with letters."

If troglodytes used visual cues to talk, it probably explained his affinity for pictomancy. "We could use sign language, if you prefer," Valdemar said. "I learned the basics."

"It's . . . alright . . . I need to master . . . speech." Hermann massaged his throat for a few seconds before speaking up again. "Lord Och sent you to me."

"Yes, about that . . ." Valdemar scratched the back of his head in embarrassment. "I'm sure you're researching something very interesting, but I'm working on something highly complex and time-consuming. No offense, but I would rather focus on my own project."

"I heard of it. You are trying to . . . to prove the existence of another world . . . called Earth. Your grandfather . . . came from it."

Clearly, word of Valdemar's activities had spread. He wondered if Lord Och or the Knights of the Tome were to blame. "I suppose you think it's a fool's errand too?" the summoner guessed. "And that I should move on to another project?"

But to his surprise, the troglodyte shook his head. "I'm . . . actually on a similar quest."

Oh? That caught Valdemar's attention. "How similar?" he asked, before connecting the dots. "Does it have anything to do with . . . with that *thing* inside your painting?" After seeing it, the necromancer couldn't chase that strange, hooded figure's picture out of his mind. The image had imprinted into his brain, and he could vividly remember each detail. The strange, alien colors beneath the hood, the swirling tentacles . . . The image had been *alive*. Valdemar was certain of it.

"Yes . . . and . . . it may concern you." Hermann rose from his seat of books, before handing one of them to Valdemar. "Look . . ."

On the surface, the book appeared to be a standard painting portfolio, a catalog of art pieces reproducing the originals. Except Valdemar had never seen any of them, and they all shared something in common. At first glance, the pictures varied in style and subject. Some followed the *Danse Macabre* artistic style which had been the craze during the early days of necromancy, showing representations of Death attending undead parties or being repelled by powerful magicians. Others were highly detailed representations of castle gates or of streets with the houses' doors opened. Another showed the famous assassination of Surtr Niflson, the dark elf general who had nearly enslaved all of mankind during the early days of the descent, in an allegorical style. So many different works of art, but *it* appeared on each of them.

Sometimes, the hooded figure hid so well that Valdemar needed a few minutes of observation to notice it. In one case, the mysterious creature appeared among a banquet's guests lost in a crowd. In another, it appeared on the threshold of a house, but when Valdemar looked into the open door, he only saw the faintest glimpse of a land of sand with a pitch-black sun. Whether it discreetly peeked through a crack in a castle's wall or openly stood at the forefront of a picture, it was *always* lurking somewhere . . . watching the onlooker.

As Valdemar finished examining the portfolio, Hermann gave him another book called *Tales of the Strangers* and opened a specific chapter. Less of a research paper and more of a compendium of stories, the book mentioned a list of cases where this strange creature had manifested.

One tale spoke of the famous artist Arnold Vitruscus, one of Valdemar's personal heroes, and of his secret collection of paintings which the inquisitors burned to cinders rather than release to the public. Another included a secret, anonymous interview of an artist speaking at great lengths about her hooded "muse" and how much it meant to her. The ghastliest story detailed the case of a madman slaying fourteen people to use their blood for his magnum opus, a macabre fresco where a hooded figure took center stage. The artist applied the finishing touch with his own life.

"Ancient scholars called him . . . the Silent King," Hermann explained. "It appears in finished paintings or frescos . . . inspiring artists with visions of . . . a land with a black sun. I suspect that it . . . comes from another plane of existence . . . and it cannot properly manifest in ours."

"It's a Stranger," Valdemar guessed as he kept reading, ill at ease.

"All entities that exist . . . outside the Church of the Light's worldview . . . are considered Strangers. They are not . . . a unified group. The Coiled Ones which my kind worship . . . have nothing to do with the Mother of All or . . . the Nightwalker . . . but the Church calls them all Strangers . . . because it cannot explain them."

At least this one doesn't seem to eat souls for breakfast, Valdemar thought. But still, these eldritch creatures were not to be trifled with. There were dozens of tales about this Silent King, some sinister accounts of murder and suicide, others puzzling stories of unexplained occurrences or the secret life of famous artists.

"Does Lord Och know what you're dealing with?" Valdemar asked.

"Lord Och sees value . . . in my research."

"That's . . . interesting," Valdemar admitted. "But I don't see what it has to do with me."

"Keep reading."

Valdemar followed the advice and read until he reached a very unusual tale. On a first reading, the story sounded relatively normal by the book's standards. A mental asylum patient in the Domain of Saklas had drawn a fresco on his cell's wall with his blood, one where the Silent King appeared.

But when Valdemar saw a copy of the fresco in question, he almost choked. The drawing represented a strange circle, with a metallic structure similar to an arrow pointing at a clouded sky within. The Silent King showed up at the bottom, right above a short sentence which Valdemar assumed was the work's title: *La Dame de Fer.*

"I investigated . . . all of these cases . . . to the best of my ability," Hermann said. "This man was found . . . in 451 After Empire . . . forty-five years ago . . . in the tunnels near the Domain of Sabaoth."

The same year of his grandfather's arrival.

He wasn't alone, Valdemar realized, his heart skipping a beat in his chest. *He wasn't alone.* He didn't know whether to feel relieved or scared.

"Nobody could understand him and . . . he turned violent," Hermann explained. "The authorities couldn't identify him . . . or any relatives . . . couldn't understand his gibberish."

"So they mistook him for yet another mad vagrant and shipped him to the first asylum that would accept him." In fact, that man had probably been simply disoriented and unable to speak the local language. "Is he alive? Hermann, if this man is still alive, then he can prove Earth exists!"

"Unfortunately . . ." Hermann shook his head, to Valdemar's horror. "Asylums . . . when nobody can pay for a patient that they cannot cure . . ."

"They often make them available for biomancers and spellcasters as guinea pigs," Valdemar shuddered in horror, but he refused to let that chance go. "Maybe we can still track the corpse! If there's anything left, we can gather information from it!"

"I could not . . . find where it went. Some mage . . . bought the corpse anonymously. The paper trail . . . it goes cold."

Valdemar let out a groan of frustration. He had found his first lead in years, *decades,* and it led nowhere.

Hermann glanced at the fresco's picture and at the words at the bottom. "They could never . . . decipher the text. Thought it meant . . . nothing. I agreed with them . . . until Lord Och approached me with a . . . with a book in a language he didn't . . . didn't understand."

"My grandfather's journal," Valdemar guessed, squinting. Normally he would have been mad at Lord Och for showing his journal to anyone, but not this time. "You saw the illustrations and connected the dots."

"Yes . . . I recognized . . . the picture and the words . . . but not what they meant. Do you . . . understand them?"

"I learned the language," Valdemar admitted. The French tongue. "It reads *La Dame de Fer*, or the iron lady. It's a nickname for a building called the Eiffel Tower."

Hermann had gone completely silent, and Valdemar knew he had the troglodyte's full attention. Finally, an intellectual who took him seriously!

"My grandfather spoke of this tower," Valdemar explained. "He said it ruined the landscape of his hometown, but he missed the sight."

Hermann nodded to himself, taking his words at face value. Valdemar found the experience incredibly rewarding. And . . . and he might have finally found a clue about how his grandfather ended up in Underland! He could finally prove his grandsire's story as the truth, the absolute truth!

"You think there is a connection between my tale and this Silent King," Valdemar guessed.

Hermann scratched the back of his left horn, removing an insect that managed to climb its way there. "I have tried to . . . to study the Silent King's pattern." Saying that out loud would have caught the deadly attention of inquisitors in any other place, but clearly, the Institute was laxer about these things. "Do you know . . . the primary colors?"

Weird change of subject. "Red, yellow and blue?" They were the best basic colors for painting pigments.

"Yes . . ." Hermann replied, before nonchalantly swallowing the bug with a swipe of his forked tongue. Valdemar did his best not to show his disgust. "I tried with cyan, magenta, and yellow too . . ."

"Was that the reason for your strange art style and color choice in your workshop?" his fellow scholar asked. "You wanted to check if specific associations of colors or forms would make the Silent King appear?"

The troglodyte nodded. "But it doesn't change . . . anything. I have narrowed down . . . the rules. The Silent King only appears in paintings or drawings . . . that include thresholds . . . doors . . . rifts . . . murder or death . . . and only those that include blood among the pigments. It is why . . . it has a bad reputation with the Church."

"Or maybe it considers death as a door," Valdemar pointed out. "So all paintings include a door or pathway of some kind."

"I reached the same conclusion," Hermann replied with a nod. "The paintings all represent . . . doors. Except . . . this fresco. Or so . . . I thought."

At first glance, it didn't make sense indeed. The Eiffel Tower appeared inside a circle, not a window or a gate. Unless . . .

"That man was drawing a portal," Valdemar guessed, his fingers shuddering with excitement. "A gate to Earth, the one he used to get to Underland. And since the Silent King only appears in pictures with a threshold inside, it means it can detect them." This entity might know the portal's location, or at least have information on it. This could change *everything*.

"I believe that the Silent King's visits and visions are . . . instructions . . . for a ritual," Hermann explained. "Showing the way to . . . to its realm. The blood is . . . the key."

"You're trying to use pictomancy to create a portal between worlds," Valdemar guessed, amazed by his audacity. "A pathway between the Empire of Azlant and this Silent King's realm."

A Painted Door between worlds. No wonder Lord Och supported the project and thought Valdemar would do the same. If Hermann was correct, and a painting could work as an interdimensional portal . . . and if the Silent King could detect conceptual thresholds . . . maybe it could show the way to whatever portal to Earth this madman had seen. Maybe even create one.

This might have been the same phenomenon that summoned his grandfather to Underland.

"Okay." Valdemar gathered his breath. "Okay, I see how our goals align."

Hermann nodded. "I thought we . . . that we could learn from each other. Cooperate to . . . to create a portal."

"Gladly," Valdemar replied. "Do you have any experience with summoning? If you're trying to contact an entity from outside our reality, you'll need it."

"I . . . I struggle," the reptilian painter admitted. "I can . . . make the Silent King appear . . . reliably . . . but I couldn't create a true gateway so far. Pictomancy alone . . . may not be enough to create the portal."

"Maybe we could combine your pictomancy with my summoning expertise." However, Valdemar could see the danger inherent to this plan. "I hope you realize that if we create a door between our worlds and his, it might gain the ability to transfer to ours. What if he is dangerous or plainly malevolent?"

"What if it is . . . misunderstood?" Hermann countered. "What if it is only trying to . . . communicate . . . but struggles with our minds?"

"It drove some painters mad."

"Not all . . . for one bad case, there are ten where nothing went wrong." Hermann coughed, and Valdemar had to wait a few seconds for the troglodyte to recover his breath. "That the Silent King is dangerous . . . is a possibility. But . . . we cannot let unproved fear stop us . . . we cannot understand the secrets of the world . . . by running away from them."

A line of thoughts Valdemar agreed with. And truthfully, the possibility of finally proving Earth's existence made taking the risk all the more worthwhile. "If this creature follows specific laws, it means it can be studied, countered, and maybe even communicated with. The fact that we *don't* understand it now, doesn't mean that we *can't*."

"Yes . . . it is frightening because of the unknown. If we know and understand . . . we won't be afraid anymore."

"Alright, I'm in," the summoner said. "I will still focus on my ecto-catcher first and foremost, but I'll help you as much as I can. However, if we progress far enough to create a functioning portal, we will only finish this Painted Door with Lord Och's assent and presence." However powerful this Silent King might be, a Dark Lord would be more than enough to deal with it.

"Agreed," Hermann said. "There is . . . another thing . . . to consider. A portrait worthy of a godlike being . . . needs rare and potent pigments. The three . . . primary colors at least."

"Well, our blood is red and will be needed for the painting anyway," Valdemar pointed out. "That leaves only the blue and yellow pigments. I think I could help with it, but I need to learn more about how pictomancy works first."

"Yes, yes . . . of course. I will teach you my art . . . and you will teach me yours." The troglodyte's tail wavered, and Hermann's facial expression turned into what could pass for a reptilian smile. "I am . . . I am glad that we met. My project . . . many wouldn't understand."

"Many don't understand mine either," Valdemar admitted, having found a kindred spirit in the troglodyte. "I do wonder why you're going down this path though. I mean, I have a very strong personal reason to prove Earth's existence, but . . . why do you seek to contact this Silent King so much?"

Hermann's smile faltered, and he became as still as a statue. "It's not . . . not about me. It's for my people. I . . ."

"You don't need to say it if you don't want to," Valdemar replied, sensing his unease. "I'll respect your privacy."

"Alright . . ." Hermann didn't hide his relief. His fellow scholar could tell that whatever pushed him on, it was something eminently personal. "Thank you."

"I have one last question." An idea had crossed Valdemar's mind. "You mentioned that you could use pictomancy to capture a soul?"

"Yes . . . what of it?"

Valdemar thought of the day of his arrest and of his grandfather's ectoplasm struggling to manifest before dissipating into the ether. "Does it work with ghosts too?"

6

OLD SHAMES

In Marianne's opinion, the cities of Ariouth were all the same: old, dusty, and overflowing with wealth. Also known as the red desert, the Domain of Ariouth was one of the most inhospitable caverns that mankind colonized over the centuries. Its high temperature, second only to the volcanoes of Sabaoth, made it difficult for vegetation to thrive; even though Marianne used magic to strengthen her body, her throat felt dry and thirsty. The landscape wasn't much better, with rocky hills and gulches bordering a vast desert of red sand. Only the undead could thrive in this hostile realm.

The Dark Lord of Ariouth, Phaleg, was the empire's greatest summoner and wouldn't let a hostile climate get in the way of his ambitions. The summoner had called upon hordes of extraplanar servants to improve his realm, using earth elementals to dig water wells, air elementals to make the atmosphere more bearable, and fire elementals to illuminate the layer. Hundreds of these burning creatures seethed inside magical cages attached to the cavern's ceiling.

Though poor in food and water, Ariouth was rich in metals and mineral resources. Hordes of undead workers toiled in its mines and quarry, fueling the empire's economy and Lord Phaleg's coffers. His capital city of Balamon was proof enough of his wealth. Most of the buildings were made of purple porphyry, with mazelike marble streets and obsidian walls. None of its spires and towers could rival the lair of the Dark Lord, a gargantuan statue of a faceless sphinx. Made of golden stone stronger than steel, the structure rivaled the Pleroma Institute in size and age. An ancient civilization had raised this monument long before men built a city around it, and some said that Lord Phaleg spent all his time trying to unlock its secret chambers.

But Marianne wasn't here to visit the sphinx. Her investigation had led her all the way to the local cathedral of the Light and to an audience with its head inquisitor. Originally, she had thought she would receive answers from the Knights of the Road. This knightly order had coordinated the Verney purge, but their master Phaleg had been the former apprentice and now bitter rival of Lord Och. Few people knew what happened between them, and Marianne wasn't one of them. The last time the Dark Lords had directly clashed, eight decades ago, the resulting civil war nearly annihilated the empire. Even today, only the threat of external enemies like the derro kingdom or incursions by surface monsters kept them loosely united.

Marianne had expected that the Knights of the Road wouldn't care about her being an envoy of Lord Och, especially since she had consulted them on a case they solved many years ago. She had been wrong. The Knights of the Road had welcomed her with gruffness on her first day and asked her to come back tomorrow if she wanted an audience with their commanders. She obeyed, only to be told that the people involved in the Verney case were still unavailable and that she should come back the next day. After wasting half a week, Marianne wised up and looked elsewhere for answers.

Thankfully, not all knightly orders answered to the bickering Dark Lords. The Knights of the Light were the church's inquisitors and as such followed the ecclesiastic hierarchy. It had taken a while, but Marianne eventually found someone involved in the Verney purge and willing to talk to her.

Priests in white garb led her through the cathedral's majestic halls and fiery altar to a more discreet sanctuary deep in the basement, where Inquisitor Penhew awaited her. Marianne had to go through three security checkpoints before reaching her host's office and noticed plenty of protective and alarm wards. Though they didn't hold a candle to the Institute's defenses, no thief could raid these halls undetected.

Inquisitor Penhew had been transformed into an undead many years ago, and only bones remained beneath his colorful plate armor. He was signing parchments behind his desk when Marianne entered his office, a yellow glow shining from within his empty skull.

"Welcome, Lady Reynard," the undead inquisitor said with a ghostly voice, though his jaw didn't move. He invited her to sit on a chair before him. "Please give me a moment to finish, and I'm all yours."

Marianne politely followed his suggestion and took a moment to observe the trove of parchment scrolls and holy texts on the shelves. She was slightly worried by the number of candles in the room so close to the books, but priests of the Light didn't fear the flames. Many gruesome items decorated the room. The dry and mummified hand of a troglodyte; an eerie golden goblet shaped like a skull; a black cube covered in eldritch symbols; a broken mirror made of purple glass; an allegorical illustration of the cursed Whitemoon, the ghoulish rogue moon that obscured the sun in ancient times. The two craters on its surface seemed to gaze at Marianne like soulless eyes, making her look away. The inquisitor even had a picture of a dissected monster from the world above. The alien creature looked superficially like a worm, with three eyes on each side of its elongated skull. Powerful mandibles protruded from its mouth, the drawing revealing them as larval forms of the adult creature forming a perverse symbiosis with their parent. The dissection revealed the monster's organs, from its elongated brain to a mazelike circulatory system.

"Our order's words are 'We light the way,'" the inquisitor said as he put down his pen and focused on his guest. "How can I illuminate yours, Lady Reynard? I can see questions forming in your mind."

Indeed. Almost all the items on display were magical in nature, though their power was suppressed. Marianne sensed secret wards in the room's walls, lessening her own power as well. "If I may ask, do these items—"

"They belonged to cults," the undead confirmed. "It is customary for our church to destroy everything related to the Strangers when we wipe them out. Dangerous ideas kill more than swords, and knowledge of the Strangers alone is often enough to give them a foothold in our world. However, we always keep some artifacts and information behind, in case we face a similar cult in the future."

Marianne wondered if one of these artifacts had belonged to the Verney family. "Why are you allowed to keep these artifacts?" she asked. "I thought prolonged exposure to some Stranger artifacts was dangerous."

"As an undead, I am naturally resistant to mind-magic; I am not tempted by the earthly pleasures or promises of immortality that the Strangers usually use to attract converts; and I have handlers to keep check on my sanity. Finally, our security systems will destroy this room and most of the floor if any of these items leave the room. You are actually fortunate to see this room."

Marianne couldn't help but blush. "Thank you for the honor."

"It wasn't meant to be one," the inquisitor replied coldly. "I wanted to show you why you should execute the cultist you allowed into your Institute."

Marianne bristled at his words. As she had worried, she hadn't been invited to an interview out of altruism. "You are speaking of Valdemar Verney?"

"I recommended that the Knights of the Chain execute him when he was caught, but Lord Och vetoed it. Sparing him is a mistake."

"Are you questioning the Dark Lord's judgment, inquisitor?" Marianne regained her composure. "Valdemar Verney's crimes were completely unrelated to the Strangers."

"That you know of."

"Where I come from, we do not execute people without proof," Marianne replied defiantly. "If you have any, bring it to me."

Penhew joined his armored fingers together. "Citizens have a wrong vision of our inquisition, Lady Reynard. Over the course of my century-long career, my order prosecuted over one hundred thousand people for cultist activities. We only ordered the execution of five thousand of these criminals. Five percent. The rest we usually let go with warnings, fines, or after a short jail time. Do you know why? Because nineteen cultists out of twenty are relatively harmless."

Marianne couldn't help but raise an eyebrow in skepticism.

"I said *relatively*," the inquisitor clarified his words, "as most cultists don't understand what they're dealing with. Jaded bourgeois invoke the name of the Mother of All to spice up one of their private orgies. The young rebel against their parents by professing obedience to another deity than the Light. A local congregation is led astray by a charismatic con man saying that the Nightwalker will lead them to a hidden paradise on the surface. Most of these people we let go with a fine, a short stay in jail, or a memory alteration spell, because they're harmless."

"And the one cultist out of twenty?"

"They're the madmen and the monsters." Penhew pointed a bony finger at the drawing of an alien monster. "A group of them assaulted one of the gates to the surface to let that thing come through. They believed that it was a messenger of the Nightwalker and that those it devoured would be reborn as its brood. In their mind, feeding innocents to an alien beast was kindness." Then he glanced at the various items, explaining what each of them did. "The hand belonged to an undead troglodyte shaman-priest, whose revival ritual involved the ritual murder of five innocent men and women. The cube in the corner? It actually holds a pocket dimension full of monsters, and the last owner used it as a convenient way to dispose of business rivals. The mirror, at its full power, could enslave the mind of anyone—"

Though it was impolite, Marianne interrupted the inquisitor's spiel. "Nobody denies the work that the Church does in keeping people safe."

"Truly?" The inquisitor's bones rattled. "If you sincerely respected our work, Lady Reynard, you would have killed the Verneys' brood when you had the chance. When we hesitate about these things, people die."

"All I ask for is an objective account of the Verney purge," Marianne insisted, at her wit's end. "I do not have the power to slay Valdemar Verney. My master alone holds that right. I shall make a report to him in due time, but for now, I am not asking for your *opinion*. I am asking for the *truth*. If you will not give it, we can end this meeting here and now."

Her harsh tone silenced the knight. He didn't say a word nor move a finger. Instead he looked at her with his burning eyes, as if he could peer into her soul.

When he didn't advocate for Valdemar's execution again, Marianne took it as a sign to go on. "You were not my first pick as a contact," she admitted. "I looked for all the inquisitors involved in the Verney purge. Imagine my surprise when I learned a fourth of them had either committed suicide or asked for a discharge within five years of the operation."

"Many of them asked to have their memories of the incident erased," Inquisitor Penhew confirmed with a nod. "I can't blame them. The reason I didn't follow their example was that someone had to remember what the Verneys did. And what they can still do."

Of course he hadn't given up. "Valdemar was a child when his family was purged," Marianne countered. "Whatever his sire and grandsire did, he took no part in it."

The inquisitor glanced at the Whitemoon's illustration, his gaze hollow and distant. "Lady Reynard, do you believe in evil?"

"What do you mean?"

"Do you believe in *evil*?" he repeated, putting particular emphasis on the last word. "Not subjective evil, but true, objective *evil*. A malice born from the annihilation of everything good in a human being. An abyss of pure darkness so foul, that after gazing into it once, you will see it each time you close your eyes?"

Marianne considered her answer for a moment. Was that a philosophical question? Or was he leading up to something else? The Church of the Light believed that the sun would return once all living beings in Underland lived a just life free of sin. Redemption was an integral part of their credo. All souls could be purified, either in life or death.

"No, I don't," Marianne replied. Evil was but a word, and entirely subjective.

"Then be thankful for your ignorance, because that was what the Verneys were. Pure evil. Especially Baron Aleksander Verney, may his soul rot forever." Inquisitor Penhew raised a hand to grab a scroll off from the nearest shelf, right below the golden cup Marianne had noticed earlier. "Look into his eyes, and tell me what you see."

As it turned out, the scroll contained the official, illustrated genealogical tree of the Verney family. Though Valdemar and his mother weren't on it, his father, Isaac; his aunt Lavina; and his paternal grandfather, Aleksander, all received a picture. Lavina was almost a carbon copy of the portrait of Valdemar's mother Sarah, with a leaner face and amber eyes; and though Isaac Verney was more handsome than his son and with dark hair, he shared his son's gaze.

In truth, Valdemar looked more like his paternal grandfather Aleksander. The man must have been in his seventies when the church made the illustration, with a gaunt, wrinkled face and red-rimmed, pale gray eyes. He dressed all in red in the picture and gazed back at Marianne with frightening intensity. The face reeked of aristocratic arrogance, but Marianne could perceive something else inside the eyes.

"A sense of purpose," she said. This man had believed in something greater than himself, with unshakable faith.

"A dark one," Penhew said before taking back the scroll. "I have been dead for decades, and I still shudder remembering this madman and that cursed rat familiar that always followed him . . . that beast's face almost looked like that of a man, and his paws were like hands. I wish we could have finished the job back then and extinguished the family line."

"Why didn't you then?" Marianne asked harshly after losing patience. The idea of persecuting someone for his sire's crime, however odious they might have been, didn't sit well with her. "From what I gathered, you were especially thorough in stamping out the Verney family. Why didn't you kill Valdemar yourself, instead of trying to convince others to do it?"

The inquisitor let out a cavernous sound, which she took for the undead equivalent of a sigh. "The Knight-Commander of the time explicitly forbade us from prosecuting Sarah Dumont; her father, Pierre Dumont; and her son, Valdemar."

Marianne's head perked up in interest. Pierre Dumont was Valdemar's grandfather and the supposed visitor from Earth. "Why is that?"

"It's a long story."

"I have time."

The inquisitor put the scroll back in its place before focusing on his guest. "Where do we start then?"

"How about the Knights of the Road?" Maybe he would give her the answers she couldn't get from them. "From what I understood, they coordinated the purge."

"Yes and no," the inquisitor replied. "A purge was far from everyone's mind at first. At first, the Knights of the Road were simply investigating the disappearance of a young woman. I think her name was Mona or something. Pretty standard procedure for them."

Each knightly order had a specific focus. The Knights of the Road specialized in finding people. Kidnapped individuals, escaped convicts, enemies of the state on the run, bounties, the victims of disappearances . . . All of these targets fell under the order's purview. They were by far the best investigators in the realm and usually mobilized when local militias faced trouble far over their head.

"The local authorities couldn't find her?" Marianne asked.

"No. There were no clues, no motive for the kidnapping. She was some no-name apprentice nurse in Saklas. In fact, I'm sure the Knights of the Road only paid attention because they had been investigating the asylum where she worked for another reason entirely. They used magic to follow a trail to the village of Vernburg, in the Domain of Horaios."

"Vernburg was the Verneys' seat of power," Marianne remembered. "Their castle oversaw it."

"It still does. The ruins we left at least. The village was never resettled after we torched it."

Marianne did her best not to show her unease. The flat, bureaucratic tone he used made her wonder if the papers he had been signing were execution orders.

"In any case," the undead continued his tale, "the Knights' lead went cold, so they came to us . . . and, as it turned out, someone had already reported something similar to the local clergyman. This person claimed to be part of a cult called the Followers of the Grail run by Aleksander Verney and that they were the masterminds behind hundreds of disappearances over the last century."

A shiver went down Marianne's spine. "Hundreds?"

"That we know of. The cult mostly targeted young women, especially freshly flowered maidens." The glow inside Penhew's skull seemed to falter into nothingness for a moment, like light swallowed by darkness. "The clergy had dismissed the informant's claims at first, but when the latest victim's description eerily matched that of Mona . . ."

"Why dismiss it?" Marianne asked, horrified. "A man comes to you reporting hundreds of disappearances, and you did nothing?"

"Haven't you heard a word of what I said?" The light in the inquisitor's eyes burned brighter than before. Her remark had struck a nerve. "We get hundreds of such reports, and usually they don't amount to much. Aleksander Verney appeared to be the image of respectability. We thought he was just being slandered, and since the Verneys controlled the local militia in their territory, the cult mostly stuck to it and buried any investigation. We had nothing but one questionable witness."

Or more likely, the inquisitors were eager to investigate common people but not Oldblood families. The privilege of birth excused many things, to Marianne's disgust. "How was this Mona any different?" she asked. "Why pay attention to her rather than all the others?"

"She was an anomaly," the inquisitor admitted, "taken because she had been touched by otherworldly forces or some other bullshit. From what I understood, what happened to her was the last straw for our informant and he spilled everything."

Marianne hesitated to continue asking questions, as she could tell that she would find the answers disgusting. But she had a job to do, and Lord Och wouldn't take her squeamishness for an excuse. "Why did the cult kidnap young women? To sacrifice them?"

"I shouldn't even tell you. We were asked to burn all the cult's texts and prevent knowledge of their beliefs from spreading, in case it would inspire other madmen."

"So far, these people only inspire revulsion."

Her answer seemed to have satisfied Penhew, for he gave the gory details. "The Verneys worshipped a Stranger who tasked them with the creation of a powerful artifact called the Red Grail. The cup would grant immortality to anyone who drank from it, and it became the cult's symbol." The undead inquisitor's glowing eyes glanced at the golden, ghoulish cup on his shelf. "Only death can pay for life."

It didn't take long for Marianne to put two and two together.

"It's gilded bones." The noblewoman put a hand on her mouth, horrified. She had seen bone weapons and items before, but the *implications* . . . if the cult had kidnapped hundreds of people over the years . . .

The inquisitor nodded slowly. "A beast slumbers in every human being, Lady Reynard, and some are *very much* in tune with their animal side. Our laws are harsh, and our punishments often appear unfair . . . but they protect us."

Marianne lowered her hand and gathered her breath. "How could . . . how could they even reach such a sick conclusion?"

"Through trial and error," he replied, still looking at the ghastly cup. "We found early versions of these grails made from troglodyte, dokkar, and even dragon bones. This particular cup was crafted more than eighty years ago from a human male. After decades of experiments, the cult eventually identified that human maidens were the best material for their Red Grail."

"Why would *anyone* do that?" Marianne sneered in disgust. "For immortality? Couldn't the Verneys already afford it?"

"The Verneys committed these atrocities for the same reason so many good people worship the Light," the undead inquisitor said with a hint of bitterness. "They believed that their vile god would reward their faith by granting them entrance to some promised land full of sunlight. Gaining immortality from the grail was only meant to be the first step to access their deity's paradise."

The empire's laws were harsh but never cruel. Criminals were put to work in life and death, but citizens had rights and were entitled to imperial protection. Even the people who became the Earthmouths were willing martyrs. Nobody forced them to undergo the transformation.

Could desperation truly justify this cult's atrocities? No. It had just been madness and pointless cruelty. The Verneys had murdered so many innocents for a pipe dream.

The inquisitor observed Marianne closely, waiting for her to recover her composure. "Now, you understand why so many of my colleagues chose to die or forget, Lady Reynard. It's one thing to hear it . . . and another to be there, finding the bones, seeing the horrors these madmen kept in their castle's basement, witnessing the worst humanity has to offer. We are trained for it, and we even have oneiromancers to help us deal with our fears. But sometimes, even all of these measures aren't enough. The Verney purge was the breaking point for many knights."

She could almost taste the sorrow in his voice. "It was one for you as well," Marianne guessed.

"I asked to be transformed into a skeletal knight after it," Penhew confirmed. "My kind of undead is . . . less susceptible to emotions, and we do not dream. We do not suffer from nightmares."

"I'm sorry for you." This experience had clearly been the most harrowing of his existence. "And sorrier for the victims."

"I wished we could have saved them, but we were too late," the inquisitor replied. "We coordinated with the Knights of the Road to raid Aleksander's castle and run an inquisition in Vernburg. Almost everyone in that cursed town was in on it, Milady. *If* they weren't part of the cult, they supported its activities. So we torched the whole place, castle included, to make sure nobody was left to pick up where the Verneys had left off."

"Except Valdemar," Marianne said. "Why did your commander decide to spare him and his mother's side of the family? Was it related to the informant?"

"Probably, but I cannot confirm it. Our Knight-Commander took the secret with him to the grave." Penhew waited a moment, briefly hesitating to tell her something. "But between us, I have a theory. Only a theory . . . if you are interested in my opinion after all."

Marianne encouraged him to speak up with a nod. "You told me the truth. I guess I can listen to your advice."

"Good," he said, before confessing. "Mona's kidnapping was incredibly brazen, and I took it as a sign that the cult was getting desperate. Maybe their god had run out of patience with their failures, and the Verneys only had a limited time to finish their artifact. I think that they were considering . . . extreme measures."

Marianne caught on. "You think that they considered sacrificing Sarah Dumont, even though she wasn't a maiden."

"She was almost part of the family—but not quite. Anyone can kill an outsider, but your own daughter-in-law? I think Baron Aleksander decided to sacrifice her as a show of faith to his god, and Isaac turned informant to save her. It would explain why we were asked to let her, her infant son, and her aging father go, even though they had to at least be aware of the cult's activities. I can't confirm it, since I was never privy to our informant's identity, but I trust my instinct."

That . . . that would neatly explain everything. Only a high-ranking member of the cult could have provided such detailed information about the disappearances. Isaac Verney made perfect sense as the informant. And yet . . . Marianne felt something didn't add up with that story. She couldn't put her finger on why, but her intuition told her that the inquisitor had overlooked something important.

"How did Aleksander Verney perish?" she asked.

"We burned him at the stake," Penhew answered with relish.

"And his son Isaac?"

This time, the undead inquisitor avoided her gaze. "The rats, Milady. The rats ate him."

The rats? "What . . . what do you mean?"

"They . . ." The undead's armored fingers shook, and the light within his eye sockets dimmed. "No, I . . . I'm sorry, Lady Reynard, but no, I . . ."

He was there when it happened, Marianne thought. *He saw it, and it still terrifies him decades later.*

"I have already told you everything that matters." The inquisitor seemed to regain his composure but went into a rant right afterward. "I did it so that you may understand who you are dealing with. I knew this Valdemar was up to no good the moment I heard of what he was trying to achieve. Reaching that other world full of sunlight . . . he took the words right out of his family's book! The same madness possesses him!"

Marianne winced. The similarities were . . . worrying indeed.

"If you let him live, he will repeat his family's crimes all over again, and they will be all on your conscience," the inquisitor said harshly. "Lady Reynard, I beg of you. Return to Paraplex, hang that blackblooded bastard, and let the dead rest. For their sake, and yours."

* * *

Marianne left the cathedral with just as many questions as answers. When she reunited with Bertrand, her retainer was busy preparing their carriage for the return trip. The giant beetle pulling it enjoyed a tasty meal made of dung and other substances Marianne couldn't identify, its antennae rising up in happiness.

At least one of us is happy here, Marianne mused, as she petted the beast's back. Even Bertrand looked dismayed with the results of his own investigation.

"I couldn't find any birth certificate for Pierre Dumont," her vampire retainer admitted with a dejected look. Bertrand prided himself in his thoroughness. "As far as the empire is concerned, he appeared out of nowhere."

This was highly unusual. The imperial bureaucracy was slow, but extensive and efficient. Few things completely evaded its gaze, and never without the intervention of the Dark Lords or powerful figures.

"So he did come from another world," Marianne said.

"Or from a distant, lawless corner of the empire, Milady." Bertrand clearly didn't believe in Valdemar's story. "In any case, the first time Pierre Dumont appeared on any document was for the birth of his daughter, Sarah. Her mother was listed as a certain Alayne Marne, a very common name. Too common, I would say—"

A promised land where the sun still shines, Marianne thought while listening to her retainer's report. *Pierre Dumont died pretending that he came from another world full of light . . . What are the odds that his daughter would frequent a cult looking for one such paradise?*

Marianne didn't believe in coincidences. She didn't think Valdemar was a cultist, but Penhew might have been partly correct in seeing a connection between his beliefs and his family's cult.

"—yet I couldn't find any marriage document involving Pierre Dumont," Bertrand continued. "At first, I thought it likely that Sarah Dumont had been born out of wedlock, but considering that marriages are overseen by the Church of the Light, I am tempted to entertain another possibility."

Marianne quickly guessed the implications. "You suspect her birth certificate was forged."

"It is not unlikely. The Verney family ruled their territory with an iron fist and had a relatively free reign in nominating local bureaucrats. But priests of the Light are chosen by the Church." Which was why the cult informant went to them. If Inquisitor Penhew had been truthful, then the Verneys had subverted everyone else in their lands. "Hence, while the cult could hide the girl's true parentage, a false marriage document would have been quickly identified."

"But what would be the point of such deception?"

"I do not know," Bertrand admitted. "Milady asked me to consider all possibilities, and so I am."

Marianne reviewed the elements of her case and immediately identified the problem. "Valdemar's genealogical tree is full of suspicious holes," she stated out loud, trying to put her thoughts into words. "Aleksander Verney, a vicious cult leader, made him a secret heir. And yet he, his mother, and his grandfather were spared from the purge."

Did the Verneys believe Pierre Dumont's tale of coming from another world, and did their best to keep it a secret? Did they believe his grandson was important to their cult's goal?

"The more I learn about these people, the fishier this all smells," Marianne said. And the more she felt that the Knights had overlooked something critically important during the Verney purge.

"What do we do then, Milady?" Bertrand asked. "Do we return to Pleroma?"

"No." The report to Lord Och would wait until Marianne had found something tangible. "We will look for more clues at the source."

It was time to visit the lost Verney lands.

7

INVISIBLE EYES

The sound of bubbling liquids filled Valdemar's room as he painted his grandfather's portrait on a canvas. The Elixir of True Sight boiled in a flask, releasing colorful magenta fumes. The smell reminded the necromancer of formaldehyde, and it mixed terribly with the odors of fresh paints around him. Hermann and Liliane shared Valdemar's workshop, both of them reading books around his table. The former was utterly absorbed by his *Expert's Guide to Magical Pigments* grimoire, while the latter occasionally raised her eyes away from her alchemy manual to anxiously check on the potion. While Liliane had offered to prepare the Elixir of True Sight for him, he had insisted on doing it himself. He wanted to learn alchemy, not watch someone else do it in his stead.

A week had passed since the summoner started working with Hermann. Iren had proved himself as good as his word, delivering the derro tech pieces that Valdemar needed to complete his ecto-catcher. The device looked as good as new, with his grandfather's journal resting safely beneath a glass dome inside the machine. Unfortunately, Valdemar had noticed a terrible problem while preparing the ecto-catcher and he needed a portrait container to house his grandfather's ectoplasm more than ever.

Valdemar put his paintbrush away and disabled his alchemical boiler. The Elixir of True Sight had turned into a substance as black as oil, with a few magenta bubbles rising to the surface. "I think it's done," he said.

"Finally!" Liliane snapped her manual shut. "It's been four hours. I told you, you should have raised the temperature by two degrees."

"I didn't want to risk botching the potion," Valdemar replied. "The recipe said—"

"The potion's inventor didn't have the technology we have today, and nobody updated the cookbook," Liliane interrupted him. Valdemar had noticed that, while usually shy and kind, the young witch turned assertive and passionate whenever alchemy was concerned. She clearly took pride in her expertise. "Next time, Valdy, raise the temperature."

"As you wish, Mistress Lily," Valdemar replied with a smirk, before putting on his gloves to manipulate the flask. He shook it slowly, watching the concoction take on a violet hue.

"Lily?"

"Well, you do call me Valdy," he pointed out. "That makes us even. I'm still sore that you gave *me* a nickname and not Hermann."

This made Liliane giggle. "How about Hermo?"

"Please . . . do not . . ." Hermann pleaded, before looking up from his own book. "Congratulations . . . Valdemar."

"For the potion or the painting?" the summoner asked.

"Both." Hermann glanced at the newly painted portrait. Valdemar had painted his grandfather Pierre in the twilight of his years, sitting on the rocking chair he loved so much. The old man smiled at the onlooker, his blind white eyes and long beard making him look like the very picture of wisdom. Valdemar had given him a simple white shirt, breeches, and stacked-heel shoes. "It's . . . good. The colors are vivid enough . . . and you blood-soaked the pigments."

Hermann had proven himself a good teacher, if slow due to his speech impediment. The principle behind pictomancy was simple in theory: the painter mixed their blood with the paint, captured the essence of the target, and then established a metaphysical link between the portrait and what it represented.

In practice, it wasn't enough to capture the target's form. You had to capture their *spirit* too. Much like normal painting, one needed genuine artistic sensibility to become a pictomancer. Additionally, as a Blood-based sorcery, pictomancy could only affect dead or living beings. Inanimate objects like stone were beyond the magic's grasp. Hermann practiced on plants and animals because it was easier to capture the essence of simpler life-forms than a human being. Besides encouraging Valdemar to paint a portrait of his grandfather for the sake of his experiment, the troglodyte had asked him to practice on the local vampire bats as a trial run.

"Are you sure I can capture the ectoplasm with that canvas?" Valdemar asked, as he waited for his elixir to cool down. "I don't want to botch the procedure. I *can't* botch it."

"It should be . . . fine," Hermann reassured. "Ghosts and ectoplasms are . . . easier to bind since . . . since they aren't anchored to a body. You also know . . . your grandfather more than anyone . . . and you share the same blood. Your portrait will be . . . the perfect receptacle. It would have been harder if . . . he had a body."

"Wait, you can rip out someone's soul with a portrait while they're still alive?" Liliane asked, horrified.

"Yes . . . and no," Hermann replied. "Pictomancy can turn a portrait into a . . . a soul trap. If the target dies . . . the soul will move into the portrait . . . regardless of the distance."

"So like a soulstone?" Liliane scratched her cheek. "But what if the painted person has one? Or if they're turned into an undead?"

"The pictomancer's portrait trap and the soulstone . . . will conflict to catch the soul. It's a . . . a contest of magical strength between the creators of . . . of both devices. Same if . . . if the target's soul is transferred into a golem . . . or an undead body. You cannot sever a soul from a living body with . . . with pictomancy."

"But you can still trap anybody's soul with none the wiser the moment they die." Liliane shuddered. "Don't take it the wrong way, Hermo, but I'm glad there aren't more pictomancers running around."

The troglodyte cleared his throat. "My name is . . . not Hermo."

"Great, I will call you Not-Hermo now," Liliane replied playfully. Hermann looked at her with an expressionless face for a moment, before giving up. "So, Valdy, where do we start? Will you drink the potion now, or attempt your experiment?"

She sounded quite eager to see both. Valdemar wondered if she intended to drink an Elixir of True Sight herself in the future, or if she had a ghost of her own to summon. "The potion," he declared. "I need more experience in pictomancy before I attempt to summon my grandfather's ectoplasm again. The experiment might fail otherwise."

"Huh? Why's that?" Liliane asked with a frown. "Did Iren give you defective pieces?"

"No, no, my ecto-catcher is perfect." Valdemar clenched his fists in rage. "It's the journal that the inquisitors damaged."

This confused Hermann. "It . . . it looks fine to me."

"The text is fine, the psychic imprint is not," Valdemar explained. "I was in the middle of coalescing my grandfather's ectoplasm when the Knights interrupted me. The process couldn't finish and exhausted some of the psychic energy that remained."

"And . . . you think you can't . . . summon it again?"

"I think I can, but it may be damaged." Valdemar couldn't tell much until he actually attempted the spell, but he worried that another failure might destroy the ectoplasm outright. "That's why I want to have a perfect soul portrait in place to catch the psychic echo, as I fear it might dissipate otherwise."

"That's horrible," Liliane said with compassion. "Is there anything we can do to help?"

"Not much, I'm afraid. It's up to me to paint the best portrait."

"Speaking of portraits, I . . ." Hermann said, before showing a page of his book to Valdemar. "I have done research for the blue pigment . . . for our project."

Our project? Valdemar couldn't help but smile as he read. The text described a rare plant called colophryar; the exotic flower grew no more than five petals at once, each a vivid shade of blue. Though highly dangerous in its natural state, the plant's toxins could be refined into a variety of things from sleeping drugs to pigments.

"It grows only in . . . the Domain of Astaphanos . . . among its crystal ecosystems," Hermann explained. "The flower is . . . a powerful magical reagent."

"Oh, Astaphanos!" Liliane smiled with enthusiasm. "I was supposed to go there with Lady Mathilde and Frigga to collect rare ingredients. We could go there together!"

"I can't leave the Institute, remember?" Valdemar pointed out, his friend's expression deflating. "Besides, couldn't Iren get us a sample?"

"He could, but . . . I'm not sure that they will be of the . . ." Hermann struggled a bit to find the right word. "The quality that we require."

"You could always ask Lord Och for authorization to go outside," Liliane suggested to Valdemar. "He might grant your request."

"It costs nothing to ask," Valdemar conceded. "As for the yellow pigment, I think summoning a Collector is our best bet. Their blood is golden and the creature possesses the ability to affect space and time in a limited capacity."

"I've . . . never heard of such a creature," Hermann admitted.

"Collectors are intermediate Qlippoths," Valdemar explained. "They're extraplanar creatures resembling giant spiders with the ability to freeze people in time. That's why they're called Collectors, as they enjoy gathering trophies. I've never summoned one though. The higher you go into the Qlippoth hierarchy the stronger and smarter they get." Gnawers were so bestial that they couldn't be interacted with, and eating everyone but the summoner was usually the extent of their service. Collectors were almost as intelligent as humans and twice as vicious.

"Maybe we could . . . convince it to give some of its blood?" Hermann suggested. "We have much to . . . to offer."

"I doubt it will listen. Collectors are born greedy, and they always want more. Worse, more powerful Qlippoths like the Collectors bargain for their services ahead of time before they can be fully bound, and they usually ask to be released into our reality after their service is finished. We'll have to wound the beast on arrival and then banish it back home."

"You know, I'm worried that you know so much about fiendish creatures," Liliane admitted. "Lady Mathilde told me summoning Qlippoths was outlawed by the church. She said that while elementals are mostly passive and usually try to return home, Qlippoths actively try to remain in our world to cause mayhem."

"Which is true," Valdemar agreed. Summoning Qlippoths meant playing with fire, and no summoner was entirely safe from them. "When I couldn't get a true magical education, I went to the Midnight Market. I managed to buy some occult texts. The most complex summoning grimoire I could get my hands on was an incomplete copy of *Concordance of the Planes*. Only the Qlippoth chapter was exhaustive." Valdemar suddenly wondered if Lord Och had access to a full copy. The sorcerer had always resented never finishing his education.

"I still don't get why you're taking so many risks for a portrait," Liliane admitted. "It's maybe because I don't have a passion project of my own yet, but . . . you might die trying."

"Besides proving my grandfather wasn't a madman, I'm doing it for everyone," Valdemar replied. "I serve a purpose greater than myself."

"What do you mean?"

"Do you like living in the dark? Being forced to raise the dead to meet our basic needs? Confronted by derros and dokkars, sandwiched between monsters from the surface and whatever creatures inhabit the world's depths?" Valdemar glanced at his grandfather's painting. "The world he described was much brighter, in more ways than one. There was no ceiling over anyone's head, food was plentiful, and though there were wars, mankind wasn't caged inside a prison of stone."

"It's . . . a noble goal . . ." Hermann said. He hesitated about saying more, before finally finding the courage to do so. "I'm . . . doing something similar. I'm . . . trying to find a new homeland . . . for my people."

"You're looking for a world to colonize?" Valdemar asked. This surprised him, as troglodytes had inhabited Underland's caves long before humans descended from the surface.

"This Domain . . . and others . . . were my kind's home before humans . . . before humans forced us out." Hermann let out a sigh. "Even now, we . . . we are not tolerated. Lord Och gave me . . . permission to learn here, but . . . he is an exception. Our kinds . . . can't coexist."

"But we coexist right now," Liliane pointed out with optimism. "It's not impossible."

"An exception . . . proving the rule . . ." Hermann replied. "If I were to visit another Domain without disguise . . . I would be looked at with distrust at best . . . or stoned at worse. This planet is . . . too small for all of us."

"You're being a pessimist," Liliane replied. "Sure, we don't have a sun above our head, but we have the magic and resources to prosper! We just need to better manage our wealth, change people's opinions, and we'll get along."

"You are kind, Liliane . . . but you do not understand. You never had to . . . to run away from violence."

Liliane pouted. "What is that supposed to mean?"

"That you've been spoiled too much," Valdemar replied with a grin.

"I should toss that potion into your mean face," Liliane replied. "I think you're just running away with a few extra steps. It would be amazing if you could find another world, but it won't fix this one. If we don't solve our problems here, we'll bring them elsewhere."

"Maybe you should ask the empress to run reforms then," Valdemar deadpanned.

"I will, Valdy." Liliane winked at him. "But until I can get an audience, I will support your project."

"Thanks." Her moral support, and Hermann's, meant a great deal to him after so many years of being ridiculed for his theories. Was this how friendship felt? If he had known, Valdemar would have struck one up much earlier. A shame he had met these people only while under Lord Och's yoke.

Speaking of Och, Valdemar glanced at his Elixir of True Sight. It had cooled enough to become drinkable. The lich had all but ordered him to take it, but if anything, Valdemar was more afraid of not knowing the truth than the Dark Lord's punishment. If invisible things watched him, he wanted to notice them too.

"So, ready?" he asked his new colleagues.

"Shouldn't we bind you first?" Liliane asked with a worried voice. "In case you go mad?"

"I can . . . restrain him if needed," Hermann pointed out. Valdemar didn't doubt his word. Troglodytes were naturally stronger than humans, and that was without taking their spellcasting abilities into account. Hermann might have been a pictomancer first and foremost, but he probably knew the basics of combat magic as well.

"Here goes nothing then." Valdemar took a deep breath and drank the potion. He almost vomited the moment the liquid hit his tongue. The brew had a fouler taste than the sorcerer expected, more bitter than anything he had ever tasted. It felt like swallowing viscous, poisonous mud. The substance didn't even wait to reach his stomach, dissolving into his flesh while halfway down his throat. It was a struggle to drink the whole thing, and Valdemar put away the empty flask on the desk the moment he finished.

"Are you alright?" Liliane asked, immediately giving him a bottle of water. "Here, take it."

"Thanks . . ." Valdemar said, but the water didn't help wash away the foul aftertaste. Worse, a sense of unease filled his body, traveling from his throat and stomach through his blood. His eyes started to hurt. "Uh . . ."

Hermann quickly grabbed a chair to let his fellow scholar sit, and Valdemar was thankful for it. He didn't remember ever feeling like this. He had never suffered any disease, and most poisons or toxins barely left him winded. Yet the Elixir of True Sight blurred his vision, stiffened his muscles, and made his belly growl. And the heartbeat! He could hear it inside his head, as if his heart and brain had switched places!

"I . . . underestimated the effects," Valdemar admitted, before wincing as a flash of pain coursed through his eyes.

This didn't reassure Liliane. "Valdy, your eyes . . ."

Valdemar glanced at the empty flask and his own reflection in the glass. His gray irises had turned into a deep shade of crimson, like when he used magic.

Even the unflappable Hermann looked a bit concerned. "Can you see . . . Valdemar?"

"Yes. Yes, I can." His enhanced metabolism finally kicked in, the feeling of unease washed away. Though he still felt tired, his vision slowly returned to normal. "I can see normally."

"Your eyes haven't returned to normal though," Liliane pointed out. "Do you notice anything different?"

Valdemar frowned, squinting at his fellow scholars. He saw a red aura coming off their clothes, the invisible energy produced by the spells woven into the fabric. He also noticed the same glow around his grandfather's portrait. It was barely a step-up from the Potion of Insight he had drunk earlier.

It wasn't until he looked at the journal that Valdemar noticed something odd. He rose from his seat, slowly lifted the glass dome protecting the book, and examined the cover as his fellow scholars watched in puzzled silence. A strange symbol had appeared on the previously featureless book, its lines glowing with a pale red glow. Two curves joined in the shape of an eye held within a rhombus, with a line slashing the rune vertically. Valdemar didn't remember it, and yet it felt intimately familiar. Like a childhood treasure that he had never truly forgotten.

Valdemar flipped the journal's pages and quickly noticed new pictures among his grandfather's drawings. These additions were not visions of earthly wonders, but odd anatomical designs. A swirling mass of flesh trapped inside a circle; a rat with human hands and an almost human face; an eldritch, shadowy humanoid without a face, but with eyes on the chest, hands, and shoulders. These images were disturbing enough, but the last one bothered Valdemar the most. Something about the eerie humanoid silhouette contrasting with the inhuman exterior shook him to his core.

Did I see it before? Valdemar thought. He had the feeling he had but couldn't remember. "Hermann, do you see these pictures?" he asked the troglodyte.

"Which pictures?" Hermann asked, confirming he couldn't see them. "I have not taken . . . an Elixir of True Sight."

But Lord Och had. Or if he hadn't drunk one while alive, he could still see the invisible. *That bastard,* Valdemar thought. *He knew but didn't tell me. He wanted to see how much I knew about the journal.*

"So it's working?" Liliane grabbed Valdemar's hand without warning to check his pulse, before applying her warm fingers to his neck. He sensed her using magic to analyze his body but let her do her thing. "Mmm, besides an abnormal current of blood flowing into your eyes, I don't sense anything wrong. You're as resilient as a dragon, Valdy."

"I do see things I didn't notice before, but honestly it's nothing worth going mad over," Valdemar replied. "And my heartbeat is killing me."

"Huh?" she asked while removing her hands. "Your pulse is fine. It's even slower than usual."

Valdemar closed his eyes, and to his surprise . . . Liliane was right. His psychic sight didn't detect anything abnormal about his heart. But then, where did the sound in his head come from? He focused, trying to locate it . . .

"It's . . ." Valdemar's eyes snapped open. "It's . . . everywhere?" Valdemar could hear the heartbeat coming from below, echoing through the ground like some twisted symphony. He put his grandfather's journal aside to touch the nearest wall, sensing the imperceptible vibrations going through them.

You can't see them, Lord Och had warned him. *But they can see you.*

"Valdemar . . ." Hermann cleared his throat. "You should . . . wait a—"

Possessed by a feverish urge to clear his doubts, Valdemar rushed to the door. Hermann immediately rose from his seat to stop him, perhaps thinking he would make a mistake. But though he quickly caught Valdemar by the shoulders, the necromancer still kicked his door open.

An eye looked back at him from the other side.

Valdemar was so shocked that he didn't even struggle against Hermann's grip. He simply gazed at the eye, at the yellow iris and the fleshy redness around it. The organ protruded from the stone wall on the other side of the floor, right above another workshop's door. It was large enough to have belonged to a giant, and it *was gazing back at Valdemar with an unblinking focus—*

"There's one above my door," Valdemar realized, as he noticed a shadow above his threshold. Only then did he notice the veins in the ground beyond his threshold. Not a mere line of red as his Potion of Insight showed him, but a black vein pumping invisible blood through the floor.

Hermann and Liliane were saying things, but he couldn't hear them over the slow, thunderous heartbeat. The troglodyte suddenly released his grip over the necromancer, and the world felt all the colder for it. Valdemar took a step forward without looking back, unable to resist the vile fascination possessing him.

He walked beyond the threshold, and he *saw*. There were eyes everywhere.

There was one above each door, in the ceiling, in the corners; some as small as human ones, others larger than his workshop. They were yellow, and blue, and red, and violet, and colors he had never seen before; all fleshy mounds linked together by invisible veins coursing through the tunnel.

They were all looking at him with unblinking stares.

Valdemar struggled to breathe, his fingers shaking. He tried to escape the eyes by looking at the clock echoing in tune with the heartbeat below, but it offered him no comfort. Something else floated in front of the device, a burning, fleshy orb of light sitting atop a tentacled body with black bat wings. The creature blinked at Valdemar, before phasing through the clock as if it was made of water and vanishing.

"Fascinating, isn't it?" Lord Och's voice echoed at his student's side, sounding as amused as an undead could be. "And you haven't even seen the second floor."

Valdemar turned his head to face his mentor, who had dropped the old man disguise. The lich beneath the illusion had revealed himself, his ancient bones wreathed in a shroud of cold blue mist and tattered robes. Hermann and Liliane stood behind the Dark Lord, though they were clearly more worried for Valdemar's safety than anything else.

"Lord Och?" Valdemar asked, his throat sore. The heartbeat around him had become background noise, easy to ignore . . . but the eyes' gaze remained unbearable. "You're . . . not using your glamour?"

"You pierced the veil, my apprentice. You see me as I am, and the world as it is."

After a moment of hesitation, Hermann found the courage to interrupt the lich. "Lord Och, if I may . . . he should rest."

"What he should do is my concern alone, Hermann," the lich replied dismissively. "Your concerns are unwarranted. My apprentice has no wish to throw himself out a window."

The Dark Lord gazed at Valdemar. "Will you?"

Valdemar glanced at the eyes, at the dreadful implications behind their existence . . . they had *always* been there, watching him. And now that the potion had opened his mind, he would see them forever. Valdemar would never escape their gaze. He would hear the heartbeat beneath his feet, always wonder if a creature was waiting to pass through a wall to ambush him. His fingers shook, his throat felt sore. If a tunnel looked like this . . . how did the rest of the world? What things outside the Institute's walls had caused so many to go mad after taking that elixir? And the implications . . . the heartbeat, the force coming from below, the eyes in the walls . . .

Valdemar wasn't one to flinch away from the truth, but . . . for the first time in many years, he asked a question whose answer he dreaded. "This place," Valdemar said, gazing back at the eyes. "Is it . . . is it alive?"

"My fortress?" Lord Och's teeth transformed into a ghastly smile. "Or the world?"

8

VERNBURG

The carriage drove along a black seacoast, toward the Verneys' lost lands. Also called the Lightless Ocean, this immense body of water flooded half of the Domain of Horaios and many caverns mankind had not yet explored. Its presence had made this particular region the most fertile in the empire, with farmers and fishermen making up almost all of its working population. Some even called Horaios humanity's granary. It was also the largest of the Dark Lords' dominions, so huge that it took weeks to ride from one side to the other. Earthmouth portals made traveling easier, but there were only so many of them. The Verneys' old lands were located in an isolated region to the cavern's northeast, days away from the closest city; even the crystal lighthouses that illuminated the Domain had grown scarcer.

Marianne spent the whole ride examining pictures of the Verney family tree that Penhew had gladly given her. She knew something had eluded the inquisitors, and now that she could compare them with drawings of Valdemar and his mother, she could tell exactly what.

"Bertrand," Marianne called out to her retainer through the carriage's window.

"Yes, Milady?" Bertrand answered while keeping his attention on the road. He had driven for hours now, showing no more signs of fatigue than the giant beetle pulling their carriage.

"How old was Lavina Verney when she perished?"

"Thirty-seven, according to official records."

"And Sarah Dumont?"

"She was nineteen when the purge happened. Why is Milady asking?"

"Because they look too much alike," Marianne said, as she compared the two pictures. Indeed, Valdemar's "aunt" looked almost exactly like an older version of his mother. As for Isaac Verney . . . "While Valdemar doesn't look all that much like his father." The hair color was wrong for a start, and while he had the Verney look, Valdemar could have inherited these genes from his paternal grandfather, Aleksander. Valdemar had been a baby when the purge took place, but as an adult, the differences were too numerous to ignore.

"Lavina Verney was old enough to be Sarah's mother and never married as far as we know," Marianne said. "It would explain the forged birth certificate." Noble families were extremely traditionalist, as Marianne could attest. Noblewomen were expected to remain virgins until they married, so Lavina Verney having a bastard would have caused a scandal and destroyed her chances to marry into the Oldblood.

"Is Milady suggesting Isaac Verney bedded his secret niece?"

Somehow, Bertrand said these words with such a flat, deadpan tone that Marianne couldn't help but chuckle. "I don't think he's actually Valdemar's father," she replied. "Or at least, not if my theory is correct. I would expect Valdemar to be less robust if his family tree was a tangled vine."

"But if Isaac Verney isn't the father, who is it?" That was the real question.

Aleksander Verney intended to let Valdemar inherit everything should something happen to him, which meant the so-called bastard was a lot more important than he appeared. Then there was the small matter of his unnaturally efficient metabolism, the magical signs that Lord Och detected, and the unnatural stench Bertrand noticed around him . . .

Was he even a natural Verney at all? He had the family look, but . . . powerful biomancers could create homunculi and clones, and Valdemar exhibited abilities Marianne would expect to see in mutants. The Verney cult had done so many terrible things; creating an artificial heir wouldn't even surprise her.

"Let's hope the inquisitors left a clue or two when they torched the family castle," Marianne replied as she put the drawings aside in a compartment beneath her seat. "How far are we from it?"

"We can already see it, Milady."

Marianne looked through the window. The crumbling walls of Verney Castle awaited a few kilometers away from the road, standing over a cliff like a twisted black candle. Ancient crystal beacons along the shores allowed Marianne to see the fortress's shadow. Its five broken towers reminded her of a wicked hand reaching for the skies. At its peak, it must have been a modest castle by imperial standards: fitting for a lesser noble but unsuited for a wealthier household. Marianne's mother would have derided it as a pauper's den. The castle's cliff overshadowed a small fishing hamlet along the Lightless Ocean's shore. It looked large enough to accommodate a few hundred souls but no more. Lights came from the houses, like embers in a fireplace.

"Is this the village of Vernburg?" Marianne asked Bertrand, as she started to wonder if they had reached the right location. "Have we veered off track?"

"I am certain that this is our destination."

Then something was wrong. "Inquisitor Penhew told me that it had never been resettled." All the guards they met on the way said they would only find ruins, but the village looked perfectly normal. Lively even.

"Milady, this place stinks," said Bertrand while pinching his nose.

"We will go there and investigate," Marianne replied with a nod. With luck, it would just be squatters having taken over the ruins.

"That is not what I meant," her vampire retainer replied. "The place smells like Mr. Valdemar. It's the same stench all over the village."

"Oh?" Marianne's hand instinctively brushed against her rapier. "Approach it quietly, but be ready for anything."

"As Milady wishes." Bertrand had the beetle veer off the road, and they made their way to Vernburg in silence.

It took them less than an hour to get there, but the smell reached them first. If anything, Bertrand had undersold the stench of the place. Vernburg reeked with the odors of rotten fish, rats, and burnt oil. The streets were made of planks covering a muddy ground, dimly lit by faltering lanterns. Though they looked functional, the wattle-and-daub houses were in poor condition, their walls covered in dung. Marianne noticed rats crawling on the wooden roofs, some looking at the approaching carriage without any fear of man.

Bertrand stopped the coach at the town's entrance, and Marianne didn't wait for him to open her door to get out. She activated her psychic sight the moment she stepped away from her vehicle. Her senses were not as sharp as most sorcerers, but it should give her an inkling of the situation. She only saw darkness. An invisible crimson mist covered the hamlet, shrouding it from her magical sight. She couldn't even detect the rats within its walls. A power eclipsing her own had taken over the village as its playground.

"Something interferes with my magic, Milady," Bertrand warned her.

"Mine too, which means a sorcerer is involved." Marianne had hoped to find clues but not something of this magnitude. "How far are we from the nearest guard station?"

"I would say three days. Our beetle is tired and needs rest."

So they couldn't expect to gather reinforcements and come back in short order. The fact that nobody had mentioned this phantom village bothered Marianne as well. The Knights occasionally patrolled this area, so why hadn't they noticed something?

"Scout the outskirts in mist form, look for wards, and report back to me," she ordered Bertrand. "I will send a messenger bat in the meantime."

"As Milady wishes." The vampire turned into a misty cloud and flew away, leaving Marianne alone. The noblewoman immediately looked into her carriage's hidden compartments, where a black vampire bat with four wings slept inside a small cage.

Biomancers had enhanced these animals to fly nonstop for days and instinctively seek out the magical signature of the Knights' beacons; the Dark Lords distributed them to their agents in case they ever needed to communicate quickly. Marianne wrote a small message on a parchment letter, attached it to the animal's back, and then let it fly away.

Bertrand returned from his errand a few minutes later, more distressed than ever. "I have not detected any ward in the outskirts," he admitted. "Although I noticed an abnormally high amount of wild rats in the area."

The Verneys' last patriarch had been quite fond of those rodents. "Did you try to fly over the houses?"

"I did, but whatever obscures my sight also forces me to transform back whenever I fly too close." The vampire's jaw clenched. Bertrand did that when he was under stress. "I would have expected a derro antimagical device to be the cause, but it would disable the spell shrouding this village. I could not transform either on the Institute's grounds before Lord Och altered the wards not to affect me."

So the magic at work within these walls rivaled that of a Dark Lord's fortress. "This can't have gone unnoticed." Marianne stated the obvious. "Did we interrupt a magical ritual of some kind?"

"I cannot say, Milady," Bertrand replied while examining the houses. "However, one does not raise a full village in the blink of an eye. If these houses were burned to the ground, it would have taken weeks, maybe months to rebuild."

This conundrum gave her a headache. The sensible thing was to establish a camp nearby and wait for reinforcements, but what if they had stumbled into something they shouldn't have? If a ritual was at work in the area, waiting for days would let it run its course. Marianne couldn't let that happen.

"We go in and try to locate the mage behind the protective spell," Marianne said. "If we face resistance, we retreat at once. Gathering information is our priority."

Bertrand responded with a nod, his eyes briefly turning red. "Shall we split up to cover more ground?"

"Absolutely not." Divided they would make an easier target. "Stay close to me."

Marianne took a step forward, Bertrand following her like a shadow. The street planks creaked as she moved, and the noblewoman worried that they might collapse beneath her feet.

Though the village appeared empty at first glance, it didn't take long for the investigators to meet one of the locals. An old man with a crooked back and dusty, tattered clothes cleaned the threshold of a house with a broom.

"Greetings, sir," Marianne said. The old man didn't raise his head to look at her, nor did he respond. "Forgive me for interrupting you, but is this Vernburg?"

Up close, the man reeked of rot and alcohol. The light of a street lantern reflected in his tired white eyes. "There are rats all over the shop," he replied with a gruff voice. "All those dirty rodents, biting my fingers at night."

"Sir?" Marianne asked, slightly worried by the answer. The man seemed . . . absentminded.

Bertrand's response was far less polite. "Milady asked you a simple question," he said firmly. "Answer by yes or no."

"I told the baron to keep his rat in check," the old man replied. He didn't seem to have registered Bertrand's existence, and the baron's mention left Marianne puzzled. "'It's not a rat at all,' he said, 'not a rat.' Like that made it alright."

Marianne looked up at the houses' roofs, but to her surprise, the rodents had vanished. "Sir, are you talking about Baron Aleksander?" she asked, trying to change the subject.

"Doesn't matter," the man said, but his tone made Marianne doubt he was answering her question, "just have to wait until the egg hatches. Just a little longer, and it'll be all over soon."

Only then did Marianne notice that he kept cleaning the spot, over and over again. After watching his repetitive actions for a full minute, the noblewoman and her retainer silently walked past the madman.

While sparsely populated, the hamlet turned out to be far from empty. Marianne crossed paths with a few locals: a washerwoman cleaning clothes by the shore; old vagrants sleeping near a small, crumbling church dedicated to the Light; fishermen tending to their boats. The village appeared gloomy but unremarkable at first glance.

A closer examination revealed worrying oddities. The fishermen tended to rotting boats unable to take to the sea. The washerwoman's clothes were full of holes. And the vagrants didn't respond when Marianne tossed them a few coins.

None of them answered her questions, instead replying with inane nonsense. "Soon I'll be young again," said the washerwoman, "with perfect skin and juicy flesh." "I wonder when Shelley will come back," muttered a fisherman, but he wouldn't reveal who he was talking about. "We weren't meant to be like this," whispered a vagrant with empty eyes, "we'll be our true selves soon."

They looked alive. They had a heartbeat and breathed as far as Marianne could tell. But they behaved like soulless automatons.

"They smell like Mr. Valdemar, Milady," Bertrand warned her as they continued their search. "All of them. The odors are much weaker, but similar enough."

"And they don't seem to notice each other any more than they pay attention to us," Marianne said as she looked through the window of a house. She saw three bowls on a table, full of mud and worms. "Zombies?"

"They breathe," Bertrand replied with a frown. "Although . . ."

"Although?"

"Their blood smells wrong to my senses," the vampire replied. "It feels fake, for lack of a better term. Same for the odors of fish, alcohol, rot . . . Only the rats and Mr. Valdemar's stench appear genuine to me. It reminds me of the homunculi Lady Mathilde raises in her lab."

"Then they're artificial creatures?" That would explain their near-mindlessness. "Is this a biomancer's work?"

"To clone an entire village would take too many resources for a single biomancer," Bertrand pointed out. "Such an operation would require a Dark Lord's backing."

Marianne remained silent a moment, as she tried to make sense out of this mess. What was going on here?

"Does Milady want me to rough one of them up?" Bertrand asked. "This would be quicker."

"No violence, please." Besides the fact that it was just plain wrong, she had the feeling it would escalate into something far worse than a muscled interrogation. "Do you smell anything else?"

Bertrand closed his eyes. "I sense a strong odor of dried blood at the town's center."

Dried blood . . . Valdemar's stench . . . rats everywhere . . .

"This place was once a den of cultists worshiping a dangerous Stranger," Marianne said. "Could it be that one of their rituals had a delayed effect and warped reality? Could it be possible to transport a village through time?"

"I do not know," Bertrand replied. "That seems unlikely."

"This whole scenario feels unlikely." If the cult had permanently damaged reality in the area, why hadn't the Knights quarantined it? Either the place must have appeared completely normal when the last patrol checked on it, or the force that obscured Marianne's arcane sight had managed to hide the truth for years. "Let's check the town's center."

She had the feeling many things would become clearer once they checked this area . . . and hopefully, they wouldn't have to resort to violence.

Bertrand walked through the streets with the confidence of a bloodhound on the hunt, and their path led them through a small graveyard behind the old church. A dozen tombstones were erected in the backyard, and Marianne took a moment to examine them. To her surprise, almost all of them were blank. There were two exceptions.

"Wait," Marianne called Bertrand, as she examined these anomalies more closely. "Let me see."

Not only were these two stones the only ones with words, but they each also had a hole dug before them. Though a layer of dust covered them, the carved epitaphs were clear and easy to read.

Marianne Reynard
475–496 A.E.
She talked too much.

Bertrand Dugéclin
149–496 A. E.
Loyal to the bitter end.

Marianne immediately generated a layer of bone armor beneath her clothes, and she called upon the Blood to strengthen her flesh.

"Milady." Even the usually unflappable Bertrand spoke with worry. And he should be worried. Only Marianne and he himself knew his birthdate, which meant that whatever force wrote these words had read his mind without being noticed. "I *strongly* suggest that we leave."

"Not yet." Marianne looked around herself, but nobody seemed to be watching them. "Whoever you are, you do not frighten me. I shall not be intimidated."

Only silence answered.

"Stay hidden then," Marianne said with a shrug. "I will get to the bottom of this anyway."

Though she remained steadfast, Bertrand's hand never left his longsword's pommel and his eyes remained red as blood. The vampire retainer led the duo to the center of the hamlet, a nearly empty plaza with an old well at its center. Unlike the rest of the village, the structure was made of strong gray stones and large enough to pull an ox through. A young woman in her early thirties sang a tune to herself next to the well, oblivious to the strong smell of dried blood coming off from it. At this distance, the odor choked the air so much Marianne struggled not to pinch her nose.

"Oh, hello!" The woman greeted the investigators with a smile, spooking Marianne. It was the first time a villager acknowledged their existence. "Are you visitors?"

"Of a sort," Marianne replied, examining the woman carefully. She was pretty, with doe eyes, and wore her light brown hair in an outdated bun. Her light dress was out of fashion, and she didn't carry any weapon. Marianne knew better than to drop her guard, however. For all she knew, the woman might be the sorcerer behind everything. "Is this Vernburg?"

"Why, yes it is," the woman replied with a look of concern. "Are you lost?"

"No, no, this . . . this is the place we were looking for." Marianne sensed Bertrand tense up behind her, as if he half-expected the mysterious woman to attack them. "What is happening here?"

"What do you mean?" The woman seemed genuinely puzzled. "Are you from Saklas too? I recognize the accent."

"Yes, indeed." Marianne wasn't sure what to make of her. Either that woman was an amazing actress, or she was another absentminded denizen of this town. "What's your name?"

"Mona," the woman replied. "Happy to meet you."

A chill went down Marianne's spine. "Would you happen to be a nurse?" she asked, her hand tightening around her rapier's pommel.

"Yes, how did you know?" The woman's eyes lit up. "Oh, are you knights? Did you come for me?"

Marianne didn't know how to answer, so Bertrand took over. "Yes," he lied. "We are knights investigating your disappearance."

"You shouldn't have," the woman replied in an innocent way that Marianne found more and more eerie. "It's all a big misunderstanding."

"You weren't kidnapped?" Marianne found the courage to ask the dead woman. *Not a biomancer,* she thought, *a necromancer.*

"In a way. I was very frightened when the masked men seized me after work, but they brought me to the baron instead. He was such a gentleman. He said I hadn't been abducted, but rather *chosen.* That I had a destiny. *Me.*" Mona chuckled to herself, oblivious to the sinister tones of her words. "He gave me beautiful jewels and said I would have more if I did my job well. Such a kind man. His rat frightens me though. Its face is almost like a human's. Creepy dirty thing."

"Baron Aleksander Verney?" Bertrand continued the interrogation with firm focus, while Marianne tried to make sense out of the situation. The woman in front of her looked too alive to be an undead. Even a vampire had telltale signs, if you knew where to look. "What was your destiny?"

"He asked me to take care of his grandson," Mona answered to Marianne's surprise. "He's growing unruly, and his mother can't calm him anymore. I took care of old Paul, so I could take care of a little boy. The baron was very happy that I took the job, as Crétail is a very important child. The previous two nurses weren't good enough for him, so they were fired."

"Crétail?" Marianne asked in confusion, doing her best to ignore the "fired" part. She had the feeling the maids faced the same gruesome fate as Mona herself. "You mean Valdemar?"

"Valde . . . mar?" Mona squinted at Marianne. "What is that?"

"Valdemar Verney. The baron's grandson."

Mona frowned while trying to remember. "I'm sorry," she apologized after a few minutes. "I never heard of a child with that name. Are you sure the name is not Crétail?"

"Yes." Baron Aleksander's testament explicitly named Valdemar as his heir, not "Crétail." What was going on here? Was this all a ghastly prank of some sort? "Who is this Paul?"

"Old Paul," Mona answered with a sad sigh. "The doctors at the asylum thought he was mad, but they were wrong. He came from another world, but nobody understood him. I taught him a few words in our tongue when I brought him his meals. Poor man, he didn't deserve it . . . I asked the baron if he could help, and he said he would. It wouldn't be the first time."

The more Marianne listened, the less it made sense. "What do you mean?" she asked.

"The baron said old Paul wasn't alone. Pierre, they called him. The other man."

"Pierre Dumont?" As odd and insane as this encounter sounded, it might give Marianne some clues.

Mona's eyes lit up in recognition. "Yes, that was his name," she confirmed. "I never met him, but they say I will meet him soon. He's a very important person."

Marianne was about to question her some more, when Bertrand unsheathed his longsword. "Milady, the roofs," he said with an alarmed voice.

Marianne looked up.

Dozens, hundreds of rats were silently crawling on the houses' roofs around the square. The black-furred beasts varied in size, some of them almost as large as cats. They glared at Marianne and Bertrand with bloodshot, red-rimmed eyes. Marianne tried to look for a human-faced one among them but found none. However, she could sense an inhuman intelligence in their gaze.

"So that's how it is . . ." Marianne muttered to herself as she grabbed her rapier in one hand and her pistol in the other. Ignoring the puzzled Mona's confusion, the noblewoman pointed her firearm at the rodents. "Whoever you are, attacking us will be an affront to Lord Och of Paraplex. We will fight, and even if you prevail, others know we came here. You won't be able to cover your tracks."

The rats answered with a maddening chitter.

They're laughing, Marianne realized. Since she had very little time ahead, the noblewoman took a few seconds to glance into the well.

The pit went on and on into pitch-black darkness. Though Marianne couldn't see the bottom—if it had one—she could smell the odors of burnt blood all too well. Using her psychic sight up close, she grew certain that the strange power clouding it came straight from this black abyss.

There's something at the bottom, Marianne realized in horror. *The source of all this madness.*

A rift in space and time to an eldritch realm? A magical artifact? Maybe a living creature controlling the rats on the surface?

"Is something wrong?" Mona asked, utterly oblivious to the situation happening around her.

"Excuse my boldness, Miss Mona but . . ." Marianne tried to find the right words as she looked away from the well. "How can I say this . . ."

"Say what?"

"I think you are dead," Marianne admitted.

Mona blinked in confusion. The words didn't seem to have registered. "What do you mean?"

"You were killed almost two decades ago by the Followers of the Grail," Marianne said. The rats stopped chittering all at once. If anything, their silence felt twice as threatening. "Your bones were found in Verney Castle's ruins."

"The Followers of the Grail? What, that silly church?" Mona giggled. "Why would they need me to make a cup? They made their grail long ago!"

Somehow, Marianne found that answer more horrifying than all the others. "Miss Mona, don't you remember?"

"Remember what?" Mona grew more and more agitated, while Bertrand looked for a way out. But though they made no move to attack, the rats had them surrounded. "Why are you saying these awful things?"

"Crétail? Do you remember this Crétail?" Marianne asked, trying to get any answer she could. She was close to uncovering this mystery. She could feel it in her bones. "How does he look?" Was that Valdemar's true name? Something linked to the grail? Marianne knew she didn't have much time left before something terrible happened.

"Crétail? He's a sweet child. He's a very sweet child . . ." Mona began to shake. "He . . . he likes the music box very much. He likes the music, but . . ."

"But?"

"He's a very unruly child. But he's sweet, he's . . ." Mona held her head with her hands, her eyes widening. "That's the blood, they said. He can't help it, he was born wrong. There's something wrong with him, it's not his fault if he's like this . . . and he's hungry, he's always hungry . . ."

To her horror, Marianne noticed *something* crawling beneath Mona's skin. The dead woman's back started to grow, to burst like a bag too small for its content. "Mona?" Marianne asked, instinctively preparing a basic healing spell. "Mona, calm down, it's going to be alr—"

White tentacles erupted from inside Mona, tearing the skin like a cloth.

Marianne took a leap backward before the squirming appendages could catch her and fired a shot midair. The bullet hit the monster in its eyeless face, causing it to screech with its triangular, fanged mouth. No blood came out of the wound, but its tentacles thrashed around in pain all the same.

The monster might have looked vaguely humanoid at a distance, but white as milk and utterly featureless save for a gnawing maw. Both its hands and legs ended in sinuous tentacles instead of fingers, and they lunged at Marianne like a net. Bertrand swiftly intervened and cut one of its arms with his sword. Marianne shot the monster in the chest while it wailed, sending it falling into the well.

There was no trace of blood or flesh left from Mona; only dry skin which the horror had worn like a suit.

Marianne ground her teeth, her pistol's tip smoking. "What was *that*?"

"A Qlippoth," Bertrand said with a scowl, as they heard more screeches around the hamlet. The rats echoed them with a chittering cacophony, like twisted hosts inviting other monsters to a feast.

The villagers were coming.

"Bring it," Marianne said while cocking her pistol.

9

VERMINTOWN

The rats watched as Vernburg's streets were drenched in blood. Marianne and Bertrand had tried to flee the cursed hamlet, only for the villagers to intercept them in the graveyard. The noblewoman felt somehow relieved that they still wore human clothes, for that was the only vestige of humanity they had left.

The vagrants near the church had grown white tentacles, the skin torn apart to reveal the same monstrosity that had impersonated Mona. A sailor had melted into a pile of red goo with human faces screaming beneath the slime. A fisherwoman's neck had elongated alongside her arms, her neck growing fanged gills. The rats observed from the roofs, their maddening cacophony droning into Marianne's ears.

And so she danced. With her rapier in one hand and her pistol in the other, Marianne charged into the fray. The mutated fisherwoman lunged at her, determined to bite her head off. Marianne made the beast eat a fistful of bullets, before gutting her chin to groin with her rapier. The mutant stumbled and a kick to the chest sent it falling backward. The monster collapsed on the tombstone the dark power behind the hamlet had made for Marianne, shattering it utterly before falling into the open grave.

"You won't bury me," Marianne said softly while swinging her blade. "But I *will* bury you if you don't back down."

The monsters showed no fear and charged. Marianne counted half a dozen, but she could hear the screech of their kindred coming closer.

This entire hamlet was a death trap that they had to break out of before getting overwhelmed.

Bertrand covered her flank, slashing one tentacled monster with his longsword while telekinetically slamming another against a gravestone. His movements were a blur but Marianne could still sense him fighting at her side. Their swords slashed everything around them in a deadly dance of steel long rehearsed. Only old, trusted friends who had fought side-by-side for years could achieve this level of natural coordination, where each anticipated the other's action without stepping on each other's toes. Whether Marianne shot a target that Bertrand had telekinetically restrained, or the vampire slashed a monster attempting to throttle his mistress, they acted as one. They had been through worse situations and would escape this one too.

"Marianne."

His voice cut through the noise like a sword through butter.

"Marianne, please."

Marianne flinched as if she had been struck, almost slipping on the bleeding remains of a tentacled horror.

A red ooze as large as an ox crawled into the graveyard, its surface slowly shifting into a dozen copies of a handsome young man's face. The noblewoman froze at the sight of those accusing blue eyes, that aquiline nose twisted in an expression of bitter contempt. "Marianne, why?" he asked, blood pouring out of his mouth like it had on that cursed day. "Why did you do this to me? Why?"

She felt . . . she felt cold, and numb, and lifeless. As if someone had opened a wound and drunk her blood until she was too tired to fight.

"It was an accident," Marianne muttered, her breath short from the surprise. "Jérôme, I swear—"

"You *swear*?" The voice echoed inside Marianne's head, sharp and condemning. The swordswoman felt her confidence weaken with each word. "You think swearing will let me live again? That it will give me back the life you stole? I wanted you to kiss me with your lips, not your steel."

"I didn't mean it." It was to the first blood only. "I missed—"

"You missed my sword because you were playing the man, Marianne. What, you thought carrying that sword would make another grow between your legs?"

Marianne flinched as if she had been struck in the face. It took all of her willpower not to drop her rapier, and even then she simply couldn't move anymore. An invisible force nudged her to surrender, to beg for forgiveness.

"Milady!" She heard Bertrand's voice trying to shake her off out of this trance, but the vampire was too busy stabbing a tentacled horror trying to exploit Marianne's paralysis.

"Would you like it, to bury me again?" Jérôme's voice scolded Marianne as the slime slowly approached her. She took a step back to avoid being smothered by that . . . that *thing*. "You didn't even weep at my funeral, you heartless murderer!"

"I didn't . . . I couldn't," Marianne said while trying to shake the slime's psychic influence. "You're not him. Jérôme would never have said something so vicious. He's dead and he's . . . he's not coming back."

"Because of *you*."

"How could I know you didn't carry a soulstone?" Marianne blurted out. She raised her pistol at the ooze, her fingers trembling. "Why didn't you?"

"Because I trusted you!"

Marianne pulled the trigger in fury. The bullet pierced the ooze and blasted a hole in its surface. A telepathic screech echoed in Marianne's mind, the spell that numbed her willpower broken. Or perhaps it was the anger she felt at this cruel monster that gave her the strength to resist. "You will pay for this," Marianne snarled as her heart swelled with anger. That creature had dared to put salt on that wound, to besmirch his memory with its filthy words!

Whatever the case, the slime abandoned all attempts at emotional manipulation in favor of attempting to devour Marianne where she stood. The noblewoman stepped to the right while shooting the creature, but the wounds her bullets inflicted closed immediately. Her pistol soon jammed, forcing Marianne to holster it and fight with her rapier. Using magic to strengthen her legs, the noblewoman ran circles around the creature and stabbed it in a dozen parts.

Wherever her rapier struck, the slime evaporated, its telepathic screams echoing in Marianne's mind like the beating of drums. Bloody bubbles erupted on the creature's outer layer, as if it boiled from within. Marianne's soulbound steel hit the monster at the very heart of its essence, destabilizing it. Within seconds, the slime evaporated. Only a trail of dried blood remained behind.

And yet it didn't assuage Marianne's anger, nor her guilt.

The noblewoman immediately moved to assist Bertrand, but the vampire had the situation well in hand. Tentacled corpses littered the ground, and the vampire seemed to have fun adding more to the pile. Marianne would have rejoiced, if she hadn't noticed something wrong with this picture.

The rats have stopped chittering, she thought as her eyes wandered to the roofs. The mocking rodents had vanished from the roofs, even though they could have tried to overwhelm Marianne and her retainer. This didn't bode well.

A pulse of magic coming from the town's center confirmed her worries. It was the same force that had obscured the hamlet from her magical sight, a sinister power that chilled her to the bone. It was raw, like a festering wound, and yet so mighty that it made Marianne lose her breath. She hadn't felt anything like this since seeing Lord Och at work.

"I sense tremors, Milady," Bertrand warned her. No sooner did he say that that the ground began to shake beneath their feet, as if some slumbering beast woke up from below them.

"We have to go," Marianne said, putting all her strength in her legs. "Follow me."

Using her enhanced strength, the noblewoman leaped into the air and landed on the ruined church's roof. Bertrand simply climbed the walls to follow her, his nails turning into claws. From this observation point, Marianne had a better view of the village's well . . . and it seemed to get closer.

On a second look, the noblewoman realized her mistake. From her vantage point, she witnessed the plaza around the well shrinking like a puddle of water down a drain. Houses crumbled under the phenomenon's weight, their ruins swallowed by the well.

The hamlet is dying, Marianne realized. The pit devoured the village, folding space itself like paper. Whatever force created this place was now taking it back.

And if the rats' flight was any indication, it would kill anyone inside the city's limits too.

"Run!" she ordered Bertrand, as she took another leap toward another house. The duo jumped from roof to roof as the hamlet shrank. The graveyard vanished alongside the church as the ground collapsed beneath them, mud, stone, and corpses all consumed.

Putting all her magic into strengthening her body, Marianne took a glance at the streets below. The locals had reverted into Qlippoth monsters, but they didn't flee from the phenomenon. Instead, they all looked in the well's direction, letting themselves be dragged toward it like animals awaiting death in a quicksand pit.

No. It wasn't acceptance that motivated them. Some knelt, others raised their tentacles to the cavern's ceiling high above their heads. Marianne had only seen a scene like this while attending the Church of the Light's sermon. It was an expression of blissful worship.

Marianne almost slipped from a roof as one of the house's walls collapsed, but Bertrand caught her by the wrist before she could fall. The two managed to reach the hamlet's entrance, even though the hamlet had shrunk by a fourth of its size.

No sooner did they land outside its confines that a fearsome howl boomed from within the village. It was a thunderous burst, stronger than any explosion Marianne had ever heard. The scream didn't belong to this world, and yet . . .

And yet it sounded so eerily human.

Marianne caught her breath, as she and Bertrand watched the hamlet collapse into nothingness. The houses' ruins swirled like a whirlpool of stone and wood, gathering into a single point. The howl lessened in strength, and when it finally ended, nothing remained of Vernburg. Marianne and Bertrand found themselves facing a muddy beach and the Lightless Ocean.

The veil of power that had obscured the place had vanished, and the well too. It was as if the place had never existed.

"Milady," Bertrand said, his hands firmly holding his sword. "Behind us."

"Val . . ." A chittering whisper reached Marianne's ears. "Val . . . de . . . Marne . . ."

Marianne turned around to look at her carriage.

A black, squirming mass of rats covered it like a dense layer of fur. The swarm had cracked the windows and ate the leather from the seats, alongside whatever they could sink their teeth into. The giant riding beetle had been the first meal of the banquet, its carapace split open from its back as rats devoured it from within. One of the rodents peeked through a crack in the insectoid husk's face like a window, while others severed one of the mount's legs to eat its flesh and marrow.

Marianne struggled to suppress her nausea at the disgusting sight . . .

And then the swarm began to *speak*.

"Valde . . . mar . . ." the rats croaked as one, their screams somehow sounding like coherent words. The more it spoke, the better the swarm became at articulating words. "Valdemar . . . Valdemarne . . . is it alive? Where?"

It?

"Does it matter?" Marianne replied while defiantly raising her blade. Bertrand bit his thumb, shedding calcified blood. "You will never get him."

"You will speak," the rats spoke as one with perfect clarity, their eyes shining with ghastly red light. "Or the good Shelley will crawl under your skin to strip the flesh from your bones! Shelley will eat your eyes and work his way to the brain!"

The beetle burst open like an egg, and a verminous army swarmed Marianne and her companion.

The noblewoman managed to leap back to escape the tidal wave of fur, but a few rats managed to jump on her clothes. They sank their teeth into her flesh, but they broke against the bone armor she had manifested over her skin. Marianne skewered them with her rapier, but one rat managed to climb onto her exposed face. Realizing the danger, Marianne started manifesting a layer of bone over her cheeks and neck, but she couldn't protect her eyes nor mouth without blinding herself or suffocating. The rodent managed to bite her lips and ripped out the flesh, before trying to force its way past her clenched teeth and down her throat.

Marianne suppressed a wince of pain as she grabbed the rat with her free hand. She tried to pull it away from her but stumbled as the swarm climbed on her legs by the hundreds. It didn't matter how many she impaled with her blade, more came.

Marianne thought she would die here, eaten alive by rats, when a red light flash blinded her. The rats let out a maddening screech of pain and they fell from Marianne, allowing her to shake them off. The one trying to eat her lips, she simply impaled with her sword.

Bertrand's bloody hand shone with a crimson light, his body fluids evaporating the moment they poured out of his wounded thumb. The swarm couldn't stand the sight of it and immediately dispersed, leaving the half-devoured beetle and carriage behind. Marianne noticed that their eyes had lost their unnatural glow and returned to normal. All signs of intelligence had vanished from their gaze, replaced with animalistic cowardice. They were no longer the fearless thralls of an outside force, but scared scavengers facing larger animals.

The vermin fled into the countryside, leaving their dead behind. Marianne took the opportunity to take a good long breath, before removing the six rats impaled on her rapier. Their corpses fell to the ground as the light in Bertrand's fist vanished.

"That was an exorcism spell, wasn't it?" Marianne asked her retainer, her lips bleeding. She used her psychic sight to analyze the damage and, to her horror, immediately confirmed that the rats carried multiple diseases. She called upon the Blood to expel the plagues and close the wounds. "I think I saw you cast it once or twice."

"I used it to banish unwanted ghosts from the mansion of Milady's mother," Bertrand explained. "I assumed the sorcerer needed all his concentration to control a swarm this size, and any disruption would cause his power to falter."

Good call.

"So that was an animancer?" Marianne asked as she examined the rats. Animancers were sorcerers specialized in manipulating animals, or even plants in some cases.

The warlock behind the swarm had to be a powerful one, to direct such a large amount of rats at once. Even the Institute's animancy specialist could only control a small flock of birds before suffering from heavy headaches.

"I assume so," the vampire replied as he glanced at the empty spot where Vernburg had stood a few minutes ago. "Though I have no explanation for this . . . this place."

"I think the two phenomenons are mostly unrelated," Marianne replied, as her wounds closed. She dissipated her bone armor, as maintaining it taxed her magical reserves. "The rats were as frightened of being trapped inside as we were."

And the thing she had sensed inside the well . . . its power rivaled that of Lord Och, but she didn't feel any finesse in it. Only raw, naked strength. And the howl at the end . . .

"The cause wasn't a ritual or some other artifact," Marianne said. "It was a living being. Maybe even a Stranger. The animancer was probably trying to make use of it, though I don't understand how."

The village's disappearance explained why the Knights never noticed it. Perhaps it existed in a pocket dimension of some kind, or it could move from one spot to another. Marianne couldn't be sure, but Lord Och would certainly identify this hamlet's true nature.

She had to warn the authorities, but the rats had sacked the carriage beyond repair. The wheels were broken, the seats torn apart, the food spoiled or devoured. All documents that Marianne kept in her hidden compartments had vanished, probably stolen . . . including her notes on the Verney investigation.

Whoever caused this, they would learn that Lord Och had caught Valdemar soon enough. Marianne couldn't shake the feeling that she might have endangered the last Verney, and it shamed her.

"You said we were three days away from the nearest guard station?" she asked Bertrand as he picked up a dead rat on the ground.

"Three days ride," the vampire replied while sinking his teeth into the rodent's corpse. Bertrand must have exhausted some of his blood casting his exorcism spell and needed to replenish it. Rats weren't as good a sustenance as humans or artificial blood, but beggars couldn't be choosers.

So it might take them a week to reach it on foot. Using the Blood to increase their pace would diminish their strength, and they didn't have any food left. They might be able to reach a coastal village, but moving in the open would make them vulnerable to an attack by the rat swarm. Marianne didn't think for a second that the magician behind everything would let them escape the region alive. They had seen too much.

"The best defense is a good offense," Marianne mused as she looked up at Verney Castle. Unlike the cursed hamlet, its ruins remained atop a cliff.

The Knights had clearly missed someone during their purge.

And Marianne would finish the job for them.

10

FRIENDS OF THE LIGHT

The ecto-catcher hummed as the shadow of Valdemar's grandfather returned from the dead. The workshop's walls trembled as technology and magic merged into a single force. The ring of blood around the machine undulated as a tired Valdemar fueled it. With his slashed right hand, he gave his life force to call his grandfather's remaining psychic energies back to the world of the living; and with the left, he tried to guide them toward the portrait on the nearest wall. Doing one of these tasks was already difficult, and the two at once even more so . . . but this time, no knight would kick down his door.

"Continue," Hermann encouraged his friend as he provided assistance. While Valdemar's blood was the ritual's key ingredient, the reptilian pictomancer had added his own to the mix. His pale body fluids formed a second ring around his colleague's, stabilizing the ritual. "We are . . . almost done . . ."

Green ectoplasm was rising from the journal inside the ecto-catcher, coalescing into the shape of a human skull. At first glance, it seemed the experiment would go almost exactly like the first time Valdemar tried it.

But when only half of the skull manifested, the necromancer realized the problem.

"Damn it!" Valdemar cursed. "Curse the Knights, there's not enough psychic energy for a full echo!" By interrupting the ritual the first time, the inquisitors had depleted most of the emotional energies left in the journal. Less than half of it remained!

Hermann, however, remained optimistic. "We must . . . press on. Take everything . . . into the portrait. You won't have . . . a third chance."

Grinding his teeth in frustration, Valdemar gathered every ounce of emotion, every forgotten memory soaking the journal's pages. He then directed the ectoplasmic construct toward his grandfather's portrait, letting the ghostly echo fuse with the enchanted pigments. The ecto-catcher fell silent as the canvas gained a life of its own. Valdemar watched with amazement as the colors in his grandfather's portrait started to shift. The painted eyes closed and opened again, while his chair rocked by a few millimeters. For a brief moment, Valdemar thought his grandfather had returned from the dead.

But the painting's movements were slow and stiff, like those of a doll rather than a human being. The eyes of Valdemar's grandfather moved from his grandson to Hermann, but though he seemed to detect them, his gaze was without warmth or life. The portrait was animated but lifeless.

Valdemar applied a healing spell to close his wounded palm, while the circles of blood on the floor dried up. "Grandfather?" He addressed the portrait, praying for an answer as his hand's skin stitched itself back to normal. "Grandfather? Can you hear me?"

The portrait's eyes moved to Valdemar, but his grandfather didn't answer. The necromancer refused to give up so soon. "Grandpa?" he asked the portrait, his eyes peering into his grandsire. "It's me. Valdemar. Don't you remember?"

The portrait observed him in silence for a moment, but the lips arched right as Valdemar thought he had failed.

"Valdemar?" The voice was nothing but a faint whisper, but a familiar one. Valdemar hadn't heard this tongue spoken in many years. "Are you off playing outside again? Don't wander too far, or your mother will worry."

Valdemar let out a breath of relief, suppressing tears in his eyes. How good it felt to hear that wise voice again after so long. Half the reason the necromancer ran this ritual was to return his family to him, beyond his research.

And he had succeeded.

"I do not . . . understand the language," Hermann said while using magic to close his own wounds.

"I do," Valdemar replied in Azlantean, before switching back to

French to address his dead relative. "It's alright, Grandfather. I can't wander away from this place, even if I wanted to."

The portrait smiled but didn't answer.

This reaction spooked Valdemar, who suddenly realized his grandfather had asked for his mother when he had outlived her. There were holes in the echo's memories.

The necromancer grabbed the journal and presented it to the portrait. "Grandpa, do you recognize this?" Valdemar asked, as he flipped the pages.

"Valdemar, did you look into my books again?" the portrait asked with a familiar frown of disapproval.

"I'm sorry, Grandpa." Valdemar couldn't help but apologize, as he pointed at a passage written in the indecipherable language. "I didn't understand that passage. What tongue is it?"

His painted grandfather's eyes looked at the text, reading it. "It's English," he whispered. "John the British, he taught it to me."

The British? Valdemar thought. *What was that? A troglodyte tribe?*

"We talked. We drank mud and breathed gas together in Picardy . . ." His grandfather scowled, the pigments turning white from fear and horror. His voice shook when he spoke. "Oh, our poor lands, what did the Germans make of you? You were so beautiful once . . ."

"Grandfather?"

But Valdemar's words fell on deaf ears.

"Where is the grass?" his grandfather muttered, his painted visage looking left and right as if surrounded by invisible foes. "I can only see the shrapnel. Paul, where are you? I can't see anyone . . . it's all dark out there . . ."

The pigments shifted again, and his grandfather returned to his original position. His painted cheeks regained colors, and his horror turned to confusion.

"Grandfather?" Valdemar asked, his throat dry. "Grandfather?"

The portrait looked at him, as if suddenly noticing his presence. "Valdemar, did you look into my books again?"

Valdemar sighed in defeat. "I went off to read outside," he said, dreading the next words.

"Don't wander too far, or your mother will worry," his grandfather advised with paternal warmth.

"She won't. I swear." Valdemar closed the journal, his fingers trembling in silent frustration.

Hermann, who had observed the interaction in silence, looked at his colleague with concern in his eyes. "Is something . . . wrong?" he asked Valdemar. "You look . . . distraught."

"It's not him," the necromancer lamented in Azlantean, as his grandfather's eyes wandered around the room. "When the picture answered me, I thought he was back. But as I feared, this replica is incomplete. Broken."

"You knew that . . . it would be an echo. Echoes cannot think."

"Yes, but . . ." Valdemar shook his head in sadness. "I hoped for more than that."

A reminder of his family was better than none, but it still broke his heart to see his grandfather like this. If only the ritual had worked the first time, maybe the painting would have become so lifelike that Valdemar wouldn't have noticed the difference from the real deal.

Hermann put a scaled hand on his friend's shoulder. "I am . . . sorry."

"It's not your fault, but the Knights." Though Valdemar believed vengeance was a sucker's game, if he ever crossed paths with the squad that interrupted his ritual . . . "At least he recognizes the language, so I can translate the missing parts over time."

"Be gentle . . ." Hermann advised, as his scaled hands brushed against the portrait. Valdemar's grandfather didn't seem to notice the troglodyte. "This painting's ego is fragile . . . it will only answer to you . . . its creator . . . and it cannot handle strong emotions."

"Do you mean it might break?"

"No, but . . . it will revert to its prior state . . . like a thought coming to a complete stop." The troglodyte observed his colleague carefully. "You should take a rest . . . before interrogating him."

"Do I look that tired?" If anything, Valdemar wanted nothing more than to fall on his bed and close his eyes. "Honestly, I almost suggested that we delay the ritual."

"I would not have . . . blamed you for it," Hermann replied, his tail wagging behind him. "Is it . . . the eyes?"

"No." Though Valdemar hadn't emerged from the Institute's lower floors since he drank that damn potion. He was afraid of what the rest of the world might look like. "I suffer from nightmares, and tonight was more intense than usual."

"Dreams are a . . . dialogue with ourselves," Hermann said while clearing his throat. He struggled to find the right words. "Perhaps your mind is . . . trying to tell you something? What did you . . . dream of?"

"It was strange," Valdemar admitted. "I was trapped at the bottom of a well I couldn't escape from, and then Marianne looked at me from above."

"Marianne . . . Reynard?"

"Yes." It was the first time Valdemar had dreamed of her. "I heard a woman's voice, and then gunshots. But when I tried to climb the well to escape and look for myself, a pile of rocks buried me alive. I don't know what to think of it."

"It is quite natural for . . . mammalian males to . . . dream of female company." Hermann scratched his left cheek with his claw. "Maybe you simply feel . . . sexually frustrated?"

Valdemar remained silent for a moment out of sheer disbelief. "No," he said.

But to his horror, Hermann remained adamant about pitching Valdemar his theory. "The well collapsing . . . before you can reach her . . . the sound of bullets firing . . . the imagery . . ."

"She had clothes."

"Oh," Hermann replied in disappointment.

An awkward silence followed, made worse by the confused gaze of his grandfather in the background. Valdemar felt blood rushing to his cheeks. "Hermann, if you say a word of this conversation to Liliane, I won't talk to you for a month."

"Her friend Frigga . . . is an oneiromancer." Though Hermann had changed the subject, Valdemar could tell that he still believed in his crass theory. "If you have nightmares . . . She can help."

Valdemar considered the proposal for a moment. *And why not?* he thought. *I wanted to consult a specialist for a while.* "She's good?"

"The best . . ." Hermann appeared a bit embarrassed all of a sudden. "But selfish."

"I'll have to pay her?"

The troglodyte nodded in confirmation. "Not with gold though . . . she will ask for a favor."

Service for service? Valdemar could live with it. "Fine, I'll consult her after we summon the Collector."

"About that . . . I have done research . . . on the Qlippoths. Are you sure . . . blood will remain behind once we kill it?"

"Qlippoths may be spiritual creatures, but if allowed to manifest, their bodies become real enough," Valdemar reassured him. As psychic entities from the extradimensional realm of madness called the Outer Darkness, Qlippoths needed to either create a body of ectoplasm or possess a living creature to manifest on the material plane. "We'll need gold coins for my method, as greed drives it."

"So it's true . . ." Hermann nodded to himself. "I read that Qlippoths . . . are manifestations of mortals' sins. The greater the sin . . . the stronger the beast."

"Where did you read that? In a Church's book?" Valdemar snorted. "It's more complicated than that. There is debate about whether the Outer Darkness is *fueled* by emotions or *causing* them, although all ten species of Qlippoths do draw their power from a particular thought. Collectors are associated with greed and ownership."

The more complex and powerful the emotion, the stronger the beast. At the bottom were gluttonous Gnawers and the envious Facethieves, who tried to mimic humanity by stealing others' identities. At the top of the Qlippoth hierarchy stood the creative Nahemoths, mad demigods whose vile wishes their Lilith handmaidens immediately fulfilled. Collectors were in the middle, too powerful to serve as common summoning fodder but weak enough to be bound.

"So when will we proceed with the summoning ritual?" Valdemar asked.

"Soon," Hermann answered. "I asked my master, Loctis . . . to rent the Hall of Rituals for our purpose. He wishes . . . to be present."

Valdemar winced. The Hall of Rituals could only be entered from the Institute's first floor above. "Can't we do it in my workshop?" he pleaded. "I mean, it's small but I summoned Qlippoths in far worse conditions."

"Summoning is only authorized . . . only possible . . . in the Hall of Rituals . . ." Hermann pointed out. "And you should go outside . . . for your health."

"I know." Valdemar hadn't left his workshop in days. Liliane delivered him the day's meal each morning. "I know."

"I . . . I researched ways to help you . . . forget," Hermann admitted. "But . . . once the body has taken the Elixir of True Sight . . ."

"You can't close your eyes."

Nor ignore those outside.

After a short, peaceful rest, Valdemar found the courage to leave the Institute's basement and explore the outside world. The eyes were waiting for him. They infested the cavern's ceiling like mushroom growth.

Some were so small that Valdemar could barely see them, but others were larger than the Institute itself. The stone's surface was blistered with crystal cysts and metallic fibers. The dark and foreboding ceiling had transformed into an alien tapestry, with none the wiser.

And yet, in spite of all its terrible eldritch grandeur, Valdemar couldn't help but see the beauty in this spectacle. Strange tangles of fibers linking the eyes together glittered like a web of light. Weird, lurid colors danced on a metallic skin stretching as far as the eye could see. Strange entities floated beneath these alien auroras, from formless shadows to shimmering masses of colored dust and gemstones.

Valdemar had flayed the false skin of the world to see the truth underneath, dreadful and beautiful in equal measure.

His True Sight also allowed him to see the wards and protections around the Institute. Fiery glyphs and arcane symbols formed a vast sphere around the fortress's walls, preventing the shadows outside from crossing its perimeter. The design was so complex that looking at it gave Valdemar a headache; how many sorcerers had woven spell after spell to raise such a perfect barrier?

Valdemar wandered the Institute's ground, before making his way to the local cathedral of the Light. The temple was almost deserted, but the necromancer noticed the red aura around the gargoyles on the walls. The statues had been animated with magic and would defend the building from attackers if needed. Valdemar crossed the gates anyway, looking for the light beyond the threshold.

He didn't know what brought him here. Valdemar had never been religious, and his experience with the Church had been mostly limited to avoiding its inquisitors . . . but the building and its fires felt reassuringly familiar compared to the alien ceiling outside.

The cathedral's hall was almost deserted when he arrived, with only a few Knights of the Tome sitting on the benches in silent contemplation. A hooded priestess chanted deep songs dedicated to the light behind the central fiery altar, feeding a brazier with wood and paper letters. The congregation had written their sins and dark thoughts on them, so the flames could purify them.

Valdemar silently sat a few rows behind them, taking a look at the area and basking in its warmth. The ceiling was made of thousands of scintillating scales surrounding a crystal shaped like the mythical sun. When Valdemar paid more attention to them, he noticed scenes carved on them: a scene of the ancient humans worshipping the sun on the surface; the Whitemoon's appearance in the skies; the age of darkness and frost that followed; mankind's descent into Underland; the wars against the troglodytes, the derros, and the dark elves; the pact between the first Enlightened One and the Dark Lords, that made the Church of the Light the empire's official religion; and the glorious future when the Light would shine again on a world free of sin.

Valdemar's inquisitive eyes then wandered to another part of the architecture, a towering pillar of chiseled purple crystal. Pictures of skulls had been carved on the surface, shining with otherworldly light. The structure reached more than ten meters in height, pushing toward the ceiling and the scintillating false sun above.

A Reliquary.

"Impressive, eh?" Valdemar turned his head toward the speaker and blinked in surprise. A golem no taller than a human stood near his bench. Made of wood and purple soulstones, the creature was clad in tattered robes, heavy scarves, and a pointed hat that obscured most of its face. Valdemar could only see darkness beneath, and the glow of two yellow crystal eyes. "I made it myself."

A handsome old woman in her late fifties followed the creature, her skin brown, and her eyes darker. Valdemar had rarely seen that coloration before and wondered if she came from a faraway cavern. Her black hair was tied into a disheveled bun, and her black robes reminded the summoner of a bat's fur. She gave Valdemar a sharp look as if he were some kind of savage beast.

"You stink," the woman said to Valdemar with the bluntness of a mace, her wrinkles creasing. "Wash yourself."

"I took a shower thirty minutes ago," Valdemar protested.

"It wasn't enough," she replied. "Your stench frightens the animals."

"Amie, please," the golem said, before pointing at the bench. "Can we sit with you? You look like better company than the Knights."

Valdemar answered with a nod. "I never saw a Reliquary so large before," he admitted, as the strange golem and his companion sat with him. "How many souls does it contain?"

"By my latest count, two thousand eight hundred and fifty-three," the golem replied. "It's not much, I'll agree. The Church of the Light's Reliquary in Saklas contains hundreds of thousands."

It didn't surprise Valdemar. Reliquaries were larger versions of the soulstones used by nobles and rich individuals to catch their souls after death, allowing them to be revived as sentient undead. Unlike individual soulstones, Reliquaries didn't capture souls at the moment of death but could hold more than one at once. As such, poor individuals could ask to have their spirit transferred into it while alive if they couldn't afford a soulstone and sensed their death approaching.

There was a catch, however. Souls inside a Reliquary fused together and lost their individuality. Their knowledge and memories melded together into a single pool of information, allowing the collective to give advice and guidance to the living.

"I'll choose quality over quantity anytime though," the golem argued, though he whispered softly enough not to disturb the religious ceremony. "This Reliquary contains the souls of esteemed scholars and researchers who either failed to achieve immortality or grew tired of it. Their collective pool of knowledge rivals even our own."

Valdemar made a note to question the Reliquary in the future. Lord Och's tutelage was already a lot to deal with, but he was interested in what this undead library had to say.

"Name's Edwin by the way," the golem introduced himself and his friend. "Edwin Crowborn. And this is Amie Malherbe."

"Valdemar." The summoner squinted. "*Master* Malherbe?"

The woman answered with a nod, although her eyes focused on the fiery altar. While Edwin looked more interested in chatting, his female colleague had come to pray and nothing else. "Hermann told you about me, I suppose?"

"How did you guess?"

"All the bats and half the rats in our walls report to her," Edwin explained. He sounded vexed that Valdemar had heard of his colleague and not him. "We're both Masters at the Institute. I'm specialized in soulcraft, while Amie teaches biomancy and animancy."

Soulcraft? Valdemar quickly put two and two together. "So the golems around the Institute—"

"They're my handiwork." Edwin nodded with pride. "The gargoyles outside too. I imbued them with life and purpose."

All Masters needed to achieve immortality. Valdemar assumed that Edwin's method involved binding his soul to an immortal golem body, though he wondered what his colleague did. Amie Malherbe reeked of magic, but she neither looked undead nor young.

"I tried to make a sentient golem once," Valdemar admitted. "My plan was to put somebody's brain in it and to have their mind animate it."

"Like the derros?" Edwin asked. "What went wrong?"

"I experimented with rat brains, but I couldn't translate the brain's electrical signals into psychic or magical pulses," Valdemar admitted. That failure was why he eventually started working on the ecto-catcher. "Since I couldn't make a golem work with something as simple as an animal, a human would have been beyond my grasp. That, and the original soul had long departed anyway."

"Your efforts were doomed from the first day," Amie said with firmness. "Even derros transfer the brain while the subject is alive. Once the soul is gone, only knowledge and memories remain. The emotions are gone."

"I thought you had success with giving life to flesh golems without the need of a soulstone?" Edwin asked his colleague.

"It was another soul that took over the vessel, like a newborn. The brain's original occupant did not return, and though the new one kept the memories, he didn't feel any connection to them."

Valdemar immediately thought of his grandfather, his eyes lighting up in hope. "Could I see this golem?" he asked.

"No," Amie replied bluntly. "Not unless Lord Och orders me."

"What?" Valdemar refused to give up. "Why's that?"

The Master looked at him with disgust. "Your stench disturbs my friends."

What kind of scientist refused to share their knowledge over hygiene? "If I put on a perfume—"

"Still no."

Valdemar sulked, causing Edwin to cackle. A knight on the front row looked at the group with disapproval, making the golem lower his tone.

"So you're Och's new protégé," Edwin whispered before examining Valdemar closely. "Well, it was nice knowing you."

Valdemar shuddered upon remembering his "initiation." "I survived so far."

"So far," Edwin replied while rolling his shoulders. "But I would invest in a soulstone if I were you. Och kills as easily as he breathes . . . well, as when he breathed." He had to be close to the Dark Lord, to name him without his title.

The ceremony ended a few minutes later, and the Knights of the Tome dispersed to return to their posts. Her prayers finished, the priestess walked away from the burning altar and removed her hood, revealing a well-groomed mane of red hair and sharp amber eyes. She was exceptionally graceful, her beauty further enhanced by an emerald diadem and a soulstone necklace. Valdemar noticed pouches of ingredients and a belt stacked with potions beneath her cloak, along with spells woven in her clothes.

"Greetings, child," she addressed Valdemar with a warm smile that reminded him of Liliane. "It is the first time I've seen you here."

"I'm not religious," Valdemar admitted.

"But you seek spiritual guidance. I can see it in your eyes." The redhead joined her hands together. "Liliane informed me of your predicament."

This confirmed Valdemar's suspicions. "You're Mathilde de Valnoir. Liliane's teacher and the creator of the Elixir of Life."

"I am a humble servant of the Light, nothing more."

Valdemar would have normally considered her words false humility, but Mathilde of Valnoir sounded quite sincere. Nor did she sound like these "holier-than-thou" type of inquisitors he had grown to despise.

"And the world's best alchemist too," Edwin flattered the priestess, while Amie rose from the bench and left without a word. She struck Valdemar as preferring solitude over social activities. "Forever young like an eternal flower."

"Thank you, Edwin," Lady Mathilde replied politely. "Though I hope you did not come to my evening prayer just to flatter me."

"And why not?" The golem chuckled. "We barely see each other unless Lord Och calls us to a meeting nowadays. I enjoy toiling in my lab as much as anyone, but eternal life isn't all about research. Besides, it's not like you get many followers. Shouldn't you try to convert me?"

"The Institute is not fertile ground for worship," the priestess admitted. "But I am not a missionary. I offer comfort and guidance to those who fear the dark, regardless of whether they believe or not."

Valdemar shifted on the bench. "Yet you hoard the secret of immortality, condemning people to death."

To his surprise, Lady Mathilde's expression shifted into one of sadness. "You cannot fathom how many times I've regretted my decision to keep my Elixir of Life a secret, young man. Alas, it is for the greater good. My elixir's preparation is extremely complex and dangerous. Very few alchemists could reproduce it. The others would create poison disguised as a cure, their botched potions spreading cancers and illnesses."

Valdemar remained skeptical. "I thought no knowledge was forbidden within these walls?"

"More knowledge is always good, but there is a right moment for all things. Just as releasing information about the Strangers to the unwary spreads their influence, sharing my formula as it is will do more harm than good. However, 'not now' doesn't mean 'never.' I am looking into ways to simplify my recipe into something every alchemist could create safely."

"Even your adorable apprentice?" Edwin mused.

Lady Mathilde smiled warmly. "Liliane is a sweet and talented girl. If I ever share the original formula with anyone, it will be with her."

Valdemar couldn't argue with that part. Though he did question Mathilde's decision to keep her elixir a secret, as the more people aware of the formula the greater the odds of someone improving it, he could understand her reasons. If there was a dangerous component to his own ecto-catcher, he would try to patch out the flaws too before releasing the schematics into the wild.

"I heard of your troubles with inquisitors, Valdemar," Mathilde said. "So I admit that I didn't expect to see you knock on my doorstep."

"Honestly, neither did I," Valdemar confessed. "I don't know what I was looking for here."

"Comfort about what the Elixir of True Sight revealed to you, I suppose?" the priestess guessed. "I am afraid that what you have seen is the truth."

Valdemar already knew that, but to have it confirmed made him shiver. "The world is alive, and we are in its bowels."

No wonder the Domains were so large.

To his surprise, Lady Mathilde shook her head. "No one understands yet if Underland itself is alive or if the ecosystem you see outside is an entity spreading through the tunnels. Perhaps it is simply no different than moss."

Somehow, Valdemar doubted the truth would be so comforting. "Did you know all along?"

"You mean the Church? Of course we know, though my superiors will deny it. In many cases, it is easier to suppress the truth than to accept it." The priestess let out a sigh. "I understand how traumatizing it is, to see the truth for the first time. My own revelation shook my faith too . . .

which is why I begged Lord Och to reconsider when Liliane informed me of his plans. I said you were too young, that you needed a few more years. 'The younger the better,' he replied."

"If it were up to Och, no sorcerer would learn magic without taking an Elixir of True Sight," Edwin said. "If you couldn't accept the truth, then you weren't fit to master sorcery in the first place. He follows a survival of the fittest mentality as far as the arcane arts are concerned."

"You all took the elixir too?" Valdemar asked.

"It is one of the required steps to become a Master," Lady Mathilde confirmed. "Lord Och has long-term plans that require special awareness of magic. If he asked for you to take the elixir, it means you factor into them."

Valdemar wasn't certain if he should take it as a compliment or a warning. Maybe both.

"But we can discuss that around a cup of tea, if you want," Lady Mathilde said with a motherly smile. "I can tell you have a lot on your mind, and as a priestess, it is my duty to ease your burden. Liliane will be here as well."

"That . . . that's kind of you, but I'll pass," Valdemar replied. Though seeing the truth of the world and his failed attempt to fully copy his grandfather's soul weighed on his shoulders, he didn't feel good about sharing his fears with a servant of the Light. Lady Mathilde remained a member of the organization that had forced him to go on the run, even if she seemed to have a kind heart.

His reaction amused the priestess. "Are you afraid of a warm drink? But it's alright, I won't force you. Liliane will be disappointed though."

"She already guilt-tripped me once," Valdemar replied. "It won't work again."

Lady Mathilde chuckled. "Valdemar, while I believe in the Light, I do not condemn others for following their own path and I do not look down on yours. Besides, our journeys share the same destination. We seek to bring back the Light to the people of Azlant, whether in this world or another. Though I do question your decision to summon Qlippoths to reach your end."

I can keep a secret, Liliane had said. But she forgot to say: *But not from everyone else!* "I know how to deal with Qlippoths."

"All summoners think that, until they call something they cannot put down," Lady Mathilde replied with skepticism. "One day, you will learn that to your sorrow."

"Summoned monsters are just inferior golems," Edwin declared. "Make your own protector."

"However, I will happily take you and Hermann with us to the Domain of Alogi to look for this plant of yours," Lady Mathilde said. "Although I must warn you that it might be a dangerous journey. Have you talked to Lord Och about leaving the Institute for a research trip?"

"Not yet," Valdemar admitted. The lich hadn't contacted him since he drank the Elixir of True Sight. "And I thought Alogi was the safest Domain?"

The priestess chuckled. "That's what the local Dark Lord says to bring visitors and tourists, but some islands are still half-untamed . . . including those where your flower grows."

"All I know of combat magic is summoning allies and telekinetic thrusts," Valdemar admitted. "I don't think you will like me calling a Qlippoth for help."

"If that is the root of the problem, I will teach you some combat spells." Lady Mathilde winked at Valdemar. "It is alright to ask for help, but even better to rely on your own strength."

"Oh, if you want I am testing a new variant of combat golem," Edwin said with excitement. "If you want to practice, I can bring them out of storage. Don't worry, my lab has its own infirmary."

Somehow, Valdemar didn't think that was a good thing.

11

SLOW PROGRESS

Hermann's master was just as odd as he was. The droning song of flies and cavern locusts heralded his coming in the Hall of Rituals, alongside a black mass of spiders creeping down the walls. A swirling tide of maggots fell from the ceiling, piling up next to one of the twelve columns holding up the underground dome. Valdemar watched in amazement as the insects and arachnids gathered in the shape of a giant humanoid whose head reached the ten-meters-tall ceiling. The swarm's spiders worked as one to form a cloak of silk covering the monster's gruesome appearance. Twin yellow stars glowed beneath the hood, gazing down at Hermann and Valdemar.

"Master . . . Loctis." Hermann bowed deeply before the monstrous swarm. "Thank you for coming."

Though the insects continued to drone, chitter and sing, one word cut through the noise.

"Student." The swarm's voice was as mighty as a dragon's roar, deep, sinister, and undoubtedly male. "Are you ready to begin?"

"Yes . . . as you can see." Hermann raised his chin and waved a clawed hand at the center of the room.

As per the procedure, the pair had rented the Hall of Rituals for their experiment and outfitted it with the necessary equipment. A summoning circle of blood, salt, and silver surrounded a pile of gold and a dozen rodents' corpses. The wealth would serve to attract the Collector and the flesh to help it take physical form. Valdemar and Hermann had also set a mounted canvas outside the circle, more than two meters tall and almost as large. Though the duo had originally intended to either wound or sacrifice the Qlippoth once they extracted its blood, another idea came to mind as they prepared. They had soaked the canvas with their blood, to serve as a spiritual anchor for the creature.

But Valdemar preferred to focus on the walking swarm rather than the summoning circle. He had already crossed paths with a similar creature when he arrived at the Institute, but he couldn't observe it up close. Thousands if not millions of critters made up this entity, this Loctis. Valdemar analyzed them with his psychic sight, sensing the threads of magic binding them together. They were like droplets forming a large pool connected to others by invisible drains.

"You are not really here, are you?" Valdemar guessed, after offering Hermann's master a polite nod.

"I am everywhere you hear the song of my swarm, manling," Loctis replied as it turned its "face" to the speaker. Valdemar felt the will of something ancient and sinister looking through the vermin's eyes. "But you are correct. This avatar is but one of many. As is the one you met when you crawled into this den of stone."

For a moment, Valdemar thought he faced the most powerful animancer he had ever seen, but the reality turned out to be far more impressive. Each insect contained a piece of soul, so small the summoner could barely perceive it. Together, all these small lights formed a brilliant tapestry radiating with power. One that rivaled even Lord Och's.

"You bound your soul to a hive of insects, Master Loctis?" Valdemar knew some animancers could transfer their soul into an animal's body, but he had never heard of someone doing it to *millions* of them at once. "May I ask how?"

"Each insect holds a piece of my consciousness," the sentient swarm answered, though he didn't go into the details. "My intellect waxes and wanes with their numbers. I am one, manling, and I am many."

All breeds of insects share a familial bond, Valdemar thought as he observed the swarm. *They tasted blood and were bound by it . . . as would all their descendants.*

But could a human soul resist being torn apart in so many pieces? Very few sorcerers could afford cutting off pieces of their essence without damaging their sanity and sense of self. Yet Valdemar detected no madness in the swarm's aura. If anything, it stood out by its focus, its singularity of purpose. The fact Loctis called Valdemar "manling" made the sorcerer wonder how human the swarm remained though.

"A skilled sorcerer can sculpt their soul like clay, and polish it like a stone," Loctis buzzed as he sensed Valdemar's confusion. Though disturbing to look at and listen to, the creature's calm, educational tone somehow felt reassuring. "Lord Och already guided you through the first steps. Perhaps one day, you shall transcend individuality and achieve the peace of the multitude."

Valdemar would rather achieve a less disgusting form of immortality, but he couldn't help but respect Loctis's feat.

"My Master . . . is a biomancer," Hermann said. "A sculptor of life . . . an artist of flesh. Life is his . . . canvas."

"I can see why he became your teacher then," Valdemar replied with a smile. "Master Loctis, may I ask why you chose to join us today?"

"The creature you intend to summon shares characteristics with arachnids," the swarm explained. "We shall see how many. I have studied all the life-forms inhabiting this world, but paid little attention to the Qlippoths and denizens of other planes so far. This is an opportunity to cover a gap in my knowledge."

"Master Loctis . . . wishes to assimilate the Qlippoth into his swarm . . . if we fail to bind it," Hermann explained. "To consume its knowledge . . . and subsume its mind."

"Assimilate a Collector? Is that even possible?" Valdemar asked in shock. A Collector wasn't truly a spider, it only had the shape of one.

"I do not know either . . ." Hermann cleared his throat, while Loctis remained as quiet as a giant pile of insects could be. "We shall . . . find out."

Valdemar didn't hide his skepticism. The attempt was more likely to end with the Qlippoth's essence overwhelming Loctis's mind than anything. And yet . . . no common sorcerer could bind their soul to millions of creatures at once either.

"Begin," Loctis ordered.

"Yes, yes," Valdemar replied as he knelt before the summoning circle. "Hermann?"

The troglodyte nodded slowly as he grabbed his paintbrush, waiting next to the portrait. Hermann raised his magical defenses, an invisible shield of psychic energy forming around him. Valdemar mentally probed his defenses to test them, and he didn't like what he saw.

"Hermann, your shield is passable but a bit weak," Valdemar warned his colleague. He knew he shouldn't complain since the likes of Och could shred through his own like tissue paper, but the summoner had no idea how powerful the Collector might prove to be. "Can't you strengthen it further?"

"I . . . I admit I focused more on practical uses of magic . . . than combat-related applications." Hermann sounded a bit embarrassed about that. "You said your summoning circle . . . would hold the creature."

"It should." Valdemar had checked multiple times. "But 'should' doesn't mean it *will*."

"I will step in if anything happens," Loctis droned with impatience. "Carry on."

If the hive insisted . . .

Hermann and Valdemar had originally planned to wound the creature on arrival, extract its blood, and then banish it . . . but the troglodyte had suggested a more daring alternative. They wouldn't kill the Qlippoth, but rather bind its essence and trap it into a painting to achieve a great feat in pictomancy.

They would create a *painted place*.

At least, that was the best-case scenario. Valdemar had faith in his summoning abilities, but he knew better than to underestimate a Qlippoth. He felt Loctis's gaze on his back as he knelt next to the circle, channeling the Blood through it.

"Collector of names and member of the fifth caste, I call thee from the depths of the Outer Darkness!" Valdemar chanted as a red glow coursed through the summoning circle. "Spinner of wealth, I offer you this tribute by the grace of the Nahemoths!"

Valdemar felt a chill run down his spine, as his Blood weakened the invisible veil separating the planes. His call echoed beyond the material universe and didn't go unheard. A powerful presence immediately took notice. The world grew cold as Valdemar sensed his life force drained away. The circle funneled his magic toward its center, soaking up the treasures and flesh like water. An alien force sank its teeth into this offering, using it to manifest. The rodent corpses inside the circle started to dissolve into goo, mixing with the coins. The metal melted and expanded into a sphere, as an invisible force reshaped it into a vessel for its otherworldly essence.

Valdemar watched in amazement as this bubble of gold and flesh grew into a tangle of red spidery legs topped with sharp blades . . . and far too many for a single spider to support. A chitinous body of red plates formed at their center, topped with a dozen yellow gemstone eyes. A mouth opened in their midst, filled with insectoid fangs.

"MINE!" The word echoed inside Valdemar's skull through the summoning bond, as clear as water. "Mine, mine, mine! It's all mine! You are all mine!"

The monstrosity grew larger than a giant beetle, its many legs pushing the summoning circle in all directions. When they touched the boundaries of blood and salt, a barrier of red energy formed to stop them. The creature thrashed against its prison, its eyes glowing with otherworldly madness.

A pulse of psychic energy erupted from inside the circle, and Valdemar sensed this telepathic wave crash against his magical defenses. *Did I make an error with the circle?* the summoner thought in alarm.

"Your souls are mine!" The abomination raged through the telepathic link. Valdemar ground his teeth, as the beast's hits against his barrier reverberated through his bones. One of the Qlippoth's eyes glared at Hermann, and another at Valdemar himself, bathing them in golden light. "Your bones are mine, and this land too! Let me out! LET ME OUT!"

"Hermann, now!" Valdemar shouted. Now that the creature had fully manifested, the summoner needed assistance to bind it in the painting. "Hermann!"

But nobody answered.

Valdemar turned his head at the troglodyte, only to find him frozen in place by the Qlippoth's luminous gaze. A golden, weblike ectoplasmic substance coated Hermann's body, preventing the pictomancer from moving. His eyes were lifeless, his limbs as still as his paintings.

Damn, the summoning circle contained the beast but not its power!

"Hermann!" Valdemar shouted, trying to shake his friend out of his temporal paralysis. "Hermann, damn it, I can't hold him alone!"

While struggling to maintain the summoning circle's integrity, Valdemar psychically probed the troglodyte's magical defenses in the hope of strengthening them and found them intact. Whatever spell the Collector had cast, it completely bypassed Hermann's protections.

Worse, the same substance had spread to Loctis's silk cloak, freezing it in space and time. But unlike his student, the Master somehow remained capable of moving.

"Enough," Loctis's voice buzzed across the room and inside Valdemar's head. "Submit."

Valdemar had no idea how the insectoid warlock managed to hijack the telepathic bond, but the trapped Qlippoth clearly heard the command. Half of its dozen golden eyes glared at Loctis in anger, the paralyzing substance spilling from the sorcerer's cloak to entrap flies and spiders. For a brief instant, Valdemar thought Hermann's master would suffer the same fate as the troglodyte.

Loctis spoke a single word, and the golden substance dispelled from Hermann and his cloak.

The troglodyte stumbled against his painting, while his teacher returned the Collector's hateful gaze. "What?" Hermann asked in confusion.

"Alas, its resemblance with spiders is indeed purely cosmetic," the swarm observed with a cold, clinical tone. He sounded neither disappointed nor frustrated. "Its mind is deaf to my song. You may proceed with the capture." The casual, arrogant way he dismissed the Qlippoth chilled Valdemar to the core. The creature the summoner struggled to contain was no more intimidating than a fly to the senior sorcerer.

Hermann quickly recovered his composure and assisted in the binding spell. The canvas's surface shifted like a whirlpool, a cell calling for a prisoner. Using the summoning bond connecting him to the Qlippoth, Valdemar attempted to transfer it into the painting. His mind grabbed the monster's essence the same way he took over a human's blood.

The Qlippoth immediately resisted, its alien will pushing back against its would-be captor's psychic grip. And unlike the Knight of the Tome Valdemar once threw at a wall, the Collector refused to budge. All the Qlippoth's eyes focused on its summoner, trying to paralyze him. Valdemar faced the golden glow in the beast's glare without flinching. Whatever warding spell Loctis had cast, it canceled the Collector's power.

The Qlippoth's eyes suddenly lost their luster, as if the creature had recognized the futility of its efforts. Valdemar felt all resistance to his control falter and crumble, like a dam breaking. The Collector's essence became as malleable as clay to his mind. Though wary of a false surrender, Valdemar immediately worked to complete the ritual. The summoning circle's shape changed, its outer layer of blood expanding to include Hermann's canvas. The painted whirlpool on its surface swirled as the Collector's legs touched it, the painting sucking the creature in. The Qlippoth vanished inside the portrait within seconds, and the summoning circle shrank into nothingness. Only a single leg remained on the ground, releasing a fountain of golden blood.

Hermann immediately applied his paintbrush to give shape to the painted whirlpool, while Valdemar continued to shape the Qlippoth's essence. Collectors had the capacity to freeze objects in time and space, and the two warlocks worked together to harness its power. Hermann's paintbrush skillfully gave shape to the canvas's chaotic surface; half of it was pure skill, and the other advanced pictomancy spells. After a few minutes of work, the researchers no longer gazed at aimless blood, but at the detailed picture of an exquisite square room with golden walls and cobwebs tapestries. The details were so intricate, so perfect, that it looked almost real.

"It is done . . ." Hermann said as he lowered his paintbrush. "Valdemar, do you . . . sense its power?"

Yes, he did. The painting radiated a faint aura of magic, one that belied the new artifact's true power. Valdemar slowly approached the portrait, raising his hand at its surface. The paint felt smooth under his nails, and the pigments shuddered when he touched them.

"Incredible," Valdemar said in amazement. "So fast . . ."

"Fighting is not among my talents . . . but I am not helpless either," Hermann said with pride. "I can . . . bind an essence in a minute. I do not even need . . . a canvas to paint on."

"You did well," Loctis calmly congratulated the two researchers.

Hermann's pride turned to shame. "No, I . . . I apologize for my weakness, Master. This spider's power . . . it bypassed my defenses. I didn't even notice. I'm sorry, Valdemar."

"I would have been trapped too, if not for your master's help," he reassured Hermann. "And my summoning circle wasn't up to the task. We're both at fault here."

"I did not protect you," Loctis replied with amusement. "I applaud your mastery of space-time sorcery, by the way."

Valdemar frowned in confusion. "You didn't protect me?"

The Master's countless insects gazed at Valdemar. It reminded him of the eyes outside the Institute, and not in a good way. "Curious," the swarm droned. "You shrugged off the Qlippoth's time-space binding but not out of any conscious effort on your part."

"Maybe the summoning bond shielded me," Valdemar guessed, though a part of him doubted it. The circle hadn't protected Hermann.

"What was it?" Hermann asked. "That attack . . . it wasn't a spell."

"The Collector altered reality on a fundamental level," Loctis explained. "Weaving the threads of space and time to isolate you from the rest of existence. I doubt anyone unfamiliar with teleportation and advanced space-time manipulation could resist this effect."

Which begged the question of how Valdemar had shrugged it off. He could sense Loctis was asking himself the same question.

"I see . . ." Hermann focused on his new painting. "Good to know . . . studying this art piece may . . . teach me how to resist such ability in the future."

"Do you want to go in first?" Valdemar asked, his hand still on the painted surface.

"The honor . . . is yours, my friend."

Valdemar held his breath and pushed.

His hand vanished through the painting, its surface rippling like water. His fingers had entered a warmer space than the cold Hall of Rituals, and soon his arm followed. With a smile, Valdemar stepped inside the painting.

The crossing felt like walking through a wall of water, his boots stepping on a smooth metal surface. The pocket dimension took the shape of a cube of gold with a single portrait-shaped doorway behind them, with a space smaller than his workshop. Still, Valdemar couldn't help but grin as his fingers trailed against the cobwebs on the ceiling. Though they felt like paint rather than silk, they were real.

Hermann followed him into the painting, his tail flapping happily. "It . . . it worked," he said with quiet joy.

"Yes, it did!" Valdemar knocked the golden wall. "Do you think we could expand it?"

"We could . . . if we connect multiple paintings." The troglodyte scratched his left horn, as he calculated the room's size. "Twenty cubic meters . . . maybe twenty-five."

Valdemar suddenly realized that Loctis hadn't sent any insects after them, the swarm waiting on the other side of the painted barrier. "Are we the only ones who can enter this place?" he asked Hermann.

"Yes . . . and no," Hermann replied. "We used our blood to craft this gate . . . and our blood is its key."

"So Liliane can't enter until we spray her with our blood?" Valdemar shuddered. "Well, I guess we can use this portrait as an additional closet."

"I will take this painted place . . . study it." Hermann's claws trailed against the walls. "This is a small world . . . too small . . ."

"Too small for your kind?" Valdemar guessed. "Is that why you wanted us to go through with that ritual?"

"It was a test run . . . practice for the day we will create . . . the Silent King's door." Hermann shrugged. "And if we cannot open it . . . maybe it could be the draft of a new world. A new reality where my kind . . . could settle."

"I think it would take a Nahemoth for that, and I doubt they can even be bound in a painting at all." Valdemar considered how to expand this pocket dimension. "Now that the Collector's essence gives this space structure, we could strengthen it. What if we bound a soul echo to the portrait, like my grandfather's? Will it take a solid shape inside? Will it increase the pocket dimension's boundaries?"

"I do not know . . ." Hermann replied, though with excitement rather than surrender. "We shall see . . ."

They were just starting.

The duo stepped out of the painted space, though Hermann attempted to bring a strand of cobweb with him. The substance vanished when it crossed the threshold, proving that painted elements could only survive inside the pocket dimension. Valdemar's hopes to bring painted gold to the real world died with this demonstration.

"Once you are done with the fluid extraction, you shall transport the beast's leg to my workshop," Loctis ordered his student, as Hermann collected the Qlippoth's blood on the floor inside a bottle. The Collector's severed leg still wriggled on the ground as if alive. "I wish to study it."

"Yes, Master," Hermann replied with obedience.

The living swarm wordlessly scattered, the spiders among it cannibalizing the silken cloak. The hordes of insects crept up the walls and vanished through small cracks in the stone.

Valdemar suddenly remembered Edwin's quip about all bats reporting to Master Malherbe. "Do all animals in the Institute answer to a sorcerer?" he asked Hermann before grabbing the canvas for transport. It was a lot heavier than the summoner had expected.

"Not only . . . the animals. Fear . . . the plants. They have ears too . . ."

"Really?"

"No," Hermann replied with a deadpan tone, as he moved to help Valdemar. "It was a joke."

* * *

"I am pleased by your progress, apprentice." For once, Lord Och sounded halfway honest. The lich had finally deigned to contact his student again, inviting him to a stroll through the Institute's hedge maze. "Turning an intermediate Qlippoth into a pocket dimension's power source was a stroke of genius, if you pardon me using the expression."

"The idea's credit goes to Hermann," Valdemar replied. He took a moment to observe the black thorns making up most of the maze and noticed a few colorful flowers growing out of them. "Has it been done before?"

"Many pictomancers created pocket dimensions, but none used a summoned creature as its fuel," the lich answered with a shrug. "You can achieve a similar result with five human sacrifices and a kitten."

That was oddly specific. Thankfully, Hermann had more ethics than the lich.

"I didn't know you were familiar with pictomancy, my teacher," Valdemar admitted. "Do not take it the wrong way, but you do not look the artistic type."

"I do not have your appetite for the arts nor Hermann's talent with a paintbrush, but I studied all forms of magic. A few pictomancers achieved a form of immortality similar to lichdom by binding their soul to their own portrait, and I sought to understand the process better."

"Did you bind your soul to a portrait, my teacher?"

"Are you fishing for information about my phylactery, apprentice?" The lich sounded more amused than anything. "I decided against using a painting. I do not denigrate the great feat of achieving immortality through pictomancy, but I found this method . . . imperfect."

"Because the painting degrades?"

"That can be solved easily enough with the right spells," Lord Och replied dismissively. "The problem is simpler, my apprentice. A sorcerer binding their soul to a portrait will always reflect it. They will never grow old, their wounds will close. But they remain unchanging, and slaves to their vanity, their passions, their lusts. Lichdom is the superior form of immortality because it frees the mind from these foolish temptations."

The answer made Valdemar smile. "I suppose you have a poor opinion of vampires?"

"I do." The disdain in the lich's voice was real enough. "I will never understand their appeal. I do not even consider them true undead, since they still need to feed. Vampires are a botched work."

The lich eventually led him to a small fountain inside the maze. A statue of a hooded cyclopean creature poured water in a marble basin full of algae and translucent fish. Valdemar analyzed them with his psychic sight and realized a biomancer had enhanced both animals and plants to make the small ecosystem self-sustaining. The fish's excretions nourished the algae that then produced oxygen and nutrients for the local animals.

"What life lesson did you take from this adventure?" Lord Och asked his apprentice, as he gazed at the pure waters.

Considering the "life lesson" part, Valdemar guessed the lich asked for wisdom rather than practical knowledge. "The Collector was more powerful than I imagined. I shouldn't have underestimated it and prepared better."

"A wise answer, apprentice, but not the one I wished to hear."

Lord Och glanced at a fish and telekinetically pulled it out of the water.

"Let me tell you a secret about the Strangers, the Qlippoths, and all these arrogant creatures inhabiting our world," the lich said, as he coldly watched the captive animal struggling to escape his invisible grasp. "You may meet a few pretending to be as old as the world, to have created mankind, or to claim godhood. It may even be true."

Valdemar raised an eyebrow, knowing such claims would have given an inquisitor a dire case of apoplexy.

"But no matter how powerful they look, we can overcome these entities." The lich released the fish, letting it sink into the basin. Valdemar let out a sigh of relief upon seeing it flee for the bottom, as far away from the surface as possible. "The gods do not deserve our worship, let alone our suffering. If these beings achieved great power, so can we; for there is no limit to the human genius."

There was something oddly reassuring in the Dark Lord's cold, calm arrogance. Inspiring even. "Impossible is but a word," Valdemar said. Countless people told him reaching Earth was impossible, and he would prove them all wrong.

"Indeed." Lord Och put his hands behind his back while glancing at the cyclops statue. "This realization should have given you clarity, and yet your mind remains clouded."

"I'm . . . I'm asking myself questions," Valdemar admitted, his own gaze turning to the water. "I've noticed a few strange occurrences, and I don't know what to make of them."

The lich scoffed. "Enlighten me."

"The Collector's power didn't affect me and it stopped resisting my attempts to bind it, even though it had more than enough strength to fight back." Valdemar had wondered if it had been a trick, but the summoner had felt the creature's essence bend to his will as he reshaped it into a pocket dimension. "It simply . . . submitted."

"You should take pride in your power."

"It felt too easy," Valdemar replied. "Also, before the ritual took place, other people commented on my stench."

"I suggest perfume," the lich quipped. "It works wonders for me."

"Except that Hermann informed me that I smelled like the Collector we just bound. I also heal far faster than anyone I know. I didn't think much of it beforehand, but when I add all these details together . . ."

"You feel there is something *unnatural* about you, young Valdemar?"

"I don't feel, I think." Valdemar scowled at the Dark Lord. "And I know you suspect something too, my teacher. You sent Marianne to dig into my family history to confirm whatever hypothesis you made."

The lich's silence spoke louder than any word.

"How did you learn to summon Qlippoths?" Lord Och eventually asked, though he refused to turn around and face his apprentice.

Valdemar frowned in confusion. "I bought a manual at the Midnight Market."

"Did you?" the lich asked innocently.

"You can ask my empty purse," Valdemar replied with insolence.

"Did *you* find this book, or did the *book* find its way to *you*?" Lord Och looked over his shoulder, the glowing light in his sockets faltering. "Are your dreams truly dreams? Are they even your own?"

Of course the Dark Lord would answer a question with more questions. "What are you getting at, my teacher?"

"That if you want to learn the truth, you should ask yourself the right questions." The lich turned around and faced his apprentice. "I do not ask questions to confuse you, young Valdemar, but because the journey to an answer is as valuable as the answer itself. Life is a test, and effort builds character."

"So if I want *any* answers, I'll have to find them myself?" So much for tutoring.

"Careful, young Valdemar," the Dark Lord said with cold amusement, having read his apprentice's thoughts. "I can tolerate insolence, but not ungratefulness. Have I not been helpful to you?"

"You have," Valdemar conceded. He wouldn't have met teachers like Hermann without the Dark Lord's support, nor glimpsed at the true nature of the world without his guidance. The Institute had given him more resources than he could have ever hoped for.

But Lord Och was still a manipulative *ass* who withheld information from his apprentice, while putting him through potentially deadly tests.

"Do you expect me to *coddle* you, apprentice?" The lich chuckled. "Like a blacksmith molding the perfect blade by hammering the steel over and over again, I will reshape you into the greatest sorcerer you can be."

"How does keeping secrets from me help with the tempering process?" Valdemar asked with a dubious frown.

"Because you are the only one who can find yourself, young Valdemar," the Dark Lord replied with surprising gravitas. "If I told you of my suspicions, they would influence you. I can teach you how to practice magic, to bend reality to your will, but I cannot tell you who you are. No one can do that, except you."

Valdemar crossed his arms but took the time to consider his mentor's words. Who was he? He didn't need anybody to tell him that. He was Valdemar Verney, seeker of Earth, and that would never change. Though he was angry with the Dark Lord for keeping his cards close to his chest, in the end it didn't matter. Valdemar had taken him up on his offer of apprenticeship to open a path to Earth, not to learn more about himself. He could do that on his own.

"Fine," Valdemar said. "I'll find the truth myself."

"That's the spirit." The lich decided to throw him a bone. "I did promise I would share one of my secrets with you if you proved an apt disciple, and I shall deliver. Tell me, what do you know of the ancient Pleromians?"

"That they built this place and many other monuments," Valdemar replied. "Until their civilization went extinct, though nobody knows how."

"Don't you find it strange though, that an entire population could die without leaving any trace?"

"Well, I did consider another possibility," Valdemar admitted. "That they aren't dead. That they just moved on."

"But where could an entire civilization go without leaving a trace? Underland is a vast place, but they should have left hints." The lich tilted his head to the side. "Unless they went . . . elsewhere?"

Valdemar's eyes widened, as a possibility formed in his mind. "No way . . ."

"It is time I show you what stirs beneath our feet, young Valdemar." Lord Och put his hand on Valdemar's shoulder, as space twisted around them. "And where the Pleromians went."

1 2

HEIRS TO A LOST EMPIRE

Many scholars fantasized about the fourth and deepest level of the Institute. Valdemar had asked everyone from Liliane to Iren about what the Dark Lord kept underneath his fortress, only to always receive the same answer: nobody knew. Lady Mathilde and Edwin seemed to have an inkling, but they knew better than to gossip about their master's secrets. Liliane believed that Lord Och hid his phylactery there and that its power radiated outward like a furnace; while Hermann thought that the lich instead maintained a secret laboratory underground, where he worked on ghastly experiments.

Valdemar hadn't expected ancient ruins, however. The lich had teleported them to his lair's depths, folding the very fabric of space. Unlike the Collector's stasis effect, Valdemar couldn't counter it. One instant they were in the hedge maze and inside a gallery the next. The walls were made of the same oily, pitch-black stone as the great pillar at the Institute's center, but were carved from floor to ceiling with ancient glyphs and depictions of the Pleromians.

Valdemar had to cover his mouth as he inhaled a cloud of dust, to Lord Och's amusement. "You will forgive me for the lack of aeration, my apprentice," he said with mock concern. "I rarely get living visitors."

"I suppose this floor —" Valdemar coughed. "It can only be accessed through teleportation?"

"Or by digging your way in. I can give you a shovel, if you want to build an air duct."

Valdemar ignored the jab and instead used the breathing exercises Lord Och taught him. He focused on the flow of air within his blood, using magic to maximize his respiration's effectiveness. The summoner had to use his hood as an improvised scarf, thick enough to protect his lungs from the dust but thin enough that he wouldn't suffocate.

It's not just the dust and the oxygen deficit, he thought. He sensed something putrid in the air, a foul humor that made him want to vomit. A remnant of disgust, the hideous smell of abhorrent sex, and the suffering of something devoured alive. *Horrors happened in these tunnels, and they echo even millennia later.*

Lord Och looked cautiously impressed. "Good. You understood the practical applications of my exercises."

"Thank you, my teacher."

"But you wouldn't need to breathe if you had transformed yourself into an undead," the lich said, immediately taking back his compliment. "You should at least learn to strengthen your organs."

"Lady Mathilde started giving me pointers," Valdemar said as the two walked down the gallery. The carvings represented the daily life of the ancient Pleromians: one showed a trio of cyclops offering a shining trapezohedron to a high priest of their kind, another a successful dragon hunt by spear-wielding warriors. "She said I should start with spells to reinforce my body and make it hard as steel."

Though their training sessions had so far been limited to Valdemar punching a crystal golem in the chest and breaking his hand. Edwin had been quite happy with his creation's resistance to damage, while Mathilde reassured Valdemar that he would progress with persistence.

"Wise advice, though Marianne would be a better teacher. You should ask her to give you lessons when she returns." The lich touched the walls with his left hand, his bony fingers leaving a trail of dust behind them. "Your body is the only weapon you can rely on . . . behind the mind. Once you complete your training, you will extinguish lives with a thought."

The carvings offered the most detailed representation of the Pleromians Valdemar had seen yet. Though most archeology books represented them as one-eyed humanoids, the ancient walls showed that they had sharp fangs for teeth, arms longer than their legs, and a gaunt, crooked body shape.

"Is it true some of them were more than ten meters tall?" Valdemar asked his mentor.

"It's an exaggeration. The tallest skeleton I found barely surpassed five meters." Lord Och pointed a skeletal finger at a representation of cyclopean priests praying before a black stone monolith. "The Pleromians were ruled by a powerful priesthood who guided their civilization by peering into the future. These seers determined the place of every individual from birth, selecting their job, who they would have children with, which cavern they would settle . . ."

"It must have been terrible." Even the empire didn't go that far in controlling its population.

"This system helped the Pleromians achieve internal stability for centuries. As far as I know, they didn't even need currency, as the state organized everything. Their lineage selection process also greatly increased the number of sorcerers among their population, to the point almost every member of their population could spellcast."

"And yet they never tried to reach the surface?"

"The Pleromians feared it," Lord Och replied with a chuckle. "Their culture considered the stars to be evil forces, and deemed that everyone living under the sky exposed themselves to their malevolent influence. Their mythology said their ancestors fled underground to avoid the sun's dreadful gaze. Even trade with surface empires was shunned."

Valdemar couldn't understand the idea of retreating underground by choice rather than necessity. The Pleromians reminded him more of bats than humanoids, as afraid of the light as humans were of the darkness.

The gallery led to a broad hall as large as the first floor's cathedral, with colossal statues supporting the ceiling. Each art piece was more complex than the last, and Valdemar suspected that they belonged to different artists. This collection included an intricate stone Pleromian warrior ready for battle, a geometric nightmare of metal triangles fused together, and a disfigured horror with more mouths than fingers.

More recent devices occupied the hall besides these ancient statues, including crystal globes glowing with bottled lightning, shelves of books protected from decay by spells, and glass vats bubbling with green liquid. Valdemar noticed husks inside the containers, such as a mutated, single-eyed humanoid and a giant skeletal undead with steel for bones.

"I owe Hermann money," Valdemar mused out loud. "He thought you kept a laboratory downstairs, my teacher."

"This isn't my true den, apprentice," Lord Och replied absentmindedly. "It is a specialized workshop meant to serve a very specific purpose."

"You attempted to recreate the Pleromians," Valdemar guessed as he examined the experiments. The skeleton was around the same size as most statues, and the mutant's single eye was a giveaway. "Did you succeed?"

"I am afraid not. I have tried to summon soul echoes the same way you did with your grandfather, but the centuries erased whatever trace of sentience they had left. Only the pain remained."

The pain . . . it was faint, but Valdemar sensed an aura of suffering suffusing this place's walls, too ancient to have been the Dark Lord's work. "What happened here?"

"I have spent centuries translating the Pleromians' glyphs and understanding those who wrote them," Lord Och explained as he led his apprentice farther down the hall. "The Pleromians were among the first to delve into the secrets of the Blood, though they specialized in biomancy rather than mastery of the soul. At the apex of their civilization, they had unlocked the secrets of extended longevity, outgrew the need for manual labor thanks to homunculi slaves, and ruled their empire without competition. But immortality comes with a certain downside . . ."

"They grew bored," Valdemar guessed. The hall led to a stairway made for giants, each step forcing him to take a leap down. Lord Och simply floated through telekinesis, amused by his student's struggles.

"Indeed, apprentice, immortality bored the Pleromians to death. The centuries are long, but unlike us humans, the cyclops didn't have troglodytes, dokkars, and derros to contend with. With no need to struggle for survival, they focused inwards and embraced every vice possible. Exotic curiosity turned into debauchery, as their harmless pleasures devolved into vile practices."

The stairway led them down to a vast corridor with two vividly detailed frescos of statues on each side of the path. The creators had exquisitely chiseled every facial expression, capturing the subtlest shades of emotion. Though an artist at heart, Valdemar wished the sculptors had been less thorough. Each scene depicted on the fresco was more obscene than the last, and it *started* with a cyclopean dinner with an especially loathsome main course.

"Parents held feasts with their children as the appetizers," Lord Och said with the same passion as a museum guide. "Priests fornicated with alien things. Sorcerers reshaped their bodies into esoteric art pieces. I will spare you their other practices, as they would make even a dark elf blush."

Valdemar didn't need to imagine, though he would rather forget what he saw. This gallery of excesses disturbed him more than any Qlippoth, especially when he noticed the statue of a Gnawer physically stitched to a Pleromian sorcerer. Worse, Valdemar felt the agony in the stone. Whoever had sculpted these horrors used live models.

Eventually, the sightseeing became unbearable, and Valdemar focused on Lord Och rather than the statues. The lich showed no disgust at the horrific scenes around him, which his apprentice found infinitely more disquieting.

Lord Och stopped floating above the ground, his steps echoing through the sinister gallery. "As you can see, young Valdemar, the Pleromians pushed the boundaries of immorality farther than even the most depraved cultists. But no matter the excess, it was never enough. After a time, they realized this world had nothing left to offer them in terms of pleasure."

Valdemar suppressed a sigh of disgust and focused on the mystery at hand. Now, he started to see the pattern behind the Pleromians' disappearance. "And once they grew bored of what this reality had to offer, they went off to look for another," he guessed.

"Exactly, apprentice. And this . . ." Lord Och stopped at the end of the gallery, and the entrance to the floor's final room. "This is the door they used."

Valdemar took the first step into the chamber and held his breath.

A colossal dome as large as the Institute's courtyard stood before him, its black stone ceiling shimmering with fiery purple Pleromian glyphs. Unlike the rest of the structure, the room lacked any piece of art or any type of device . . . save one.

Valdemar's steps echoed in the dome as he approached the towering archway at its center; a door large enough to let an army of giants through. It looked so simple and yet so intricate, a twisted tangle of black stone, purple metal cables, and shining crimson crystals. The archway thrummed with power and purpose, humming a low-pitched song that rippled through the fortress, inviting the living and the dead to cross it. Yet this door was closed and led to nowhere.

But a dreamer could always wake up, no matter how deep the slumber. The magic remained vibrant in this old device, waiting for the day when a wise mind would unleash it again.

Valdemar couldn't resist touching the archway, his fingers shuddering at the contact. The stone and the metal making up the structure gave off a faint warmth. Even millennia after the Pleromians had vanished, their work endured. Whatever depraved horrors they had inflicted on each other, Valdemar couldn't help but admire their genius. This was the ultimate expression of his dream made real.

"Is it still working?" Valdemar asked his teacher.

"Yes . . . and no." Lord Och put his hands behind his back as he joined his apprentice. Even this ancient master of the dark arts looked humbled by the device. "The Pleromian Gate can be reactivated under the right conditions, but I haven't figured them out . . . *yet.*"

Amazing. Simply amazing. "It's a stable portal," Valdemar realized as he analyzed the structure with his psychic sight. The inner workings of the device were a mystery to him, but its purpose was as clear as water. "A doorway into another universe."

"Into *multiple* universes, with the right tweaking," Lord Och corrected him. "I haven't had the opportunity to study the other gate for some time, but I assume it had the same function."

Valdemar's head snapped in his teacher's direction. "The *other* gate?"

His reaction amused the lich. "You think the Pleromians could fit their entire civilization through one door? I know of at least another gate like this one in Ariouth, though I haven't been able to examine it since my previous apprentice and I had a . . ." Lord Och's voice turned cold as ice. "A disagreement."

Valdemar remembered the tales of the Dark Lord Phaleg's rise to power and how he had been Och's apprentice before becoming his sworn foe. *If only they could cooperate, we might have reached other worlds by now,* Valdemar thought.

"We might have." Lord Och's voice was heavy, though Valdemar didn't detect any remorse in it. "Alas, the living hold grudges better than the dead. In any case, if two doors exist, why not three or more? The Pleromians' empire wasn't as large as our own, but it covered a large part of Underland."

An idea formed in Valdemar's mind. "If there are other portals, maybe my grandfather used one."

"Now, you're getting it." Lord Och nodded happily. "Did your grandfather tell you how he ended up in our fair empire?"

"He didn't know himself," Valdemar admitted. "He said he was there as a medic-soldier, fighting a war between many human countries in trenches of churned mud, hungry rats, and sharp shrapnel. A living Hell, he called it. His hands shook whenever he remembered it."

"My sympathies," the lich said without really meaning it. "Did these human countries use magic?"

Valdemar shook his head. "They hadn't discovered the Blood, but their firearms were better. He said they didn't break half as often as ours, and some could kill a dozen men at once."

"You look a bit tall for a half-derro, child," Lord Och teased Valdemar. The derros couldn't use the Blood, but their engineering prowess far surpassed that of mankind. Many technological advances came from reverse engineering those madmen's inventions.

"Derros can't mate with humans," Valdemar replied, vexed.

"Not naturally, but everything is possible through the Blood." Lord Och turned serious again. "It does not surprise me that humans from other worlds do not practice magic. Our civilization learned of the Blood from troglodyte tribes after the Descent. We feared the dark and its wonders back then."

"My teacher, you speak as if you lived during those times."

The lich chuckled.

"You did?" Valdemar asked, his eyes widening in shock. He had heard Och was older than the empire, but he would have to be nearly a thousand years old to predate the Descent.

"If your grandfather's civilization hasn't discovered the Blood," Lord Och said, superbly ignoring his apprentice's question, "then how did he end up in our world? What did he remember?"

"Not much," Valdemar admitted as he remembered his grandfather's tales. "He and his unit were sent to hold a village destroyed by the *Kaiserreich* tribe. When they arrived, the place was a blasted minefield. Grandpa remembered working to remove the mines when a booming sound interrupted his work. He thought it was the Kaiserreich tribe attacking, but a light swallowed him before he could flee. He lost consciousness and woke up in a tunnel."

"Which color for the light, and which tunnel?"

"Grandpa didn't remember well, as it happened quickly. As for the location, he woke up in the tunnels between Horaios and Sabaoth."

Lord Och considered his apprentice's words for a few seconds, before speaking up again. "I suspect the sound came from a short-lived spatial rift opening. The sudden change in air pressure between an open space and our caverns could have triggered an explosion. As for what caused this rift to open, a red light would have been a telltale sign of a Blood magic ritual. Question your painted echo until you learn all its secrets."

Valdemar flinched at the way Lord Och referred to his grandfather, but he didn't comment on it. "Someone could have opened a Pleromian Gate with a ritual?"

"Perhaps . . . though I entertain another solution." Lord Och joined his fingers in a thoughtful pose. "The region between Horaios and Sabaoth is close to the derro kingdom of Andvari. King Otto Blutgang spent the last decades clashing with our forces in the area. Considering his fondness for esoteric machinery, it's possible one of his devices opened the breach."

"You think Otto the Demented experimented with planar travel?" If so, Valdemar was thankful that his grandfather rejoined human civilization rather than falling into the derros' clutches. If even half the tales about Otto's brutality were true . . .

"The Demented? Lesser minds call him that, but having had the opportunity to confront him, I find this nickname demeaning. Otto the Nail possesses a superior intellect, the kind that only comes once every few centuries. He operates differently than most." Lord Och shook his head in genuine contrition. "It's such a shame that he was born a derro, or he would have risen to become a Dark Lord. Truly a shame."

"How is impaling your countrymen along a road a show of intellect?" Valdemar asked with heavy sarcasm.

"Weeding out idiots is a favor to the universe," the Dark Lord replied dismissively. "The information gathered by Hermann indicates that our late asylum prisoner saw a portal similar to the Pleromian gate and painted it on his cell's wall. He might have belonged to the same warband as your grandsire."

"I thought the same," Valdemar said. "It's possible that my grandfather passed out during the planar transport."

"Perhaps . . . or maybe something separated him from the others. We will have to locate the tunnel where he landed, but not now. You would not survive the journey in these tunnels." The lich examined his apprentice head to toe and clearly found him unsatisfactory. "While you continue to assist young Hermann on his pictomancy project, we will focus your studies on combat spells. You need to broaden your perspectives beyond slamming knights against walls and summoning thralls."

Though Valdemar considered fighting a last resort, he had to admit he wouldn't mind getting better at it. His life would have been very different if he had been powerful enough to fend off the inquisitors. "Will you teach me combat spells?"

Lord Och shook his head. "I have a better combat instructor in mind for you."

Valdemar thought he had misheard. Did the arrogant lich just admit to being second best at anything? "A *better* one?"

"I give credit where it is due, but the person I have in mind is less . . ." Lord Och hesitated on the right word, "*delicate* than I am."

Valdemar shuddered. Considering Lord Och's idea of a test was to pit him against monsters, he dared not imagine what the lich considered indelicate.

"Young Mathilde will teach you the basics of spellcasting combat for now, as will Marianne when she returns from her latest errand," Lord Och decided. "I will send you to my chosen tutor afterward. Once he has made a proper battle mage out of you, you will be ready for my direct tutelage."

"Thank you." Valdemar bowed slightly. He was always eager to learn. "If I may ask, who else knows about these gates?"

"The other Dark Lords and some of my most trusted lieutenants. Count yourself lucky." The Dark Lord waved a hand at the Pleromian Gate. "How do you feel, now that you learned of this secret?"

That if Lord Och was correct about the device being capable of reaching multiple universes, then Valdemar's quest might finally reach its end. Earth awaited beyond these doors, alongside mankind's hopes for a better life. And yet, a cynical part of Valdemar's mind remembered a common saying all too well.

If it looks too good to be true, it probably is.

"You will forgive me, my teacher," Valdemar said, "but I found an inconsistency in your tale."

"Do you accuse me of lying to you, apprentice?"

"I believe you are withholding some elements." Valdemar crossed his arms. "We all know that in a population, there are always headstrong individuals who go against the majority's wishes. Cultists are proof enough of that. Even if most Pleromians had grown bored with Underland, some would have elected to remain behind. Maybe not many, but a few."

The lich listened in silence.

"I can only see one reason for why the entire population would willingly move away, down to the last man," Valdemar said. "It wasn't a migration, but rather an evacuation order."

The Dark Lord nodded in satisfaction. "Your insight does you credit, young Valdemar. Indeed, the Pleromians first built the doors in the pursuit of a higher understanding, until their seers predicted a disaster that would soon befall their empire."

"What disaster?"

"The Pleromian glyphs do not give details," Lord Och replied with a shrug. "Though according to my research, the Pleromians escaped a few decades before the Whitemoon entered our solar system."

"They predicted its arrival?" It still didn't add up. "*We* survived it well enough, albeit at a cost."

"Perhaps they overestimated the danger or predicted that we would slaughter them like we did the troglodytes once we made our way down," Lord Och said with a ghoulish, skeletal grin. "Though truthfully, I have no answer to this mystery. Whatever disaster the Pleromians predicted, it didn't prevent us from surviving a thousand years."

He had a point. The Pleromians had good reasons to fear the Whitemoon, as mankind learned to its sorrow, but it couldn't extinguish the light of mankind. The cyclops had run away rather than stand their ground.

"The Pleromians left these artifacts and all their secrets in our capable hands," Lord Och continued. "I know that together we will uncover them all."

"Is this why you revealed this gate's existence to me?" Valdemar asked while gazing at the gate.

"Skills can be learned," Lord Och declared, "but a drive is innate."

"One day, we shall open this door into humanity's new home," Valdemar replied with firm determination. "I swear it."

His people would finally see the light.

13

NEST OF EVIL

Even as a crumbling ruin, Castle Verney looked foreboding. The fortress's dark walls hadn't aged well. Marianne scarcely saw a roof without a hole, or a battlement without a breach in its stone. The Knights' fires had consumed most of the wooden parts of the architecture, leaving only ashes and black stone. Most towers had collapsed, and the few that still stood looked like broken fingers. The absence of vines or mushrooms also disturbed Marianne. The castle had been abandoned for nearly two decades, and yet nature hadn't taken it over.

A place so evil even plants won't enter it, Marianne thought as she looked at the archway entrance. A defaced stone gargoyle loomed over the rusted iron doors and the darkness beyond them.

"I smell rats inside the walls," Bertrand said, eyes red as blood and fangs out. Ever since the rat attack, Marianne's retainer had chosen to stay in his true form. "This is their nest."

"I don't sense any magical defenses," Marianne said as she raised a lantern she had managed to salvage from the carriage. Its faint light illuminated the archway and showed a dark corridor leading inside the castle. "Makes sense. The Knights' patrols would have noticed."

"I could go in alone and scout ahead," Bertrand suggested. "We are entering the enemy's territory, and they know of our arrival."

"We are more vulnerable while separated, and our foe can target us from afar." Bertrand had taught her the basics of his exorcism spell on the way to the castle, but lack of practice made it unreliable. Marianne was confident in her abilities, but she was no spellcasting genius. "We must force the sorcerer's hand."

Wielding her lantern with one hand and keeping the other on her sheathed rapier's pommel, Marianne stepped inside the keep. Bertrand made no sound as he followed her, but she sensed his sharp gaze on her back.

After a short walk through a dusty corridor, the duo reached the castle's crumbling great hall. Most of the ceiling had collapsed, and the Knights had defaced the bas-reliefs decorating its walls. The room smelled of dust, and a thin layer of ashes covered the ground. Nobody had visited this place in years.

Marianne relied as much on her psychic sight as her physical one. She often sensed the presence of rats hiding in the walls and the ceiling, lurking at the edge of her magical senses. The rodents scampered off whenever she moved in their direction, but she knew that they followed her. The sorcerer controlling them had learned their lesson and refused to offer a direct battle.

A cursory search through the ruins proved fruitless. The stables were a desert of dust and rot; the towers' stairways were for the most part broken and led nowhere; the library had no books, though Bertrand found a pile of ashes where the Knights gave them to the pyre.

Lord Verney probably slept here, Marianne thought as she examined the dusty remains of an opulent bedchamber. Rats and vermin had devoured the bed's mattress, while the cushions had rotted. The remains of a small lab occupied a stone chamber to the bedroom's left, with broken alembics and a shattered workbench covering the floor. *Did he murder his victims here, I wonder?* The more she and Bertrand explored the keep, the more Marianne found the place's silence oppressive. Even old tunnels felt more alive than this open tomb.

They found the first corpse in the castle's bathrooms. Bertrand smelled something at the bottom of a pool of murky water and fished out human bones. They found a larger collection of charred skeletons piled up in a dining hall, their legs shattered and their skulls split open by swords.

"They were sanctified after death," Marianne said as she examined the remains with her lantern. "To make sure no ghost would rise from the ashes."

Lord Penhew hadn't lied. The inquisition had been very thorough in extinguishing the cult.

"Is Milady looking for something?" Bertrand asked, as he watched Marianne examine the charred skeletons.

"Lord Penhew said he burned Aleksander Verney at the stake," she replied. "I wonder if his corpse is among these."

"All men look the same in death," Bertrand pointed out. "Milady might as well look for a needle in a haystack."

"Maybe his remains smell the same as Valdemar." *Or a Qlippoth,* Marianne thought.

Lord Och had mentioned an abnormal quantity of Orgone in Valdemar's blood, a telltale sign of summoned creatures. After visiting that village and the strange creatures inhabiting it, Marianne had immediately noticed the connection.

Is Valdemar even human? Marianne thought grimly. *Blood scans should have identified his true nature if he were a shapeshifter.*

Bertrand chuckled. "Milady, that is not how scents work. These bones smell the same."

"What about the smell of rats? Can't you follow them to their nest?"

"This castle *is* their nest. They are everywhere."

"Then try to locate the stench you noticed in the village and around Valdemar," Marianne ordered. "It might lead us to our culprit."

The noblewoman sensed the rats growing agitated at the periphery of her psychic sight. *I need to find the animancer before he deciphers my notes and goes after Valdemar,* Marianne thought with determination. She refused to endanger a guest of Lord Och, even if indirectly. Valdemar's family legacy had hurt him more than enough already.

Bertrand sniffed the air, inhaling ash and dust. It took him minutes and a lot of backtracking, but he eventually found a lead in the bathroom. "I sense a stench coming from below," he said while staring at the murky pool. "It is faint. Almost unnoticeable. I don't think a hunting hound would notice, unless it knew exactly what to look for."

"The stench travels through the plumbing?" Marianne asked as she examined the pool. The water had festered, but the bathrooms remained connected to whatever well they drew the liquid from. "An underground cistern, perhaps?"

"Or a hidden cavern," Bertrand suggested.

Marianne hardened her free hand with a layer of bone and punched through the wall closest to the pool. She heard a rat screech as she smashed her way through the stone, her fingers closing on the rodent.

Marianne squeezed the animal to death as it attempted to bite her, before tossing its corpse in the pool.

The hole she made revealed a complex array of bronze pipes going through the wall. "I think we found how the rats travel through the keep," she muttered out loud. The pipes went down and down underneath the castle.

Marianne grabbed a pebble and tossed it into the hole. She didn't hear it hit the bottom, though Bertrand's sensitive ears proved more effective. "It echoed," he warned his mistress after a few minutes. "The pipes lead to a larger cavern underneath."

Marianne and her retainer took down the wall one stone at a time, revealing a narrow shaft barely large enough to accommodate one person. They could use the pipes as support to climb down.

"I must warn Milady that it will be easier to go down than to climb up," Bertrand said. "If the culprit awaits us at the bottom, it will be difficult to retreat."

"The same will go for the sorcerer." Unless their foe could use another secret passage. "If we wait too long, they might escape."

"Then allow me to go in first."

Marianne nodded in agreement, and her retainer transformed into a cloud of mist. The vampire flowed down the shaft, while his mistress grabbed a pipe with her free hand. It was difficult to climb all the way down while holding a lantern, but Marianne's magically improved strength helped her a great deal.

She expected the rats to attack her during their descent, but though she heard the rodents crawling through the pipes and drains, they stayed out of Marianne's reach. Were they gathering to attack her at the bottom, or preparing to close the way out? Or did Bertrand's exorcism shake the animancer's control over his swarm more than she thought?

Whatever the case, Marianne found Bertrand back in his vampire form when she reached the shaft's bottom. After making a safe landing, the noblewoman raised her lantern to see through the thick darkness.

The duo had entered an old boiler room, a tangle of old machinery and rusted pipes. Marianne heard the sound of running water in the distance and suspected this area was connected to the Lightless Ocean. The devices once drained the water and treated it for the Verneys, only to decay over the decades.

Twenty meters below the castle's first floor, maybe more, Marianne thought as she tried to calculate the shaft's length. *Close to water level. Maybe even below.*

"Milady," Bertrand said as he examined the boiler's levers. "No dust."

Marianne frowned as she observed the device. Indeed, the machinery looked rather well-preserved for something left to rust for twenty years. Some pipes and drains had fallen into disrepair, but others looked surprisingly polished. Marianne followed them as they dug into the rock walls, leading to a steel door with rusted hinges. Its doorknob hadn't gathered dust either. Marianne extended her psychic sight and sensed multiple life-forms on the other side.

"Trap," Bertrand suggested while unsheathing his sword.

"Trap," Marianne confirmed before grabbing her own rapier. "What do you smell?"

"Mr. Valdemar's stench, formaldehyde, and blood." Bertrand squinted. "Blood most of all."

The vampire transformed into a cloud of mist and traveled through the keyhole to scout ahead, while Marianne gathered her breath for the battle she knew would come soon. "Bertrand?" she called through the door.

"Milady may not wish to look," her retainer replied on the other side with a hint of disgust.

Marianne responded by kicking the door open. The rusted hinges gave way and the noblewoman stepped inside a dark cavern. Her lantern's light reflected on a glass vat, a set of dead human eyes looking at her on the other side.

Marianne held her breath, as she watched a woman's corpse float inside a container filled with formaldehyde. Her lower half had turned into bloodred bones, and her upper body parts were white as milk. The corpse's face was frozen in a hollow expression, like a mindless doll. And yet, Marianne immediately recognized her from the Verney pictures.

"Sarah Dumont," she whispered as she examined the vat. The container was old and cracked at one spot. It was a miracle none of the liquid inside had leaked through. "It's . . . her."

"It's *them*," Bertrand replied. The vampire was looking at a second container to his mistress's left . . . and the thing inside *moved*.

Marianne flinched in horror.

Another Sarah Dumont was held prisoner in the second container, but she was missing more than her legs. Only her beautiful head floated in a vat of green liquid, along with her spine, a beating black heart, and cancerous lungs. The creature's gaze snapped between Bertrand and his mistress, but her eyes lacked any hint of intelligence.

Marianne's thoughts froze as she tried to process the sight before her. The noblewoman slowly raised her lantern to take a better look at the cavern around her.

Or rather, the lab. Her lantern wasn't bright enough to see everything, but what little it showed shook Marianne to the core. The two vats near the entrance were but the first of many, some broken, others relatively intact. One held a mutant human embryo with an oversize head; another a twisted mockery of Sarah Dumont with elongated arms and a fanged mouth. Both appeared alive to Marianne's psychic sight, bronze pipes supplying their glass prisons with water and nutrients.

A metallic tang hung in the air, while small puddles of alchemical substances stained the stone ground. Marianne carefully walked past workbenches covered with dusty bloodstains before noticing a hideous cup carved from a human skull on one of them. Someone had filled it with black hair and a pair of half-rotten gray eyeballs.

Marianne's horror was replaced with fury, as she connected the dots. She moved on to the next table, finding a macabre assortment of butcher tools, vivisection treatises, and half-scribbled anatomy notes.

Someone was trying to recreate the Followers' grail and had used clones of Sarah Dumont as raw material.

The grim laboratory seemed to stretch on forever. Whoever used it had cobbled it together by scavenging broken containers and second-hand instruments. Their work was gruesomely grotesque and unbefitting of any professional biomancer. Whoever used this place was a novice. A *deeply deranged* novice, but a novice all the same.

But why Sarah Dumont of all people? Marianne wondered. The biomancer's obsession with her was obvious, and this lab's resources could have been used to do so much else. What made Sarah special? Was she the best material for the grail somehow?

And what did it mean for Valdemar?

Marianne glanced at Bertrand to ask him if he smelled anything, but the vampire put a finger on his lips before she could open her mouth. He then pointed at his ears, and his mistress immediately understood. They weren't alone.

Marianne silently scanned her surroundings, ready to strike at the first sign of danger. Her psychic sight sensed life-forms in the room, but whenever she looked in their direction, she only found herself facing a deformed clone.

Bertrand pointed at his nose and then to an area of the lab shrouded in darkness. The lab was chaotic and haphazard with little organization to speak of, but this part of the cavern lacked any form of equipment whatsoever. A wide space more than twenty meters in diameter had been left untouched.

This part of the cavern was entirely unremarkable, save for a strange, circular pool at its center. An unknown substance bubbled in it, a vile tar as black as the purest darkness. The sight of it filled Marianne with a mix of thirst and revulsion. She felt the primal call to drink this vile oil, to let it flow inside her. It would make her *better*. She would never grow old, and her skills would never rust. Her senses would be sharper than any beast, her skin as smooth and strong as steel. No one would match her strength, and no one would try to force her to wed again.

Marianne would be free.

Or she would die.

Marianne knew, on a primal level, that taking this oil might kill her. Her survival instinct screamed at her to run away, to avoid the temptation. It was the medium for something powerful, too strong to be contained. She would burn from the inside, a moth consumed by flames.

Life or death.

Marianne felt like a woman dying of thirst being offered a cup of poison as these two instincts pulled her in different directions. Her psychic sight went wild, as it struggled to grasp this substance's true nature. It felt *alive*, incomprehensible yet familiar. Something that called to her flesh and soul, telling her to join this divine union. The call was insidious, and by the time Marianne realized what was happening, she had already walked three steps toward the pool. *No*, she thought, using all her willpower to look away. She canceled her arcane sight, briefly blinding herself to magic, closing her eyes to the vile promise of that . . . that *thing*.

Bertrand fared no better. Her vampire retainer gazed at the pool with horrified fascination, licking his fangs while his body trembled with tension. Though he hadn't walked forward, he struggled to hang on to his weapon's pommel. His eyes were redder than ever, like a man possessed.

"Bertrand," Marianne whispered. Although her retainer had told her to remain silent, she saw he was losing the fight. "Bertrand, look away. Bertrand—"

A black droplet fell into the pool from above.

Marianne instinctively looked up and raised her lantern at the ceiling.

An enormous symbol glowed faintly in the stone above, so faintly she could barely see it. Two curves joined within a cube, slashed by a vile organic rift. The lines making up this symbol closed and opened without rhyme or reason, festering with the black oil like a bloody wound on the world's skin.

It was blood.

That black oil was the blood of *something* greater than any human, something that called to all living beings the same way a flame tempted moths to their doom. This was the divine nectar the grail was meant to contain; the primordial fluid that would grant either immortality or oblivion.

Marianne couldn't look away from this bleeding eye of stone and barely noticed the black-furred shape crawling on the ceiling right above—

The swordswoman suddenly snapped back to reality. "Bertrand!" she shouted a warning far too late, as the rat dropped a shining flask on them. Her retainer didn't move an inch, unable to look away from the black pool. Without another alternative, Marianne tackled her vampire retainer. The blow broke Bertrand's trance and the vampire transformed into a cloud of mist right as the flask hit the ground. The substance inside erupted in a bright flash of light.

Marianne instinctively covered her head with her arm, saving her eyes from blindness. The white light was strong enough to illuminate the cavern, but it did more than that. Bertrand screamed in pain, his cloudy body reforming into a humanoid shape and collapsing on the floor.

"Bertrand!" Marianne tried to rescue her friend, but though she avoided the worst of the flash, the sudden bright light had weakened her vision. She could barely distinguish the vampire's shape near the pool.

Something landed to Marianne's left with a loud thump before she could reach him.

Only years of training allowed the noblewoman to dodge the dagger aiming for her throat, and she still dropped her lantern in the motion.

The container shattered against the ground, its flames erupting between Marianne and her attacker. She immediately used magic to heal her eyes.

Her foe didn't let her recover from her shock and leaped over the broken lantern with lethal speed. Marianne quickly dashed forward with her rapier and surprised the creature, their blades clashing. And she gazed into the bloodshot red eyes of her foe, the noblewoman remembered one of the Qlippoths' words at the hamlet with perfect clarity. What Baron Aleksander Verney had said about the strange, hideous rat that followed him everywhere.

It's not a rat at all.

The monster before her was neither man nor rodent, but a gruesome intermediary step between the two. Rags and a layer of black fur covered the beast, except for its clawed hands, dirty face, and elongated tail. Its head had curved ears and long sharp fangs which snapped at her with bestial fury. His two daggers were crossed, barely stopping Marianne's rapier from impaling him through the throat.

The Knights had mistaken this *thing* for a mutant rodent, instead of the infant form of something far, *far* more dangerous. Something intelligent—and deadly.

"You're a cultist," Marianne realized. Bertrand wriggled on the ground at the edge of her vision, with burns all over his skin. "The last Follower of the Grail."

"Master Aleksander is dead," the monster rasped with an all-too-human voice, before pushing Marianne back with inhuman strength. "But good Shelley never wavered in his devotion!"

Marianne attempted to gut the monster and finish him off, but his tail lunged at her head from the side like a whip. She lowered her back to dodge it, and the beast immediately attempted to stab her from another angle. The swordswoman disarmed one of her foe's hands with a well-placed parry and dodged the other dagger. Moving with astonishing speed, the man-rat used his newly freed hand to grab her by the throat. Marianne tried to stab the beast in the heart while gasping for air, but the rat dropped his other dagger and grabbed her wrist. Her rapier managed to cut his chest and draw blood anyway, but not deep enough to pierce the heart.

"And now," the man-rat said while lifting Marianne above the ground with one hand and pushing her sword away with the other. "Shelley will feast!"

His fangs lunged at Marianne's face, sharp and hungry.

14

THE WOUND

Reacting quickly, the swordswoman raised her free left hand and stabbed the monstrous rat in the eye. A layer of bone grew over her thumb as it crushed the eyeball and hit the soft flesh underneath. Shelley's fangs stopped within an inch of Marianne's face as the monster let out a screeching roar. The noblewoman channeled the Blood through her arm to strengthen it, frantically keeping the monster at bay. She tried to wrench her other hand and rapier free from the monster, but his grip remained strong as steel.

Shelley frantically tried to shake Marianne off him, but she refused to give ground. Though his clawed fingers tightened around her throat and prevented her from breathing, she kept pushing her thumb deeper into the rat's eyeball. A fountain of blood erupted onto her gloved hand, and she sensed Shelley's skull slowly crack under her tight grip. A little longer and she would tear his head apart.

Eventually, the pain became too much for the cultist to bear, and he tossed her off him with inhuman strength. Marianne rolled on the cold hard floor as she gasped for air, but her foe lunged at her again the moment she got back to her feet. The beast charged at the noblewoman on all fours, claws out. He pounced at her like a cat on a mouse, but Marianne dashed to the left to dodge his claws. The rat's tail swiped at her head, forcing her to keep her distance.

He's faster than me, Marianne thought while gritting her teeth. She still struggled to breathe correctly, and worse, Bertrand still wriggled helplessly on the floor not so far from her position. *But completely unskilled.*

Shelley assaulted her with a whirlwind of claws and bites, screeching all the way. The left side of his face dripped with blood, making the beast look even more savage. Having learned the lesson from their last clash, Marianne kept her distance and remained on the defense. She sidestepped and backflipped, letting the beast exhaust himself while she waited for an opening.

Her chance came when Shelley attempted to pounce on her again and left his flank exposed. Moving to his blinded left, Marianne stabbed him in the chest with her rapier right between the ribs. The monstrous rat's hide felt strong as armor, but her soulbound weapon pierced him all the same. Marianne knew next to nothing about rat anatomy, but she hoped to have hit a major organ.

Shelley pushed her back with his tail before covering his wound with a hand. The cultist let out a screech, and Marianne heard a chittering symphony answer his call. A horde of bloodred eyes looked at her from the laboratory's shadows, and a tide of vermin rushed at her from all sides.

With few options, Marianne attempted to use the exorcism spell Bertrand taught her. Using the Blood, she projected a part of her soul outward like a blast; the magic took the shape of a red light radiating from her, disrupting the invisible bond between Shelley and his rats.

Unfortunately, her lack of practice showed. While the light caused many of the rodents to recoil in fear, not all of them did. A few rats pursued Marianne and forced her to move toward the black pool to avoid being encircled.

"You will be the new sacrifice!" Shelley shouted, as he brought a flask from beneath his tattered rags. Recognizing the same blinding substance the cultist used to burn Bertrand, Marianne quickly grabbed her pistol with her left hand. She didn't have many bullets left and her weapon was prone to jamming, but she banked everything on one shot.

Her aim remained true, and she blasted Shelley's flask before he could throw it at her. The substance inside ignited, and Marianne barely had time to cover her face as it unleashed a flash of bright light. Shelley let out a roar of surprise but didn't scream as loudly as the helpless Bertrand. Marianne winced as she heard her retainer's cries of pain, the light burning his skin to reveal the festering flesh underneath.

Though the noblewoman's eyes struggled to adapt to the lighting, she heard some rats scampering in her direction to exploit her distraction. Marianne fired a warning shot, but one attempted to leap at her face. She backhanded it with her pistol midair, sending the beast flying into the black blood pond.

And the dark oil erupted. Marianne held her breath as an immense mound of black slime rose from the pool; a monstrous mass of oozing darkness larger than a carriage. The rodent she had thrown into the pool screeched from atop this protoplasmic horror, the vile substance tearing its flesh apart and filling its skin like a bag.

"No, you fool!" Shelley screamed in genuine terror. His left hand was missing two fingers where Marianne shot him, with glass shards piercing his palm. "They're not worthy! Not worthy!"

Marianne couldn't take her eyes off the black slime. The call that almost led her to throw herself into the pond was now replaced with primal revulsion as she witnessed the black substance change the rat in its grasp. A second head grew out of the rodent's neck, one with three mouths. New eyes opened all over its tainted fur, and they soon overwhelmed the rat's body mass. The rodent's screeches turned silent, as the cancerous mutations devoured him from within.

Eventually, they became too much. The poor rat's skin burst open like a pierced balloon and exploded in a shower of blackened blood. "Bertrand!" Marianne shouted a warning as she dashed at her wounded friend. "Get away!"

Too late.

Though Marianne managed to avoid getting soaked by the black rain, a droplet hit Bertrand as he recovered from his wounds. The vampire's skin had started to regenerate from exposure to the bright alchemical light, but the black slime touched his festering shoulder. The infection spread through him like a wildfire, blackening his dusted flesh.

"Bertrand!" Ignoring all caution, Marianne rushed to her retainer's side, sheathed her rapier, and prepared to put a hand on him. Maybe a healing spell could help him—

"Back off!" her retainer snarled before her palm could touch his shoulder. His mouth had transformed into a maw of sharp fangs, and a layer of translucent skin covered his eyes.

Marianne flinched and took a step back, right as the black slime returned to inside its pool. A booming sound echoed across the cavern, and its walls shook. Shelley's rats scampered off in fear, perhaps because their natural cowardice overwhelmed his control. The monstrous cultist bandaged his wounded hand and face with his rags, while glancing at the ceiling with religious awe.

The horrified Marianne ignored him. Instead, she watched powerlessly as Bertrand's body started to change. His hair fell from his skin as it turned translucent, making his bones and organs visible. His claws grew as long as spears, his muscles melted away into a gaunt and elongated figure, and his human ears turned into those of a twisted bat.

"Bertrand, let me help you," Marianne insisted.

"Back off, Milady . . ." The vampire crawled away, refusing physical contact. He clawed at his clothes and the skin underneath as if he could extract the infection with his bare hands. "I can't . . . it's inside me . . ."

"You can fight it off," she encouraged her friend. "You're strong. You can—"

A terrible noise boomed from the ceiling above. Marianne had never heard a sound like this. It was deep and yet high-pitched, an eldritch cacophony not of this world, a maddening song that rippled through reality itself. Marianne instinctively dropped her pistol and covered her ears, but the noise traveled *inside* her head. Thousands of voices screamed at once within her skull, their screeches traveling through her nerves and blood. Marianne thought her head might explode as she looked up at the screaming ceiling.

The symbol above her had started glowing. The stone wound that fed the pool no longer spat blood, but rather smoke. A magenta shroud of eldritch energies floated out of the carved rune, as ephemeral as a ghost. The simmering mass coalesced into the shape of a swirling eye, its design so hypnotic that Marianne couldn't look away from it.

"A sign!" The rat cultist yapped with rapturous joy, so loud that his voice cut through the noise. "The Master of Masters heard Shelley's prayers!"

The eldritch noise died down, but the stone symbol kept glowing with a bright red light. The cavern trembled, a quake rippling from it and shaking the tunnels to their foundations. The ceiling cracked and a boulder fell just left of Marianne and Bertrand.

It's going to collapse, the noblewoman realized in horror.

The cultist didn't share her fear. In fact, he looked almost giddy.

"Yes, yes, the good Shelley doesn't need this place!" he muttered to himself, as he grabbed another flask from beneath his rags. "The grail is alive! Alive!"

Reacting quickly, Marianne grabbed her pistol from the floor and attempted to shoot the rat cultist's head off. However, Shelley dodged the bullet with a leap, before throwing his flask at his laboratory. Instead of unleashing a bright flash, this potion erupted into a burst of green flames. They quickly spread across the lab, while Shelley himself escaped into the darkness. Marianne shot the cultist twice but wasn't sure if she managed to hit him.

The cultist had set his own lab on fire, leaving his foes and the rats alike to die.

"Come, Bertrand!" The noblewoman ordered. "We need to get out!"

"Can't . . . control . . ." Her friend shook as if suffering from the cold. Translucent wings grew out of his arms, his body shape twisting into a monstrous hybrid between a man and a bat. "It's calling me, Milady . . . everywhere . . . inside me . . . inside *you* . . ."

Inside her? But she hadn't been touched by the black oil, she was certain of it. "Bertrand, you must fight it," Marianne tried to encourage her friend. "You're strong. You can—"

"I can't!" He snarled at her, his voice twisting into a beastly roar midway. "Go!"

"I'm not abandoning you here—"

Marianne's retainer snapped his jaws at her like a savage animal, nearly tearing off her arm. She barely managed to avoid the attack by taking a step back, her heart skipping a beat in surprise. Her transformed retainer grabbed his head with his clawed hands as if suffering from a headache, his words transforming into a beastly hiss.

Even in spite of his warnings, Marianne prepared to cast a healing spell on her retainer, only to remember the eldritch cloud above her head. She barely had the time to raise her eyes to see it fall toward her.

Marianne dashed away toward the lab to escape it, but the alien entity followed her. She shot the eldritch cloud with her pistol, hoping the bullets would disperse it. Instead, the projectiles harmlessly went through the fumes and the cloud continued its pursuit.

Marianne sent one last glance at Bertrand as she ran away. Her retainer had fully transformed and flew in the opposite direction as her, toward the clones of Sarah Dumont. He had reverted into a savage beast, hungry for blood; *any* blood.

"I'm sorry . . ." Marianne apologized to Bertrand. After one last regretful look, she fled in Shelley's direction, knowing the cultist would have an escape route ready.

The cloud followed the noblewoman even as she ran between cloning vats and workbenches, but Marianne channeled the Blood through her legs. Her speed increased twofold, and she soon left the eldritch fumes in her dust. The cloud persisted until a large stone fell from the ceiling, shattering a glass container and spraying the ground with fluids. A warm, half-formed clone of Sarah Dumont rolled on the ground, and the eldritch entity stopped pursuing Marianne to feast on this easier prey.

It seemed the pistol's bullet had hit Shelley on his way out, as the noblewoman noticed a trail of blood on the ground. It was faint, only a few droplets, but clear enough. Marianne fled into the heart of the lab as it burned behind her, following the trail toward a small tunnel dug into the crumbling wall; she and Bertrand had missed it on their way in, as it was so small that a human needed to crouch to move inside.

Marianne bent as she rushed inside, leaving the collapsing, burning lab behind her. She heard a boulder block the way behind her and felt dust falling on her head as the tunnel trembled. *I need to get out*, Marianne thought as she frantically crawled through the tunnel. The whole place was collapsing on her.

Never before had Marianne felt so frightened. Each time the walls shook, she worried about being buried alive. The air grew thick and dusty, making her cough. All the way, she prayed that Bertrand found a way out; so long as he lived, even as a monster, he could be cured.

Marianne had no idea how long she crawled through the tunnel, as she lost herself between twists and turns. Did it go to the center of the world or to a darker horror than the one she left?

I won't die here, Marianne told herself. The soulstone necklace around her neck seemed to pulsate against her skin, waiting for her soul to pass on to better catch it. But in this place, nobody would find it. Her spirit would remain trapped beneath Verney Castle, forgotten until the end of days. Marianne prayed to the Light for deliverance. The tremors weakened the deeper she went, though they were followed by a loud and terrible noise. The noblewoman pressed on nonetheless. She *refused* to perish here, buried and forgotten. She had too much to do.

She didn't die. At long last, Marianne heard the sound of crashing waves and reached an exit. Her boots hit a thin layer of water as she emerged from the tunnel into a small cove roughly one kilometer away from Verney Castle.

Speaking of the fortress, a quick look showed Marianne that it had started to crumble. A good part of the cliff supporting the keep had collapsed into the Lightless Ocean, leaving only a pile of rocks rising from the waters. Smoke rose from the ruins, though Marianne couldn't tell if the fumes belonged to Shelley's flames or the eldritch creature he had released upon the world.

Maybe Bertrand was buried under these rocks, or maybe he managed to fly away to safety. Marianne needed to inform the Knights. To uncover the rubble, to bring biomancers to cure him. She refused to let her retainer and old companion perish as a monster.

The noblewoman walked along the cove, following droplets of blood along the sand with her pistol in one hand and her rapier in the other. She couldn't see far in the dark, but she wouldn't relent. She would find that abominable cultist and end his life here and now. The trail continued for a while, before abruptly stopping. Marianne looked around with her psychic sight, trying to detect the presence of magic. She expected Shelley to get the drop on her, but no ambush materialized.

A horrible doubt formed in Marianne's mind, and her gaze turned toward the Lightless Ocean. She squinted and focused, until she distinguished a small shape on the water far away from her. A boat.

Marianne let out a cry of frustration as she opened fire on the escaping vessel. She fired two more shots before her pistol ran out of ammunition. It was all for naught. As the boat vanished from her sight, Marianne lowered her weapon in silent rage. Shelley had gotten away.

For now, Marianne thought as she glanced at her left thumb and the rat blood soaking her glove. With these fluids, the Knights' spellcasters could locate Shelley almost anywhere.

But though Marianne had managed to send a messenger bat to the nearest guard station, it might be days before reinforcements arrived and Shelley would get a head start. It wasn't hard to figure out where he went.

"The spawn is alive." Marianne remembered the cultist's words. Considering who he had been trying to clone, it didn't take long for the noblewoman to connect the dots. *He's going after Valdemar.*

If Shelley was foolish enough to get near Lord Och's protégé, the lich would slay him easily enough. But why would he? Why was Valdemar so important to the cult? Marianne thought of the black blood in the cave, about the force lurking inside the phantom hamlet of Vernburg.

Shelley was a dangerous foe, but only the maddened thrall of something far worse. A dark force was at work in the region, and Marianne had barely scratched the surface of its activities.

Inside me, Bertrand's words resonated in her mind, *inside you.*

Marianne needed to get to the bottom of this. Not only for herself, but for her retainer. Shelley knew the nature of the substance that transformed the vampire into a monster; perhaps he knew how to cure it.

"I'm going to hunt you," Marianne swore as she looked at the Lightless Ocean, her fingers clenching on her weapons. "Like a *dog.*"

15

THE DREAMLANDS

Lady Mathilde believed in traveling light. Valdemar had expected such an esteemed alchemist to gather a large escort of knights for her trip to Astaphanos, but the priestess did not. As he reached the Institute's stables with a bag full of painting supplies, he only found Liliane, Hermann, and Iren waiting next to the carriage. They had all dressed for the trip. Liliane had traded her usual robes for a more casual blue traveling dress and a chic red beret, while Hermann hid his face behind a plague doctor's mask and his hands beneath a pair of gloves.

"Is that really necessary?" Valdemar asked the troglodyte. "Can you even breathe with that apparatus?"

"Locals . . . will lynch me otherwise," Hermann explained. "Your merchants . . . will refuse to sell their wares . . . or overcharge me. It's better that they . . . think I'm human."

"Probably," Valdemar admitted. Most humans saw troglodytes as savage barbarians, and they weren't tolerated in Azlantean settlements without an escort. By hiding his tail beneath his robes and lying about his profession, Hermann could pass for a human.

"I will punch anyone who tries to shortchange you," Liliane said while pumping her fist.

"They're more likely to laugh than feel fear," Iren teased—and was punched in the arm for his trouble.

"Didn't your mother tell you not to pick on fair ladies?" Liliane asked with a pout.

"You're too young to count." Iren easily dodged Liliane's attempt to pinch him again, before glancing at Valdemar. "You look like shit, my friend."

"I couldn't find sleep." For once nightmares weren't responsible though. Valdemar's mind simply refused to abandon itself to slumber, though he couldn't explain why. "I didn't know you were coming with us."

"I'm surprised by your presence as well," Iren replied with a raised eyebrow. "Weren't you forbidden from leaving the Institute?"

"Lord Och gave me permission to go out and gather material for the Painted Door project." The lich seemed rather confident that he could track down his apprentice if needed, though Valdemar wasn't foolish enough to flee. "Though I have to, I quote, 'follow all of young Mathilde's orders as if they were mine.'"

"Don't worry, Valdy, everything will be fine," Liliane reassured him with a pat on the back. "It'll be like a picnic! A relaxing experience!"

"I'll pass for the picnic, as I've got some private business to take care of in Astaphanos," Iren replied before making a mock bow. "Until then, I'll be your chauffeur. You'll need a good one."

Indeed. Though Lady Mathilde traveled without an escort, Valdemar couldn't say the same about her wagon. A house on wheels might have been a better descriptor, as it needed two giant beetles to pull it. Made of wood and metal, the vehicle included a second floor with windows, a bronze chimney, and even an alchemical reservoir. A small ladder allowed people to climb to the back door.

"It's a mobile lab," Liliane explained. "Some alchemists use them to travel across Azlant and sell potions on the road."

"It's too big to go through some tunnels," Valdemar commented.

"The major roads are more than large enough for these vehicles," Iren countered. "The Dark Lords made them wide enough to let armies through them. You got a point though. I wouldn't travel to the border towns in this wagon. Those regions have narrow tunnels and way too many carriage robberies."

"I thought . . . you had friends in . . . every criminal enterprise?" Hermann asked.

"Friends and foes, my scaled fellow," Iren commented with a chuckle, before dusting his clothes. "And here comes our revered Master."

He had a sharp ear. Lady Mathilde indeed rejoined them, though not alone.

A stunning dark elf followed the priestess, and her appearance made even Valdemar pause.

Liliane was a pretty girl and Marianne Reynard had an austere beauty, but they looked downright bland compared to this otherworldly creature. Her figure was graceful, her face a lovely sight. Her skin was as smooth as a polished mirror, nearly black, and her pale blue eyes shone in the dark. Her light violet hair fell down to the bottom of her back, and she walked with the arrogance of someone used to getting her way. Her regal black and purple dress embraced a weblike motif, while a gold and ruby necklace sparkled around her neck. A spidery veil on her hair completed the ensemble.

Only a pair of curved ears, hooved feet, and a serpentlike tail betrayed her inhuman origin. Neither did Valdemar sense any warmth in the woman. She was attractive the same way a cave lion was: deadly, exotic, and dangerous to approach.

"Greetings, everyone," Lady Mathilde said with a polite nod. "I believe we are all here."

"Frigga!" Liliane greeted the dark elf with a smile. It was a warmer welcome than Hermann's, who ignored her entirely, while Iren's own smile looked false. "I'm so glad you could come."

"My dear Liliane, how could I let you visit Astaphanos without me?" the dokkar said with a beautiful clear voice. She kissed Liliane on the cheeks, making her blush. "I can't wait to show you our embassy's Pleasure Gardens. You will love them."

"That reminds me, the oneiromancers of the Ardent Dreams await your next visit with anticipation," Iren informed the dark elf. "They have developed a new mind experience just for you."

Frigga sneered. "I hope it is better than the last one. Their dreamscapes cater to vulgar tastes, and I strive for finer experiences."

Valdemar took a moment to observe Frigga in silence, trying to get the handle on her personality. His experience with the dokkars, or "dark elves," was limited to what he had learned in books. The humanoid race had ruled one of the largest territories in Underland alongside the Pleromians until repeated wars against Azlant and the derros caused them to fall from preeminence. Their empire had fragmented into city-states barely kept united by the threat from other species.

Valdemar didn't pity them though. The dokkars had nearly exterminated mankind during the Descent, and the massacres perpetrated by their generals remained a trauma in humans' collective consciousness. Were it not for his ancestors' choice to resort to mass-drafting of undead and extensive use of necromancy, Valdemar might not have been alive today.

But those were old times, and neither Azlant nor the dokkars wanted a war that would only serve to strengthen the derro kingdom's position. So humans and dark elves engaged in a policy of reconciliation.

It was a slow and difficult process. The few dokkar communities in Azlant had been expelled two hundred years ago for worshipping a Stranger called the Mother of All; and though the empire had since allowed dark elf merchants to trade in their territory, they were limited to a few border cities. Considering the mention of the dokkars' embassy, Valdemar supposed that Frigga was something of a diplomat. She seemed quite friendly and Liliane appeared to like her, but Valdemar remembered Hermann's warnings about the dark elf's selfishness. Indeed, he detected a hint of cruel cunning in Frigga's gaze. Like a cat, she played nice when she wanted something but could prove more vicious otherwise.

The dark elf noticed Valdemar's gaze and gave him a lovely smile. Most men would have blushed, but the summoner remained cautious. "And who might you be?" Frigga asked.

"Valdemar Verney," Valdemar introduced himself.

"Frigga of House Fredegund." She offered her hand to Valdemar. The sorcerer was puzzled for a few seconds, before realizing that he was supposed to kiss it, which he did. Damn noble etiquette . . . "My dear Liliane spoke highly of you."

"I speak highly of everyone," Liliane responded with a chuckle.

"And we all love you for it," the dark elf replied courteously as Valdemar let her hand go. "You seem wary of me though. I swear I won't bite."

"It's the first time I've seen a dokkar in the flesh," Valdemar admitted. "All I learned of your civilization comes from imperial propaganda, and I'm not sure what to think of it."

"Oh, your inquisitors will tell you that we dark elves eat babies, enslave the weak, and sacrifice our kinsmen during orgies dedicated to the Strangers, but they're wrong." Frigga chuckled. "Babies don't have enough meat, slavery is tightly regulated, and we abolished dark elf sacrifices since animals worked just as well."

"Charming," Valdemar deadpanned. He noticed that Lady Mathilde looked uncomfortable about the "sacrifice" part for obvious reasons. "You don't believe in the Light?"

"I worship the Mother of All," Frigga replied, and Lady Mathilde's expression turned into a blank mask. The Mother of All was considered a Stranger, and her cult was outlawed in the empire. "But don't worry, I follow the laws of your land while in it and I do not proselytize."

"Frigga is here as part of a scholarly exchange," Lady Mathilde explained to Valdemar. "Lord Och allows her to study our magical traditions, and one of our colleagues receives tutelage from dokkar archmages."

"Between us, I'm also supposed to spy on Lord Och and report everything he does to my house," Frigga said while winking at Valdemar. "I would be thankful if you could tell me everything you know about the lich."

"Shouldn't you keep that part for yourself?" Valdemar asked with amusement.

"Well, everyone already knows," Iren pointed out with a smirk. "I had her pegged as a spy on her first day."

"I'm not telling you anything about my teacher," Valdemar replied. "Though I would be interested in learning more about the dokkars from you. I've been researching ancient civilizations lately, and your empire is second only to the Pleromians in age."

"We are far more ancient than your empire, that's for certain," Frigga replied with racial pride. "I would be delighted to enlighten you on our culture while we solve your sleeping problem."

Valdemar glared at Liliane.

"What?" she asked.

"You can tell me anything, I won't tell anyone?" Valdemar quoted her.

"I was trying to help!" Liliane protested. "Frigga is the Institute's best oneiromancer! Her dreams are so vivid, it's hard to distinguish them from reality."

"You paint with pigments, while I sculpt desires," Frigga told Valdemar. "We're both artists in our own way."

"How is Poingcarré's project going by the way?" Lady Mathilde asked the dark elf. "Were the dream crystals I provided up to the task?"

"They were," Frigga replied with a sharp nod. "But alas, he needs more. Hence my visit to Astaphonos, besides entertaining my dear Liliane."

Poingcarré, Poingcarré . . . "Isn't Poingcarré the Master who created the well outside?" Valdemar asked Hermann.

"He is . . ." the troglodyte confirmed. "Master Poingcarré is a . . . a specialist in occult mathematics and . . . dimensions."

"Master Poingcarré is studying the world of dreams; particularly the Nightmare of Kazat at its center," Frigga explained. "Where every onei-romancer has failed to physically enter the dreaming world with magic, he believes he can succeed with technology. In exchange for my expertise on oneiromancy, he took me as an apprentice."

"I'll pass on your help for my sleeping troubles," Valdemar declared. "If you're out to learn more on Lord Och, I'm not letting you anywhere inside my head."

Frigga laughed. "Spying on the lich is what I'm *supposed* to do, but I think in the long-term. If Lord Och took you as an apprentice, it means you might grow into a powerful and influential magician. Hence, it will be in my house's interests to cultivate good relationships with you so you can be of use to us later."

Valdemar suddenly wondered if her friendship with Liliane was with-out ulterior motive. Probably not. Liliane was the heiress of a powerful weapon magnate, and a good friend to have for a dark elf diplomat.

"I will vouch for Frigga," Liliane insisted.

"So will I," Lady Mathilde added.

Valdemar didn't hide his surprise. "Do you trust her?"

"I trust her self-interest," the priestess said. "Frigga was required to sign a soul contract when she arrived here, which allows Lord Och to punish her no matter where she is. She will not dare to displease him."

Frigga's smile turned colder. "I would rather that you didn't spread word of this particular arrangement, Lady Mathilde."

"And I would rather that you behave in public," the priestess replied with a dry tone.

Liliane looked plainly uncomfortable, and Valdemar couldn't blame her. Lady Mathilde and Frigga did their best to hide it, but they clearly didn't get along.

"In any case, out of respect for my dear Liliane, I would gladly help you with your nightmares." Frigga put a hand on her waist. "But when you're good at something you never do it for free. Since you're a friend of a friend, I will give you a discount."

"How much?" Valdemar asked with a sigh, having expected some-thing like that.

"You will paint me a pictomancy portrait as payment," Frigga decided. "I cannot deny Hermann's talent, but his special style cannot capture my beauty. Liliane seemed very impressed with your mother's portrait, so I suspect you shall prove up to the task."

A portrait? Valdemar could live with it. "Sounds simple enough."

"But it won't be any portrait," the dokkar said with a coy smirk. "I want something sordid and scandalous. A painting that will make your priests blush."

Ah yes, *dark elves*. Valdemar prayed she wouldn't ask for him to paint her torturing a mole rat. "How sordid?" he asked warily.

"If I were at home, I would ask you to paint me during an orgy," Frigga said with longing. "But alas, your Empire's citizens are too tight-laced for such festivities. Maybe you could paint me naked with a corpse at my feet? No, that would be too quaint . . . we'll use a giant bat instead, and I'll take a very suggestive pose . . ."

"Frigga!" Liliane protested in horror, her cheeks turning red. "Why?"

"Because it will be *fun*." The dark elf sounded more and more excited with her idea. "Imagine if I sold it and used the money for charity. A naked dokkar's portrait made by the child of cultists, helping fund your orphanages. I can already imagine the scandal!"

"I already know a few people who would pay a fortune for a naked picture of you, beautiful," Iren said. "I would be first in line."

The horrified Liliane glanced at Lady Mathilde, but she remained imperturbable. "The Light shines on all that is beautiful," the priestess said. "There is no shame in celebrating our bodies . . . within acceptable limits."

"The Light, yes," Frigga said with disappointment. She had wanted to infuriate the priestess and lost interest when she didn't take the bait. "See, Liliane? I would be doing holy work. You can come to watch the painting process, if you want . . ."

By now, Liliane was so red that Valdemar started to worry for her health. "When are we leaving?" she asked Lady Mathilde.

"Right now," the priestess replied. "Our journey will take a while, so make yourselves at home."

Much like the Institute, Lady Mathilde's wagon benefitted from space alteration spells. Already large on the outside, the inside proved large enough to fit multiple rooms. The alchemist had set bunk beds on the second floor for her trainees and allowed Valdemar and Frigga to use one for their dreaming experiments.

"This is a sleeping draught," the dark elf said, as she gave her patient a cup. The blue liquid inside tasted like mint. "Just lay down on the mattress and relax."

"My metabolism clears drugs quickly," Valdemar warned her as he followed her directives. Lady Mathilde had decorated her ceiling with the painted symbols of surface constellations, which he found tasteful.

"So Liliane told me, but I gave you enough to put a dragon to sleep." Once her patient was laying on his bed, Frigga touched his forehead with her soft fingers. Valdemar sensed a jolt of electricity travel through his skin as she made contact. "Close your eyes, and clear your mind. It will be easier that way."

"Hypothetically, could you enter my dreams even if I resisted?" Valdemar asked.

"Of course I could," she replied scornfully. "But it will be more pleasant for both of us if you don't struggle."

Valdemar closed his eyes and did his best to relax, but as he expected, the potion was slow to affect him. Or perhaps he was still wary of letting the dark elf inside his head, even if others vouched for her.

Valdemar's mind remained restless, and he tried to find a distraction. "May I ask you something?"

"Go on," Frigga replied while calmly massaging his forehead.

"If you are called dark elves, does it mean there are light elves? The question always bugged me."

"There were, sort of." Frigga decided to give him a full history lesson. "In ancient times, our civilization discovered the Blood but split over what to do about it. Most dokkars were primitive people who feared witches and sorcerers to the point of imprisoning them. Our spellcasting ancestors, rejected by all, decided to create a new home underground. They believed that magic originated from something deep below the earth and sought to commune with it."

Valdemar shuddered as he remembered the eyes on the walls. Could this strange organic superstructure have a connection with the Blood? "And what happened to these surface cousins of yours?"

"We slaughtered them when they tried to flee the Whitemoon and the chilling cold," Frigga replied with an eerily casual tone. "'Beware of serpents with long memories' is a famous dokkar proverb."

"I'll keep that in mind," Valdemar deadpanned. He was pretty sure magic wasn't the only reason that the light elves had exiled their darker cousins.

Frigga asked Valdemar questions of her own as he relaxed. When did he start dreaming? What did he dream of? Had he already seen the well of his nightmares in the waking world? Valdemar answered them all, though his focus slowly slipped. His body started to feel numb as it entered a torpid state of inactivity. His breathing slowed down, and darkness soon overwhelmed his mind.

When his eyes opened again, Valdemar found himself in a place stranger than any Pleromian ruin. He stood alone on some kind of plateau drenched in a thin layer of pure water, the surface reflecting the half-formed images of his grandfather's wizened face, his mother's sad smile, Liliane's giggles, and Hermann's reptilian eyes. Small statues rose from the waters, from a broken Eiffel tower to a shattered planetary sphere. Only Lord Och's representation stood absolute, its bones made of rusted steel.

This dreamworld's ceiling was made of yellow fumes coursing with colorful electrical bolts, though their light didn't hurt his eyes. The current had its source in a strange city on the horizon, one that didn't look like any human settlement. Valdemar distinguished a tangle of bulbous black towers, spiraling stone buildings, and floating islands of stone. The lightning circled it like a halo or the eye of a magical storm.

The more he squinted at it, the more this city disturbed the dreamer. Its towers appeared to be made of countless statues of humans, troglodytes, elves and other creatures bound together in a macabre fresco; its architecture shifted as if alive, a building flickering and reappearing on another spot.

Valdemar attempted to use his psychic sight to analyze the area, but his magic failed him. While his body felt real, no magic coursed through his veins. He was an illusion, a mirage without substance.

"So this is your dreamscape." Valdemar raised his eyes and noticed Frigga sitting on empty air above his head. Somehow, her voice cut clearly through the noise of the thunderbolts above. "It's a complete mess."

"I didn't expect *this*," Valdemar admitted. He thought that his inner world would be a physical representation of his old family house, or maybe a copy of the Institute. "I never dreamed of this city. I don't even know what it is!"

"This is the Nightmare of Kazat, a landmark of the dreamworld," the dark elf said while glancing at the strange city on the horizon. "Without going into the gory details, it's an invasive nightmare that grows by consuming dreamers. Exploring it is dangerous for all but the most powerful oneiromancers, so I would suggest enjoying its dark beauty from afar. The fact you can see it from your dreamscape is a bad sign."

Valdemar flinched. "How bad?"

"I will need a moment to check," she said. She reminded Valdemar of a cat stretching on an invisible sofa. "This doesn't look like it, but I'm delving into the fabric of your dreams."

"Sure, make yourself at home," Valdemar deadpanned, though he let her work in peace.

He took the opportunity to explore the plateau, which turned out to be much smaller than he had anticipated. It was half as large as the Institute's first floor and almost entirely devoid of decoration. It disturbed Valdemar that out of all the images of his friends and family, only Lord Och's statue seemed complete. The Dark Lord cast a large shadow even in his subconscious.

Since it was a dream, Valdemar attempted to summon things from the ether, and then to fly. His imagination should rule in his mind, but he couldn't summon anything and his feet remained anchored to the ground. Maybe his subconscious enforced some limitations on his dream? He couldn't fly because he didn't believe he could?

After a few minutes of observation, Frigga leaped from her invisible seat and gracefully landed in front of Valdemar. Her black hooves made no sound when they hit the ground, nor did the water ripple at her contact.

"You are ill, my dear human," the dark elf declared. "First of all, I can tell you have absolutely no oneiromancy training, which means your psychic defenses fade away when you sleep and leave your mind unguarded. Second, you possess an abnormally strong connection to the Primordial Dream."

"I thought all souls were connected to it?" Valdemar asked, having done some research on the subject when he tried to banish his nightmares on his own. The Primordial Dream, also known as the Collective Unconscious and the Dreamlands, was the magical dimension from which all dreams originated.

"Yes, but not directly." She waved a hand at the plateau on which they stood. "This is your dreamscape, a sanctuary unique to an individual soul that serves as a filter between your mind and the Primordial Dream. It's a bubble that shields your mind from unwanted attention.

However, the Nightmare of Kazat exists deep inside the collective unconscious."

"Which means my dreamscape is thin and not working properly," Valdemar guessed with a frown. Wonderful. "I suppose that's not a good thing?"

"Not for you, it isn't," she replied with a chuckle. "Your home's door is unlocked and anyone can get in. Besides making you a lot more vulnerable to nightmares than most of your kind, I'm surprised you weren't attacked in your sleep by a night hag or incubus already. Or maybe you were and don't even remember."

Okay, this was much worse than expected.

Damn it, he should have consulted an oneiromancer years ago! Valdemar had thought his nightmares were the result of a childhood trauma, not a magical deficiency. He already didn't like Lord Och reading his mind, and the idea of any criminal oneiromancer infiltrating his dreams angered him.

"How did it happen?" Valdemar asked. "From the way you make it sound, it's unusual."

"I will need more sessions to answer that question," Frigga admitted. "Dreamscapes naturally form during infancy and yours simply didn't grow as it should. It's possible your mind was tampered with or you survived a terrible experience that left your subconscious permanently scarred."

Valdemar clenched his fingers. "My grandpa said I fell into a well while young," he explained. "I've been having nightmares ever since."

"Poor you," the dark elf replied without really meaning it. She reminded him a bit of Lord Och, going through the motions of courtesy without truly believing in them. "A childhood fear could have weakened your dreamscape, but not enough to leave it dead. I can't stress it enough, you won't even feel any intruder slipping inside you."

"Is the phrasing intentional?"

"Yes," Frigga replied coyly. By now, Valdemar had grown certain that she took joy in teasing and embarrassing people.

Valdemar gave her a false smile. "Then how can I *protect* myself from bad girls like you?"

This made the dark elf chuckle. "Good one. Learning the basics of oneiromancy will let you strengthen your dreamscape, protect it from intrusions, and prevent your sleeping mind from wandering into dangerous places. Alternatively, you could buy a dreamcatcher, though it will be horrendously expensive." Frigga waved her hand, and a strange device formed in her hand. It resembled a circular amulet with a complex web design at its center.

Valdemar couldn't help but feel a tinge of envy. The dark elf had better control of *his* dreams than he did!

"A dreamcatcher is a nifty amulet that prevents you from dreaming at all," Frigga explained. "It seals your subconscious shut while you sleep. No dreams, no intrusions. You won't be able to use oneiromancy though."

Valdemar frowned in skepticism. "I spent some time in the custody of inquisitors, and they preferred to keep me awake rather than put an amulet on my neck."

The dark elf licked her lips like a cat. "Did they torture you?"

"They strapped me to a wheel and pumped me full of drugs."

"What, that's all?" She looked downright disappointed. "Your inquisitors lack imagination. Their method is understandable though. A dreamcatcher is a very complex amulet that must be adapted to a specific mind, making it extremely costly."

And Valdemar's funds were extremely limited. Lord Och afforded him a research budget, but he spent most funds on his ecto-catcher and various elixirs. Besides the cost, he would rather avoid relying on an item he could lose. "Could you teach me how to repair my dreamscape?" he asked the dark elf.

Frigga conjured a throne of black mahogany from nowhere and slouched on it as if she owned Valdemar's mind. "Not for free."

"I already promised you a portrait!"

"To pay for my expertise," the dark elf replied mirthfully. "Which I'm generously providing. But tutoring you would demand a lot of my free time, and I am a busy woman."

"I should have listened to Hermann," Valdemar complained. The troglodyte had called Frigga selfish, but she was even worse than expected.

"The lizard is a goody-goody," Frigga said with a cackle, "while I know what I'm worth."

"I don't have an inexhaustible purse," Valdemar warned her. "How much do you want?"

"Then let's agree on a future favor. Nothing comes to mind right now, but I'm sure I will find a use for you." The dark elf licked her lips in a predatory way. "Now, about that portrait you owe me . . ."

16

THE EYES OF HEAVEN

When the next morning came, Lady Mathilde summoned the scholars to her workshop. While it probably paled before her true laboratory at the Institute, her wagon was truly an alchemist's dream. The workshop resembled a cozy wooden cabin, clean and brightly colored. Clever use of space and hidden compartments allowed Lady Mathilde to store a wealth of potions, ingredients, dried mushrooms, and shelves packed with esoteric grimoires. A coal boiler served to heat the wagon and fuel the flames of boiling flasks. From alembics to blood-filled show globes, Lady Mathilde had collected every tool in the alchemical repertoire.

Valdemar also noticed other devices that he had only ever heard of before. The largest was the athanor near the boiler, a very special metal furnace used to mix multiple alchemical substances at a constant temperature, but he paid more attention to a strange projector. A black soulstone was attached to it, ready to be activated.

"Is that a phantom projector?" Valdemar asked Lady Mathilde in astonishment. Frigga observed a green homunculus fetus in a flask to his left, watching tubes feed the artificial creature with nutrients.

"It is," the priestess replied with a kind smile, before giving him a demonstration. She pushed a button and the device projected the crimson image of a wizened old man.

"Day 30, Viveka month, year 304 After Empire," the specter muttered to himself. Valdemar recognized it as one of the last years of the so-called

Spore Plague that killed a third of Azlant's population. "File 253. Observation of Spore plague in action among adult female subjects. Subject: Andrea Torras, fourteen days after infection. Observation: the spore appears to spread through the air before infecting the cerebrospinal fluid and higher brain functions. Humor analysis shows an increase in adrenaline. Subject's neurons are slowly replaced with fungal tissue, while biological functions are repurposed to produce more spores. Hypothesis: modification of cerebrospinal fluid might be the key to checking the infection. Note: must create a control group to observe further developments."

"I've never seen one before," Valdemar admitted as the ghost continued reporting his findings. Phantom projectors allowed the user to extract a soulstone's memories and showcase them.

"He was a . . . biomancer?" Hermann asked, as he and Liliane approached the device.

"An unlicensed one," Lady Mathilde explained as she turned off the projector and caused the ghost to vanish. "Human biomancy was illegal in 304 A.E., but many spellcasters turned to the art in an attempt to cure the Spore Plague."

"And three of them were successful in the end," Valdemar remembered from the history books.

"This soulstone belonged to one of them, the alchemist Johann Baptista," Lady Mathilde explained. "While he and his colleagues did find a cure, they committed atrocious human experimentations in the process. Even infecting healthy families to study the disease's progress."

"That's horrible," Liliane said with a frown.

"They killed hundreds and saved millions," Valdemar replied. "It's a net gain. Desperate times call for desperate measures."

Lady Mathilde's smile lacked any warmth. "That was their defense, but they still abducted and experimented on people without their consent. However, since Johann and his colleagues *did* save the empire's population, it was decided that their souls would be preserved in soulstones for the benefit of future generations. Lord Och came into possession of all three of them and entrusted Baptista's spirit to me."

"Your kind would not have needed to sacrifice anyone if they had allowed biomancy from the get-go," Frigga said after losing interest in the homunculus. "Our people have never suffered from diseases for millennia thanks to health treatments and inheritable mutations. Nor do any of us die of old age, and we don't even need a potion for it."

"A process that . . . decreased your fertility," Hermann pointed out. "You still haven't . . . recovered from the last human war's losses."

Frigga's expression twisted into one of disdain, but Valdemar could tell that Hermann's words hit a nerve. "I would rather stay forever young than have more than three brats at home," the dokkar argued.

"Lady Mathilde's elixir makes both possible," Liliane boasted with a bright smirk.

"Thank you, Liliane," the priestess replied serenely, while Frigga sulked. "In any case, I didn't gather you all for a biomancy lesson. Valdemar, a few days ago I gave you pointers about combat spells. I would like to check on your progress."

"I've been practicing the reinforcing spell," Valdemar answered with a nod.

"You too?" Liliane seemed strangely competitive today. "Let's compare!"

In response, Valdemar channeled the Blood through his hand until his fist turned black as coal. His skin and flesh strengthened until they were hard as steel.

While Lady Mathilde's eyes widened in surprise and Frigga looked on with interest, Liliane outright whistled. "Valdy, how did you do that?" she asked. By comparison, when the heiress reinforced the skin of her fist, it simply looked thicker and stiff.

"I rearranged the chemical composition of my skin while reinforcing it," Valdemar explained. "From what I gathered, reinforcing works by channeling blood to thicken the skin. I figured that since blood contains iron and carbon, it would be better to restructure my skin into a flexible alloy of organic steel. It turned out great."

"It's a highly advanced use of the reinforcing spell only found among trained battlemages," Lady Mathilde congratulated him. "I'm impressed you picked it up so soon . . . and that you didn't collapse immediately. Your blood needs iron to transport oxygen through your body, so using that much should have left you *at least* winded."

"I heal and regenerate blood quickly," Valdemar said with pride as he returned his hand to normal. "I think I could harden my entire body."

Frigga snickered for some reason.

Lady Mathilde shot the idea down immediately. "Don't. Reinforcing your entire body's surface will consume an enormous amount of resources and, most importantly, it's useless. The human anatomy is astonishingly resilient, so focus on covering your weak points. The neck, the head, the torso . . . you will consume less resources this way."

"I'm jealous," Liliane complained. "I can only enhance my arms so far."

"Don't worry, my dear Liliane," Frigga reassured her while putting a hand on her forearm. "You will make a far better mind mage than him."

"By the way, Valdy, did you sleep well?" Liliane asked with curiosity. "Oneiromancy is amazing, isn't it?"

Frigga laughed while Valdemar gritted his teeth in embarrassment.

"What?" Liliane asked with a surprised frown.

"He's hopeless," Frigga said with a wide, mocking grin.

She has such a punchable face, Valdemar thought while struggling to keep his calm. Liliane looked at him with astonishment, which somehow made him feel even more ashamed.

"No way!" she said. "But oneiromancy is so easy!"

It was Valdemar's turn to look at his friend in astonishment. "You can do it?" he asked Liliane.

"I taught her the basics of dream defense," Lady Mathilde said with a raised eyebrow. "What is your problem with this science, Valdemar?"

"I don't get it!" The necromancer admitted in frustration.

He had spent the entire night receiving "tutelage" from Frigga about strengthening his dreamscape . . . but he would have asked for a refund if he could. The dark elf had given him exercises such as detailing child-hood memories to build things in his dreamscape, or focusing on his feelings.

It didn't work. Valdemar tried for hours to conjure things in his dream, to give them shape, to no avail. Frigga's support turned to frustra-tion at his slowness, then at astonishment before his terrible results, and finally into mockery.

"It astonishes me that an artist would be so poorly in tune with their feelings," the dark elf said, as she finished her tales of Valdemar's failures. Lady Mathilde listened with a frown, Hermann scratched his head in confusion, and Liliane looked at Valdemar as if he were sick.

"What does that even mean?" Valdemar rasped. "I know who I am."

To the necromancer's surprise, Lady Mathilde didn't look convinced. "From what you tell me, I am not so certain."

"Let's do a thought experiment," Frigga suggested. "Liliane, Valdemar, imagine you get an idea for a new source of energy. What do you do with it? You can answer the question too, Hermann."

"I will start considering the practical applications," Valdemar replied as he tried to figure out her point.

"Mmm . . ." Liliane took a longer time to formulate her answer. "I would try to see how it could help everyone."

"I would study . . . understand it as much as possible," Hermann declared after considering the question for the longest time.

Frigga nodded without judgment. "Now, that energy you discovered is limitless. Your whole civilization will benefit from it. However, it will put your coal miners out of work. They will lose their jobs and suffer. What do you do?"

"The answer is in the question," Valdemar pointed out. "The greater good and the big picture trump everything. So long as the many benefit from it, the feelings of the few are secondary."

"Valdy, you're too hasty," Liliane scolded him. "I would find a middle ground. Introduce it progressively, so the miners can find new jobs."

"And so make the whole civilization lose out on the new energy's advantages in the meantime?" Valdemar asked.

"Everyone should prosper, Valdy," Liliane replied with surprising firmness. "Common prosperity isn't worth hurting people in the process."

"Please, my dear, no judgment yet," Frigga chided her, before glancing at Hermann. "What about you?"

"I . . . I do not know," the troglodyte admitted. "I . . . I suppose I would ask everyone . . . to reach a consensus."

Frigga nodded in agreement. "From your answers, I can tell dear Liliane will make the best oneiromancer among the three of you. No wonder we get along. Even Hermann has some potential, but you, Valdemar? You will never be more than passable."

Valdemar frowned in anger. "Watch me."

"No, she has a point," Lady Mathilde declared. "Oneiromancers need to be in tune with their feelings, Valdemar. Not only those of others, but also their own. They understand themselves and their values."

"So do I," the necromancer replied.

"I do not . . . see the problem," Hermann agreed with him.

"Valdemar, imagine you fulfill your goal and reach this other world full of sunlight," Lady Mathilde said. "What will you do then?"

An easy answer. "I will keep the path open so my people can settle on the other side."

"That's not what she asked." Frigga smiled. "What will *you* do? How do you imagine your life after you fulfill your objective?"

Valdemar opened his mouth. And immediately closed it. What would he do after opening a pathway to Earth? He . . . he would probably try to visit his grandfather's tribe if it still existed, and . . . maybe explore this brand new world?

"You never . . . never considered what you will do *after* reaching your goal?" Hermann asked.

No, he hadn't. Valdemar's life had revolved around fulfilling his grandfather's dream, and he never imagined what his life would look like afterward.

"You see the big picture but forget to include yourself in it," Frigga explained. "And that's why you will never be a great oneiromancer. You have a *goal*, yes, one that you borrowed from someone else; but you don't have *dreams*."

"Why think about the future if I haven't achieved my objective yet?" Valdemar asked back. "I'll cross that bridge when I reach it."

Lady Mathilde had the grace to explain things better than the dark elf. "Frigga makes a poor effort at getting her point across. What she means, truly, is that you are a *thinker* and not a *feeler*. Your mind reasons in terms of tangible results, of problems to solve, but with little consideration for your own feelings or those of others. It's not a bad thing. Your disciplined mindset heavily contributes to your engineering and summoning prowess. But this will make learning oneiromancy and all forms of mind-magic difficult. These spellcasting traditions heavily rely on intuitive feelings and empathy."

"Lord Och has no empathy for anyone, and yet he can read minds," Valdemar countered. "And Frigga is, forgive the expression, a selfish ass."

Valdemar ignored the glare Liliane sent him, but Frigga didn't seem to care anyway. "You wound me," the dark elf replied without meaning it. "It's not because I put my feelings and person above others that I don't consider them. I wouldn't be half as good as riling up your kind if I weren't such a sensitive, caring soul."

"As for the Dark Lord, he had centuries to cover his weaknesses," Lady Mathilde replied. "Anyone middling in a field of magic can become talented with enough time. I'm not saying you can't master these skills, Valdemar; only that you will have a harder time with them."

"You can't . . . be good everywhere," Hermann tried to reassure Valdemar, who crossed his arms in defeat. "You should focus . . . on building your strengths."

"Come on, Valdy, you're already amazing in so many fields." Liliane patted him on the back. "Don't be greedy."

Valdemar sulked, but after a moment he realized that his friends had a point. He couldn't expect to become a master of all forms of magic. Besides, he didn't need to invade others' dreams or read minds. The necromancer only had to learn enough to protect himself from those who used these forms of magic. And if not, he could simply summon a creature that would solve the problem for him.

"But we have digressed from our original point," Lady Mathilde said while trying to refocus her lesson. "Liliane, Valdemar, I am very proud of your progress. Now that you have learned the basics of the reinforcing spell, it's time I teach you a long-distance option."

The priestess raised her hand, extended her fingers, and pointed them at a wall. Blood erupted from below her nails, before taking the shape of five sharpened, crystalized projectiles. They hit the wall so fast that Valdemar's eyes couldn't keep up, impacting on the steel with the strength of arrows.

"This is the Blood Bullet spell," Lady Mathilde explained. While Liliane examined the point where the projectiles hit, Valdemar focused on the priestess's fingers instead. The wounds below her nails had closed immediately, leaving no opening. "You use this technique by solidifying blood below the nail, crystalizing it, and then apply pressure to launch the resulting projectile at high speed. Of course, it decreases the amount of blood in your body. The more you use it, the quicker you will exhaust your reserves."

No wonder I haven't seen many Knights cast this spell, Valdemar thought. *Reinforcing or telekinetic slams didn't exhaust reserves nearly as fast as throwing these projectiles.*

"I know a stronger version," Frigga commented lazily, trying to show off. "Except I use bones and reinforced phalanges rather than blood."

"The Bone Bullet spell is indeed a stronger variant, but one that needs more resources and finesse," Lady Mathilde replied calmly. "For now, blood will suffice."

"Master, doesn't it hurt?" Liliane asked with a frown. "You're cutting through your skin."

"You will feel pain, dear child." The priestess smiled. "But you'll get used to it with effort."

"I . . . I would like to learn as well." Hermann cleared out his throat. "I need to . . . get better at fighting."

"You're thinking of the Collector?" Valdemar asked, his troglodyte friend nodding in confirmation. It seemed his defeat had affected Hermann more than he expected.

"Cool, we can practice together," Liliane chirped with a grin. "Could you show me your Bone Bullet technique too, Frigga? I would love to learn it."

"Of course, my dear," the dark elf replied before kissing her friend on the cheek in a way Valdemar didn't find chaste at all. "Everything for you."

It took a while, but the group finally reached their destination. Iren informed them that they had crossed the right Earthmouth portal, and Valdemar emerged from the wagon to take his first step in Astaphanos's capital of La Dorada. Famously known as the Pearl of the Empire, the city lived up to its name. Raised on an island surrounded by the Lightless Ocean, the settlement mixed impressive architecture with exotic beauty. Shaped from brass, tin, and gold, the buildings used curved forms rather than the rigid lines favored in Paraplex and other rival Domains. Domes and rounded roofs were more common than spires and towers, while vast canals allowed cowled undead boatmen to transport travelers on lavish skiffs.

The city buzzed with activity. The Earthmouth opened on the group's wagon to a sprawling bazaar where merchants from all corners of the empire came to sell their wares. From licensed necromancers selling mindless undead servants to dokkar tradesmen importing expensive silk, La Dorada was a commercial crossroads where many pleasures could be fulfilled. Biomancy-enhanced whores invited clients to lavish brothels for unforgettable trysts, while oneiromancers openly peddled dream-drugs. Some magicians even offered wealthy clients the ability to experience the memories of others, or live out their darkest fantasies in dream worlds where their will was law.

Of course, not even this place was exempt from the Dark Lords' surveillance. The mirror-faced Knights of the Mind observed the bazaar from the safety of the rooftops and the shadows of alleys. They didn't just survey the streets to prevent crime, they also patrolled dreams and thoughts.

All fantasies could be satisfied by oneiromancers; all but those that the local Dark Lord, Lady Phul, deemed unacceptable. She allowed more freedom and debauchery than her colleagues, but it was all an insidious illusion; a calculated spectacle meant to lure citizens into complacency with meaningless sensations. Those who succumbed to darker temptations, who mistook the liberty of dreaming of torture, sex, and ephemeral power for a license to turn to the Strangers or question the Dark Lords, were never seen again.

But both people and buildings paled before the beauty of La Dorada's gardens. Sprawling rows of plants, phosphorescent mushrooms, and bioengineered trees decorated the streets. The smell of flowers mixed with the smell of sex and drugs; in La Dorada, beauty and decadence coexisted in equal measure. Liliane and Frigga immediately asked Lady Mathilde's permission to visit the garden, and Hermann seemed tempted to join them.

And yet, for all of the city's beauty, the eyes were here too. They were on the cavern's walls and the ceiling, big and small. An army of squamous orbs observed the oblivious human ants toiling beneath them. The watchers judged men and women in silence, unseen and yet all-powerful.

Valdemar looked up at the ceiling, at the largest eye of them all. It was so red, and so big that it probably matched the city below in size. Its black pupil seemed to watch the bazaar, and Valdemar wondered if this creature could notice him specifically.

"Can you understand me?" the necromancer whispered, his voice drowned by the shouts of oblivious merchants and the cacophony of tourists.

The eye of the world did not answer. Maybe it didn't hear. Maybe it didn't understand human language. Maybe it watched but didn't truly care.

"Blink if you do," Valdemar asked, afraid of the answer.

For a moment, the necromancer found solace in his ignorance.

But then the giant eye closed. Lids of hideous festering flesh emerged from the stone flesh of the living cavern, covering the eyeball in a protective mantle. They were so huge, and yet moved so fast that they made no sound when they joined.

And when they snapped open again, Valdemar felt the thousands of eyes of Astaphanos adjust their gaze. Their pupils turned from watching the thousands of civilians to a single person in their midst with unwavering intensity. Valdemar sensed the burden of their vigil on his shoulders, on his back, on his face. He felt from every direction, from above and below. When he looked down at the ground to escape the watchers' attention, he noticed tiny golden eyes growing from the pavement, so small he hadn't noticed them.

But they had seen him. They had heard him, and they had answered.

Whatever this thing, this superorganism was, it wasn't just alive. It was *sentient* too.

Letting out a breath in silent anxiety, Valdemar tried to focus on something else. His gaze wandered to the crowd in the bazaar, but the people had eyes too. Most didn't pay attention to the necromancer. Some looked through him, focusing on stands behind his back.

But a pair of eyes peered into his own, as pale and gray as his own.

Valdemar froze in shock as he noticed her long raven hair and oh-so-familiar face; the same face that sang him songs as he learned to talk, who carried him in her arms whenever he cried. She looked younger, far younger than when she had died, but it was *her*. Even hidden below her black hat, he could recognize her anywhere.

He blinked, and she was gone.

Valdemar immediately rushed into the crowd, pushing away people. He heard shouts and Liliane calling his name, but he didn't care. He rushed between the stands, toward the alley where he glimpsed her, but he only saw fleshy eyes on the walls and shadows.

But he hadn't dreamed. He knew what he had seen, even if he didn't understand how it was possible.

"Mom?" Valdemar asked.

The eyes didn't answer.

17

THE SHOPKEEPER IS YOUR FRIEND

Are you certain . . . it was her?" Hermann asked. The disguised troglodyte attracted many curious gazes with his plague doctor outfit, with people stepping out of his way. "It could have been . . . a trick of the mind."

"I know what I saw," Valdemar insisted. "My True Sight protects me from illusions. I can even see Iren's real eye color now."

Iren put a finger on his lips, as he guided the trio through La Dorada's narrow alleys. "Shush," he said. "The ladies prefer me with purple eyes."

Speaking of eyes, Valdemar had had his fill of them. The organic orbs were less common in the suburbs, but the necromancer couldn't find an alley without at least one of them gazing at him. Attracting the entity's attention had proven to be a mistake, as it refused to let Valdemar go out of its sight.

No wonder most of the people who had consumed an Elixir of True Sight went insane. The feeling of being watched all the time was maddening and fueled Valdemar's paranoia. Though he valued his life enough to bear this burden in silence, he understood how some magicians might have considered death a release from the constant surveillance.

Valdemar would have been happier sailing the Lightless Ocean, but fate got in the way. The group should have taken a flesh ferry toward a half-savage island to find samples of the Colophryar plant, the last ingredient needed for the Painted Door project. Unfortunately, the ship had apparently suffered from a technical mishap, delaying their departure.

Iren had then suggested going to the Midnight Market's local chapter and buying the plant from smugglers; Hermann had reluctantly agreed to it for a lack of a better option. Since Lady Mathilde's own errands were more legal in nature, the group had split in half with orders to meet again at the dokkar embassy afterward.

Iren had led them to the dirtiest parts of the city. Far from the splendor of the main square and bazaar, the distant districts of La Dorada were a hive of shacks, houses in squalor, and crumbling buildings. The alleys formed a maze without rhyme or reason, though Iren seemed to know the area like the back of his hand. Beggars asked for money at every crossroad, and even the Knights of the Mind were less present in the district.

This was the lair of Astaphanos's underclass: The pox-ridden whores unable to afford a biomancy treatment, the servants, the waiters, the carriage drivers. Valdemar suspected a few of them were miners and farmers put out of the job by the ever-increasing use of undead labor, with no choice but to migrate to the larger cities to find work.

Was his mother hiding among them? Valdemar knew he had seen her, deep within his bones; even if he couldn't explain it himself.

Hermann noticed his unease. "Maybe it was . . . a look-alike?"

"Maybe," Valdemar admitted. "But . . . I can't explain why, but I *know* it was her."

"It could have been her ghost paying you a visit," Iren said. "Is your mother entombed in this Domain?"

"No." His mother was buried in Horaios, and ghosts didn't rise from the dead years after their demise. "A specter can look almost real, but their true nature is easy to discern for those with the right knowledge. She was made of flesh and blood."

"A hallucination then," Iren suggested while shrugging his shoulders. "You don't sleep enough and you suffer from a lot of stress. Both combined can drive a man mad."

Maybe. Valdemar hated to think himself as mentally unwell, but he had barely started treating his insomnia; even his sessions with Frigga left him tired, as dreaming exhausted him mentally.

Hermann scratched his mask's beak. "What if . . . it was the eyes' doing? You said she appeared after . . . after you addressed them. The two events might be . . . related. A telepathic projection . . . an attempt to communicate. We should . . . test it out."

"I would rather not," Valdemar admitted. "Not now at least." The watchers' gaze weighed on him enough already.

Iren finally led them to their destination, some kind of lost pawnshop inside a dead-end alley. It did not inspire confidence from the outside. Time and dust had degraded the storefront's paint job, while the entrance sign "Elias Emporium" was clearly missing a few letters. The metal door's hinges were rusted, while the cracked window showed an odd assortment of items including jewelry, figurines, musical instruments, and even a pistol. The alley was empty, as if the locals feared approaching it.

"This is the place," Iren said.

"Looks a bit too small for a Midnight Market haunt," Valdemar pointed out. "The smugglers prefer larger places such as hidden tunnels to do their business."

"This is just the entrance, my friend." Iren knocked on the door three times in quick succession, then two more times after a short wait. Valdemar guessed that it was a signal. "I'll lead you there and you'll be free to ask around for your flower while I solve my business."

"Why did you . . . come here?" Hermann asked with curiosity.

"A pal of mine found an item I've been looking for," Iren explained. "A rare coin from before the Descent. I'm wary of forgeries, so I'll check it myself before making the purchase. I'm something of a specialist."

Valdemar chuckled. He had expected Iren's business to involve blood money or worse. "You collect *coins*, of all things?"

"Everyone's got a hobby, friend. I'll show you my collection when we return home. I've got stuff that goes back to the Pleromians."

Valdemar sensed someone approaching the door from the other side with his psychic sight, even before he heard the lock turn. The gate opened to reveal a spry old man in his seventies, with pale skin and a balding head. His clothes were simple and inexpensive, his eyes whitened by age.

And yet, Valdemar immediately sensed something unusual about this shopkeeper. A sense of wrongness exuded from his gaze, as if his eyeballs didn't fit the wrinkled eyelids. He wasn't a sorcerer and released no magical aura, but . . . Valdemar couldn't put his finger on it, but something about this man struck him as unusual.

Unaware of Valdemar's thoughts, Iren greeted the shopkeeper with a pat on the shoulder. "Elias, my old friend, how's the family?"

"Fine, fine," the shopkeeper answered with a smile missing half its teeth. He invited the group inside his shop and closed the door behind them.

The place was larger than it looked from the outside, dustier than a tomb, and a complete bazaar of the strange. The sheer number of items piled up in every corner astonished Valdemar, as he wondered how the shopkeeper managed his inventory. Besides the usual assortment of pawn shop goods, the emporium had gathered quite the collection of odd goods as well: a drum made from a cave leopard's skin, a pre-imperial era curved sword, a broken soulstone . . . and even a tattooed dokkar's mummified hand. Candles provided a modicum of light, though some shelves remained obscured.

Valdemar and Hermann took a moment to scan the shop for anything interesting, while Iren made small talk with the shopkeeper. The troglodyte immediately focused on a collection of carved stone masks representing reptilian creatures. Some took inspiration from snakes, others from cave lizards, and a few were completely fantastical. Hermann grabbed a mask with six eye openings and a fanged, open mouth. His hand brushed against the surface with nostalgia.

"These are troglodyte masks?" Valdemar guessed.

"They represent the Coiled Ones . . . that my kind worship. Priests wear them to take . . . the persona of the god." his reptilian friend whispered too low for the shopkeeper to hear. "This is Ashgar K'ris . . . the Hunter of Souls . . . god of the dead. I wonder how . . . it ended here."

Valdemar guessed that some tomb robber found the mask and sold it without understanding its significance. Neither did the Knights, or they would have fed these troglodyte artifacts to the flames even if none of them carried magical properties.

The shop had collected thirteen masks in total, though one of them stood from the rest. This particular artifact wasn't made of stone, but rather some kind of black substance that reminded Valdemar of wood. It lacked openings for the mouth, the nose, or even eyeholes. A chalky white symbol expanded from the forehead, before ending in tentacles as it reached the mask's borders.

"Which god does it represent?" Valdemar asked, as he peered into the spiral. His gaze lost itself in its center, in this never-ending white abyss. "A god of knowledge?"

To his surprise, Hermann shook his head. "This is not . . . one of ours."

Truly? Valdemar touched the mask and shuddered. The "wood" felt cold as ice. *Definitely not normal,* the sorcerer thought, *but I don't sense any Blood magic coming from it either.* The back part of the artifact was as black as the purest darkness.

Pushed by curiosity, Valdemar put the mask on. The substance felt unbearably cold against his skin, though it didn't hurt either. Even stranger, the mask seemed to adapt itself to the wearer's face, latching to his mouth and nose like a second layer of skin. Valdemar breathed, and chilly fresh air filled his lungs. Though the mask lacked any opening, the sorcerer started to see through the wood. This magical vision was sharper, focused at the center; the unlit parts of the shop became clearer, as if the mask had lifted the veil of darkness. Valdemar glanced at Iren and the shopkeeper, and while the former found the scene amusing, the latter frowned in confusion.

"Now you look like a real cultist," Iren said with a smile.

"We must bring Frigga to the sacrificial altar!" Valdemar joked back. The mask made his voice reverberate like an echo. "The dark gods will have their due!"

Even Hermann joined in. "I can hold the knife . . . while you restrain her."

"Aw, you're cruel," Iren replied with a chuckle. "Trust me, she's a paragon of virtue by dokkar standards."

"She is vulgar . . . arrogant . . ." Hermann looked fit to gag. "Tasteless!"

Clearly, the troglodyte hadn't digested Frigga's contempt for his art style.

"Anyway, Valdemar, what's up with that mask?" Iren asked. "You sound like some bad novel's villain."

"Besides the voice change and feeling cold to the touch, it improves my ability to see in the dark." Valdemar removed the mask easily, as it detached itself from his skin. "Pretty underwhelming for a magical item, but practical. How did you guys manage to hide it from the Knights?"

"The Knight-captain in charge of the district loves money and whores more than he fears his superiors," Elias replied while crossing his arms. "We pay him and his men a generous sum each week to look the other way. Sometimes, we also give them a few items to confiscate or traitors to arrest. Pretty sweet deal if you ask me."

Why couldn't the Knights of the Chain have been so accommodating?

Valdemar examined the mask, trying to understand the enchantments woven into it. To his surprise, he didn't notice any. His True Sight had identified the lines of bloody energies fueling Och's fortress, but this mask only oozed cold and darkness.

"Where did you get it?" Valdemar asked the shopkeeper. The longer he examined this artifact, the more fascinated he became.

"I do not remember, but I can look in the registry," Elias replied gruffly. "Do you want to buy it?"

"I will," Valdemar replied as he put the mask back on. He was curious about how this item worked and why his True Sight couldn't identify the enchantments used to create it.

"I will take . . . the others," Hermann declared while grabbing all the troglodyte masks.

"All of them?" Iren asked with a raised eyebrow. "Are you a collector too?"

"They belong . . . to an ancient and proud people," Hermann replied. "Not to . . . *tourists*. This is cultural appropriation!"

Valdemar could read between the lines. Hermann worked tirelessly to find a new homeland for his people and considered these artifacts troglodyte property. He would have paid any price to get them back to his kind.

Thankfully, the purchase didn't amount to much. A few hundred silver coins for Hermann and a handful of gold for Valdemar.

"Are you well, Elias?" the rogue asked their host as he put the troglodyte masks in a cloth bag. "It's not like you to underprice your wares. You didn't even argue."

"I don't care about those," the shopkeeper replied as he handed the bag of masks to Hermann. "The good merchandise lies below."

Something in his tone made Valdemar suspicious. Elias sounded a bit too unenthusiastic for a pawnbroker. *Maybe it's just the eyes getting to me,* the sorcerer thought. *Now I'm starting to see shadows in every corner.*

Their transactions done, the shopkeeper moved behind his shop's counter and lifted a carpet. He touched the floor, and Valdemar heard the sound of a lock opening. "The others are already downstairs," the shopkeeper said while opening a trapdoor in the floor and revealing a narrow staircase. "If you want to see the real stuff."

"Where does this lead?" Hermann asked.

"To a smuggler cavern," Iren explained as he confidently walked down the stairs. In all likelihood, he had done so countless times before. "That's where the market gathers at this hour."

"I'm still not . . . convinced that they will have quality Colophryar," Hermann said as he climbed down after the rogue. "This is a . . . very rare plant."

Valdemar followed the march but stopped at the trapdoor's threshold. "You're not coming with us?" he asked the shopkeeper.

"Someone has to keep the counter," the man replied as if he were an idiot.

It made perfect sense, and yet . . . a lifetime of evading inquisitors kicked in, raising all kinds of alarm bells.

Valdemar trusted his gut, and something didn't feel right here. The shopkeeper, a pawnbroker, hadn't even argued about the price of his wares; nor did he seem to remember their real value or origins. And though he did his best to appear aloof, Valdemar sensed an undercurrent of nervousness coming from him.

"Valdemar?" Hermann asked inside from the stairs. Iren had long since vanished from sight, delving into the darkness below the shop.

Elias the shopkeeper was growing impatient. "You're going in or what? I ain't leaving it open forever."

Something felt wrong about this man, though Valdemar couldn't explain why. The sorcerer locked eyes with the shopkeeper and finally realized what bothered him about the eyelids.

"You don't blink," Valdemar said while Hermann emerged from the stairs in confusion.

They had been in the shop for minutes, and Elias hadn't blinked *once*.

Valdemar swiftly raised his hand while the shopkeeper flinched in surprise, his gloved fingers grabbing Elias's eyelids and lifting them. There was another patch of skin below the first, white as chalk.

A derro steel dagger sprang from the man's sleeve and aimed straight for Valdemar's stomach. The sorcerer reacted faster and hardened his chest into steel. The dagger's blade cut through his reinforced clothes like butter but grazed against the impenetrable shield Valdemar's skin had turned into.

Hermann let out a roar and rushed at the shopkeeper, but the man swiftly leaped to safety with inhuman dexterity. He never landed, as Valdemar telekinetically grabbed him in midair and tossed him against the counter with enough force to break it. Splinters flew all around the shop in a catastrophic crash, and blood flowed from the shopkeeper's nose. He tried to struggle, but Valdemar held him firmly with the power of his mind. The man's blood bent to his will.

And as he established firm control over the shopkeeper's flesh, Valdemar began to notice many unusual things. A substance in the eyes, to change their coloration; an abnormality in the vocal cords, as if they were made of different muscles than the throat; iron bars in the limbs, neck, and spine to extend them; more livers than a man should have; a metal device inside the brain; and an alchemical powder grafting a second layer of skin over the first.

"He's some sort of mutant," Valdemar warned Hermann while keeping the shopkeeper restrained. His captive tried to scream, but his mouth refused to open. "Do you smell anything?"

Hermann briefly removed his plague doctor mask and revealed his true troglodyte visage. "It's strange," the pictomancer said as he sniffed the horrified captive's face. "There are two people's smells . . . and the second is . . . not human."

The troglodyte removed his gloves, grabbed the shopkeeper's forehead with his hands, and started peeling the skin away with a claw. Hermann's incision was as precise as a scalpel as it cut through the man's visage and revealed a second face beneath the first.

Ghoulish cheeks and chalky skin, strands of a white beard, hateful lidless eyes . . . The creature was humanoid and yet inhuman. Yet both sorcerers in the room quickly recognized Azlant's ancestral enemy.

"A derro," Hermann said with astonishment. "How did he . . ."

"How did *they*," Valdemar interrupted him. No way he acted alone.

. . .

And Iren hadn't come out of the stairs.

Shit.

"Hermann, bring this spy to the Knights and sound the alarm," Valdemar said, as he knocked the derro into unconsciousness by slamming his head against the counter. The summoner loathed the inquisitors from the bottom of his heart, but the situation was too terrible to be picky. "I'm going after Iren before he gets himself killed."

"Alone?" His troglodyte friend was aghast. "This is madness."

"That derro's false skin came from a living human," Valdemar replied grimly. It wasn't hard to guess what this monster's compatriots would do to Iren if they caught him, and the rogue didn't deserve it. *Nobody* did.

The necromancer began his descent while Hermann reluctantly obeyed his command and exited the shop to call for help.

The stairway went down for at least ten meters below the shop, the stone steps trembling below Valdemar's feet. His mask allowed him to see perfectly in the dark, to notice the magical symbols etched into the walls. They had been used to shield the basement from supernatural scrutiny but had degraded from lack of maintenance. The derros couldn't use the Blood, after all.

They must have been here for days, Valdemar realized, as he reached an archway at the bottom. He was starting to hear voices in the derro language; though the sorcerer wasn't particularly good at it, he understood that the speakers were having an argument of some kind.

As Iren had warned, the stairway indeed led to a natural cavern hidden deep below the city, one large enough to accommodate an underground bazaar. The derros had turned the marketplace into what Valdemar could only describe as a twisted laboratory.

Tall pylons reached as high in the ceiling and crackled with electricity, their light powerful enough to illuminate most of the cavern. Unlike the bric-a-brac above, the nightmarish factory was a model of cruel organization. A row of six operation tables was lined up against the left wall, though only two were occupied. The first housed an unconscious derro with elongated legs, the second a shackled human male. A masked derro surgeon two heads smaller than Valdemar was opening his fully conscious victim's forehead with a saw, the man gagged to muffle his screams.

The right side of the cavern looked even ghastlier. Six human brains floated inside a glass container hooked to a strange machine-maze of steamy pipes and pumps, while flayed human skins dried on a vast cupboard. Each had been treated with alchemical substances and marked with a three-digit number.

A dozen undead workers toiled among the pylons and operation tables, but a closer look informed Valdemar of their true, ghastlier nature. Their skin had been cleanly removed, leaving their raw bloody flesh exposed; and their skulls had been scooped open above the eyes, their brains replaced with metal antennae pulsating with flashes of lightning.

Two of these workers were carrying an unconscious Iren to an operating table. The rogue profusely bled from the chest and head, his clothes tainted red. Valdemar's eyes widened in horror and fury behind his mask, his heart turning cold as ice.

Two derros with daggers argued not far from him over the corpses of a third and fourth; the cruel dwarves both wore leather armor and carried daggers, perhaps because firearms would make too much noise. One of their dead brethren had Iren's shortsword impaling him through the chest, and the other's head had rolled a few meters away from the neck.

The first derro was admonishing his compatriot, and Valdemar distinctly heard the words for "idiot," "need alive for surgery," and "brainless lobotomite" among the litany of insults. They were so busy arguing that they didn't notice the sorcerer entering the room.

Valdemar did not hesitate. The warlock raised both his index fingers at the cruel dwarves and fired two blood bullets. He winced in pain as the projectiles erupted through his skin, but they both hit their target in the head and killed them on the spot. He had killed beasts and summoned monsters before, but never sentient humanoids. *No,* Valdemar thought as he glanced at the brainless corpses of his kindred. *They're beasts who can speak, nothing more.*

The derro surgeon among the operation tables let out a screech of surprise and rushed at Valdemar with his saw, but the warlock telekinetically squashed him against the ceiling. While the dead doctor crashed on the ground, the sorcerer rushed to the wounded Iren's side. The undead workers didn't stop him, too mindless to act without direct orders.

Valdemar applied a hand to Iren's chest and head. The derros had stabbed him *eight* times, broken his ribs, and savagely beaten him into unconsciousness. The rogue was losing blood and risked permanent brain damage if not treated quickly. Valdemar used magic to treat Iren's wounds the best he could, knitting flesh together and redirecting his blood to prevent a stroke. The other human victim, strapped to a bed, looked at the sorcerer with pleading eyes. Blood flowed from his forehead where the derro surgeon had cut him.

"I'm sorry!" Valdemar replied while focusing on saving Iren's life. He had stabilized the rogue for now, but he needed more time to help him fully recover. "One at a time!"

Yet a thought couldn't escape Valdemar's mind, as he remembered the numbers on the flayed skins.

How many?

How many?

Heavy steps echoed in the cavern, alongside the clinking of steel. Having closed Iren's wounds, Valdemar raised his eyes to see a golem emerge from a deeper area of the cavern. The steel machine was twice as tall as a human, and the glass tank serving as its head almost reached the ceiling; a disembodied, cadaverous derro skull with a cable spine floated inside green liquid. The golem's chest was a furnace, its shoulders steel pipes. Its left hand was large enough to crush a man's skull, and its right ended in a cannon.

The machine raised its weapon at Valdemar without a word and opened fire.

18

THE BRAIN COLLECTORS

Lady Mathilde had advised Valdemar not to reinforce his entire body, as it cost a great amount of energy and he only needed to protect a few vital areas. But she probably hadn't expected her student to be subjected to artillery fire. As he heard a click echo from the golem's cannon arm, Valdemar instinctively jumped between the unconscious Iren and the line of fire. His skin turned to steel from head to toe, while his flesh grew denser from the sheer concentration of iron within his muscles. His sense of touch numbed into nothingness as he became a living statue of metal.

A cannonball the size of a human fist hit Valdemar in the chest, the impact's blow reverberating through his body as the projectile flattened against his magical armor. The blast propelled him backward against one of the cavern's walls, his back shattering the stone. A sharp pain spread through his ribcage, perhaps from a bone fracture.

Valdemar saw stars and stumbled, the flattened cannonball falling to his feet with a loud clang. The golem froze for a few seconds in surprise, the skull inside the machine's glass dome of a head glaring at the iron sorcerer.

Unlike the brainless workers, that thing had a mind of its own.

Valdemar attempted to telekinetically take over the golem's skull and crush it. He sensed a mental response, a brain and a spine connected to machinery, but no blood to control. The derros had replaced veins with cables, and body fluids with alchemical components.

The golem immediately charged at Valdemar with frightening speed, the ground shaking with its heavy steps. It raised its left hand and prepared to rip the sorcerer's head from his shoulders.

Reacting quickly, Valdemar glanced at the derro surgeon's corpse lying on the ground and telekinetically tossed it at the golem's face. The body hit the machine's glass visor with enough force to crack it, but it didn't slow down. Valdemar attempted to free Iren and the other bedbound prisoner before making a break for the stairway, but he almost tripped while taking a few steps.

Damn it, his iron armor might have been strong enough to resist a cannonball, but it lacked the flexibility of skin!

The golem tossed aside the infirmary's beds in its charge—thankfully missing Iren's—and attempted to punch Valdemar. The sorcerer leaped to the side at the last second, the machine's metal hand piercing the cavern wall like a sword through butter.

Worse, the noise was starting to attract attention. Valdemar heard voices deeper in the cavern and realized that another group of derros was moving his way.

Hastily undoing his metal armor to move more freely, the sorcerer rolled to the ground, got back to his feet, and fired a few blood bullets from his fingertips. The projectiles hit the golem's glass tank and widened the existing cracks, but not enough to pierce the shielding.

It didn't matter though, as Valdemar's blood slipped through the cracks and the sorcerer telekinetically reshaped it into a small summoning circle. As the golem freed its hand and pointed its cannon at the sorcerer, he snapped his fingers and activated the spell.

The summoning circle ignited, and the golem's visor exploded in a fiery blast. Valdemar raised his arms to shield himself from both the bright light and glass shards as the golem violently fell on its back. A self-sustained conflagration materialized over the machine's metal body, tongues of flames looking for fuel. The fire elemental raged like an inferno as it incinerated the golem's piloting skull to a crisp and turned its strange fluids to steam.

The machine didn't rise again.

Valdemar had yet to see *anything* survive a monster being summoned inside it.

"Enjoy yourself," the sorcerer said, as he left his summoned bonfire to its fury. Valdemar glanced at the derro surgeon's guinea pig, whose bed had been tossed aside by the golem. The human, a man in his forties, bled so profusely from the forehead that his hair had turned red. He struggled against the manacles chaining him to his bed, his eyes widening in relief upon seeing Valdemar approach.

"Calm down," the sorcerer said as he applied a hand to the man's forehead. The derro surgeon's saw had cut through the bone, which Valdemar couldn't repair, but he quickly stitched his skin back together. The summoner then reinforced his hands, breaking the man's manacles. "Hey, my friend is wounded, can you help me carry—"

Valdemar never finished his sentence, as the prisoner fled for the stairway the moment he could. He didn't even bother to remove the gag around his mouth.

That coward!

It was an all too human reaction, but Valdemar would have hoped for a little gratitude.

"I hope you get shot!" the summoner shouted on impulse.

And the derros fulfilled his careless wish. A bullet hit the nameless prisoner in the back of the head, shattering the skull in a shower of blood and brain. The corpse collapsed at the bottom of the exit stairways, and Valdemar immediately regretted his words.

A trio of derros emerged from the cavern's depths, wearing primitive respirators and glass visors on their faces. The shooter carried a long, spindly firearm Valdemar had never seen, the second a blunderbuss, and the third an alchemical flamethrower.

The trio noticed Valdemar and his elemental, with the blunderbuss wielder opening fire. The sorcerer ducked down in time to dodge, but his summoned elemental was hit directly. It only enraged the entity, who abandoned its futile attempts to burn the golem's corpse to charge at the derros. The vile dwarves fired bullets, but their projectiles harmlessly passed through the creature's flames.

An idea crossed Valdemar's mind. Glancing at the two derros he slew earlier, the sorcerer manipulated the blood bullets encased in their skulls and telekinetically reshaped them into summoning circles.

The two corpses erupted in a shower of blood, as twin masses of eyes and tentacles manifested within them. Two Gnawer Qlippoths materialized, sandwiching the derros between the elemental and themselves. One of the dwarves activated his flamethrower and bathed the summoned creatures with green flames, but their tentacles swiftly coiled around his neck and started choking him to death. One of his allies attacked every-one with his rifle, while the fire elemental caught the last member of the trio and melted the flesh from his bones.

The nice thing about being a summoner, Valdemar thought, *is that you're never outnumbered.*

With his foes distracted by his summoned allies, Valdemar hastily returned to Iren's side and checked his vitals with blood magic. The sta-bilization process had worked, though the sorcerer noticed abnormal chemical reactions in his body. Having focused on the stab and head wounds in priority, Valdemar started paying more attention to the rest. He noticed an abnormal balance of hormones, hints of biomancy manip-ulations, and— Oh.

Valdemar was thankful that his mask had merged with his face's skin, or he would have probably blushed in embarrassment.

Carrying his ally in his arms, the summoner prepared to make a dash for the stairs when he noticed movements coming from it. Briefly fearing derro reinforcements, the sorcerer instead froze in confusion as a swarm of col-ored vipers slithered down the stone steps. The creatures, which numbered in the hundreds, lacked eyes and depth; they appeared two-dimensional, like sheets of paper. Their scales were all red in color, rippling like . . .

Like fresh paint.

"Valdemar!" Hermann's voice called out as he emerged from the stairway. His painted snake horde spread across the room and chased after the derros. While the derro had managed to burn the Gnawers to a crisp, the fire elemental had turned the blunderbuss wielder to ashes in return. Hermann's vipers coiled around the flamethrower-user and crushed him under their weight, the last derro fleeing deeper into the cavern with Valdemar's elemental in hot pursuit.

"You can do that with pictomancy?" Valdemar asked Hermann, as two mirror-faced Knights of the Mind entered behind the troglodyte. They flinched upon seeing the room, and especially the brainless worker corpses walking around, before chasing after the last derro. For perhaps the first time in his life, Valdemar was happy to see the authorities.

"I was in a . . . hurry," Hermann replied, as he rushed to his ally's side and glanced at Iren. "Is he . . ."

"No, but he will need help," Valdemar reassured him. Hermann took Iren from Valdemar and shouldered him, the rogue as light as a feather to the troglodyte.

A strident screech suddenly echoed through the lab, while the electrical pylons' light became unbearable, electrical arcs jolting between them with increasing frequency. The mindless, brainless workers stopped their tasks as the noise turned sharper, clearer. *Derro words,* Valdemar thought, as his ears struggled to make sense of them.

The workers swiftly answered the signal, the brainless animated corpses rushing to the harvested human brains' containers and removing them from the machines to which they were connected.

"Stop them!" Valdemar shouted, as he realized the danger. "They're trying to get away!"

Hermann let out a hissing whistle, and his painted snakes immediately attacked the brainless workers by coiling around their legs. A single kick was enough to dissipate them into harmless paint however; Hermann's creations were more obedient than Valdemar's summons, but far more fragile.

The light from the pylons brightened, and the electrical bolts they emitted spread between them. A bolt vaporized half a dozen snakes, while another hit a Knight of the Mind rushing down the stairs and struck him to the floor.

His vision went white with a crashing boom. For a brief instant, Valdemar's world slowed down to a crawl. A bubble of white light seemed to surround him, spreading over his blurred body; he went deaf for a moment, all sound stopping, all images dimming.

And then came the pain. The excruciating pain. A wave of burning heat spread over his flesh, as if it were melting off his bones. Invisible ants crawled beneath his skin, from his toes to his eyes, the thrumming wave of suffering consuming him entirely. Every inch of Valdemar's body *hurt*, and yet he stood in place, unable to move. His fingers trembled, his nerves ablaze. He didn't even have the strength to scream, his brain paralyzed by the monstrous current racing through its neurons.

Another lightning bolt hit Valdemar in the chest, and the white turned dark.

Valdemar oscillated between darkness and consciousness afterward. Each time he opened his eyes, the pain took over. Even his treatment at the inquisitors' hands couldn't compare to what Valdemar was experiencing in these moments; he felt as like a piece of meat being cooked alive, his blood boiling as invisible ants devoured him from the inside.

Sometimes he woke up facing Liliane's panicked face. At other times, he vaguely remembered Lady Mathilde pouring liquid into a syringe. Valdemar actually welcomed the brief moments of dreamless oblivion that followed, right before his eyes snapped open again. The only part that didn't hurt was his face, his mask providing him with fresh air, its cold surface soothing the pain.

And cold he felt when he awoke.

The world was dark and chilling. The frost numbed him to the bone, though he didn't shiver. He was dead, and yet he breathed. He walked on thick ice, with only a distant howl for company. He thought it was some beast calling out to him, until he sensed something brush against his naked chest. A movement in the air, strong and fresh. Fresher than anything. Was that . . . the wind?

There were no walls around him, no ceiling to keep him down. Only a white desert and an all-consuming darkness. He walked alone in the ruins of frozen cities, past the corpses of mammoths and monsters forever trapped in cages of ice. When he looked at their faces, he could only see fear and despair.

What was worse? To be slain without knowing it . . . or to see death and yet be powerless to escape its grasp?

Valdemar looked up at the small distant lights in an ocean of cosmic darkness. He had heard of the stars, from the records of the world before the surface went dark; some were blue, others a baleful shade of green. He watched a hundred fall down like droplets while twin demonic flames danced in the void. The stars looked beautiful and terrible in equal measure.

And then, he noticed the Whitemoon looking down on him. A pallid white sphere blurred the heavens, obscuring a smaller moon and the constellations. It was smaller than the world, the way a derro appeared so frail next to a human being. It dominated the skies, hanging above the surface like a vampire bat over an open wound.

And it had eyes too. They were not the flesh eyes of Underland, no. They were as soulless as its surface, two black bottomless abysses over vertical rifts. The Whitemoon's ghoulish visage would have reminded Valdemar of a skull, were it not for its expression. Something in the eyes told the watcher everything he needed to know about why this rogue moon had emerged from the coldness of space to orbit around this world, why it had obscured the sun and cast the surface in eternal darkness.

Hate.

That face *hated* Valdemar. It hated life, and warmth, and all that was. Its hateful eyes didn't look at the surface, but below; at the living creatures festering beneath the stone skin of the planet, hidden but never safe.

Valdemar lost himself in these hateful eyes, but he looked beyond. Beyond the darkness, beyond the death it promised. And no matter how deep the blackness, the light shone through it. Soon the sorcerer found a glowing star beyond the Whitemoon. A fireball greater than the world, beautiful and bright.

Is that the sun? Valdemar thought as he gazed at the light, his fingers reaching for it. It looked so close and yet so distant. *It's . . . beautiful.* His fingers looked so ugly and shadowy in comparison, claws of blackness trying to approach something they could never possess. The closer he got, the warmer he felt; but the sun forever remained out of reach.

His vision sharpened, revealing the candles beneath the fireballs, the chandelier, and the pale yellow ceiling. Valdemar's hand became clearer, covered in lightning-shaped scars, and he noticed the bedsheet against his naked chest.

"Valdy," Liliane's soft voice said to his left. Valdemar struggled to turn his head but did notice his friend sitting at his bedside with a look of concern and a bouquet of blue flowers in her hands. Iren occupied a bed behind her, his chest bandaged like a mummy and his eyes open. "Valdy, how do you feel?"

"Like shit," he replied slowly, his voice twisted into an alien growl by his mask. His body didn't hurt anymore, but it was numb and slow.

"I had to triple the anesthetic dosage," Liliane said while biting her lower lips. She seemed relieved to hear him speak, but bothered by his voice change. "Your body eliminates it otherwise. Your regeneration is . . . it's amazing."

"You would be dead otherwise," Iren said from his bed.

"It was just a flesh wound," Valdemar replied with a chuckle, only for his chest to contract. The pain was sharp but lasted less than an instant.

"Don't you dare," Liliane scolded him with a deep frown. "Lady Mathilde and I didn't nurse your ass back to life for days to hear you joke about it."

"Two bolts, that's all," Valdemar groaned. Liliane fidgeted in her chair. "What?"

"Hermann said you were hit *six* times," his friend said, her face turning as pale as milk. "I . . . I didn't recognize you at first. I could see the flesh, and we couldn't remove your mask."

Six times? Also, she said he had been asleep for *days*? "Why couldn't you remove it?"

"It sank into your flesh when we tried. Lady Mathilde feared it would reach the bone and fuse with it if we tried too hard. We had to give you the healing potions intravenously."

That . . . that didn't bode well for him. Had the mask fused with his flesh permanently?

Valdemar moved his hands to his face, his numbed finger fumbling as they touched the wooden surface covering his skin. Liliane looked on with worry. "Valdy, be careful," she asked.

"I . . . it's alright." The mask detached itself without any trouble, allowing the sorcerer to remove it and put it on the blanket. It felt strange to breathe normal air again; he sensed dust flowing into his lungs, and the smell of flowers. "It must have been a defense mechanism."

"Maybe." Liliane shifted in her seat. "Where did you find that thing, Valdy?"

"In the shop," Iren replied for Valdemar. "I don't think the fake Elias understood its true value."

Valdemar thought there was more to that. He examined the mask, finding its surface as perfect as the day he first touched it. Lightning powerful enough to burn its wielder alive hadn't even dented it.

"How did you try to remove it?" Valdemar asked Liliane, his voice raspy and his throat sore. "How?"

"I poured acid on it for a start," his friend admitted. "We escalated from there."

And yet, it had survived everything. And the dream Valdemar had of the Whitemoon looking down on him . . . it felt far too real for it to be a figment of his imagination. The sheer amount of details, that sensation of infernal cold and loneliness . . . Clearly the mask was related to the surface in some way.

"Valdy, what is that thing?" Liliane asked.

"I don't . . . I don't know." Certainly not a pawn shop item. "The shop . . . does it have sales registers?"

"You'll need to ask the Knights," Iren said. "They confiscated everything."

Valdemar would consult them, and yet his thoughts moved to the fake Elias. The derro had looked confused when he had the mask. Maybe it was just inexperience, as the imposter couldn't possibly know everything the true shopkeeper did. But why hadn't Hermann's masks bothered him?

He had never seen this particular artifact before, Valdemar thought, a shiver going down his spine. *The mask was never there.*

Liliane clenched her fists. "Damn it, Valdy," she said, her voice breaking. "Please don't do that again."

"What was . . . *that* actually?" Valdemar asked, as he remembered the horrific sight of human skin dried like clothes. He knew some Qlippoths used a similar process to impersonate mortals, but he never imagined derros could replicate it with surgery. "Did . . ."

"From what I understood, some of the dwarves escaped through tunnels with the brains they harvested," Iren said from his bed, looking at the window. "Not all of them though. The Knights are interrogating them and recording Hermann's testimony; Lady Mathilde is studying the skin samples they recovered."

"Lady Phul is furious," Liliane said, before showing Valdemar her blue flowers, which he identified as fresh Colophryar. The petals smelled so sweet. "She asked us to remain discreet and gave us these flowers as thanks. They come straight from her personal gardens."

Thanks? More like a bribe to keep quiet. The Dark Lord didn't want people to know that a derro cell had been operating right under her nose. What did the dwarves even want with the brains they took? And how many people had they managed to replace?

Valdemar chased the thoughts from his mind. It was the inquisitors' problem now, not his own. With the Colophryar plants in their possession, he could finally complete the Painted Door with Hermann. "When will we leave?"

"Not for days." Liliane put the flowers on a bed table, then glared at Valdemar. "If I find you out of your blankets, I'll spank you like a child."

"Not even my mother spanked me," Valdemar replied with a smile.

"She should have, it would have taught caution. Why did you think going alone in this dwarf den was a good idea?" She pointed a thumb at Iren, as if he were an afterthought. "To save this guy?"

"I know you care," Iren teased her, though Valdemar sensed a hint of pain beneath the playfulness. "Your life would be too dull without me."

"Pfft, of course I would have saved you, but Valdy is supposed to be smarter than I am." Liliane sighed. "Now that we can access your mouth, it'll be easier to feed you. I'll come with potions, and you better drink them all."

"Yes, Mom," Valdemar replied with a deadpan voice. Liliane exited the room through a door while rolling her eyes, leaving him and Iren alone.

"You should ask her out," the rogue commented with casual bluntness. "I mean, you almost died without passing on your genes."

"So did you," Valdemar deadpanned back. "Frigga is all yours."

"You know, she didn't even visit us. I expected her to do weird stuff to us while we were asleep." Iren looked at Valdemar with a playful look.

Valdemar slowly turned his head at the rogue, blinking repeatedly. "What do you mean by that?"

"All those times she talked to you in your dreams? Well, she could still move in the real world. Alone in a room, with your unconscious body."

No way, Frigga didn't strike him as that kind of . . .

But . . .

A doubt formed in Valdemar's mind, while Iren grinned ear to ear. "Why did I save you again?" the summoner asked, while trying to suppress the horrifying mental image of Frigga sneaking into his bed.

"I dunno." His voice turned from playful to serious. "Honestly, friend. If you had been the one shanked in a derro basement . . . I wouldn't have risked my life for you."

Valdemar remembered that nameless prisoner who made a run for the stairway and ended up dead for it. He wondered if Iren would have reacted the same, if the positions had been reversed. "Then why do you call me friend?"

"I call everyone friend, because that's my job." Iren shrugged. "I'm the guy that gets you what you need."

"The guy, or the lass?"

"Depends." Iren's voice swiftly changed from masculine baritone to high-pitched and feminine. His—*her*—facial features grew softer, more ladylike. "Does it matter to you?"

"No," Valdemar replied immediately. "Well, yes, it does, but . . ." Damn it, how could he say it? "Iren, you're not fully human," the warlock stated. "Are you?"

Iren looked away. "If I answer, will you tell me why you saved me? Because I really don't get it."

"I would even if you kept quiet." Valdemar shrugged. "Why wouldn't I have saved you? Liliane would have, you heard it yourself."

"Liliane is as naïve as a newborn, and she'll probably get killed for it. You struck me as smarter."

"Honestly, I might have hesitated if you had been an inquisitor or wronged me before." Though nobody deserved to be flayed alive and their skin used as a warm disguise.

"And if you hadn't known me?"

"I would have helped anyway." *And I did,* Valdemar thought as he remembered the derros' other victim. "After my mother and grandfather died, I was all alone. It was a tough life. Nobody helped me without expecting anything in return."

"That's how the world works," Iren said with cynicism.

"Well, it's *wrong,*" Valdemar declared firmly. "Just like it's wrong to have a roof of stones above our head rather than a bright blue sky, or to have inquisitors burn our books because the knowledge inside *might* be dangerous. If we worked together rather than constantly keeping each other down, mankind would have expanded beyond this cold tomb by now. We're *better* than this."

Iren looked at him with an indecipherable gaze. "You spent too much time around Liliane," he mocked Valdemar.

"Maybe," Valdemar admitted. "But she isn't wrong. I don't think we can change everything . . . but someone has to try. To start somewhere. Or nothing will change. Even if I fail to reach Earth . . . I hope someone will pick up where I left off."

Iren smiled, and this time it reached the eyes. "You're an idiot," he said while looking at the window. "Lord Och is going to eat you alive and shit you out."

"He can't, he doesn't have intestines."

"He will grow them, just to mess with you." Iren marked a short pause. "Have you ever heard about doppelgangers?"

"The shapeshifters?" Valdemar raised an eyebrow. "You're one?"

"Yeah." Iren's face darkened, literally; his pale skin took on a browner shade, and his hair became blacker. His eyes didn't change though, which might explain his use of illusions to hide their colors. "It's complicated."

"You don't have to tell me," Valdemar replied.

"Maybe I will one day." Iren pulled his blanket closer to his shoulders, his appearance returning to "normal" and his voice becoming masculine again. "I hope I'll live long enough to see that bright blue sky of yours."

"Me too," Valdemar replied while looking at the ceiling, trying to imagine the sun beyond it. "Me too."

1 9

THE RED GRAIL

You should have let him die," the Knight of the Beast told her, his eyes squinting behind his horned helm. A lantern's glow reflected on his plate armor's steel. "You made a mistake."

Marianne ignored him as she and a dozen armored warriors searched the beach of rocks that had once been Verney Castle. Her messenger bat had reached its destination and allowed a warband of the Knights of the Beast to answer her call. This military order, bound to Horaios's Dark Lord Hagith, specialized in hunting and slaying monsters, patrolling tunnels to protect trade, and studying dangerous creatures. They were professionals and set out on arrival to search the fortress's wreckage for clues.

They had upturned most stones, finding the crushed remains of burned clones or broken alchemical tools. Precious little evidence had survived the castle's destruction, but inquisitors were nothing if not thorough. The remains of Shelley's lab were compiled for psychometric analysis, while specialized black warhounds memorized noteworthy smells.

They had found no trace of the black blood or of the monster it had summoned.

No signs of Bertrand either.

If that thing is still Bertrand, Marianne thought grimly.

The Knights' captain continued scolding her. "By prioritizing the life of a servant over the greater good, you not only allowed a dangerous cultist to escape, but also let him summon a dangerous eldritch entity in imperial territory. Worse, you failed to finish off your vampire before he could transform into an abomination. Hundreds might die because of your weakness—"

"With all due respect, sir," Marianne interrupted him with a glare, as she turned a stone to reveal the crushed hand of a Sarah Dumont clone, "*fuck you.*"

A few knights looked in their direction, while their captain's eyes peered at Marianne through his helmet's visor.

"Bertrand was not only my servant, but also a friend and companion. Perhaps you consider it alright to abandon your own allies to their death, but I do not." Marianne's tone turned even icier as she continued. "I acted to the best of my abilities in a situation that your order should have dealt with."

"Abilities that were found lacking," the captain replied.

"*You* let a cultist act in your territory. Were it not for my investigation and my retainer's efforts, you would still be in the dark about Shelley's activities. If *you* had done your job and correctly surveyed the region, I wouldn't even be here."

The captain grunted. "I will admit our patrols failed to pick up on suspicious activities, but you should still have followed proper procedure and joined us at the nearest station, and then we would have assaulted the castle. Going in alone with your retainer was madness."

"Shelley would have escaped anyway, with no blood sample to track him down." Bertrand's loss had made her deeply furious, as did her failure to catch the cultist. If not for her need to report the truth to competent authorities in case she perished on the job and her carriage's destruction, Marianne wouldn't have waited for these reinforcements at all.

"Maybe. Or maybe your early interference caused the premature summoning of whatever creature you saw. And my point stands, you should have prioritized the cultist over saving your retainer. Some people are simply too dangerous to live." The knight prepared to argue further, when one of his alchemists approached the rocky shore. "Squire József?"

"Captain Léopold, Lady Reynard," the alchemist made a military salute, fist against his chest. "We finished analyzing the suspect's blood sample."

"Did you find anything?" Marianne asked. She had tried to preserve the blood she took from Shelley the best she could, but most of it had dried before the Knights arrived.

"I am the one asking questions here," Captain Léopold said with annoyance. Marianne wondered if he was simply unhappy with his job in general; this area was one of Horaios's most remote, and not the most prestigious of assignments. "Report, József."

The alchemist answered with a sharp nod. "The cultist is almost certainly a mutant lycanthrope, sir. We found traces of a modified Beast Plague, inoculated during infancy. It's possible Aleksander Verney got his hands on a sample and modified it to include rat genes."

The Beast Plague. When the Dark Lords last came to blows, Horaios's master Hagith had his biomancers create this biological weapon to transform humans into hybrid monsters susceptible to an animancer's mental influence.

"What was the point?" Captain Léopold asked his subordinate.

"Rats are intelligent but weak-willed creatures, pliable but capable of complex tasks," the alchemist theorized. "Exposure to the Beast Plague usually results in the victim losing higher intelligence and self-control; while this wererat was not as powerful as a werewolf, he clearly kept most of his human intelligence. Enough to run a lab."

And since Shelley had been in his master's employ while an infant . . . Marianne tried not to think too hard about the ghastly implications. *Whatever his origin, he is a threat to the empire now,* she thought.

"And the blood-trackers?" Captain Léopold asked.

"We are synthesizing one as we speak," the biomancer replied. "We have enough blood for two, maybe three."

"I would like to have one," Marianne asked. She had sworn to hunt the beast and she would deliver. Besides the danger he posed, maybe Shelley held the keys to returning Bertrand to normal.

"Certainly not," the captain replied. "Hunting monsters is our order's prerogative."

Marianne frowned. "Fighting dangerous spellcasters is the Knights of the Tome's duty."

"True, and we will ask for the order's support . . . but you are not a Knight of the Tome." The captain shrugged. "We thank you for your assistance, but it is no longer necessary."

"I do not work for you," Marianne pointed out, struggling to keep her calm. The sheer ingratitude and condescension got on her nerves. "Lord Och asked me to get to the bottom of the matter, and I will."

"You are free to pursue your hunt but not with our trackers."

"I brought the blood needed to make them." By now the other knights were all watching their argument. "And Bertrand?"

"He will be caught alive, if possible."

His tone made Marianne clench her fists. "Do you truly want to bring Lord Och's wrath on your head?"

"I do not answer to him." Léopold's eyes gleamed with scorn beneath his helmet. "A case like this shouldn't be entrusted to a noble dilettante and husband killer."

Marianne's cheeks turned red. *So that was what it was all about*, she realized. *I knew his accent sounded Saklasian. He must have studied at the officers' academy too.* "You knew Jérôme."

"He was ten times the man you were . . . or would have been, if you were a man." The captain glanced at her rapier. "And you killed him over a *sword*."

"It was an accident," Marianne said while clenching her teeth.

"Then why did you run away and seek Lord Och's protection?" Léopold shrugged, uninterested in her answer. "He must have loved you a lot to let you win."

"You're wrong. I was a better swordswoman than he ever was." Even Bertrand had called her a saint of blades, and she had surpassed him in spite of his centuries of experience. "And that is why I asked for a duel." Her soulbound rapier was her heritage as a Reynard, and though her father had wanted Jérôme to wield it, she could never bring herself to surrender it to someone who couldn't best her at swordplay.

Even if she had loved that someone.

"I won fair and square," Marianne said. "I regret Jérôme's death, more than you could possibly know . . . but I don't regret winning that duel."

"Regret all you want, he's dead and you live unpunished. I suppose you can add your retainer to the list of your victims—" Captain Léopold froze, as the tip of Marianne's rapier stopped within an inch of his left eye. Her movement had been so swift, that she could have slain the man before he even reacted.

"You won't finish that sentence," Marianne warned coldly. The noblewoman noticed the other knights raise their spears at her, but she ignored them. "One way or another."

The air grew cold and tense, as the captain looked at her sword without a word. Neither Marianne nor the knight backed down, and a fight seemed almost inevitable.

What is this? she thought, as a heavy presence hovered over the shore. The sound of crashing waves grew dimmer, as if the Lightless Ocean itself receded. *It's not the force I encountered below the castle . . . it's something else.*

Her psychic sight noticed an invisible force manifesting among the rocks, as overwhelming as the tide. She felt the texture of rotting flesh on her palate, smelled rot in the air. It was the stench of inevitable death.

The Knights around her threw down their weapons and kneeled. Marianne imitated them. She recognized the presence from her childhood, the few times other Dark Lords visited the empress in her Domain of Saklas.

"My, my, what a mess." The voice was deep and jovial, closer to a friendly merchant than a powerful archmage. "If you wish to fight, we have arenas."

The Dark Lord Hagith manifested on the shore in a bright silver flash. When Marianne's eyes recovered, the ruler of the Domain of Horaios floated in front of her and Captain Léopold, overshadowing them both.

The tallest among the Dark Lords, Hagith's height reached almost two meters and a half and his body was so obese that he looked more like a mountain of stitched, putrescent flesh than a man; to the point where Marianne couldn't even see his nose. Thick strings prevented his hairless skin from falling apart due to overstretching, and also kept a second, colossal mouth on his belly closed. His eyes were entirely black, without an iris or pupil, and he wore naught but oversize breeches.

He was not physically present though. His body looked as ephemeral as a ghost, a silver cord growing out of his chest and vanishing into the ether. Marianne wondered what spell he used. Her surprise must have shown on her face, for the Dark Lord gave her an answer.

"Astral projection, fair maiden." The specter moved his hand to his mouth and chewed, as if he was eating something invisible. In all likelihood, the Dark Lord spoke to her over dinner. "A spell every mage should master, though few are capable of casting it."

"My lord." Captain Léopold bowed his head so low that his helmet's horns almost touched the ground. "To what do we owe the honor of your visit? Has our messenger reached you already?"

"Oh, you sent a messenger?" The Dark Lord caressed his naked paunch in a motion Marianne couldn't help but find obscene. "No, I have not received any message. I sensed a surge of magical energy coming from this hideous . . ." The specter glanced at the castle's ruins and then at the shore. Only then did he realize that the castle was gone. "My, this does improve the sea view," the Dark Lord noted to himself with a chuckle before glancing at Marianne. "Are you the cause of this destruction, Milady?"

Marianne hesitated before answering. Of the Dark Lords, Hagith was by far the most popular for organizing grandiose festivities, running gladiatorial tournaments, and supporting farmers in his territory. Hagith preferred to rule with bread and circus rather than an iron boot . . . though he was just as capable of the latter as his fellows. "Yes and no, Lord Hagith."

"I would have preferred one or the other," the Dark Lord replied. "But I have time. Tell me everything, dear. The truth and nothing but the truth. Starting with who you are."

Marianne noticed Captain Léopold about to say something, perhaps a slander attempt . . . but his words died in his throat the moment he looked at the Dark Lord's second, closed mouth. "I am Marianne Reynard," she said. "I have been sent by Lord Och to gather information on the Verney family . . . but I'm not certain that I'm allowed to disclose everything."

Her response amused Lord Hagith. "Lord Och is far away, and I am here. You would rather risk my wrath than disappoint him?"

"I swore my loyalty to Lord Och," Marianne replied. She hoped the Dark Lord wouldn't begrudge her faithfulness to her employer; he probably expected the same from his own men. "However . . ."

"Your investigation involves dark secrets about Och's newest apprentice." Lord Hagith laughed at Marianne's surprise. "The empire is a small world and news travels fast between us Dark Lords. Do not worry, dear. Lord Och and I enjoy a cordial relationship. If I find your answers lacking, I will get them from your master."

Marianne nodded slowly and gave the Dark Lord a report while omitting only a few details relating to Valdemar. How she had tried to look for information on the Verneys at the source, only to discover a ghost hamlet and a cultist operating under the family's castle. Hagith listened to her words with rapturous attention, his black eyes narrowing when she mentioned the hamlet and the black blood beneath Verney Castle.

"I see," he said simply. "Léopold? Do you corroborate her tale?"

"We haven't found any trace of the black blood she mentioned or of the creature that it summoned," the captain replied. "But the rest of our findings match Reynard's story, sir. We are currently preparing to hunt the perpetrator."

"Do so immediately," Lord Hagith said with firmness. "This ratling may have failed to summon the Nahemoth once, but we can't let him live long enough to try again."

Marianne's head jerked up in surprise. "Nahemoth, my lord?"

"A Nahemoth, dear," Hagith's lips pursed, revealing rows of sharp teeth. "Your retainer identified this ghost hamlet's villagers as Qlippoths, correctly so. But he didn't know enough about them to understand what you had found. This 'Vernburg' was almost certainly a Nahemoth's demiplane."

"I . . ." Marianne gulped, slightly ashamed of her ignorance. "Sir, I . . . I do not understand much of what you say."

Hagith observed her with a calculating gaze, before turning at the knight next to her. "Léopold?"

"Yes, my lord?" the captain replied.

"You will provide Lady Reynard with a blood-tracker, your Bestiary, supplies, and a mount."

Marianne's heart skipped a beat in surprise. Captain Léopold, though, didn't sound happy for her. "My Bestiary?" He tried to hide his displeasure, but his voice betrayed his true feelings. "Sir—"

"You will receive another, and Lady Reynard clearly needs a crash course on Qlippoth pest control." The Dark Lord's tone remained warm, but it was clear that he would brook no dissent. "I will have no quarrel with Lord Och over such a trifling matter, and if she wants to assist in the rat hunt, I shall indulge her."

"I . . ." Marianne was at a loss for words. She had expected to be sent home, not given assistance. "I don't know what to say."

"Then say nothing," Lord Hagith said with a chuckle. "Another Dark Lord would have accused you of starting trouble or slain you for withholding information, but you have done me a great service in uncovering this sordid mess. You will do me a greater favor by killing that rat. And this black blood bit, it's truly fascinating . . . Yes, we will take your retainer alive. We must study him."

Marianne's hope immediately turned to horror. "My lord, I . . . he's a friend, and my retainer."

"Oh, don't worry." Lord Hagith waved a hand at her dismissively. "If he dies, you will be compensated for your loss."

Marianne wanted to argue further but bit her tongue. The man was generous when it cost him little, but he clearly put his interests first. If she were to save Bertrand, it would be by capturing Shelley or through Lord Och's influence.

And the way he spoke of this black blood . . . Marianne had aroused a dreadful curiosity in this archmage and feared what might come out of it.

There was not a moment to waste.

Captain Léopold was true to his master's orders, affording Marianne everything she needed. Marianne decided to hunt on her own though, separate from the Knights, and he didn't stop her. If anything, she would have been happy never to see Léopold again. That behavior was why she had fled from Saklas. Most people she knew despised her now, and the reasons that had driven her to duel Jérôme in the first place remained. Nothing had changed. Nothing *would* change.

Riding on a giant beetle's back as it ran along the Lightless Ocean's shore, Marianne observed the blood-tracker. Taking the shape of a red crystal of fossilized blood, the device shone with a crimson glow depending on the direction she pointed it at. It hadn't taken her long to identify Shelley's most likely destination.

Paraplex, she thought. *He's going to Paraplex.*

Shelley couldn't use the Earthmouth portals; now that the Knights had his blood, if he tried he would be immediately detected and caught. He would use longer tunnels. Though the cultist had a heavy lead on her, Marianne might beat him to the Domain thanks to this. And her vampire bats would inform Lord Och long before either of them reached Paraplex.

But Marianne knew better than to underestimate Shelley. Otherworldly forces supported him, and they might rival even the Dark Lords in power.

The grimoire in her supply bag was heavier than she'd thought. As it turned out, the Bestiary was a hefty grimoire distributed to the Knights of the Beasts' captains, compiling detailed information on monsters they might be expected to fight. Léopold's book numbered thousands of pages. The information within was confidential, and only meant for high-ranking members of the Knights of the Beast. No wonder Léopold had been so displeased about giving up his own, to a nonmember no less.

When her beetle took a pause to drink, Marianne took a moment to check the information on the Qlippoths. The interdimensional species had a whole chapter dedicated to them in the "extraplanar dangers" subsection. The pertinent chapter opened on a picture of ten orbs connected together by a twisted tree of flesh.

"The Tree of Death," she read out loud, to better memorize the content. "Flowing from the root of the Nahemoths, who dream the other Qlippoths into existence, the Tree of Death represents the Outer Darkness's hierarchy."

Each orb contained a picture of an eldritch creature, some of whom Marianne recognized as beasts who attacked her at the hamlet. "Satoriel, or Facethief," she read below a picture of the creature which had impersonated Mona. "Second caste . . . born of envy and jealousy . . . capable of limited shapeshifting . . . seeks to steal the life of others, often to the point of self-delusion . . . easy to identify due to being unable to fully emulate emotions . . ."

Marianne's jaw clenched upon recognizing the picture of the slime creature that taunted her about Jérôme in the third caste's sphere. Called Ghogiel, or Egoid Ooze, the creature was apparently fueled by sloth; it delighted in convincing people to lay down their arms and spiritually waste away, usually through telepathic attacks.

The worst of the Qlippoths occupied the tree's bottom, and the picture itself gave Marianne nausea. A disembodied, monstrous face looked back at her on the grimoire's pages; a fiery maw surrounded by eyes and swirling tentacles, spitting out the flames of creation. Pictures of the other Qlippoths floated around this monstrosity like fleas around a colossal vampire bat.

"The embodiment of selfishness and solipsism, Nahemoths generate a magical field where their desires are laws, allowing them to spawn lesser Qlippoths into existence," Marianne read. "While absolute in the Outer Darkness, this ability is limited by the inherent order of our reality. The summoning of a Nahemoth on the material plane instead results in a bounded space-time anomaly where the creature can twist our reality but not fully control it. A place that is neither the material realm nor the Outer Darkness, but both. A *demiplane*."

Or a ghost town where Qlippoths played at being humans. Marianne tried to remember the well at its center and shuddered as she realized what slept at the bottom.

The more she read, the more she found cause for concern.

"Summoning a Nahemoth is an extremely difficult task for all but the most powerful conjurers, and an act of pure madness," she whispered, her lantern the only source of light. "Nahemoths are malicious entities that cannot be bound to servitude. At best they can be unleashed as living disasters on unsuspecting populations. Fighting a Nahemoth head-on is a feat worthy of a Dark Lord. If you encounter one, contact the nearest headquarters for immediate reinforcements."

Most information about fighting these creatures amounted to containing the lesser Qlippoths while conjurers banished the Nahemoth back to its home plane. Thankfully, powerful spells could achieve such a feat; the Bestiary even detailed a procedure to do exactly that, though it was so complex that it gave Marianne a headache from trying to understand it. Only a powerful sorcerer could pull it off, and certainly not without support.

The thing at the well's bottom had probably been a Nahemoth, true. It checked perfectly.

But according to the Knights' Bestiary and Lord Hagith's own words, only an exceptionally powerful conjurer could summon one. Shelley's knowledge of magic seemed limited to rat-related animancy and alchemy. At no point had the mad cultist tried to summon reinforcements during their battle at Verney Castle.

He didn't summon the Nahemoth, Marianne thought. *He was only studying it.*

But then who summoned that creature? She looked into the general parts of the chapter, trying to see if the Qlippoths could invade the material plane without a conjurer's support. She quickly noticed a section that had been recently edited, with some sentences slashed and notes added below the pages.

"Most scholars theorize that the Outer Darkness is a dimension of pure chaos and festering madness," Marianne read. "Recent oneiromancy research in Astaphanos suggests instead that the Primordial Dream shared by men, dokkars, and lesser races may be a subsection of the Outer Darkness. It is possible that the collective unconscious evolved as life's dreamscape, a protective cocoon created by sentient life to protect itself from depredations; this would explain the intimate link between Qlippoths and the emotional spectrum."

Marianne rarely dreamed, but she shuddered at the idea of something like the false Mona looking at her innermost thoughts. Worse, the Bestiary's theory begged a very important, and terrible, question.

If the Outer Darkness is a dream, Marianne whispered to herself, *then who is the dreamer?*

The Bestiary's writer answered her question. "Oneiromancy researchers suggest that the Qlippoths are the will of a Stranger made manifest," she read. "The same way the Nightmare of Kazat was created by dreamers perishing in their sleep, the Outer Darkness may be an almighty Stranger's dreamscape. In this interpretation, the mightiest Nahemoths are no more than the conduits of a larger being's creative impulses. Considering the Primordial Dream might have been unconsciously created by life to protect itself from Qlippothic influence, we must assume that this entity's desires are antithetical to mankind's survival. As such, every member of the species found unbound must be executed on the spot."

Marianne closed the book, considered this information, and then tried to put everything in order. She reviewed every part of her case and tried to see how it all fit.

The Verney cult was heavily associated with Qlippoths. A Nahemoth had recreated a copy of Vernburg for a reason Marianne couldn't fathom, and Shelley clearly cooperated with it. The Qlippoths found in the hamlet also smelled like Valdemar, suggesting a connection.

If the Bestiary's theory was correct and Qlippoths served a Stranger . . . then it might have been the creature that the Verney cult worshipped. The entity that had manifested its will through the rune beneath Verney Castle—it was its blood that the cult had tried to harvest by creating their unholy grail.

But why clone Sarah Dumont? What made her so important? Because she was the daughter of a human from another world? The Verneys had been interested in travelers from this "Earth" according to the False Mona. What made them important?

"They're not worthy!" Shelley had screamed, when the black blood had consumed both Bertrand and his own rat familiar. *"Not worthy!"*

It made them worthy.

Everything fell into place, and Marianne's eyes widened in horror. She searched for a feather and ink among the supplies given to her and scribbled down a genealogical tree. One far simpler and far more terrifying than she had thought.

Pierre Dumont and Lavina Verney were Sarah Dumont's parents, two worlds united through a single bloodline with special powers. One that was *worthy* of the cult's greatest honor. One that could *survive* it.

This accounted for Valdemar's maternal side.

As for the paternal . . .

Perhaps the truth is even stranger, Lord Och had told Marianne when she asked for his opinion on Valdemar's true nature.

Stranger.

The Dark Lord had hinted at the truth, dangling it right under her nose.

"The grail is alive! Alive!"

The Red Grail. A vessel capable of holding a god's blood and binding worlds together. One made of bones and flesh, that promised immortality. A living bridge between the cult and their vile deity.

Marianne wrote the bloody rune she had seen below Verney Castle in the place of Valdemar's father.

"We must assume that this entity's desires are antithetical to mankind's survival."

I pray, for all our sake, Marianne thought grimly, *that he takes after his mother's side of the family.*

20

MOUSE TRAP

A giant rat, you say?" The old man smiled with a crooked tooth, his eyes hidden behind bandages and an old musket resting on his thighs. "Haven't smelled a rat in a while. My cat catches them all."

"A hooded visitor, maybe?" Marianne asked from atop her giant beetle. The farm was calm and peaceful, with giant snails lazily grazing moss inside their pens. Their owner lived modestly in a two-floor hollow stone pillar of a house. There were lights and dancing shadows behind the windows. "Someone hiding his face, traveling to Paraplex?"

The old farmer scratched his white beard as he sank deeper into his rocking chair. Though he appeared calm at first glance, Marianne could see the tension in his fingers. A wrong move and he would reach out for his weapon.

Marianne couldn't blame him for being suspicious. The closest farm was half an hour away, and these tunnels weren't frequented. The only light came from the houses or the few lanterns along the road. For all the farmer knew, she might have been a highwaywoman or worse.

"I swear on the Light," Marianne said. "This . . . man is a criminal and a murderer. If you know anything—"

"Yes, yes." The farmer shrugged. "Imperial officials only come to collect taxes or hang poachers around here."

"I'm not here for either." She had too many questions to ask Shelley before she could consider a summary execution. "If you do not remember anyone, it is fine. I will be on my way."

"There is . . . there was someone." The farmer stopped playing with his beard and looked over his shoulder, at the iron, decrepit door of his home. "Dear?"

"Yes, Da?" a younger, female voice answered from the other side.

"You said you met a leper while washing clothes at the well?"

"Yes, poor thing!" The woman answered. "Bandaged everywhere, wouldn't even show his face or approach me! Said he was looking for a healer to soothe his pain, so I sent him to Emma and he thanked me!"

"Emma?" Marianne asked.

"The apothecary," the farmer replied with a sneer. "Closest thing we've got to a healer since our last one took a nap in the dirt, though methinks a few of the village's men pray to her cunt. Her three whelps gotta come from somewhere."

"I'm sure Werner is the dad!" his daughter answered through the door. "He visits her every day!"

The farmer snorted. "None of the children look the same. Youngest one got fire in the hair, while Werner's beard is as black as they come."

Marianne wondered how he knew that detail since he was blind. "When did it happen?" she asked. If the Light had shined on her, she might have finally found a lead on Shelley's itinerary.

"My dear washes clothes every first day of the week."

So three days ago? One day after Verney Castle's collapse, Marianne counted. It could have been Shelley. Considering his inhuman endurance and speed, he wouldn't have needed a mount to cross the distance in such a short time. "Can you tell me the way to this lady's house?"

The farmer gave her directions with a chuckle—the house with the garden to the left of the road's second lantern—and Marianne tossed him a coin as she left.

It was easy to notice the lanterns in the ambient darkness and difficult to see the road itself. Most routes from Horaios to Paraplex went through Marianne's home, the Domain of Saklas, but thankfully Shelley had taken a less frequented tunnel. Since they were far away from Earthmouths, few people inhabited these pathways; this "village" probably numbered fewer than forty families dispersed across kilometers. From their sinuous shape and walls of volcanic rock, the swordswoman suspected that these caves used to be lava tubes and magma chambers. The ceiling was low, and the road would benefit from repairs.

Although her eyes focused on the lanterns' lights ahead, Marianne's thoughts turned to another matter. To a revelation and questions she had rehearsed in her head for the last few days, trying to fathom their implication. Valdemar Verney was a half-Stranger, a living ritual and cult experiment born to serve a nefarious purpose.

But which one? Was Valdemar meant to serve as his progenitor's messenger in Underland? A living gateway for the Qlippoths to enter the material plane? A vessel for the Stranger to possess? Did the Verney purge truly disrupt this entity's plans, or simply delay them? And most important of all, what was Marianne supposed to do with Valdemar himself?

Captain Léopold's words came to mind: Some people are too dangerous to live.

If there was any risk that Valdemar might yet fulfill his intended purpose, even unintentionally . . .

An inquisitor wouldn't have hesitated. Though Valdemar was unaware of his heritage, the greater good commanded that he should perish. Every breath this ticking time bomb took might bring the empire closer to a disaster. Marianne had only to spread the news and the Knights would burn the last Verney on a pyre; even Lord Och would probably let it happen, if the information became public knowledge. The lich didn't fear the masses, but other Dark Lords would pressure him into relinquishing his protégé.

Marianne only had to send a single letter, and it would be all over.

And yet . . . and yet she hesitated.

He looks so human, Marianne thought, as she remembered her short discussions with the last Verney. Even the inquisitors couldn't discern his true nature. *In spite of his origins and difficult life, he didn't become a monster. He is a dreamer who wants to help people.*

By opening a portal to another world.

Marianne couldn't help but see it in another light now. *Is that even his own desire, or his progenitor's?* she wondered. *Is this Earth even a world of sunlight, or a trap? Will a portal there lead to a den of horrors hungry for human souls?*

It had been nearly twenty years since the Verney purge, and besides his incredible resilience and skill at conjuration Valdemar had yet to cause an incident of any kind. True, he had broken the law, but he hadn't driven a town to madness or summoned a Nahemoth, as far as Marianne knew. Even Lord Och had taken the young conjurer under his wing rather than dissect him, although he certainly suspected his true nature.

Marianne couldn't make a decision rashly, and some elements still eluded her. The false Mona had mentioned a certain "Crétail" child and, unlike Shelley, had shown no knowledge of Valdemar's name. Maybe she had been lying, but the Qlippoth impersonating her was infamous for getting too much into character according to Léopold's Bestiary.

I have uncovered a piece of the puzzle, but many more remain hidden, Marianne thought as she had her beetle turn left after the second lantern on her path. *And only Shelley might be able to answer my questions.*

Emma's house was located deep in a dead-end cavity, far enough from the road that Marianne thought she had taken the wrong turn at first. Her beetle accidentally stomped on a garden of moss, mushrooms, and medicinal plants the noblewoman had seen before in the Institute's greenhouse. She and her mount approached foreboding stone walls and closed windows. The entrance door was a rusted sheet of iron so fragile Marianne could probably break the hinges by kicking it.

"Is anyone here?" she called through the door. She didn't notice any light inside the house, so maybe they were sleeping? But by now, Marianne had gotten used to bad surprises. She activated her psychic sight, trying to detect the presence of human life inside. She didn't sense much. Only the hint of smaller life-forms, of fungi and maggots. The blood inside the house was cold and dead. No human life in a home owned by a woman and three children.

Hastily climbing down from her beetle, Marianne unsheathed her rapier. The noblewoman put her ear against the door and, when she didn't notice any noise on the other side, kicked it open.

"Bertrand, cover my—" The words died in Marianne's throat before she finished her sentence. She had grown used to her retainer having her back on difficult missions, and her mind hadn't accepted his disappearance yet. She missed him dearly.

With her lantern in one hand and her sword in the other, Marianne stepped inside the house. She didn't make a sound as she walked, her heartbeat quickening as she prepared for an ambush.

The house smelled of an unpleasant mix of body odor, cooked meat, and alchemical fumes. The front room's stonework was crude and lacked paint, with only a mole rat's skin used as a rug. *Humble people, a harsh life*, Marianne thought as she examined the ground. Mud covered the rug, as if a group had walked out without bothering to clean up afterward. The many footprints in various sizes weren't fully dry yet and pointed to the exit.

People had left in a hurry, and Marianne had just missed them. The noblewoman decided to delay her hunt. She needed to determine the fate of the house's occupants, and if it was indeed Shelley's work . . . why did the cultist stay days here before continuing to Paraplex?

Marianne moved to the next room, a cramped kitchen mixed with a storing room. The table was set for four, the plates as unclean as a latrine. A cauldron rested on a stone oven, still containing some sort of cold meat stew. Marianne moved her lantern over its surface, trying to see what it was made of. She noticed something buried inside the soup, so heavy it had sunk at the cauldron's bottom. A bone, perhaps . . . but it looked too big and round for a mole rat's rib. A terrible doubt crossed Marianne's mind, and she used the tip of her rapier to bring the food to the surface.

A severed human head looked back at her from inside the cauldron, the eyes and tongue devoured by maggots.

Marianne would have loved to say that she had grown used to this kind of horror by now, but she struggled against the urge to vomit. The head belonged to a middle-aged man, grown bloated from the liquid in which it had been soaked. From the black hair around the cheeks, it probably belonged to this "Werner" the farmer spoke of. He must have visited the apothecary, only to find a dangerous guest in the house.

No, Marianne thought as her eyes briefly wandered to the plates on the kitchen's table. Her breath shortened as she realized the rest of Werner's body was missing. "Please, no . . ."

The noblewoman moved into the next room, her steps faster, her movements tenser. The bedroom was a mess, the four straw mattresses covered in animal excrements and the remains of half-devoured rats. If Marianne needed any proof that Shelley was behind this, her suspicions were now confirmed. She followed the foul smell in the air to narrow stone stairs leading to an attic. The blood-tracker glowed inside Marianne's pocket as she climbed the stairs.

Was Shelley still here? Marianne doubted that he was as she would have sensed him, but she remained on her guard. The odors of herbs and potions mixed with the terrible smell of rot and death as she climbed.

Emma had used her attic as an herbalist lab. The furniture was so old Marianne wondered how it hadn't crumbled already, the tools made of rusted iron or bones. Seeds and herbs dried on a shelf next to a small fireplace and a barrel of fertilizer, while bloodied, broken flasks lay on a workbench. The few books Marianne could find had had their pages torn apart. Potion containers had been shattered and their contents spilled on the floor.

The blood-beacon grew more agitated when the noblewoman examined the alchemical stains on the ground. Marianne soon noticed red spots among the puddles of healing potion and herbal elixirs.

Shelley's blood. Had he been trying to experiment on his own blood? For what purpose? To find a way to avoid his pursuers?

And that foul smell . . .

Marianne turned her lantern, its light revealing a corpse in the fireplace. Considering the breasts and body shape, she must have been a human woman once . . . but these were the only hints to her former identity. The corpse had an elongated rat head, the bloodshot eyes consumed by fungi growth. Pustules grew on the furred back, while maggots festered in the slit throat and stumped tail. The mutant's dried blood had been arranged into the dreadful shape of Verney Castle's rune, as if the baleful symbol had gorged itself on the creature's life. A sentence was carved into the corpse's forehead, a promise and a warning.

We always return to the Blood.

Marianne had no idea how long she gazed at the macabre spectacle, unable to say a word, unable to process what she saw. It wasn't the sight of the symbol that mesmerized her, or the worrying absence of Emma's children that paralyzed her muscles. It was everything, all at once.

Marianne's breath grew shorter and shorter. *Am I . . . am I shaking?* she thought as she glanced at her shivering hands. The noblewoman trembled as if she had walked straight into a cold chamber. First that twisted village, then Bertrand, then Valdemar's true nature and the implications of his mere existence . . . Now . . . Now this . . .

And the children . . . Four plates but no trace of the children.

It . . . it was too much. Too much all at once.

Marianne sat on the workbench, the lantern's light dimming in her shaking hands. She closed her eyes, breathing in and out in an attempt to calm herself. The noblewoman attempted to meditate, to clear her mind. She closed herself to the foul smell of this tomb, banishing the memories of the horror she had seen.

Was this how Inquisitor Penhew had felt after the Verney purge? Too many dreadful encounters at once, a dive into the darkness leaving the mind exhausted, the spirit wavering?

What was even the point in continuing? Everywhere she went, it was already too late. Maybe dark gods smiled on Shelley, looking over his work with favor. Investigating the Verney case had only resulted in the loss of Bertrand and unleashing more horrors on the world. Maybe fate was already written, and the forces Marianne fought were beyond her ability to overcome.

. . .

No.

No, she couldn't give up. Not now, not later. She *refused*. Not while she could still do *something*.

Bertrand wasn't dead and could still be saved. Valdemar hadn't become a monster. The children were missing but hopefully alive. Shelley could be slain.

Marianne hadn't lost yet. Maybe she would fail to change anything. But at least, she would have tried.

Her heart invigorated with grim determination, the noblewoman opened her eyes and returned to her search. She examined the mutated body, trying to confirm her identity. From the clothes and pouches of herbs around her thorn belt, this was probably Emma herself. Had Shelley transformed her into a monster through the black blood?

We found traces of a modified Beast Plague, the Knights of the Beast's alchemist had said, *inoculated during infancy.*

Marianne glanced at the alchemical tools and the remnants of Shelley's blood on the floor.

It's possible Aleksander Verney got his hands on a sample and modified it to include rat genes.

Shelley had extracted the modified plague that turned him into a monster from his own blood and used Emma as a test subject. Her aging body couldn't resist the changes and perished rather than fully transform.

Only a few days, Marianne thought. Shelley had ransacked this house three days ago and probably left yesterday morning. The illness was lethally effective.

The noblewoman returned to the entrance and examined the footprints with more attention. She confirmed that some were smaller than others. The children had survived the inoculation, but considering the plates and the lack of resistance, the plague had given Shelley a hold on their mind. They had become no different than the rats he controlled.

Though the cultist's cruel acts filled her with loathing, Marianne couldn't help but ponder the reasons behind them. Was he trying to recruit new minions, to indoctrinate new wererats into the Verney cult? Why hadn't he done it before then?

And why had he been so careless? Shelley had set his last lab on fire and been careful to keep his activities hidden for years. And now he had left the corpse of a sacrifice in the open like a morbid trophy. And though he had made a token effort to break the tools behind him and obscure the purpose of his experiments, it struck Marianne as half-assed. A carelessness that bordered on arrogance.

Either Shelley didn't think that it mattered if people learned of his existence and activities . . . or he actively wanted word to spread. Perhaps he took joy in finally practicing his vile religion after years of hiding in a castle's crypt and exulted in his newfound mission. But somehow, Marianne suspected a larger scheme was at work.

Even stranger, her blood-tracker still pointed in the general direction of Paraplex. Even if Shelley recruited a dozen wererats, they wouldn't be enough to bypass the Institute's defenses. If he attempted something so foolhardy as an infiltration or assault, Lord Och would slay him.

Unless . . .

Unless Shelley didn't intend to attack the Institute from the front. It would make more sense to stretch its resources thin or force a desperate situation where Valdemar would have to leave the fortress to help. A terrible disaster that even a Dark Lord would be hard-pressed to deal with . . .

Marianne's eyes widened in panic as she put two and two together, and she rushed outside. She climbed on her riding beetle and fled toward Paraplex as fast as she could, without even alerting the locals to their herbalist's fate. The danger was too great, and every second wasted would endanger more lives.

Shelley had created a plague, and he had already selected the first carriers.

21

THE DOORWAY TO NOWHERE

The Institute's Hall of Rituals had turned into an art gallery. When the time came to finally complete the Painted Door project, Hermann decided to have multiple pictomancy works set on the room's walls, especially pictures associated with death, the Silent King, or doorways. The troglodyte hoped that the presence of so many art pieces in close proximity would somehow enhance the planned ritual. It took hours for the Institute's golems to transport them all. In total, the "exhibition" included twenty pictures, from Hermann's geometric designs to a copy of the famous macabre *Pickman's Supper*. Meanwhile, Valdemar only offered one contribution to the exhibition.

"So, if I understand," Valdemar asked his grandfather's portrait, switching from his native Azlantean to English while writing down notes in his notebook. "I need to add 'ed' to the end of a verb to speak about the past. Like 'I goed to the church last month?'"

"Yes, for most verbs," his grandfather's shade replied. The painting looked outwardly the same, but Valdemar's true sight identified the countless magical wards protecting it. Lord Och had personally outfitted the artifact with his own protection spells to ensure it would survive whatever may come. "But some verbs change entirely if used with the past tense. The past of 'go' is 'went.'"

"Huh? Why?"

"It's an irregular verb. There are many others. Like how the past of 'make' is 'made.'"

"But . . . What is the point?" his grandson asked in confusion. "If you have a simple rule, why make common verbs abstain from following it? What higher grammar purpose does it serve?"

His grandfather's portrait smiled in embarrassed silence.

Valdemar sighed. "Is there a way to identify an irregular verb from a law-abiding one?"

"No, but . . . I remember most of the list."

So Valdemar would have to memorize them all? Damn it. "Alright, could you give me the list, Grandpa?" the summoner asked as he scribbled on his notebook. "'Go' becomes 'went,' 'make' becomes 'made' . . ."

His grandfather listed all the irregular words, or rather the few that he remembered. Valdemar had noticed a few other "irregular" words in the journal, but when he pointed them out to the animated painting, the portrait couldn't identify them.

Curse the inquisitors for interrupting his ritual the first time!

Despite the occasional oddities, mastering the English language had come easily to Valdemar. Contrary to his grandfather's native French tongue, the grammar rules were relatively simple, with only one word for each concept and little reliance on outside context to get the meaning of a sentence across. French had fewer irregular verbs but harder conjugation, more flexible use of word placement, and differentiated between a formal and informal dialect. He still had no idea why the British tribe called their language "English" rather than "British" though.

The holes in his grandfather's memory unfortunately made identifying specific English words difficult. Valdemar was confident he could decode most of the journal's coded pages given time, but not all of them.

"I am glad to see you are making progress, my apprentice," Lord Och's voice suddenly echoed at Valdemar's left. By now, the summoner had grown used to his mentor teleporting into his presence without warning. "Time is the most precious currency of all. The only one we cannot get back."

Valdemar closed his notebook and offered a nod to his grandfather's portrait. "I need to go, Grandpa," he said while bowing. "We'll continue another time."

"Be careful, Valdemar," the portrait advised. "Don't talk to strangers."

A bit too late for that, Valdemar thought as he glanced at Lord Och. The lich carried the spiral mask his apprentice had recovered in Astaphanos. "Are you returning it to me, my teacher?" the summoner asked.

"It is yours, my apprentice. Though I thank you for bringing it to me for study." The lich's skeletal fingers trailed on the mask's spiral design. "Your intuition was once again correct. The material making up this artifact comes from the surface."

"From the Whitemoon itself?" Valdemar had suspected a connection after his dream.

"Yes . . . and no. This mask was made from the hide of a powerful creature that traveled to our world with the Whitemoon and now roams the surface above our heads. I suspect you already heard of it."

Valdemar gritted his teeth. "The Nightwalker."

This Stranger was infamous for roaming the desolate, snowy surface above Underland. The entity had attempted to descend underground in the past, only to be repelled by powerful magical wards set by the Dark Lords. Cults worshipping it often attempted to travel to the surface, to be rewarded with transformation into "higher" beings that could thrive in the eternal night and bitter cold.

Did the mask create a psychic connection with the creature? It would explain Valdemar's dream. The summoner had seen the surface through the eyes of another, gaining a glimpse of the horrors that now inhabited the ruins of ancient civilizations.

"Why are you giving it back to me, knowing the danger this artifact represents?" Valdemar asked his teacher. "Iren couldn't find any receipt or transaction paper trail in the shop's registers. The mask found its way to the shop on its own."

"Of course it did. It was a gift, Valdemar." His reluctance amused Lord Och. "How ungrateful of you to spite another's generosity."

"I am not fond of poisoned gifts." For all Valdemar knew, the mask could give the Nightwalker a foothold into his mind.

"All gifts are poisoned, young Valdemar, because they are never free. They always come with a subtle string called the law of reciprocity. 'I give you this ring, but in exchange, you must share your life with me.' 'I offer my friendship, but you must help me in return when I need it.' Together, all these obligations form a web that we call society."

"What about selflessness? Helping someone because it's the right thing to do, without expecting anything in return?"

"Oh, but help is never truly free," Lord Och replied, his ghostly eyes flickering like candles. "Sometimes, the reward is one's own gratification, the addictive drug we call self-righteousness."

"That is a very cynical vision of the world, my teacher," the summoner replied with a frown. Somehow, the discussion had become a philosophical debate. "I hope that I never come to share it."

"Naïveté is the privilege of the young, my apprentice."

"And cynicism is the last refuge of the old?"

The lich chuckled. "I should remove your tongue for your insolence, but I will indulge you for now. Age, and the world we live in, will teach you wisdom soon enough."

Wisdom? Where was wisdom to be found in such nihilism? The world was not a fine place, true. Valdemar couldn't deny it. But someone seeing only the bad parts of it was just as blind as those who only wished to see the good ones.

Lord Och gave Valdemar an indecipherable gaze. The lich's skull was an expressionless mask, but for a moment his apprentice saw the light in it vacillate; as if his very thought had struck a chord with the Dark Lord.

"How old," the ancient undead rasped, "do you think I am?"

Valdemar considered the question thoughtfully. Lord Och predated the empire's foundation and was probably a lich already by then. Some said that the undead warlock was older than the Descent itself, though his apprentice doubted it; humans only discovered the Blood and undeath after fleeing into Underland's depths. "Between six and eight hundred years old?"

"Six or eight or ten, I had learned all I needed to know about our species by the first two," Lord Och replied coldly. "Some philosophers in my youth said that peace would be achieved when everyone lived in comfort, that we should give all citizens a voice in the government. I've listened to rulers making speeches about how, if they were granted ultimate power, they could bring eternal order and prosperity to mankind. I have survived more wars than you have years, watched nations turn to dust. And across the long centuries, I have seen our kind make the same mistakes over and over and over again."

Valdemar listened in respectful silence, trying to see what the lich was getting at.

"Human nature—no, the very nature of sentient life—is as unchanging as gravity," the ancient Dark Lord explained. "It always pulls us down. The ancients complain about the good old times, while the young believe they can do anything. The weak envy the powerful, and the strong sow the seeds of their own demise through their willful indulgence. Empires rise and fall as easily as republics and democracies. The system we Dark Lords have created is the stablest one yet because we understand human ambition and keep it tightly leashed. But even so, for all of our efforts, this great undying pyramid is always one slip, one mistake away from collapsing."

By now, Valdemar couldn't keep his mouth shut. "So *what*?"

"So what, he asks," Lord Och replied with a laugh. "You are working under the delusion that bringing the sun back to our fellow humans will make them happier. You are wrong. It will make their lives more comfortable, yes. They will swear to make it right this time, to change their ways because they feel regrets about the sacrifices they had to make . . . until they do not. They will fight for resources, for glory, for the color of their skin or for a useless patch of land. You could give our people everything, and they would still be unsatisfied."

"I do not have the benefit of your age, sir, so I will trust your expertise," Valdemar replied calmly. "But if we abandon hope for a brighter tomorrow for our kind . . . what's left to believe in?"

"Power," the lich replied immediately. "Knowledge. And yourself."

"So, giving up on everyone and everything else? That's a lonely path to walk." And not one Valdemar wanted for himself.

"Perhaps, but it is a less painful path than the one you are treading. Only bitterness and disappointment lie ahead of you, my apprentice."

"With all due respect, my teacher, I believe my beliefs and magical potential are unrelated," Valdemar argued. "Whether I face success or disappointment, I will carry on regardless."

"I hope so for you, but I have seen too many promising sorcerers wallowing in self-pity. The only way to become powerful, truly powerful, is to stand above the petty squabbles of mankind. The sooner you free yourself from others' expectations, the better." The lich chuckled. "Except mine, of course. Do not disappoint them."

Do as I say, not as I do, Valdemar thought. "Is that why you became a lich, my teacher? To transcend human frailties?"

"It played a part, along with immortality and magical power." Lord Och glanced at the paintings, especially Valdemar's portrait of his grandfather. "I do not need to feed or drink. My thoughts are unclouded by dreams and lust. I have time, enough time to learn all there is to know. I hope to improve myself and achieve a higher state of existence without the weakness of a phylactery one day, but lichdom is an acceptable intermediary step for now."

Valdemar immediately saw the flaw in his logic. "If you believe cutting yourself from others is the key to power and freedom, why become a Dark Lord? Why rule a country? And why take apprentices?"

"Because there is a limit to what I can do alone," Lord Och replied calmly. "I could rule a kingdom of the mindless dead and learn what all the 'Masters' of this place are uncovering by myself, but it is more efficient to delegate. As for our relationship, young Valdemar, we are simply useful to each other. Your talent serves my purposes, and I reward you with knowledge and power. We lift each other up. That is all."

"Sir, with all due respect . . ." Valdemar took a long deep breath, unsure how the lich would react. He considered keeping his mouth shut, but silence couldn't protect him from mind-reading . . .

"Speak your mind," Lord Och ordered, his tone colder than before. He had already glimpsed Valdemar's answer in his thoughts. "I do not punish honesty."

"I do not believe you," his apprentice stated.

"You accuse me of *lying*?"

"If you are free of others' expectations and feelings, why try to convince me?" Valdemar pointed out. "If you are truly confident in what you say and believe, then you don't need to prove anything."

Lord Och chuckled, though Valdemar sensed the falseness in his voice. "You are unshakably convinced of Earth's existence, young man, and yet you've been trying to prove its existence to all the people you have met."

"I know Earth exists," Valdemar defended himself. "But no, by your own logic, I'm not free of others' expectations. A part of me wants to prove the truth to others, and it will bring me joy when I am inevitably proven right. Just as a part of you wants to convince me because it will make you feel better."

For the first time since the conversation began, the lich became as silent as a tomb. The air became colder and dryer, as if an invisible force sucked the warmth out of it.

"Lord Och, I will take your knowledge and wisdom with gratitude," Valdemar declared with honesty as he stood his ground. "But I won't become like you. I do not want to."

Maybe his path was one of failures and disappointment, maybe his efforts wouldn't change anything in the long-term. But Valdemar would try to make things better, not only for himself, but for others.

The lich didn't answer immediately. For a few seconds, the ancient undead remained as still and silent as the stone walls around them. His eyes flickered with otherworldly light, as if his very soul waved in power.

And then he spoke, his voice echoing with the weight of centuries, each word resonating with ominous power.

"We shall see about that," was all the Dark Lord said.

Valdemar shivered as the temperature returned to normal. So did Lord Och's voice, as he summarily dismissed the matter with unnerving ease.

"In any case, to go back to our original discussion . . . Why would anyone send a gift, young Valdemar?" Lord Och asked, though he didn't wait for his student to answer. "To catch your attention. Strangers and powerful entities are not so different from any powerful patron. Some are whimsical immortals who try to lead men astray and delight in watching their destruction unfold. Others offer power and knowledge for service. Dealing with the Strangers can be very profitable for a lucky few, which is why so many fools try in spite of the dangers involved. This mask may be an opportunity to unlock powerful secrets and gain more strength."

"Or a trap to take away my free will," Valdemar pointed out. "The risks are high."

"Life is full of dangers, young man. There is a chance that the ceiling above your head will collapse once you step outside, but would you spend the rest of your existence hiding in your home?" The lich shook his head. "I suggest that you minimize the risks to yourself but study this mask with a rational mind. We cannot hope to conquer the Strangers and make their powers our own if we do not understand them."

Valdemar glanced at the paintings, in particular, at a large wood panel at the center of the Hall of Rituals. The support on which he and Hermann would paint a door to another world. *It's no different than studying this mask,* Valdemar thought as he grabbed the artifact, its surface cold to the touch. *I'll just have to avoid putting it on until I understand what it does.* "My teacher, if I may ask . . . Do you know why the Whitemoon came to our world?"

"Of course I do," Lord Och replied with a smug tone. "Though I believe you gained a glimpse of its motives already."

Motives implied sentience. "Does it hate us, humans?" Valdemar asked. "Or the eyes we share tunnels with?"

Lord Och's skeletal face morphed into a ghoulish smirk. "You should find that out on your own, young man."

Of course. Why had Valdemar expected anything else but a cryptic answer?

"Because you do not listen," Lord Och replied with a mocking tone, having read his student's thoughts. "In any case, I hope you enjoyed your little vacation in Astaphanos, because you will not leave my fortress in the near future."

"Am I grounded?" Valdemar frowned as he put his mask and notebook beneath his scholarly robes. "Is it because of the derros?"

"You will remain here for your own safety." The lich put his hands behind his back, his voice deepening. "I have received worrying reports from young Marianne and my colleague Lord Hagith. It appears the inquisitors were not as thorough as they thought, and a cultist from your grandfather's group escaped the purge. He is currently at large . . . and aware of your existence."

Valdemar froze. Even twenty years later, his family's misdeeds still haunted him. "You think he will come for me?"

Lord Och gave his apprentice a curious look. "Would you want to meet him?"

"No, of course not." That loathsome cult had already made his life hard enough. Were it not for the reputation he inherited from them, Valdemar might have already opened a pathway to Earth by now. "I could help catch this man, if you want. Act as bait."

"I considered this course of action, but I fear it might get out of hand and put you at risk." Lord Och sounded halfway concerned, to his apprentice's surprise. "Besides, I would not call a wererat a man. More like a beast gifted with human intelligence."

"A wererat?" Valdemar asked, his eyes widening in surprise. "I didn't even know that kind of monster existed."

"There is a lycan variant of almost every animal alive today and even some extinct species. Young Hagith outwitted himself when he created his Beast plague. It is far too flexible and resilient to my liking." Lord Och let out a shrug. "Lycans are an annoyance. You leave one free and a dozen pop up in your backyard the next week. Someday I might create a virus to exterminate them all and be done with this nonsense."

"Why haven't you tried that with the derros?" Valdemar asked with curiosity. After seeing the gray dwarves at work, the summoner understood why the empire had such a harsh foreign policy toward them. It had taken days for the lightning scars to vanish from his body, and while Liliane got to see the dark elves' embassy gardens, Valdemar spent his days in Astaphanos in a hospital bed.

"Oh, we tried germ warfare before against the derros, but their government massacred all their infected countrymen while their alchemists developed a cure." And the lich said that with such cheerfulness too . . . "Believe me, young Valdemar. Anyone complaining about our political system hasn't spent a day in the derro kingdom. Their ruler values life even less than I do."

Well, at least the Dark Lord didn't pretend to care.

But Valdemar couldn't help but find it incredibly creepy how Lord Och could switch from cold-heartedness to amusement so easily. It felt like watching someone go through masks in quick succession. Or maybe Valdemar had yet to see the lich's true self.

"We face a dozen lycanthropy cases each year," Lord Och said dismissively, as the buzzing of flies and echoes of heavy footsteps resonated in the Hall of Rituals. "I don't expect this one to be any different. The wererat does not worry me half as much as the forces he helped unleash, or the scrutiny his foolish actions might bring you."

Valdemar could live with that.

Hermann and his master, Loctis the Swarm, climbed down the Hall's stairways to join them. The troglodyte carried pots of paints, two ceramic palettes, and paintbrushes. "Lord Och . . . Valdemar . . ." the troglodyte nodded before the other master-apprentice duo. "Sorry for the . . . wait."

"No need to apologize, young Hermann," Lord Och replied, though his eyes focused on Loctis alone. "A few minutes are nothing to the likes of us. Loctis, my friend, how is your research going? Any new breakthroughs?"

Valdemar couldn't help but notice that Lord Och hadn't used "young" to qualify his colleague . . . and he sounded even a little respectful. *They've known each other for a very long time,* he guessed. *Centuries maybe.*

"The cancer theory seems to be the likeliest explanation for the biological oddities we observed, Lord Och," Loctis answered, the countless flies and insects making up his body buzzing beneath his tattered cloak. "Mutant cells breaking off from the body, weakening it and causing a reaction."

Lord Och thoughtfully touched his chin with his bony fingers, as if stroking a nonexistent beard. "How will the body react to these cells' behavior? Destruction and replacement? Forceful assimilation? What consequences will it have on the host?"

"It is too early to say yet."

Valdemar didn't fully understand what they discussed, though it seemed they were talking about biomancy . . . until Lord Och mentioned the derros. "I suspect Otto Blutang shares our hypothesis," the lich said. "His men gathered many brain tissue samples recently, probably for the purpose of comparative studies. My spies among the dokkar enclaves and troglodyte tribes informed me that the Astaphanos incident wasn't an isolated case."

Did . . . did the derros abduct dark elves and troglodytes too? Valdemar exchanged an uneasy glance with Hermann, neither of them willing to interrupt their teachers.

"For what purpose?" Loctis asked coolly. "His kind shouldn't be affected."

"From what we know," Lord Och replied. "They have been here for a while."

Loctis pondered the lich's words, and Valdemar sensed his countless eyes gazing at him and Hermann. "May we speak privately?" the swarm asked.

After a short silence, Lord Och waved his hand. A bubble of crimson mist formed around him and Loctis, and when the lich's mouth moved, no sound came out. None that Valdemar could hear.

Whatever they discussed, they didn't want their students to learn it. Maybe it was a state secret about the derro kingdom's ambitions.

Well, in the end, it didn't matter. Valdemar shrugged and examined Hermann's painting supplies. "Is everything ready?"

"Yes . . ." The troglodyte's tail waved behind him uncontrollably as he handed Valdemar his palette. "I'm . . . I'm nervous and yet . . . excited too."

"Same." Valdemar glanced at the pigments. His blood mixed with that of his fellow pictomancer for the red, Colophryar extracts for the blue, and the Collector's blood for the yellow. Hermann had mixed various combinations to create other colors, from green to orange, even a deep shade of purple. "I'm taking a risk by bringing my grandfather's portrait to this gathering. Frankly, if Lord Och hadn't warded it himself . . ."

"I swear it . . . it will not be in vain. It will improve our odds . . . I know that." Hermann glanced at the exhibition. "Where is . . . Frigga's portrait?"

"I barely started it," Valdemar admitted while shuddering. Frigga had proven to be a wonderful model, aesthetically speaking . . . but the more he painted for her, the more she asked for ghoulish alterations. "She wants me to represent her with half her body rotting now. To 'show life's fragility.' Between us, I would rather paint Liliane or Marianne. Frigga just rubs me the wrong way."

"You know . . . some of my kindred eat . . . dark elves." Hermann handed him a piece of charcoal, so they could make a sketch of the painting before starting with the paint job. "I . . . frown on these practices . . ."

"But you wouldn't mind making an exception for Frigga?" Valdemar chuckled. "I wouldn't recommend it. She probably tastes bitter and rancid."

"It's not about . . . the taste." Hermann's lips pursed to reveal the fangs beneath. "It's . . . about pleasure."

By now, the two pictomancers didn't even need to discuss the sketch. They acted as one, drawing a charcoal picture of a wide gate opening into a foreign world of sand dunes with a black sun in the skies. The wood panel was two meters seventy centimeters tall, with a width of two meters; large enough to let both humans and troglodytes through.

"You know . . ." Hermann cleared his throat. "The harvested poplar tree we used . . . was recreated from a fossil. There is . . . no other support . . . like this one."

"We gathered materials worthy of a god," Valdemar agreed. "If the Silent King snubs us, I will be mad."

His remark made Hermann thoughtful. "I . . . I hope it will work. I researched . . . I researched him for years. If we fail . . . if we fail, I'm considering an . . . an alternative."

"Create a painted world?"

"Yes. Create a world for my kind . . . piece by piece." Hermann hesitated. "But I . . . I will need help. To bind the creatures . . . to use as fuel."

"Say no more, I will help you depopulate the Outer Darkness," Valdemar vowed with a smile. "Each Qlippoth piece will have its place."

"Thank you . . ." Hermann's inhuman lips morphed into a smile. "Maybe we . . . could link the painted place to . . . your grandfather's portrait. Let you . . . touch him."

Valdemar's heart skipped a beat. "It's possible?"

"I do not know . . . but we can try."

Their respective masters finished their conversation, with Lord Och canceling his spell to oversee the sketch. "Are you ready to begin?" he asked, both Valdemar and Hermann nodding at once. "Then proceed."

Both pictomancers grabbed their paintbrushes and began to work.

More of their blood mixed with the pigments as they applied the first coat of paint. Valdemar sensed the gaze of his teacher on his back, the invisible pressure of his expectations. But his arm remained steady, as did Hermann's. Their paint brushes followed the outline sketch, creating sharp colored lines.

Once they had completed the outline, they started filling in the various shapes. A halo of blue for the door, a pale hue of yellow for the endless desert beyond, a dark shade of red for the sky above it. They mixed the colors with expert care, choosing the right composition for the most vivid result.

At this point, they should have let the painting dry before moving on to the next phase of the composition . . . but the pigments seemed to do it on their own. Fumes came out of the black sun at the composition's center.

Hermann's hand approached the dark star without touching it. "I sense . . . heat."

Yes. The center of the painting radiated warmth, drying the paint by itself. A fount of magic erupted from the black sun like a fountain, a power similar to the Blood and yet subtly different.

A spell that neither Hermann nor Valdemar had cast. They glanced over their shoulders, Lord Och giving them a nod while Loctis's swarm remained unnervingly silent.

The pictomancers switched from coating the wood to adding texture, depths and thickness. They added layers to the gateway and to the sun, filled the skies with blood, and gave shape to each grain of sand. The portrait's lines shifted on their own, the magic of both sorcerers suffusing every shade, every hue. Valdemar noticed his grandfather's portrait fidgeting at the edge of his eye, alongside the other pieces exhibited. They sensed an invisible pull, something that the painters could barely perceive.

The Silent King walked on the painted dunes, beyond the door's threshold.

He was small, so small that Valdemar could barely see him. His robes were a shade of dark green, tattered rags fluttering in the wind. A mass of multicolored tentacles squirmed beneath his hood, obscuring the light of his eyes. The creature took a step and then another.

The Silent King was moving closer.

By now, Valdemar painted entirely on instinct. His hand was no longer his own. Something other than his will guided it, as gentle as a parent's hand, as cold and alien as an otherworldly outsider. An invisible bond connected the summoner to the creature on the other side, using the painting as a medium, the same way Valdemar used a circle to bind Qlippoths to his will. Hermann was as transfixed as his colleague. The rest of the world no longer mattered. Only this painted door, this perfect magnum opus, deserved their full attention.

Even when the ground started shaking beneath their feet.

A deep rumble echoed through the Hall of Rituals, and dust fell on Valdemar's shoulders. The walls trembled, but he didn't care, didn't let that interfere. His hand turned into festering flesh and sick pale eyes opened all over his arm, but he didn't care.

He only had eyes for the alien world before him. The ruins of an ancient city rose from beneath the painted dunes, alongside floating structures of stone rising in a cloudless sky and spiraling staircases that no man had ever seen. Statues of alien, defaced giants appeared all over the horizon, all of them in awe of the black sun's radiance. The Silent King walked closer and closer, his open eyes revealing stars and a glimpse at forgotten cosmic secrets. Beckoning the painters to take a step into this brand new and terrifying world.

An alien howl echoed across the hall, and Valdemar's paintbrush snapped between his fingers.

Only then did the summoner regain awareness of his reality, to see it blurring with a nightmare. His hand had turned into the same festering flesh and eyes as the walls beyond the Institute, and a fanged mouth snapped its jaws inside his palm. The Hall of Rituals had gained new colors, reality blurring like a chaotic canvas. The other paintings in the exhibit appeared like islands in a sea of fresh paint.

Lord Och's voice cut through the noise, as sharp as a sword.

"Carry on."

The lich remained imperturbable, while Loctis cast spells at his side. Though he appeared an eternity away from Valdemar, Lord Och's voice reached his student's ears just fine.

"Carry on," he repeated.

And Valdemar returned to work. His paintbrush broken, he used the same technique as the blood bullet to solidify his body's fluids into a crystalized wand to carry on. Hermann had switched from using his brush to his tail, while his eyes shone with feverish madness. They added shadows on the city, highlighted the black sun's dark radiance, and worked all the disparate details into a single, unified whole.

An invisible force pushed against his face as he gazed into the painted door, small grains of sand hitting his cheek.

Wind, Valdemar thought in his creative fever. Not the cold, howling blizzard that his mask had shown him, but rather a dry, warm breeze.

The Silent King looked tall beyond the threshold, so close he was but one step away from crossing it. And yet, he did not. The Stranger stood on the other side, gazing through this portrait as he did with countless others. The Silent King didn't say a word, nor did he need to. His meaning was clear as springwater, as all pieces fell into place. His visits to painters and madmen had never been a call to summon him to the material plane. Silent or not, a true king did not visit foreign courtiers.

COME.

A true king *invited.*

Hermann and Valdemar weren't the summoners.

They were the ones being summoned.

And so the two pictomancers answered the call. They couldn't resist, even if they had wanted to. They had poured their blood and soul into this masterpiece, and it wouldn't come to life without this final commitment. They stepped through the painted door and into another world.

2 2

IN THE COURT OF THE SILENT KING

Songs reigned in the Silent King's realm. Valdemar was no music expert. His experience was limited to his mother's music box and street performers playing tunes in taverns for a coin; he had never listened to an opera or an orchestra. But as he listened to the melodies echoing across the sand dunes, Valdemar doubted that any mortal instrument could play them. Some sounds he recognized as belonging to trumpets, violins, ocarinas, and pipe organs, but others . . . others were more like animal screeches, the sound of shattering ice and burning flames. This was a symphony of chaos and madness, played by an inhuman orchestra. Valdemar couldn't help but hum the melody's tune to himself. Something in the song felt familiar, like a childhood lullaby his conscious mind had never forgotten entirely.

"This is . . ." Hermann removed his hood as he looked at the heavens above them, his reptilian eyes wet with tears. "Beautiful."

A black sun shone in the dark red skies above the two mortal visitors, surrounded by a crimson halo. The sinister star reminded Valdemar of an eye gazing down on him, a deity observing the world below from a celestial throne. The summoner had expected the crimson light to burn his eyes, to blind him with its terrible beauty; and yet the black sun's sight inspired neither pain nor horror, but awe.

It was not the fabled sun and blue sky of Earth, but Valdemar had never seen anything more beautiful in his life anyway. The colors were *real*, not painted pigments or figments of his imagination. Natural light traveling down from the greater cosmos with no stone ceiling to block it.

And the wind . . . the flowing current that brushed against Valdemar's cheek felt as warm as his mother's hand. The grains of sand were dryer than Underland's dust, but the air was fresher, *pure*. No dust or mushroom spores filled the summoner's lungs as he breathed.

It felt good.

Valdemar had tasted freedom. The pleasure of an open sky without walls or ceiling to keep him imprisoned. He had taken a look outside the stone womb of Underland and gazed at the infinity beyond.

Everyone else needed to see it too.

Valdemar looked behind him, half expecting the Painted Door to have collapsed after they crossed it. To his surprise, an enormous canvas stood out of the sands, representing the Hall of Rituals. Neither Lord Och nor Loctis appeared on the picture, but it looked so vivid, so real, that Valdemar immediately recognized it as a doorway between worlds. He touched the surface with his fingers, sensing the softness of the paint and a lack of resistance. He could push through if he wanted, crossing the boundaries between universes to return to his own.

My hand, Valdemar thought. It was as normal as it had always been, with no screaming mouth growing out of his palm. Had it been a dream? An illusion created by the ritual? Or a brief glimpse at a revelation that escaped even his True Sight?

Valdemar was not stupid. He knew of his abnormal biology and he doubted Lord Och took him under his wing only for his talent. There was more at work than he knew. *Eyes,* he thought, as he observed his arm. *It had eyes like the walls.*

"I think we can leave if we cross this painting," Valdemar informed Hermann. "But neither of our masters crossed it, and I can't hear anything through the Painted Door."

"They . . . weren't invited. Only the two of us were." Hermann's eyes couldn't stray from the black sun above them. "It's . . ."

"Hermann?"

"I'm sorry . . ." Hermann shook his head, wiping off a tear with his claw. "It's . . . I hope your Earth looks as beautiful as this sky . . . I dearly wish so. This place is . . . better than anything I imagined."

Valdemar smiled and gave his friend a pat on the back. "One day, I will show you Earth. Just like you brought me here."

"We did it . . . together."

"But it's your research, your work, that made this Painted Door possible. I only assisted you in your endeavor."

"I . . . I thank you for it." Hermann looked down from the skies and at the endless dunes surrounding them. Structures rose out of them like blind fish jumping above the Lightless Ocean's water, whether they were black pyramids standing beyond the horizon, inhuman statues reaching out toward the skies, or the ruins of forgotten cities. "But this place . . . it's dead. All dust and ruins . . ."

"There's music though," Valdemar pointed out. "You can't have a song without a musician."

"Maybe . . . maybe the Silent King's focus isn't painting . . . but art itself?" Hermann scratched the scales below his mouth, his gaze thoughtful as he observed the ancient ruins from afar. "The structures for architecture . . . the subtle symphony for music."

"Then you think the Silent King contacted other artists?"

"Probably . . . but the signs were less visible. How can you see . . . a song?" Hermann glanced at the painted portal behind them. "I wish Master Loctis . . . could be here. He would know . . ."

"They can't cross the Painted Door on their own," Valdemar guessed. Knowing the lich, Lord Och would have magically forced his way into this other world if he could. The fact he hadn't, meant that the Silent King's spell only worked on invited individuals, or that the entity had enough control over the portal to prevent intruders from crossing into his realm. "Do we cross the Painted Door again and report to our teachers?"

Hermann shook his head. "It may close forever behind us . . . if we try. Better to . . . explore this realm first. Meet . . . the ruler of this place . . . ask for answers."

True. They had seen the Silent King during the ritual, but the Stranger was nowhere to be found. Valdemar and Hermann were guests in this realm; they would have to travel to their host and pay homage, not the other way around.

The music seemed to come from the ruined city rising out of the sand, so the two pictomancers walked in that direction. Valdemar had barely taken two steps before he had sand all over his boots, in and out. "I don't think it's a Painted Place," the summoner whispered as he examined the grains. They didn't feel like pigments to the touch. "It's a natural world."

Hermann searched under his robes and brought out a compass. The needle pointed toward the black sun above them rather than the distant north. "Laws here are . . . different. Electromagnetism does not behave . . . like in our world."

Valdemar smiled at his friend's foresight. "Did you bring that tool expecting we would be transported to another world?"

"I . . . hoped we would." The troglodyte put the device back in a pocket. "I thought I could . . . bring my people to this place. Help them settle in a new world . . . with the Silent King's permission."

Valdemar wasn't sure this desert could sustain life at all. The presence of breathable air implied the presence of oxygen-recycling plants or elementals . . . or at least it would if they were exploring a cavern. He had no idea how air worked in this alien realm.

Come to think of it, how did the wind not disperse into space without a ceiling to keep it trapped? Valdemar had never asked himself the question, but now it sounded odd to him. There were so many things he didn't know, so much to learn.

"You thought, as in the past?" Valdemar asked his troglodyte friend. "You've changed your mind?"

"Only a select few . . . are let inside," Hermann replied. "I don't think the Silent King will . . . let my entire people settle in his realm."

"You can always ask, it will cost you nothing. Though I can understand if you would prefer a greener place."

"I will take . . . what I can get." Hermann's expression turned grim and sorrowful. "We troglodytes are a . . . a shattered people, Valdemar. Our tribes were long at war . . . even before mankind conquered our caverns . . . and scattered us across the tunnels. Our population decreases each year . . . killed by wandering monsters or derros. If nothing is done . . . we will disappear. Not now or in a century . . . but one day."

"Hasn't anybody tried to unite the tribes?" Valdemar knew of a few troglodyte warlords who threatened the states that preceded the Empire of Azlant in the distant past. "Not as a marauding horde, but as a peaceful state we could trade with?"

"We do not have Earthmouths . . . our settlements are scattered. Easily crushed by larger armies. And why would others trade . . . when they can steal?" Hermann shook his head. "Our civilizations will never . . . become one, Valdemar."

"We're getting along just fine," Valdemar pointed out. "I understand your desire for a place to call your own, Hermann, but I don't think the situation is so hopeless as far as our species are concerned."

"Individuals can become . . . friends. But nations? I don't think so."

Many of the imperial Domains once belonged to troglodyte tribes. Hermann had given up on recovering his people's old homeland from the Dark Lords and now sought another; to the point he had agreed to serve under one of his kind's tormentors.

Though he was a human whose kind benefited from the troglodytes' decline, Valdemar couldn't help but feel compassion for his friend's plight. If Hermann found a hospitable new world, would Lord Och let him keep it for his people? Somehow Valdemar doubted it. History would repeat itself and the Dark Lords would have their due.

The duo's long march through the desert ended at the broken fortifications of a dusty city as large as Pleroma. The architecture differed from the visions Valdemar had seen while creating the Painted Door though. The houses were joined together like tunnels in an anthill, their walls covered in geometric symbols. The roofs were ovoid in shape, while the tallest structures included elaborate domes and rounded towers.

Valdemar examined the streets with his True Sight, but to his surprise he didn't detect any hint of Blood-related magic. The walls' symbols had no supernatural properties, nor did they have eyes to glare at the visitors.

So this many-eyed entity's reach is confined to Underland? Valdemar guessed. Good. Hopefully, Earth would be free from the eyes' presence too.

The streets were desolate and empty, but strangely preserved as well. The dunes hadn't buried these ruins, nor did a layer of dust cover the paved roads. The desert had stopped at the walls as if afraid to enter the city.

"I recognize . . . the architecture," Hermann said as he examined a house's rounded roof. "I've seen a similar shape . . . at the dokkar embassy. But . . . sharper. This city . . . It looks cruder. Older."

"Could it be an elf settlement from before the Descent?" Valdemar asked. Did they somehow travel to the past? No, that was absurd. He had never heard tales about a black sun shining in the skies before the Whitemoon's arrival.

He glanced into a house's open windows and saw a stone room lacking any furniture whatsoever. Mosaics of hunting scenes or carvings of ancient rituals often decorated the various buildings, but Valdemar didn't find any table, chair, or even cooking instrument. The homes were beautiful but lifeless.

"It's like this city was never inhabited in the first place," Valdemar noted. "No corpses either. If a cataclysm destroyed this settlement, the dry air should have preserved some remains."

The summoner grabbed his notebook, recording the walls' symbols next to his list of English irregular words. Maybe Frigga could translate them when they returned home? At his side, Hermann grabbed dust and dirt samples inside small flasks for study.

Their quest led them to ascending spiraling staircases with crumbling steps and steep slopes. The city's districts were piled up on one another, and the second level proved slightly different from the first. Conic structures swiftly supplanted the rounded houses, while reptilian statues became commonplace. Each street corner, each crossroad had its personal representation of a coiling serpent or a mighty four-armed lizard.

And all of them wore familiar masks.

"Impossible . . ." Hermann froze in awe before the statue of a mighty troglodyte warrior overseeing a dried fountain. "This is . . . On'ragon, protector of the Steelscale Tribe."

"I've never heard of it," Valdemar admitted.

"They're . . . long-extinct." Hermann raised a hand but didn't dare to touch the statue. Perhaps he was afraid of bringing down the Silent King's ire, or of infuriating the cultural deity that the art piece represented.

Valdemar would have asked for details if not for an oddity in the music. The city's music had changed so slightly and naturally that he hadn't noticed at first. Drums and cymbals had replaced the ocarinas and pipe organs, the melody growing slower and more aggressive. The melody was clear and intelligible, but paradoxically no more noticeable than background noise.

Valdemar glanced at the horizon in an attempt to locate the music's origin, only to notice new oddities. *There were pyramids in that direction,* he remembered as he stepped close to a stone guardrail and observed the distant dunes. Yet the monuments had vanished, replaced instead by the shadow of a colossal tower piercing the skies like a spear. Other structures had risen out of the dunes: a giant cyclopean statue that closely matched those near the Pleromian shrine underneath the Institute; the shadow of another city with twisted, hunched architecture; and a colossal black crystal as large as the Institute.

Valdemar glanced down at the houses below. The troglodyte district was no more than four meters above the elven one, but the distance appeared far greater from the summoner's point-of-view. The houses below had become as small as anthills.

We didn't climb that high, Valdemar thought with a frown. Did the Silent King use spatial magic? Then why couldn't the summoner's True Sight detect anything? Was he too weak to perceive the magical wards embedded in the stones around him, even though he could notice Lord Och's? Or did the Silent King use a power similar to the Collectors and alter reality on a fundamental level?

So many questions and no one to answer them.

"They all come from . . . extinct tribes," Hermann whispered as he examined other statues. "Shrines to . . . fallen nations."

Lost civilizations. Valdemar remembered stories about human empires before the Descent. About how they worshipped the sun, raising pyramids and towers in an attempt to become closer to its life-giving power. As for the Pleromian statue . . . So many different civilizations, but they all had one thing in common.

"It's not a dokkar district," Valdemar said as he gazed down at the houses below. "It's from the light elves. We heard their music, witnessed their architecture, and saw their pictures. We experienced the essence of their civilization, their art."

Hermann immediately caught on. "This realm, this entire world . . . it's not a kingdom . . . It's—"

"An art museum," Valdemar completed his sentence while moving away from the guardrail. "Of ancient civilizations."

Iren collected coins.

The Silent King collected cities, songs, and paintings.

Valdemar licked his lips. *Even the taste of troglodyte cuisine,* he thought upon sensing a spicy whiff on his tongue, mixed with a sweet aroma.

Hermann's curiosity turned to dread. "Are we visitors?" he wondered out loud with a hint of terror. "Or . . . part of the collection?"

Valdemar shuddered. Had this all been a trap? A method to capture artists and preserve their civilization's culture forever? Would they be condemned to wander these endless dunes for all eternity?

"The Silent King left the way out open," Valdemar pointed out weakly. "And there's nobody else here."

"I wonder too . . . we can't be the only ones to have . . . made our way to the Silent King's realm." Hermann looked up, his eyes setting upon the highest point in the twisted city; a stairway reaching higher than the tallest tower, yet seemingly leading nowhere. "Maybe we will . . . see more from up here?"

With no better idea to suggest, Valdemar followed his troglodyte friend as they continued their ascent. The music changed once again as they reached the stairway's first step, alien sounds drowning out the mortal instruments. The symphony grew louder with each step they took, as if the singers awaited them at the summit. The stairway itself lacked a guardrail or anything in the way of decorations, but the path was wide enough to let a giant beetle through.

Valdemar didn't know how long they climbed. Minutes? Hours? When Hermann had to stop to catch his breath at the halfway point, his friend glanced at the path's side. They couldn't have risen more than a few dozen meters above the city, yet it appeared leagues below them. Domes had become specks of dust and towers no taller than needles.

They wouldn't survive a fall into the void.

The second half of their ascent became weirder and weirder. Each new step crossed caused the world's music to change slightly, as if they were the keys of a giant piano. The wind stopped blowing, and the world below . . .

Valdemar held his breath, glanced beyond the stairway, and immediately looked back at the path ahead. Heights already disturbed him, but now the city below had become almost invisible, a black spot at the bottom of an endless pit. A part of Valdemar wanted to look at the void, to throw himself into its depths. The ground was calling him.

"You won't fall," Hermann said while raising his tail as if it were a life-saving rope. "I will . . . catch you if you slip."

"Have you ever walked at such heights?" Valdemar asked, a little ashamed of his fear. Unlike him, Hermann appeared just out of breath.

"Not quite, but . . . I like climbing." The troglodyte smiled. "It's alright."

Was that what friendship felt like? To know someone would have your back no matter what? That Valdemar didn't have to fear, because another would help him?

Friendship felt nice. Almost as nice as family.

Their hellish ascent ended atop a rectangular stone platform at the apex of the world. The world had become nothing but an endless red horizon, with black lightning coursing through the cloudless heavens. The music and wind had both died out, leaving only an oppressive silence.

The Silent King liked it this way.

The Stranger awaited his visitors at the very edge of the platform, facing a portrait floating in the void. His green robes had turned red, gray tentacles wriggling underneath the cloak.

Watching him hurt Valdemar's head. His vision blurred, his eyes unable to properly perceive the thing facing him. The summoner expanded his senses with his psychic sight, trying to divine the Silent King's true nature. He saw *nothing*. No feedback, no blood, no flesh, no magic. Nothing. As far as his psychic sight was concerned, the creature in front of them didn't exist.

This figure was not the Silent King . . . it was nothing but a psychic projection. The avatar of a greater power that human minds couldn't comprehend. Valdemar's brain had attributed humanoid features to this entity in an attempt to give it sense.

As for the portrait that the Silent King's avatar observed, Valdemar immediately recognized it as a copy of the Painted Door. Or was it the original, teleported across time and space to join the Stranger's endless collection? More strangely, another Silent King walked inside the picture, his robes as green as verdant moss. From Valdemar's point of view, the Stranger appeared to look at his living reflection in a mirror. And if the Painted Door was here, before them . . . then where did the painting in the desert lead to?

What was going on here?

Valdemar glanced at Hermann, only to see his friend kneeling before the entity. After some hesitation, the summoner imitated the troglodyte. This creature possessed great power beyond their comprehension, and they should show him the respect he deserved. An insult, perceived or real, could result in their death.

The Silent King didn't say anything as lightning erupted from the black sun and coursed through the skies. He seemed absorbed in his silent contemplation of the painting, marveling at every detail, each subtle change in color. The halo around the black sun above them changed color, dyeing the red skies with a purple shade.

An alien noise buzzed inside Valdemar's head as the heavens transformed. They formed words not made of letters, but alien sounds and thoughts; like an animal trying to mimic human speech, understanding the meaning but not the subtleties.

WHAT DO YOU DESIRE?

Valdemar remembered Lord Och's words about Strangers. Some were powerful patrons exchanging service for favor, others pranksters toying with mortals at their leisure. To which category did the Silent King belong?

Valdemar exchanged a glance with Hermann, the troglodyte clearing his throat before daring to answer. "What . . . do you offer . . . Your Majesty?"

The answer came swiftly.

THE TRUTH.

"At what cost?" Valdemar blurted out, before swiftly adding, "Your Majesty?"

A tentacle emerged from the king's scarlet robes and brushed against the Painted Door's frame.

"Will we . . . stay here?" Hermann asked anxiously.

NO. YOU LEAVE. FOREVER.

They would return to Underland and never find their way here again. The Silent King would not summon them again from the other side.

Perhaps all his visitations across imperial history had been nothing but art commissions, an attempt to get mortals to paint a new masterpiece for his collection. Or perhaps this portal would serve the Silent King's aims in the far-future, whatever they were. In either case, he no longer needed the pictomancers. He would thank them for their "service" with a boon, but no regret nor explanation.

Valdemar glanced at Hermann. The troglodyte looked disappointed but not surprised. As he had expected, the deity wasn't willing to let *anyone* settle in his private gallery.

"What do you mean by truth?" Valdemar probed, trying to sound as polite and respectful as he could. He didn't want to anger this ancient entity by asking too much, but this was a once-in-a-lifetime opportunity. "Will you answer all our questions until we are satisfied?"

Unfortunately, the Silent King was not that generous.

ONE TRUTH.

"One question?" Hermann's voice died in his throat. "One for the both of us?"

ONE EACH.

Better than nothing, but less than Valdemar hoped. The summoner exchanged another glance with Hermann. "You go first," Valdemar told his friend. "It was your project. The honor is yours."

Hermann nodded slowly, before looking back at the Silent King. "Your Majesty . . . my people are scattered and broken." The troglodyte hesitated, before mustering the courage to ask his question. "Tell me how . . . how I may give my people . . . a new world of their own."

The Silent King did not answer.

Hermann glanced at Valdemar, with the summoner thoughtfully considering his next words. He had so many questions to ask.

What are you? Valdemar thought. *What is this place? Why did you bring us here? Why is this door important to you? Why is there another you inside it? What power do you possess? How may I bring back my grandfather and mother from the dead? Do you know how to turn back time and change the past? What knowledge do you have? What can you teach me? Can you teach me? Is my father truly my father? Will I die before realizing my dream? Who am I? What is the meaning of life?*

All these questions had value, but only one mattered to Valdemar.

"Tell me," he said, "how I can bring my people to this beautiful world called Earth."

The Silent King turned around to face his guests. The visage beneath the hood belonged not to a man, but to the sky Valdemar had seen in his dreams; islands of light shining in an ocean of darkness. But instead of the Whitemoon dominating this cosmic landscape, a black sun ruled absolute.

Valdemar lost himself in the darkness beneath the hood, his mind absorbed by the blackness. The black sun grew to encompass the universe itself, the shadow of eyes, mouths and tentacles wriggling beneath its surface. The stars vanished in the pitch darkness of the cosmos, the cold void of space inside which not even the stars could survive.

Valdemar no longer felt his body. He no longer breathed, no longer lived. His thoughts had escaped his flesh, becoming an immaterial spirit. The Silent King's words resonated in the void, giving shape to nothingness.

BLOOD OF TWO WORLDS.

A vision of Valdemar's grandfather appeared floating in the darkness, scribbling words in a diary. He looked as if he had lost ten years, and so oblivious to the invisible strings making him dance. Another man's shadow observed him from inside the cover of darkness, a vile rat standing on his noble shoulder. But when Valdemar tried to look at the stranger's face, he only saw blood, worms, and a wicked smile.

YOU WERE BORN FOR A PURPOSE.

The vision changed. His grandfather had grown old, singing words while reading scriptures from his journal. A copy of Valdemar stood before him, naked as the day he was born; symbols were etched into his skin, while his gaze was lost in a drugged haze. Alien fumes erupted from his nose and mouth, gathering in the shape of a living nightmare, a monster with many eyes.

FULFILL IT.

The false Valdemar opened his mouth, and it grew. It grew larger, wider, devouring his torso and his limbs. His blood melted into the earth, his flesh and bones turning into an archway.

The Earthmouth that was once Valdemar opened, and his grandfather took a step through.

His tears dropped on green grass, growing under a bright blue sky.

No.

SACRIFICE.

No, no . . .

THE GATE AND THE KEY.

No! Valdemar's mind screamed, denying the vision, denying his grandfather, denying the god's words.

TRUTH DOES NOT LIE.

Valdemar's mental scream echoed into the void, dissipating the illusion only for another to swiftly rise in its place.

A derro sat on a throne of steel and steaming pipes. The gray dwarf's hair was black as night, his face smooth like a polished mirror. A crown of dark steel pulsated with lightning around his forehead, illuminating his cold, heartless blue eyes. An archway of steel crackled with lightning behind him, twisting the fabric of space itself.

ANOTHER WAY.

The derro king collapsed into a puddle of blood, his fluids pouring down a deep dark well. The steel throne and portals collapsed into dust, while another Valdemar stepped out of the darkness. Thick black blood poured out of his veins, while eyes and mouths tore out his skin to reveal the inhuman face underneath.

The Silent King's final word drowned Valdemar's screams as an eye opened at the well's bottom, hungry for blood.

ABOMINATION.

A tide of Blood swallowed Valdemar's soul, bringing him back to his body.

The floor of the Hall of Rituals was unwelcoming, the air dusty and cold. The ghoulish visage of Lord Och looked down on Valdemar, with none of his grandfather's feigned affection. "My my," he said, his words distant like an echo. "You look unwell, my apprentice."

Valdemar didn't answer. He couldn't. His head hurt, his body shivered from the cold within. He didn't even rise up. His heart was dead in his chest, beating so slowly he could barely hear it.

Lord Och's amusement turned to . . . concern? Caution? Something Valdemar had never seen on his skeletal face. The lich gave no word of comfort or condemnation. He didn't say anything. Instead, the Dark Lord offered Valdemar his hand.

His apprentice looked at the appendage as if it were a foreign object. He almost expected a trap or a mockery, but Lord Och waited with the patience of the dead.

After a moment of hesitation, Valdemar grabbed his mentor's hand. The lich felt cold to the touch, but not as much as the floor. Lord Och helped his apprentice to his feet, his expression unreadable.

Hermann was there too, and in better shape than his fellow pictomancer. The troglodyte held his head while his master Loctis observed him with a look of concern, his reptilian face morphing into a bright smile.

"I saw . . . I saw it. The Painted World . . . I saw it." Hermann glanced at Valdemar with a look of pure happiness. "Valdemar, it's wonderful . . . I hope your Earth looks as beautiful . . ."

Valdemar didn't answer. The vision of his body twisting into an Earthmouth flared into his mind like a dream twisting into a nightmare. His eyes wandered away from Hermann, to observe the gallery of the Hall of Rituals.

The Painted Door's panel remained, but it had become a blank slate. Valdemar and Hermann's sublime magnum opus had vanished, taken away to join an endless collection in a dead world orbiting a pitch-black star.

As for the other portraits . . .

Valdemar turned to his grandfather's painting—and the ghost within it. The echo of Pierre Dumont smiled at his grandson, oblivious to his clenched hands, gritted teeth, and furious glare.

"Valdemar, are you alright?" his grandfather asked with concern that almost looked sincere. "You shouldn't talk to strangers."

23

SHELLS

aldy," Liliane's voice called through the workshop door. "Valdy, are you inside?"

Valdemar stared at the ceiling while lying on his bare mattress. The bedsheet covered his grandfather's portrait in a corner of the room, hiding it from view.

"He is . . ." Hermann muttered. "But I . . . I don't think now is the time . . ."

"Nonsense!" Liliane replied. "Valdy, I made a cake. With vanilla mushrooms. Right out of the oven. Come out before it becomes cold!"

Liliane's words sounded like whispers to his ears, distant and nearly unintelligible. Valdemar's pots of blood-paints, the unused leftovers of the Silent King project, shook in a corner. Bubbles rose to the surface as if an invisible fire boiled the substance.

"Valdy, talk to me. You can tell me everything, you know that? I swear I won't judge. It will make you feel better."

The paint burst out of the pots and climbed on the nearest wall like aggressive moss. Its color changed from red to green and black and yellow, a twisted chaos echoing Valdemar's own emotion.

"He . . . he needs time," Hermann whispered, so low Valdemar barely heard him. "To think. He is wounded . . ."

"That's exactly why we can't leave him alone, Hermann."

"Sometimes . . . The only cure for woe . . . is time, Liliane. He needs time in his lair . . . to lick his wounds. To figure it out. Only then will he . . . let us in. When he comes out . . . we will be here."

A short silence followed.

"I . . ." Liliane cleared her throat. "We will come back later, Valdy. Please . . . don't do anything stupid, alright? Be safe."

"Friend?" It was Iren this time. "You're still in your room?"

Valdemar turned on his side and stared at the left wall. The paint covered it entirely now, like an infectious growth taking over the room centimeter by centimeter. The chaotic colors had assembled into a stable form; that of a twisted, ghastly tree with eyes for leaves and flesh for bark. His magic had gone wild, letting his subconscious guide the design.

"You know I could unlock this door if I wanted, right? Someone will if you don't give us a sign. Liliane is worried you're going to hang yourself or something."

What would that change? Considering Valdemar's regeneration, it probably wouldn't stick.

Iren sighed, too loudly for it to be natural. "Hermann didn't give me all the details, but enough to figure it out on my own. He thinks you need to be alone for a while to digest what you learned and that we should respect your privacy. I would be tempted to agree, but somehow I think your mood will only get worse the longer you stay alone."

Valdemar doubted that. He had already hit the well's bottom, when depression had filled the void anger had left in his heart. He didn't even struggle to escape in his dreams either.

Iren waited a moment for an answer. Valdemar sensed him looking around beyond the door, checking if anyone listened. "I know what you're going through," Iren said. "More than you know."

No, he didn't.

"I don't need telepathy to know what you're thinking, friend." Another pause. Hesitation. "You know, when mothers don't want a child, they usually go to a biomancer. One spell and they're purged. Some sorcerers though . . . don't take money as payment. Especially when one of the parents isn't human at all."

The flesh tree spasmed, the painted yellow eyes looking in all directions. Black pigments gathered on the bloody bark, like the bud of a dreadful flower.

"I was born in a lab, Valdemar," Iren confessed. "A biomancer extracted my stillborn, half-formed fetus and perfected it into a 'viable specimen.' Once he had learned everything of value about shapeshifting by the time I reached maturity, he thanked me for my 'contribution to science' and forgot I existed."

The black paint turned into an armless hand with a yellow eye for a palm. The clawed fingers fidgeted on the wall, as if trying to tear through the invisible barrier between its two-dimensional reality and its creator.

"The reason I'm saying this . . ." Iren struggled to find his words. "Look, whatever you were born for, it doesn't matter. I've been so many people over the years, I forgot my original appearance. Boy, girl, old, young, I don't keep a face for long. If being Valdemar Verney is too painful or sorrowful . . . just become someone else. Someone who feels better."

The black hand slowly emerged from the wall, its fingers dragging it across the floor.

"I've said my piece," Iren said with a sigh. "You don't owe your gramps anything, friend. Not even your name."

The living hand collapsed into a puddle of black paint, and the flesh tree bore another fruit.

By now, the paint covered the ceiling and half the walls. The tree of flesh shared the room with a pitch-black sky full of colorful stars orbiting around a pure blue sphere. The Mask of the Nightwalker faced the ghastly picture on the right wall, like the Whitemoon glaring at the surface of the world. Painted creatures crawled all around the workshop, from shapeless green blobs no larger than a clenched fist to pale white moths with eyes on their wings.

Someone knocked on the door, and Frigga's voice came through. "My dear Valdemar, I cannot help but notice you are missing our modeling meetings," she said with a chuckle. "Unless you expect me to complete my portrait myself?"

The painted creatures lived short lives, but each new generation lasted longer than the previous one. One survived for half an hour before collapsing into lifeless pigments.

"Fine, if you won't do me the courtesy of answering, I shan't be polite either." The dark elf dropped her mask of playfulness. "I don't like you. You have a certain talent for painting and sorcery, but frankly, I don't find you particularly interesting. You're bland and forgettable."

A moth landed on the painted Earth, tainting its blue waters with thick black blood.

"However, your petulant behavior saddens my dear Liliane. She worries for you more than everyone else in this Institute combined, and I believe her pity is wasted on you. I am truly tempted to enter your dreams and put back some positivity in that empty skull of yours."

It would cost her if she tried. All Valdemar dreamed of last night was of the well and the hungry maw waiting at the bottom. When the nightmares came, he hadn't fought them back.

"Your new defenses won't stop me if I try to get in," she said. "Don't think I haven't noticed what you're doing in your sleep. I don't know what you intend to do with that trap of yours, but it won't ensnare me."

Good. It wasn't meant for her anyway.

"In any case, get out of that room before I drag you off from it. Your petty nightmares will look like childish fantasies compared to what I shall show you."

The paint had claimed every inch of the room, except the right wall. The Mask of the Nightwalker exercised a counterforce and channeled a power that rivaled Valdemar's own. Painted landscapes of alien worlds, magical glyphs, and chaotic maelstroms stopped at a circle of nothingness around the Stranger artifact, unable to cross the invisible barrier. Even the moth swarm flying around the room couldn't touch the mask.

Valdemar sensed a connection forming through the Blood between the stone floor beneath the paint and the world outside. A surge of magic, powerful and yet nearly imperceptible, created a bridge between the workshop and another place. Valdemar couldn't sense the point of origin, but he did detect the undead sorcerer traveling through it.

His painted field waited for the last moment and then pushed back.

Valdemar expected Lord Och to force his way through the magical cocoon, but he instead redirected his spell through the right wall, teleporting right in front of the Mask of the Nightwalker. The switch took less than a second, so swiftly that the Dark Lord's apprentice was convinced he had planned it from the start.

"Nice try," Lord Och said with satisfaction. "If I were a few centuries younger, I might have fallen for it. Still, what kind of unruly student attempts to prank their teacher?"

"You intended to teleport behind me without warning, Lord Och," Valdemar said as he rose from his mattress to salute the Dark Lord. "I strongly suspect that you enjoy startling people."

"And you would be correct." The lich glanced at the painted land-scapes all around the room, and at the artificial moths flying in the air. He raised his hand, with one of the insects landing on his index finger. "And here I thought you were wallowing in self-pity, doing nothing all day."

"I work or paint when I feel down," Valdemar admitted. "It distracts me."

"A productive way to deal with loss, albeit not the healthiest one," Lord Och said, the painted moth dissipating into colored smoke. "What a curious innovation, this room . . ."

His reaction surprised Valdemar. "You have never seen anything like this?"

"I have my suspicions about what you did, but I admit I never saw pictomancy used this way." Lord Och smirked, baleful light shining through his skeletal eyeholes. "You attempted to emulate the Nahemoths by creating your own demiplane."

Valdemar nodded. Truthfully, he was pleased with the lich's response. Considering his age, surprising him was a victory in itself. "When I saw Hermann create painted creatures during our fight with the derros, I immediately thought of the Nahemoths."

These creatures gave birth to lesser Qlippoths by shaping their essence through their demiplane. Since Valdemar had mixed his own blood with the pigments used to create the Painted Door, he had quickly realized that he could use them to turn an area of space into an extension of him-self. He had let his subconscious direct the growth of this "painted field" inch by inch.

The more space he had claimed, the easier it had been to manifest magical constructs from the paint. They were extensions of his subcon-scious, paint and sorcery granted a simulacrum of physical form; they weren't meant to exist in the physical reality, making them fragile. Rather than force reality to accept these constructs, Valdemar had turned a small corner of the world into an extension of himself, making his creations more "real" inside it.

The mere fact that Hermann hadn't needed this infrastructure to gen-erate a tide of painted snakes spoke volumes about his talent.

Valdemar also hoped that this Painted Field could serve as an external dreamscape since oneiromancy didn't come easily to him. Since he failed to create a sanctuary in his dreams, he would build one in the physical world instead. Frigga could boast as much as she wanted, her reaction had shown Valdemar that he was on the right track.

Valdemar once thought the nightmares plaguing him were mere repressed memories. The Silent King's visions had shown him that something far more sinister was at work, and he needed to improve his defenses. Were his nightmares even his own?

Lord Och sounded very pleased with his apprentice's progress. "I knew introducing you to Hermann would yield excellent results. And of course, since the Painted Door could open rifts between two dimensions, I suppose you intended to experiment with summoning next? Maybe open a path to Earth?"

Valdemar glared at his mentor. "You *knew*," he spat.

"Of course I did."

"Then why am I still alive?" Valdemar asked with a frown. "Why didn't you sacrifice me, like my own grandfather wanted to?"

Lord Och gave him a curious look. "You believed the Stranger's words?"

"I didn't want to, but . . . I had to check." And when he confronted his grandfather's portrait, the echo inside entered another cognitive loop. Maybe it had forgotten the original memories, or the truth was too difficult to bear. "I created this room to understand myself, to try to figure out if the Painted Door would have worked if my blood hadn't been used as fuel. But now it's all around me, I can notice the Orgone in the air. Only summoned creatures produce such an amount, and I belong to two worlds through my mother."

"Partly," Lord Och said before glancing at the blackened Earth painted on the ceiling. "Your lineage does bind our two planes together, but other factors are at play in your peculiar abilities."

ABOMINATION.

The Silent King's condemnation flared inside Valdemar's mind alongside the vision that came with it, the one where he had seen himself transforming into a monster. The summoner glanced at his veins and the red blood flowing through them.

He had always suspected his paternal grandfather's cult had experimented on him. He had mistaken his regeneration for a mere body enhancement, instead of the symptom of something far more sinister. Had this obliviousness just been mere naïveté? Valdemar had always brushed off questions about his past, even his own. Maybe he had known the truth all along but refused to accept it. It had taken a Stranger's mental assault to finally make him reexamine his life.

Or perhaps his thoughts weren't fully his own. Maybe his two grandfathers had set instructions in his mind while he was in the womb, to ensure he would fulfill their ultimate goal when the time came.

Thick black blood poured out of his veins, while eyes and mouths tore out his skin to reveal the inhuman face underneath.

Whatever that goal was.

"Lord Och," he asked feebly, "am I a monster?"

"Do you remember what I told you, apprentice, when you asked me who you were?"

Valdemar's jaw clenched. "That I was the only one who could tell who I was."

"Young Iren spoke with wisdom," the lich said, blatantly admitting to spying on his apprentice from afar. "Whether you are a monster is up to you, young man. You are who you choose to be."

A man or an Earthmouth then, Valdemar thought grimly. He had asked the Silent King how he could lead mankind to Earth, and the Stranger had answered his question literally. The summoner should have also added that he wanted to survive the experience and see that world for himself.

"If you want to sacrifice yourself, I will not stop you," Lord Och said. "Though it will be a waste and many will weep. Your grandfather didn't use an Earthmouth to enter our world, so why should we need one to reach his own?"

Because that method would work for certain. Valdemar had been bred for this purpose since the moment he was born.

"Why would I sacrifice you, when I *know* we shall eventually succeed with another method that won't cost you your life?" Lord Och asked mirthfully. "If I still needed to eat, I would say that I intend to have my cake and eat it too. The long-term benefits of your survival will outweigh the short-term gains of an interdimensional Earthmouth."

Valdemar shivered at his cold, brutal logic . . . but somehow he couldn't help but feel relieved. It might have sounded selfish, but he wanted to see Earth with his own eyes too.

His grandfather . . . Pierre had brainwashed him since his childhood with stories about his homeworld, the way a farmer fattened a snail for the slaughter. He had sown the seeds of Valdemar's devotion, hoping to reap it in the form of a sacrifice for his own rotten selfishness.

But . . . even if the dreamer wasn't a good person, did that invalidate the dream?

Mankind needed to see the light again. To gaze at the stars and the sun as Valdemar had in the Silent King's realm. The universe was a strange and dangerous place, but also beautiful beyond words. His people, his friends, deserved better than a stone ceiling.

Valdemar glanced with shame at his workshop door, remembering the individuals who knocked on it. In truth, while he was thankful for their support . . . he didn't know how to deal with it.

In his childhood, Valdemar had usually run back to his grandfather for protection whenever he felt sad. Now the mere memory soured his mood, and he had long grown used to isolation anyway. What was he supposed to do, share his dark thoughts and foul mood with others? Spread the pain around? Rant about how his grandfather, the person whose dream he had dedicated his *entire life* to, had raised him as a mere tool?

Above all things, Valdemar hated being pitied.

What he needed was time to process everything, to strengthen his mind. Sorrow and anger could only affect him if he let them be.

"I suggest that you embrace undeath," Lord Och happily suggested. "It did wonders for my good mood, and it will certainly improve your looks."

Valdemar ignored his mentor's jab. "You could clone me," he suggested. Biomancers often used that procedure for rich patrons, to cultivate fresh organs and replace the original's aging parts. "Create a soulless sacrifice."

"It will not work."

"How do you know?"

"Because I already tried the day we met." Lord Och chuckled as his apprentice gave him an offended glare. "My apprentice, you leave your genetic material everywhere, what did you expect? Between us, I always like to have a spare apprentice or two."

Valdemar shuddered, as he remembered the Dark Lord's attempts to duplicate the Pleromians. "Why didn't it work then?"

"Two reasons." The lich joined his hands. "First, Earthmouths need the soul of a *willing* martyr to function. This is why it is such an honor and we do not use, say, prisoners and political enemies for it. The creation ritual does not function if the sacrifice does not consent to it, whether out of despair or altruism."

Valdemar thought about the vision he'd had—and the dead look in his illusory double's eyes. *Despair,* he thought, *born of betrayal.*

"Second, your peculiar biology makes cloning you a hazardous prospect, as testing can attest. When I tried to duplicate you, your clone's regeneration went . . ." Lord Och hesitated. "Haywire."

ABOMINATION.

"It mutated?" Valdemar asked, although he wasn't sure if he even wanted to know.

"All I will say is, if you ever lose a body part, I strongly suggest that you reattach it as quickly as you can. Or throw it at your nearest foe." Lord Och chuckled to himself. "Come to think of it, we should explore this idea in the future."

Valdemar crossed his arms. "Speaking of the future, where do we go from now, Lord Och? You asked me to help Hermann with the Painted Door project and we completed it."

"And the experience proved enlightening for all parties involved," Lord Och mused. "You are a Scholar of Pleroma, young Valdemar. You are free to take your research wherever you want, and I suspect you already know your next destination."

Yes, he did. The Silent King had shown him the path.

"In my visions, I saw a derro with a crown building a portal," Valdemar admitted. "Probably King Otto Blutang. From what we gathered so far, it's highly probable that the derros summoned my grandfather's unit to Underland with their technology."

"Do you intend to ask the derro king to share his discoveries with us?" Lord Och asked mirthfully. "Considering the troubles in Astaphanos, I'm sure the empress would agree to a diplomatic mission."

In all likelihood, it would end with Valdemar's brain in a jar and his skin used as a disguise by some mad dwarf infiltrator. "Maybe the English parts of the diary hold information about the tunnels where my grandfather landed," said the summoner. "You could examine them. Maybe the derros left hints."

The Dark Lord scoffed. "*I* could examine them? Are you offloading your duties to me, apprentice? Or have you given up on fulfilling your dream?"

Was that dream even his own?

Valdemar still thought mankind deserved a world with an open sky, but he wasn't certain if he was the best person to find it anymore.

His family's cult had worked for a bloodthirsty Stranger. If they wanted to reach Earth so desperately and created Valdemar to achieve their goal, then it served their patron's goals somehow. Maybe the Stranger wanted to access Earth for its foul purposes.

Valdemar was afraid. Afraid not to be in control, or worse, to accidentally poison the perfect world he had dreamed of. "Lord Och, is my mind compromised? Do I want to reach Earth because I actually want it, or because an instinct embedded in my blood is pushing me to?"

The lich remained eerily silent.

Valdemar sighed. "I'm the only one who can answer that question, is that it?"

"Keep building that Painted Dreamscape," the Dark Lord replied without really answering. "It will help you figure out the truth."

A pointer was better than nothing.

"Locating the site where your grandsire appeared is a good idea," the Dark Lord said. "But as I warned you before, the tunnels in question are dangerous. Even more so now that your family's cult is active once more and that the derros are on the offensive again. Thankfully, the combat-magic teacher I had in mind has agreed to take you under his wing."

"Which Master will it be?" Valdemar asked, banishing his darker thoughts from his mind. Edwin and Loctis appeared to be the most talented battle mages in the Institute from what he had seen.

"My chosen instructor does not serve me, or anyone else for that matter," Lord Och replied. "You will have to travel to the Domain of Sabaoth to meet with him."

Sabaoth? It made sense. This Domain was the Empire's bulwark against derro invasions and monsters wandering out of the unexplored depths of Underland, a fortress of stone, steel, and magma pits.

However . . .

"Wasn't I supposed to stay at the Institute until the wererat was apprehended or slain?" Valdemar asked with a frown.

Lord Och brushed off his worries. "You will travel to the safest place in the Empire under good escort. Young Marianne is making her way back to us as we speak, albeit short a retainer. I believe a stay in Sabaoth will also help her sharpen her blade."

Marianne is returning? Valdemar was eager to see her. She had investigated the Verney family far enough to detect a hidden cultist, so maybe she had found something interesting. *I need to know the truth,* Valdemar thought. *The full truth. About who I am, and my purpose.* "Who is this instructor?"

The lich's ghastly smile sent shivers down his spine.

"It is time," the Dark Lord said, "that I introduce you to my previous apprentice."

2 4

SWORD & SORCERY

The wererat's guts had spilled all over the dead-end alley, his poisoned blood reddening the stone floor of the city of Pleroma. Marianne resisted the urge to pinch her nose from the foul smell. Her blood-tracker burned against her skin as if she had finally completed her hunt. And yet, even a cursory glance at the creature at her feet disabused her of the notion. The hunt had only begun.

Marianne had followed the blood-tracker's call as it guided her back to Lord Och's stronghold, and found the city on lockdown. The ancient lich hadn't taken any chances upon learning that a wererat was after his apprentice and restricted access to the Earthmouths. After reporting her return to the Knights and requesting an escort, Marianne had let the blood-tracker guide them through the narrow alleys of the old town.

Rats were numerous in these poor suburbs, making the swordswoman quite paranoid. When the blood-tracker confirmed Shelley's presence in the area, Marianne and her reinforcements split up to close off the area and cover more ground.

The creature before her had jumped in without warning the moment she looked into the alley. The ambush had lasted mere seconds, with Marianne's blade gutting the beast like a fish. For a brief moment, the swordswoman thought she had finally avenged Bertrand.

But while the creature before her took elements from both a rat and a human, it was too gaunt and small to be Shelley. The rodent nose was half-formed, with only one arm having claws and the other unmutated.

The beast wore rags smelling of cheap fungi alcohol, and Marianne noticed a cup with a few coins hidden behind the corpse. She examined the face more closely and found it vaguely familiar.

I tossed you a few coins near the market street, Marianne remembered. The homeless man had white hair rather than fur then. She had never paid this man much attention in the past and didn't even know his name. Yet the sight of his mutated corpse filled her with anger. If she had caught up to Shelley earlier in the tunnels, she might have saved him. *Each day I fail to bring the rat to justice, someone else pays the price,* she thought grimly.

The noblewoman sensed a presence above her with her psychic sight and instantly readied her sword. She looked at the roofs surrounding the claustrophobic alley, half-expecting another wererat to fall upon her.

Instead, a pitch-black bat descended upon the alley. The animal was no larger than a fist, but its body radiated an aura that betrayed its true nature. A crimson shroud of power surrounded the critter as it landed next to the dead wererat. The flesh expanded, the fur receding to reveal the brown skin underneath. The wings turned into black robes, the face shifted into an old woman's visage with piercing black eyes.

Marianne lowered her sword upon recognizing the witch. "Master Malherbe."

"Reynard," the Institute's animancer replied with a dry voice while she examined the corpse. Amie Malherbe didn't care for common courtesy. "When did this happen?"

"Minutes ago," Marianne replied as the Master bent down to examine the corpse. "Did you receive my messenger bat? About the Beast Plague variant?"

Amie confirmed with a sharp nod, before putting her thumb into the wound the rapier left. Once she had soaked her nail with blood, the animancer licked it.

Marianne winced at the sight but didn't try to stop the Master. Amie Malherbe was the Institute's foremost expert on animancy and a talented biomancer. If anyone had developed an immunity to the Beast Plague, it would be her. "I used this device to find him," Marianne said as she showed Amie her blood-tracker. "I thought it would lead me to Shelley."

"It did," the animancer replied as she licked her lips, not even glancing at the tracker. "Your cultist's blood courses through his veins like an infection. Along with something else."

Marianne struggled to suppress a sigh of frustration. Shelley could have bitten dozens of victims by now, turning all of them into decoys. Had this been his true goal all along when he developed his plague? To use the infected as a smokescreen to cover his tracks? "Something else, you said?"

"Blood from another source," Amie replied as she summarily removed the victim's rags to examine him; pants first. Marianne couldn't help but blush. "But not from any creature I've encountered. I would have said a vampire, but more ancient, primeval."

Marianne's heart skipped a beat. "A mutated vampire?"

"Maybe." Amie rolled the corpse over, revealing a half-formed tail growing between the cheeks and bruises on the left ankle. "Could be your retainer's blood."

Marianne hadn't dared to raise the possibility out loud. Her last letter had included a demand that the Institute could look for an antidote if possible. A request that had gone unanswered.

The swordswoman didn't know how to take the news. On one hand, finding Shelley meant locating Bertrand as well. But on the other hand, why would the deranged cultist need her retainer's blood for his plague?

Or he was looking for another substance inside Bertrand's veins, Marianne guessed, as the memory of the black blood dripping from the ceiling in Verney Castle came to mind.

Master Malherbe had reached the same conclusion. "From what you said in your letter, the original substance has powerful mutagenic properties," she said. "Too powerful. Your retainer's blood acts as a diluted substitute. Less potent but more malleable."

Amie pointed at the bruises on the victim's ankles. Some scab remained at their center, the remnant of a wound. "Look."

Marianne squinted. "Looks like a rat bite to me."

"A *normal* rat's bite," Amie pointed out.

Somehow, that made it even worse.

Shelley's rodent thralls could spread the wererat plague on their own. Marianne glanced at the streets beyond the alley, watching rodents hop out of a trash can. How many of them carried the plague inside them?

This complicated things. If Shelley found a way to infect normal rats with his blood plague, he might not even be in the city at all. Pleroma was the only city in the Domain of Paraplex, surrounded by foul bogs and marshes. The wererat could be hiding in the swamps, far away from civilization while letting his swarm do his dirty work. If he had spread his rodents over a large area, it would make it extremely difficult for the blood-tracker to find him.

Her curiosity satisfied, Amie pulled the corpse over her shoulder. Bile and blood spilled on her cloak, but the animancer didn't even seem to notice. "I need time to study it," she said. "Knowing Lord Och, he will ask me to suspend my projects until I develop a vaccine."

"What about those already infected?" Marianne asked with a frown. "What about Bertrand? Master Malherbe, do you think you could cure him?"

"I would need to examine him first, but if this is indeed his blood I tasted . . ."

Master Malherbe shook her head, and Marianne's heart shattered in her chest.

"Why?" the noblewoman asked, her voice breaking. She was no biomancer, but she had seen their work. "You can reshape life, transform yourself into an animal."

"I cannot stay in an animal shape for too long, Reynard," Amie replied. "If I do, I will stop being a transformed human and truly become a mindless animal. This is the same principle for the Beast Plague and whatever affected your vampire. If allowed to take root, that kind of magical virus bonds with the victim on a primal level. The effects can be suppressed with biomancy treatment and constant medication, but the disease only sleeps. It never goes away."

"But you could make a suppression treatment?" Marianne refused to accept Bertrand and Shelley's victims were beyond salvation. "Could they live a normal life again?"

"Maybe, if they follow a lifelong biomancy treatment that few can afford." Amie shrugged. "It will be kinder to kill them."

"It would be crueler to kill them when there is hope for an alternative." Even if Marianne would rather have a cure, she could live with this imperfect solution. She would pay Bertrand's treatment out of her own pocket and find a way to help Shelley's other victims.

Her honor demanded it. It was her fault that the cultist had escaped so far. *Is it?* Marianne wondered as she glanced at the gutted corpse. She had a responsibility in failing to catch Shelley so far, but the cultist moved unnaturally fast. As far as Marianne knew, he was on foot while she had the benefit of a riding beetle. He shouldn't have reached Pleroma before her, let alone managed to infect anyone so quickly.

Either Shelley learned teleportation in record time or Marianne had overlooked a critical clue.

"Master Malherbe, how did you locate us?" Marianne asked the animancer as they walked out of the alley to meet with the Knights. "Can you track the wererats by smell?"

"I was looking for a smell, but not that one." Amie sneered in disgust. "That stench is all over the city."

"Valdemar's?" Certainly Lord Och wouldn't be so foolish to let him out of the fortress while a Verney cultist was on the loose?

"No," Amie replied. "It's similar, but more intense. Purer. Fouler. It lurked around the Institute, like a mole rat looking for a way in. It couldn't get past the magical defenses, but it startled the animals."

Marianne's thoughts turned to the Vernburg demiplane. Could it have been the Nahemoth acting? She ruled out that possibility. The creature that lurked around the Institute had acted with too much subtlety. Could it be the strange, cloudlike entity that was summoned beneath Verney Castle?

Whatever that creature was, its goal was clear.

"It was after Valdemar," Marianne pointed out the obvious. And considering how it appeared in Paraplex at the same time as the first wererat infection, Shelley and the entity might be acting in concert. "It will try to get in again."

"It won't," Amie replied with a shrug. "But Lord Och wants us to deal with it anyway, before it makes an attempt."

A sensible decision. Even if neither Shelley nor any summoned Qlippoth could enter the fortress, they might start attacking its staff whenever they ventured out. The longer Shelley was left free to act, the more trouble he would cause.

As for Valdemar himself . . .

Marianne looked up at the shadow of the Institute overseeing the city. The fortress now looked like a prison to her, jailing the child of a Stranger with terrible potential. Her duty demanded that she report to Lord Och and let him make the final decision about his apprentice.

But . . . What if the lich was playing with forces too dangerous even for him? Lord Hagith already suspected Valdemar of being more than he looked, and the more word of Shelley's activities would spread, the more the Verney heir would gather attention. What would happen when the Church of the Light figured out what Marianne had learned and called for Valdemar's head? Surely Shelley had to know that his murderous antics would endanger his precious Red Grail . . .

Marianne suddenly froze in place, causing Amie to raise an eyebrow at her.

"That's what he wants," the noblewoman muttered as she examined the wererat. "He knows he can't get in."

She had thought that Shelley intended to thin out the Institute's defenses by starting a plague and stretching them thin. But threatening a Dark Lord was a daunting task, and Och had access to near-limitless resources and manpower. As long as Valdemar enjoyed the lich's protection, Shelley and his patron would never get within a meter of him. But as Lord Hagith had shown, the last Verney couldn't escape his family's shadow. The more atrocities Shelley committed in the cult's name, the more news would spread. Inquisitors and imperial citizens would suspect Valdemar's involvement. The alienated sorcerer would become an even greater object of distrust, isolated and vulnerable. And from what little Marianne had seen of him, Valdemar might even decide to confront his family's last cultist to get rid of the stain for good.

Shelley wasn't trying to get inside the Institute.

He was trying to lure Valdemar out of it.

Marianne's apartment felt colder without Bertrand.

After she made her report to Lord Och and received her newest mission, the lich had offered her a golem servant to replace her retainer. Marianne had politely refused. If anything, using a mindless thrall in Bertrand's place felt like an insult to his memory.

She still remembered their last discussion before leaving Pleroma. Bertrand had mused that his mistress would ruin herself in tea shops without him, and now that she had to prepare her brew herself, the noblewoman realized he had been correct. Her drink tasted bitter to her lips and burned her tongue.

Sitting at her table, the noblewoman gazed at the hedge maze beyond her window with longing. After spending days on the road with little but sorrow to show for it, stopping to rest felt odd to her. Lord Och had given her a day off before her transfer to Sabaoth for her new mission, but Marianne couldn't focus while her first job remained incomplete.

She had begged the Dark Lord to reconsider his decision, asking him to give her a task force to hunt down Shelley, Bertrand, and whatever creature had escaped the castle, or at least keep Valdemar safely inside the Institute for the moment. The lich had denied her wishes.

"The forces after my apprentice are relentless," the Dark Lord had told her. "The wererat is but a thrall to a higher power, easily replaceable. I will not always be here to protect my apprentice, and he cannot spend his existence inside these walls until the day he dies . . . if he can even perish. He has to grow strong enough to defend himself. Besides, if you stay with him, young Marianne, you might get to conclude your hunt."

Yes, she would. If Shelley dared to attack Valdemar on her watch, Marianne would greet him with steel and fire.

And there were no better warriors than Verneys' chosen combat instructor. Even Bertrand had suggested that she go to Sabaoth to perfect her swordsmanship, and Lord Och implied that his former apprentice would gladly give her some tutelage too. And while Marianne hated to admit it, she did need to become stronger.

If she had been a better fighter, she might have saved Bertrand.

Marianne heard a knock on her apartment door. "You may come in," she said, "I left the door open." She had expected his visit.

The noblewoman listened quietly as her guest opened her door, closed it behind him, and explored her home. His steps were hesitant, and she heard him briefly stop to examine the crests in her training room. *It's his first time entering a woman's private quarters*, Marianne guessed. *He feels out of place.*

When the smell of tea lured him to her, Marianne had set a second cup for him. However, his eyes paid more attention to her novel collection.

"*The Leaden Moon*?" Valdemar Verney asked as he sat across the table. "It's not the author's best."

"I haven't finished it," Marianne admitted. "I read halfway through before I left the Institute. But I do admit *The Clockstopper's Dilemma* is my favorite so far."

"You know the publisher is working on a picture book version?" Marianne nodded slowly, making Valdemar smile. "You're not a casual reader, but a true fan."

Marianne chuckled in embarrassment. "I like pulp novels, even if others look down on them."

"Have you read *The Pirate King*? It's not the best novel out there, but I think it would suit your tastes."

"I'll check." *I didn't know he liked to read novels,* Marianne thought as she stared at her visitor's face. Valdemar clearly hadn't slept in days, and though his smile was genuine, she noticed the wariness in his gaze. He had changed since their last encounter; he dressed like a scholar and seemed more confident.

Above all else, Valdemar Verney looked human.

When she outright asked Lord Och about her theory about his apprentice's origins, the lich had simply chuckled and said, "*Stranger things happened in the past.*" But the way he answered, like a teacher congratulating a child for giving the right answer . . . the noblewoman knew she had guessed correctly.

Valdemar shifted in his seat, and Marianne quickly realized she had been staring at him in silence for several seconds. "My apologies," she excused herself. "My mind wandered off."

"I know the feeling," he replied as he examined his teacup. "You learn so many earth-shattering truths in too short of a time span, and you struggle to process them all."

Marianne looked at him with compassion. "Lord Och told me about your grandfather," she admitted. The lich hadn't given her all the details, but enough to fill the many holes in her investigation. "I'm so sorry for you."

"For what? You weren't here when I was born."

Marianne glanced through the window and back at the hedge maze. "I won't say our situations are the same, but believe me when I say that I understand what you are going through. I too was born a tool, only valuable for my body."

Valdemar finally picked up his cup, letting it warm his fingers. "For what purpose?"

"To make children," Marianne admitted. "Since I was born a girl, my father decided that my only purpose in life would be to strengthen our family's political ties and give him a grandchild. A *male* grandchild, worthy of our ancestral blade."

"Since you're here, I assume your family's plans didn't work any better than my own."

Except Valdemar's "father" looked more determined to get back in his child's life than Marianne's sire. Should she even tell him? His faith in his maternal grandfather, who he admired, was already shattered. Learning about his paternal parentage might drive him over the edge.

"They didn't," Marianne replied, thinking of Jérôme. "Though it cost me greatly."

"It's never easy to stand up for yourself," Valdemar replied. He should know, he had been sent to jail for going against imperial regulations. "For all it's worth, I don't believe gender should determine your worth. I can't believe sexism still exists in a country ruled by an immortal empress."

"You can get away with many things with immense arcane power."

"I've seen that with Lord Och." Valdemar sipped his tea. He appeared to enjoy it more than Marianne. "He is sending us to Sabaoth. To meet with Lord Bethor."

"I heard," Marianne replied before locking eyes with him. "I swear by my rapier, nothing will happen to you so long as I am with you." She thought her words would reassure him, but they only made the sorcerer tense.

"I don't want your coddling. I want the truth."

Of course he did. Marianne knew he would confront her about her investigation the moment she returned to the Institute.

"Where is your butler?" Valdemar asked, making Marianne wince. His eyes immediately widened in surprise. "Is he . . ."

"No," Marianne replied with a sigh. "Not yet."

His expression turned sympathetic. "Is there anything I can do?"

"I don't know." Amie didn't think much could be done for Bertrand, but if Valdemar had inherited even a part of his "father's" power . . . perhaps he could do the impossible.

"Lady Reynard—"

"Call me Marianne," she interrupted him. "I will act as your bodyguard for the Dark Lord knows how long. We might as well work on a first-name basis."

Valdemar processed her words for a moment as he finished his cup. "Very well," he said. "Marianne, what happened? What did you find? What happened to your retainer?"

"Do you truly wish to know?" she asked him in return. His answer was a slow but firm nod. "What has Lord Och told you?"

"Only details about that wererat cultist." Valdemar's scowl deepened. "Did he forbid you from sharing your findings with me?"

"No, he did not." Though he did suggest that Marianne wait until after they reached the Domain of Sabaoth. "But you already suffered mental scars. I'm not certain I should add more to them."

"Do you remember what you told me on the day of your departure?"

Of course she did. "That I would share what I learned. That you were entitled to learn about your origins. I still believe in my words."

"And I appreciate you for it," Valdemar said, making her chuckle. "Marianne, I have been lied to since the moment I was born. I'm done with it. Even if the truth hurts, it will still be better than ignorance. And I can't help you with your problems if I don't understand them."

Marianne blinked. "My problems?"

"You said it yourself, I might help with whatever happened to your retainer." Valdemar smiled at her confused reaction. "What, you thought I would refuse? I will still try to help even if you don't tell me everything."

Marianne observed the strange sorcerer for a moment. "Why?"

Valdemar shrugged. "Why not?"

"Because whether I like it or not, I am part of the system that imprisoned you," Marianne pointed out. "And you would gain nothing from it. Bertrand didn't even like you."

"You got me out of that jail, didn't you?" Valdemar shook his head. "Lord Och believes all interactions are self-interested, but I don't want to play that game. You have been honest and straightforward with me since day one and it is reason enough for me to help you. Even if your retainer disliked me."

Marianne thought back over her investigations and the people she'd met. From Lord Hagith to Captain Léopold, every offer of help came with strings attached. Even Inquisitor Penhew only accepted an interview in an attempt to convince her to have Valdemar slain, a position that Marianne had derided at first but had almost started believing in too.

And yet, Marianne couldn't detect any hint of deceit in the last Verney's eyes. He truly meant everything he said.

Lord Och had told her his apprentice hadn't hesitated to defend Institute personnel from a derro attack in Sabaoth. Even on the first day they met, he had willingly shared information about his research with her in the hope they would improve mankind's chances to settle in another world.

Valdemar Verney had a good heart.

Others would call him an idealistic fool, but not Marianne. If anything, she saw a little of herself in him. No matter the reasons behind his birth or what disaster he might bring, Valdemar Verney deserved a chance to life. Judging him on his origins rather than his actions simply felt wrong. Even if Marianne might end up killing him to protect others . . . she would give the man a chance to prove he could avert his fate.

"Valdemar." Marianne cleared his throat. "I don't know what the future holds in store for us, but I can promise you one thing."

The summoner listened in silence.

"We will uncover the truth," Marianne swore. "About who you are. Whatever the obstacles thrown at us."

"You shouldn't make promises you aren't certain of delivering," he said with amusement. "I guess I should make one myself, to make us even. I swear, however impossible it might sound, that we will save your retainer. And more to the point, as long as you have my back, I will have yours." Valdemar offered Marianne his hand.

After a moment, the noblewoman shook it. His fingers felt warm against her own, his grip was as solid as steel. A deal had been struck, and woe to those who would try to break it.

"So," Valdemar asked after breaking the handshake. "Where do we start?"

And so, Marianne recounted her case from the very beginning to her new partner.

2 5

CASE REVIEW

The eyes were looking at him through the window. The walls of Lord Och's fortress kept them away, but as they infested the Domain's ceiling like moss, he couldn't escape them.

"Val . . . mar . . ."

They had watched him since the moment he was born, though he couldn't see them then. He thought his grandfather's death had left him orphaned, but in truth, he had never been alone in his life. Not for a single second. His family had followed him everywhere.

"Valde . . . mar?"

Valdemar looked away from the eyes outside and locked his gaze with a smaller pair of them.

"Valdemar?" Marianne asked him with concern. The teapot between them let out a small puff of steam. "Are you alright?"

"No," he replied, his throat dry. "Are you certain of it? About . . ." *About my father.*

"I can't be sure," Marianne admitted. "But it's the most likely explanation from the clues that I gathered so far. Shelley's facility and the . . . the clones inside point in that direction."

They cloned his mother.

They made a cup out of her bones.

Was his mother even the original Sarah? Had his two grandfathers cultivated her in a flask like a homunculus? Was *Valdemar* born inside a womb or a vat of glass? A piece of eldritch flesh wrapped in human skin? Maybe the derros weren't such pioneers after all.

Marianne had been true to her word. The investigator told him everything with unflinching bluntness, though she had looked more and more concerned as she went on. By the time she was halfway through recounting her case, Valdemar took everything in stoic silence. He simply couldn't muster the strength for emotional distress anymore.

He thought it would have been impossible to top the Silent King's revelations, that he had reached an emotional bottom. But as it turned out, you could always dig deeper.

"Val . . . mar?"

Valdemar blinked as he realized he had zoned out again. "I'm sorry," he apologized. "It's . . . a lot to take in."

"I understand." Marianne's eyes wandered to his hand, as if she considered taking it into her own. But she hesitated. Perhaps she thought it would be inappropriate? While they had agreed to work together, they weren't friends either. "We can continue later, if you need rest."

As if sleep would be any escape. If anything, Valdemar was afraid of slumber like never before. He would dream of the well again.

"When you visited the false Vernburg . . ." he rasped. "What hour was it?"

Marianne frowned. "I can't tell exactly. We arrived late and explored the village for a few hours until morning. Why are you asking?"

"I dreamed of you while you were away," Valdemar admitted. "I was at the bottom of a well, and you were looking down on me."

Marianne's curiosity turned to unnerving focus. "You were at the bottom?"

"And when I tried to reach you, the well collapsed on me."

His bodyguard digested the news in silence, her gaze thoughtful. "What's your sleeping schedule?" she asked, having reached the same conclusion.

"I have an irregular sleep cycle due to nightmares, but I usually go to bed late and wake up early," Valdemar admitted. "I have been dreaming of the well you saw since I was little. Sometimes I had nightmares of rats watching me from above or tossing me bones and meat."

"Shelley's rats, most likely," Marianne said, joining her hands. "So you have a mental connection to the Nahemoth trapped inside the well."

"If it *is* a Nahemoth," Valdemar pointed out. It would fit, but he was now considering another, darker possibility. "What do you know about oneiromancy?"

"I have a well-protected dreamscape, but oneiromancy is not one of my strong points," Marianne confessed. "I was only ever interested in defending my thoughts rather than invading others. I have started to research the subject after learning more about the Outer Darkness though."

"I couldn't learn the basics, because my dreamscape is dysfunctional. I haven't been able to shape my own dreams. Frigga and Lady Mathilde said it was because of my personality and subconscious thoughts, but now . . ." Valdemar glanced at the hedge maze beyond the window. "Now I wonder."

"From what I read in the Bestiary, the Primordial Dream shared by mankind is a self-defense mechanism created by sentient life to protect itself from the Qlippoths," Marianne said. Valdemar made a note to borrow and read that book later, if only to complete his own knowledge. "Maybe that's why? You can access the dream world as a human, but since you share a connection to the Qlippoths, the collective unconscious fights off your attempts to alter it."

"That," Valdemar said. "Or I have a fully functional dreamscape, but I don't materialize it in the Primordial Dream."

Marianne's eyes widened in shock. "The Vernburg village disappeared when you woke up from your nightmare."

Valdemar nodded. "Now the question is . . . do I have a connection to a Nahemoth and passively summon him when I dream, or is the thing at the bottom of the well my unconscious self-materializing the Qlippoth hamlet as a physical dreamscape?"

"What difference would it make?"

A big one. "In one case, I'm a mere summoning conduit, a living portal. In the other, my unconscious mind warps reality itself and births Qlippoths into existence."

Marianne didn't respond. Her expression became a blank mask as the implications dawned upon her.

Valdemar's laughter broke the silence.

It surprised him and startled Marianne too. For it was not laughter of joy, or even sadness. It was a laugh that burst out of his lips uncontrollably, like water overflowing out of a broken cistern. The kind of laugh that left the throat dry and the soul sickened.

"I mean, that's funny," Valdemar continued, unable to stop himself as he laughed maniacally between each sentence. "Frigga mocked me for having a defenseless, unremarkable dreamscape, but I conjured a whole town with Qlippoths as private security! They play humans in my head! Like me! If it's not my subconscious at work, I don't know what—"

A flash of anger passed over Marianne's face as she raised her voice. "Don't say that!"

Her sudden reaction startled Valdemar, the laughter dying in his throat. "Say what?" he asked.

"That you *play* human, instead of being one," Marianne said. "Because you *are* one."

"I'm not," Valdemar replied grimly. "Never was."

"A monster like Shelley is not human," Marianne insisted. "The creatures inside the Vernburg village aren't human. You might have inhuman origins and peculiar abilities, but you breathe like a man, behave like a man, eat like a man."

Shit like a man? Valdemar thought back on his grandfather's echo and how he had wished it could become the real man. "Even if a pictomancer made the perfect portrait of someone and breathed life into the pigments, it would still be a painting rather than the real thing."

But Marianne wouldn't back down. "But what if the portrait has a soul? If the copy has emotions and dreams, then its life has value."

"The inquisitors would say otherwise," Valdemar gazed down at his empty cup. He felt just as hollow. "Why am I even alive, Marianne? By imperial laws, you should have given me up to the inquisition or executed me yourself."

She frowned. "Inquisitor Penhew suggested that I execute you because you were too dangerous to live. That was before I visited Vernburg, and all that followed. If word of what I learned reached his ears, the Knights would hunt you down."

And for once Valdemar was tempted to agree with them. His very existence might serve as a portal for interdimensional monsters. Many had been executed for less.

"I am not a Knight," Marianne declared. "I will not execute people because they *might* threaten the empire, but only if they *do*."

Valdemar looked away to avoid her fiery gaze. Somehow the eyes outside seemed less oppressive. "I nearly killed you while *dreaming*."

"But I survived your nightmare, and you had no control over it. Besides, Lord Och wouldn't let you run around if you were a lost cause. Instead of dissecting you or transforming you into an Earthmouth, he tutors you. Why do you think so?"

Obvious. "Because he has plans for me."

"Because he thinks you can master your abilities." Marianne sighed. "A Master once told me that centuries of undeath had divorced Lord Och from human emotions. He plays with us like we're ants, because it amuses him. But when it comes to genuine threats? He is a supremely rational being. Many Dark Lords have come and gone over the centuries, but Lord Och was never dethroned. He has slain everyone who ever endangered him."

Valdemar couldn't help but snicker. "So you say he didn't kill me because I'm not that huge of a threat?"

"I trust Lord Och's ruthlessness and survival instincts. If he tutors you, it means he intends to exploit you in the long-term and he believes the risk is manageable."

That . . . that was the kind of cold logic Valdemar expected from the lich.

The summoner gathered his breath and tried to consider things rationally. He was not fully human. There was no denying it. After surviving multiple lightning bolts, he wondered if his regeneration would even let him die. The Qlippoths bent to his will; he could dream a village into existence and open doors to other worlds. The Stranger that masterminded his birth wanted him to serve some mysterious purpose he couldn't fathom yet.

Imperial safety demanded that he die.

But Lord Och knew all of this and yet decided to spare him. Though callous, the lich had accumulated centuries of experience and wisdom and seemed dedicated to protecting the empire's status quo; even if for purely selfish reasons.

Marianne had a point. If Valdemar were a lost cause, Lord Och would have killed him the moment he stepped inside the Institute. Instead, the lich cultivated his apprentice like a flower and encouraged him to seek answers on his own. And even though Valdemar was only half a man, he was close enough to humankind that inquisitors never identified his unholy origins.

There's hope for me, the summoner realized, though a cynical part of his mind told him hope could only carry you so far.

"But what if Och is *wrong*, Marianne?" Valdemar asked. "What if my dreams or my very existence cause a disaster, and I have to be put down for the good of everyone else?"

"If we can't find another solution . . ." Marianne glanced at the rapier attached to her belt. "Then yes, I will do what must be done. But it won't come to that."

"Hopefully not." Valdemar had too many things left to do. Too much to learn.

Where sadness once filled his heart, anger took over. He refused to be a pawn in someone else's game, whether his grandfather's, Lord Och's, or the Strangers'. No more. He would cut all the strings pulling him, and for that, he had to find them.

Marianne's expression softened. "To go back to our first topic of discussion . . . as far as I'm concerned, you're a human being."

"Half of one," Valdemar said with a dark chuckle. "At least I took more from my mother and only have two eyes."

"Is that supposed to be a reference to something?" Marianne asked. "If so, it's lost on me."

"Wait, haven't you taken an Elixir of True Sight?"

"No," she admitted. "I can request Lady Mathilde to make one if needed."

Lady Mathilde . . . she took the elixir and was close when the eyes all looked at me, Valdemar thought. *No way she didn't notice our interaction. Yet she said nothing.*

His thoughts turned to the private interaction between Och and Loctis. How they had cast a silence spell to prevent Valdemar from hearing anything. *Some of the Masters are in on it,* he thought. The Dark Lord had given them instructions.

Plots within plots, and he had to figure them all out. "Then you haven't seen the eyes outside," Valdemar said.

Her confused face told him everything. "I would like more details," Marianne said as she checked her teapot's temperature. "Do you want more tea?"

"With pleasure," Valdemar replied. "You prepared it well, even if it was your first time."

"Did I?" Marianne asked as she poured tea into their empty cups. "I'm relieved."

You're such an open book. It astonished Valdemar that this woman could fight a man-eating wererat in close quarters without flinching and then get embarrassed over something so trivial as making tea.

"Your expression gave it away," the summoner said while sipping the brew. "Between us, I could never afford this kind of tea. Too expensive."

"I let Bertrand deal with shopping duties." Marianne's gaze wandered to the hedge maze outside, her lips curving into a sorrowful scowl. "Master Malherbe doesn't think she can cure him."

Now it was Valdemar's turn to cheer her up. "Even if she's an expert, it's still just one person's opinion and she doesn't have the full picture. If we trust your theory, the same black blood runs through my veins. Maybe we could compare samples and find a cure."

"I hope so," she replied with a sad smile. "Do you have any idea what this blood belongs to?"

As a matter of fact, he did.

Valdemar spent the next minutes enlightening Marianne on the true nature of reality. To her credit, she took the news remarkably well. Valdemar guessed that after seeing the walls of Underland bleed beneath Verney Castle, learning that an invisible creature occupied the tunnels didn't sound all that surprising.

"This is disturbing," Marianne admitted, her eyebrows arching as she sipped her tea. "I will take an Elixir of True Sight to see it for myself. I never progressed past the Potion of Insight due to the risks involved, but I will need it to complete the case."

"So we think as one. The eyes and the bloody wound you saw beneath Verney Castle both belong to the same entity." *To my "father,"* Valdemar thought, though he doubted the entity even had a gender.

"It would make sense. And this Stranger is connected to the Qlippoths somehow." Marianne sipped once more from her cup. "If the Knights' Bestiary is correct, then they are psychic manifestations of this enormous creature. And if the Primordial Dream appeared to protect sentient life from them—"

"Then this entity has been coexisting with us since the beginning of life in our world." It had been here before men crawled into the depths of Underland. It had watched the Pleromians come and go, witnessed empires rise and fall.

"But if it is hostile to us, why do we still exist?" Marianne asked in confusion. "If it covers the entire world as Lord Och implied, then we literally live inside its bowels."

Valdemar didn't know. The eyes were everywhere, with no place to hide from them. Yet Shelley had been blissfully unaware that his Red

Grail had survived the purge. "What did the wererat say when the entity manifested?"

"That the 'master of masters' finally answered his prayers," Marianne quoted from memory before putting two and two together. "Ah, I see. The entity ignored Shelley until that moment. It never informed its agents on the ground."

"Maybe it can't communicate." The eyes did blink when Valdemar directly addressed them, but it could be because they were . . . related. The Stranger might have considered lesser entities beneath its notice. "Or not the way we humans do."

"I don't think so. The Verney cult received instructions from their patron, though they must have been vague or misunderstood. They mistook their Red Grail for a cup rather than a . . ."

"Than my mother," Valdemar said bluntly as Marianne struggled to find the words. His answer made her wince.

"A woman's purpose does not stop at her reproductive organs," Marianne declared.

The story hit close to home for her.

Valdemar shivered as he suddenly wondered if his mother had been born only for the purpose of creating him. He wouldn't put it past his two grandfathers to go to such lengths.

ABOMINATION.

Maybe she had never wanted him in the first place.

But whether she had been the original Sarah or a clone, his poor mother had been a pureblooded human; a frail woman consumed by mental illness in her last days. She didn't share her son's peculiar abilities, and the coroner never noticed anything wrong when she perished. Sarah Dumont had been a mere human, used to fulfill a dark purpose and then discarded.

But what Valdemar should make of her appearance in Astaphanos? If he checked Marianne's timeline of events, it happened soon after the collapse of Verney Castle. Could that have been a surviving clone?

Valdemar brushed off the possibility. The Domains of Astaphanos and Horaios were located on opposite sides of the empire. Unless the clones could teleport, they could never have made it in such a short amount of time.

Wait a minute . . .

"You said Shelley moved unnaturally fast?" he asked Marianne.

She took the sudden change of subject in stride. "Even if he used a modified rat to transmit his plague inside our walls, it shouldn't have crossed such a vast distance faster than a riding beetle. I still can't explain it. He was quicker than a man when we fought, but not nearly as much as a trained mount."

Valdemar had only ever seen Lord Och being capable of teleportation, a feat made possible because he spent the Light knows how many years coating his fortress in advanced spells. He wondered if it would be possible for a summoner to call a wererat to their location from afar, before deciding against that possibility. The Dark Lords protected vital areas of their territory with wards or detection spells.

The fact Valdemar saw a vision of his mother right after Marianne shattered a lab full of her clones couldn't be a coincidence, though the nature of the connection escaped him for the moment. Maybe another clone of his mother had escaped Shelley in the past and taken refuge in Astaphanos? It struck him as far-fetched, considering the wererat could only make malformed copies. Or maybe the eyes had toyed with his mind, as Hermann suggested?

Valdemar didn't know what to think of it. The idea of his mother being alive in some form should have been cause to rejoice, but his gut told him that her appearance only heralded troubles to come.

"So, to summarize," Marianne said, "the entity can communicate with its cult, but its instructions are either vague or very rare."

"Maybe it's restricted somehow," Valdemar guessed.

"Restricted by what? Magical laws?"

Maybe. Even Qlippoths couldn't enter the material realm without a summoner's help, although their godlike progenitor occupied every inch of Underland's tunnels. "I don't know," Valdemar admitted. "That's the root of the problem. Unless we understand what that entity is, we won't figure out what it can do or even want."

"We can surmise the latter," Marianne pointed out. "To reach Earth."

Valdemar shook his head. "I'm not so sure. That was my grandfather's intention, yes, but the cult wanted power and immortality along with their promised land."

The Silent King had shown him a vision where he transformed into a monster. Something unlike the Earthmouth his grandfather planned to turn him into.

Marianne crossed her arms and hung back in her chair. Valdemar could almost see gears turning inside her head. "Could it be . . ." she whispered.

"You figured out something?"

"Someone betrayed Aleksander Verney's cult soon after your birth and made the purge possible," Marianne explained. "Inquisitor Penhew never learned their identity, nor why your grandfather and mother were spared by the Knights. How could I miss it . . ."

No way . . . "You think my grandfather sold out the cult?"

Marianne nodded. "Inquisitor Penhew thought that your rumored father, Isaac Verney, betrayed the cult to save your mother. Maybe he was right about the motives but wrong about the culprit. If we assume that your two grandfathers had diverging agendas, Pierre Dumont makes an ideal suspect. It would explain why he and your mother were spared from any kind of retribution by the inquisition, as he would have negotiated an amnesty."

It fit. "So the fate the cult had in store was even worse than turning me into a gate between worlds," Valdemar deadpanned. "Wonderful."

"Maybe," Marianne said with a softer voice. "Or he wanted to protect you because you were his grandson."

Valdemar scowled. "The Silent King—"

"Showed you why you were born. But did your grandfather ever try to prepare you for the sacrifice?"

"He nursed me with tales of Earth, until I believed in his dream." Until Valdemar would do anything to achieve it.

"But he never tried to indoctrinate you into pursuing the Earthmouth ritual. As Lord Och told you, you only need to consent to it. Age is not a barrier. He raised you to adulthood without ever crossing the line, even after your mother perished."

Valdemar frowned in disbelief. What nonsense was that? Couldn't she see the obvious, that his grandfather manipulated him since the day he was born? That the strings had been subtle? "What are you implying? That he changed his mind?"

"Maybe," Marianne replied. "Maybe your mother talked him out of his plan. Mine said that parenthood changes people, for good or ill."

Valdemar wasn't a parent, so he couldn't tell. *Maybe she has a point,* he thought. His grandfather had been nothing but kind in their time together.

Or maybe Valdemar simply had a hard time reconciling the happy memory with the unsavory goal his grandfather created him to fulfill. Whether or not he changed his mind, Pierre Dumont worked with a Stranger cult to turn his grandson into a gateway between worlds. Valdemar wasn't sure he could ever forgive him for this, even if he balked half-way through.

"I can't say," the summoner replied, trying to banish these thoughts from his mind. They only made it harder for him to focus. "The echo inside my portrait can't answer half my questions."

"Could it answer this one?" Marianne gathered her breath. "Who is Crétail?"

"Crétail?" Valdemar raised an eyebrow. "You mean *Créteil*? With an 'e'?"

"I think it was with an 'a,' though I may have misheard. One of the Qlippoths in Vernburg spoke of a child with that name, probably you."

"Créteil was my grandfather's hometown on Earth. It's not one of my names." Valdemar tried to remember in which context he learned that information. "I always bugged grandpa about it."

"Did your mother ever use that word?" Marianne asked. "I'm grasping at straws, but any clue, no matter how circumstantial, can help."

"Grandpa only used the word once in her presence," Valdemar replied, wincing at the mere memory. "The one time he did, it caused a crisis."

"A crisis?" Valdemar looked away, causing Marianne to clear her throat. "If this is sensitive—"

"My mother was . . . unstable." The summoner shifted on his chair, the memories painful to remember. "She . . . she was very kind and gentle, but . . . moody. Sometimes she cried without warning, or she didn't answer when called. At the end of her life, she spent most of her time in an asylum for treatment."

"I'm sorry to hear that." She sounded genuine too. "How old were you?"

"Old enough to understand what was happening, too young to do anything about it." Valdemar gazed at his reflection in his tea. "I thought she was ill, but knowing everything you told me . . . I think she was just traumatized by what she went through with the cult. It can't have been easy."

She probably didn't even consent to having a half-Stranger for a son. *ABOMINATION.*

Maybe Valdemar had just been a burden she had to take care of.

"While I apologize for unearthing painful memories, I believe we should investigate that *Créteil* lead," Marianne said, oblivious to Valdemar's dark thoughts. "Call it gut feeling, I believe it's an important detail."

"I'll look for it inside the journal," Valdemar said as he rose from his seat. "And investigate that creature you saw being summoned in Vernburg Castle. I have my suspicions about its nature, but I need more time to confirm them."

"Well, it's late," Marianne said with a chuckle. "I think you should go to sleep. We have been at it for hours, and we leave for Sabaoth tomorrow."

"I can't sleep until I complete my Painted Field," Valdemar pointed out. "Or I might manifest the hamlet."

"I have potions that can give you a dreamless sleep. I'll give you a few, since your metabolism will shrug off weaker doses." Marianne smiled sadly. "I have nightmares too."

"About your family?"

"In a way." Marianne looked quite uncomfortable with the subject. "I . . . I know it sounds hypocritical after we discussed your family history, but . . ."

"You don't have to tell me if you don't want to," Valdemar replied with a chuckle. "Unless one of your parents is a Stranger? Then we could work on solving that case too."

"Not yet at least," Marianne mused. "You have a pretty dark sense of humor."

He had to. When faced with pain, he would rather laugh than cry.

26

VERMILLION

Frigga's workshop looked more like a noble's boudoir than a lab. It was a bit larger than Valdemar's own room and far better decorated. Deep red carpets covered every inch of the floor while beautiful tapestries and paintings occupied the walls. Most represented triumphant scenes of dokkars conquering each other in wars, founding cities atop the skulls of defeated troglodytes, or engaging in orgies just barely short of the Pleromians' depravity.

Only one painting was hidden behind a velvet curtain: Valdemar's newest piece.

As the summoner entered the room with Marianne in tow, he was surprised to see workbenches, shelves full of parchments, and strange clockwork contraptions in a corner right next to a king-size bed. While Valdemar thought she was mostly a dilettante, though with great skills in oneiromancy, Frigga seemed to take her studies to heart.

The dokkar awaited her guests at the table, along with Iren, Liliane, and Hermann, and a host of strange desserts and pastries. Among the goods, Valdemar noticed a pumpkin cooked in a cream pot, jelly spiders, and a hound-size bat stuffed with candies. Drinks included tea, dokkar wine, and cocktails that the summoner didn't recognize.

"Finally," Frigga said before offering Valdemar her hand. The dark elf had chosen an elegant spider-silk dress for the day and put a silver brooch in her hair. "I was starting to wonder if you had spurned my invitation."

"Not for anything in the world," Valdemar replied with falseness as he kissed her hand.

"Valdy, so good to see you again," Liliane said as the summoner greeted her with a kiss on the cheek before shaking hands with Iren and Hermann. The latter looked ill at ease with his host's choice of decoration, glaring at the portrait showing his ancestors' defeat.

"And I see you brought a friend," Frigga said as she observed Marianne. Valdemar noticed that the dark elf didn't offer her hand . . . and that she had already set a chair for the swordswoman. *She is well-informed,* he thought.

"Do not mind me," Marianne replied with formality. "Lord Och asked me to serve as Mr. Verney's bodyguard until a certain issue is resolved. I will be invisible."

"Nonsense, take a seat!" Liliane smiled at Marianne before waving a hand at the pastries. "Come, there's enough for everyone."

"I cannot turn away the heir of a noble house," Frigga added with courtesy. Of course, the dark elf would try to strengthen her political ties.

"A disgraced heir," Marianne replied as she and Valdemar sat at the table. "I am unwanted in Saklas."

"I know someone who could help with that," Iren said while giving a wink to Liliane.

"I could always have a word with Dad," the witch admitted. "But it's considered impolite for noble houses to meddle in one another's affairs."

"That is true among dokkars too, but we do it all the same," Frigga replied before giving a charming glance at Iren. "Dear, please serve drinks to our new guests."

"I knew you didn't invite me for my pretty face," Iren deadpanned before pouring a mix of mole rat milk and herbal brew into everyone's cups. To Valdemar's delight, he had completely recovered from his encounter with the derros. "It's fine. I'm glad our friend here decided to leave his room at last."

"I . . ." Valdemar cleared his throat without touching his drink. "I apologize for shutting you all out."

Iren snorted. "Friend, you don't have anything to apologize for."

"It's fine . . ." Hermann cleared his throat. "You feel better . . . that's what matters."

"Valdy, it's alright," Liliane said with a warm smile. "After what you went through, it's normal that you needed some time for yourself."

Valdemar had worried about his friends' reactions, and hearing their responses filled him with relief. *It's nice to be understood,* he thought, *without judgment.* He resolved to be a better friend to them in the future, especially if they ever faced similar troubles.

"I shall forgive you for your rude behavior if I like the result," Frigga replied while glancing at the painting hidden behind the velvet curtain. "I will give you this, Valdemar, you did fulfill your obligation on time. I'm still thinking about the other favor you owe me."

She would never let him forget it. "Sure, but only if you fulfill your end of the bargain," Valdemar said. "Marianne and I may have found the reason why my dreamscape is faulty."

"Oh?" Frigga put a finger on her lips while Marianne sipped from her cup without a word. "Do tell."

"Later, in private." Better not spread the word to too many people yet. "I would need your oneiromancy expertise to verify our theory."

While he didn't like her, Valdemar couldn't deny that Frigga was a dream expert; and since she worshiped a Stranger, she was no more friendly toward the inquisition than he was. He doubted that she would spread the information, if only because he knew she would rather use it for concessions and her soul contract with Lord Och prevented her from acting against his interests.

The dark elf chuckled. "In private? My, are you inviting me for a secret tryst?"

"No," Valdemar replied flatly.

"Valdy is above that kind of thing," Liliane added with a happy chuckle.

"Not with everyone," Iren said with a playful smirk. Liliane, in an eminent show of maturity, answered by sticking out her tongue.

Hermann, always insightful, immediately put two and two together. "Is it linked . . . to our experiment?"

"Or the wererat cultist running around?" Iren asked.

Valdemar sighed. "Does everybody know about the last part?"

"The Knights of the Beast issued orders and a bounty," Marianne said before glancing at the pastries with apprehension. She looked like a house pet surveying its dinner but unsure if she should take a bite.

Frigga smiled before taking a piece of jelly spider, wordlessly inviting everyone else to do the same. "I can't even use the Earthmouths without a health checkup," she complained. "Even though I am a dokkar and immune to diseases. The sooner your Knights catch this animal, the better."

"Is it going to be alright, Valdy?" Liliane asked with a worried face. "I mean, I don't doubt your abilities Lady Reynard, but . . ."

"Call me Marianne," she replied. "Your friend has nothing to fear."

"It is only a matter of time," Valdemar insisted, though he didn't truly believe it. He started with a piece of cake, delighting at the aroma and swiftly changing the subject. "Liliane, is this yours?"

"You like it?" Liliane beamed with pride when he answered with a nod. Good. He knew she would start to feel anxious for his safety if they kept talking about Shelley. "You better. I don't think you'll get any cake in Sabaoth, so it's your last moment of joy for a while."

"Don't expect meat either," Iren mused as he assaulted the pastries with relentless culinary brutality. "The soldiers in Sabaoth all eat the same protein-vitamin bars, while the workers must do with gruel."

"Surely officers have privileges?" Frigga asked with a raised eyebrow. Valdemar noticed Marianne listening in silence as she took a bite of a pastry.

"Those who try to skirt the rules get punished in front of their units," Iren replied. "Lord Bethor doesn't tolerate insubordination. *Any* form of insubordination. To him, overlooking any form of corruption leads to lack of discipline down the line."

"It sounds like you visited the place," Valdemar pointed out.

"I did. Lord Och often uses me as an intermediary to deliver goods to Bethor's army. I'm sure I'll get to say hello before the end of your stay."

"Maybe I will visit you soon too, Valdy," Liliane said while biting into a jelly spider's leg. "Dad owns many of Sabaoth's foundries. I'm sure I could sneak in to say hello."

"I appreciate the thought," Valdemar replied, "but you should focus on your studies."

His friend smirked. "That's the best part, I can do both! Lord Bethor commissioned many projects to Lady Mathilde, especially about reverse-engineering derro tech alchemy bombs."

"How are things on that front?" Valdemar asked, shivering as he remembered the trapped brains and skinless corpses in the derros' underground labs.

"The inquisitors still don't understand how the infiltrators managed to fool psychic scans," Iren explained. "It's one thing to disguise oneself, but the Knights of the Mind routinely peek into the minds of people to detect heretical thoughts. Derros have an innate resistance to mind-magic, but they aren't immune to it."

"Maybe they use special dreamcatchers?" Liliane suggested. "If a magical item can protect dreamers from oneiromancers, another could block mind-magic."

"But derros can't use magic," Iren pointed out. "Where would they have found these hypothetical magical items?"

"I dunno, they could have stolen them?" Liliane asked. "It's just an idea."

"The dwarves do not need dreamcatchers since they cannot dream," Frigga said, sneering. "They have no more connection to the Primordial Dream than to the Blood."

This piece of information caught Valdemar's full attention. Marianne, who had been reserved so far, turned her head in the dark elf's direction. "I thought all sentient life shared a connection to the dream world?" the swordswoman asked. "As a defense system."

"Ah, you heard of that theory?" Frigga smiled ear to ear. "This is true of all natural life with a nervous system in our world."

Valdemar didn't miss the implications. "*Natural?*"

"There are theories . . ." Hermann cleared his throat. "That derros started as . . . artificial life-forms."

"Let me tell you something," Frigga said, eager to retake the spotlight. "We dokkars descended into Underland long before your kind did. In this era, we found Pleromian ruins, the troglodytes, even the occasional talkative dragon or mindworm. Each of these races, lesser or greater, left clues of their presence."

Valdemar noticed Hermann squinting at her last words, a subtle jab against his own kind.

It wasn't lost on Liliane either. "Don't say that," she scolded Frigga with an angry glare that Valdemar had never seen her use.

"Say what?" the dokkar asked with a raised eyebrow.

"That there are lesser or greater races. It's wrong. Everyone can do great things."

"My dear Liliane, you cannot put a dragon and a rat on the same pedestal."

"Are you the rat or the dragon, Frigga?" Valdemar asked coldly, causing Iren to burst into laughter. The dokkar glared at him in response, her mask of affability faltering for a moment.

"Who cares?" Liliane asked as she raised her voice. "They are both successful in their own way, just not by the same metrics. Dragons can breathe fire and live for thousands of years, true, but there are ten million rats for each of them. Mice colonized every corner of Underland, while we're pushing the dragons farther and farther down. Which of them is better?"

"I understand your point, my dear Liliane," Frigga replied though Valdemar doubted that she meant it. "But all civilizations are made of hierarchies. Even this Institute who welcomes all species has a lich at the top and everyone else at the bottom."

"Your species . . . is as endangered as mine," Hermann spoke with eerie resignation. "There is little place for us . . . in the world the Dark Lords are building."

Frigga opened her mouth to answer, but no sound came out. Instead of arguing further, the dark elf fell into a deep, sullen silence; Hermann had beaten her with the truth.

And as he observed Frigga's thoughtful face, Valdemar suddenly wondered if her arrogance and cultural posturing took root not in her pride, but in her denial and insecurities. The dokkars were an empire in decline and might very well suffer the same fate as the troglodytes if they couldn't turn the tide.

"Alright, I see your point," Frigga conceded when the silence became unbearable. "Each of these species left clues of their presence."

"But not the derros?" Liliane asked, eager to put the argument behind them.

"No, my dear," Frigga replied slowly, regaining a little of her previous confidence. "We knew you humans existed and your push below ground, while unexpected, wasn't truly surprising. The derros though? They poured out of unexplored tunnels without warning, like savages. They hadn't developed the toys that make them dangerous today, so we thoroughly crushed them."

"But they still took you by surprise," Iren guessed.

"We missed an opportunity to exterminate them." Frigga sighed. "I believe the Pleromians are to blame. I'm sure the derros are the mongrel descendants of a slave race they left behind in stasis, woken up when the Whitemoon disturbed our planet's tectonic activities."

"But they can still be affected by spells," Valdemar pointed out, having telekinetically thrown derros around in Astaphanos.

"Of course," Frigga replied with a hint of smugness. "Like your warbeasts, the Pleromians always made their thralls unable to fight back against their control. The fact that derros lack the ability to dream makes it harder for a mind-mage to target them as they appear thoughtless at first glance, but a truly talented magician always finds workarounds."

"Like you, darling?" Iren asked with a sarcastic tone.

"I have picked derros' minds open in the past, though I wouldn't recommend it. Their emotions are as dull and gray as their skin. They're natural slaves drawn to a strong leader." The dark elf chuckled. "Maybe that's why they steal others' brains."

"Has anyone figured out why the derros needed them?" Valdemar asked, remembering Lord Och's discussion with Master Loctis.

"Not yet . . ." Hermann admitted. "Master Loctis is . . . investigating though."

"Maybe we'll get to explore the subject in Sabaoth," Liliane said. "It's the frontier with the derro kingdom after all."

"I . . . I will pass," the troglodyte said. He alone hadn't touched any of the food. "I am sorry Valdemar, but . . . another project requires my full attention."

"The Painted World?" Valdemar guessed.

"Yes," Hermann rasped with a nod. "The Silent King showed me how I might . . . create a true pocket dimension. A world for my kind."

"Truly?" Frigga asked with a sly smirk. "If you succeed, would you kindly share your findings? I know a few people who would pay a great deal for a private universe to . . . indulge themselves."

Hermann glared at the dark elf with a hint of disgust. "No."

"Come on, my scaled friend, don't be so close-minded. Certainly making a new world will need resources you cannot get on your own."

"I have all the necessary tools . . . except one." Hermann glanced at Valdemar. "I would need your help in the future . . . if you agree."

"Of course, Hermann," his friend replied. "I suppose you want to summon a Qlippoth as fuel?"

"Yes, but . . ." Hermann shifted in his seat. "Not just any of them will do."

Valdemar sipped his drink and shivered as he put two and two together.

A Nahemoth. His Painted World needed a Nahemoth to work.

It made sense, since these entities had unimaginable control over reality and could create lesser Qlippoths from nothing, including the Collector that the two pictomancers used to fuel their Painted Room.

"You realize no one has managed to bind them to servitude?" Valdemar asked his friend with skepticism. Even though he and Marianne suspected that a Nahemoth was trapped at a well's bottom, the summoner wasn't sure if it was truly imprisoned or simply unable to fully manifest in Underland.

"I'm sorry, Hermo," Liliane said with a frown. "But that plan of yours sounds highly dangerous."

"Do not . . . call me Hermo . . . please . . ." Hermann pleaded. "The Silent King showed me the way . . . I can create a special painting that once completed . . . with the right ritual . . . will trap the Qlippoth with no possibility of escape."

Marianne's eyes glanced at Hermann while Valdemar thoughtfully considered his friend's words.

"Forgive me if this sounds like a stupid question," Iren said, "but a painting is a fragile thing. Wouldn't time damage it and unleash a dangerous creature into the world? Sounds pretty risky to me."

"Once completed . . . the Painted World will be near-indestructible," Hermann replied. "An invulnerable door to an artificial plane."

Unknown to the troglodyte, Valdemar might very well need to deal with a Nahemoth in the near future. A trap capable of holding it would come in handy. "Could you translate this ritual to paper?" he asked Hermann. "So I can examine it?"

"I would like to do the same," Liliane joined in. "I know you are smart and talented, Hermann, but you shouldn't use a ritual taught by an otherworldly creature without checking it extensively."

"Yes, of course," the troglodyte agreed with a nod. "I already showed Master Loctis and . . . he was very interested too."

"So you would share that knowledge with a pile of insects, but not with me?" Frigga asked with a frown. "I feel disrespected."

"You are," Hermann replied bluntly while glaring at the painting showing his kindred being massacred. "I know . . . you put it on display to mock me."

The dokkar chuckled. "Fine. I guess it was not elegant on my part."

"It wasn't," Liliane said.

"My dear Liliane, friends *support* each other."

"Yes, which is why I'm trying to change your mind," Liliane replied plainly. "I'm friends with both you and Hermann, and I want you to get along."

"A lost cause I'm afraid," Iren said with a chuckle. "They mix like oil and water."

"I am not . . . interested," Hermann said with a sneer.

"Maybe, but I have to try," Liliane replied with surprising determination. "If I can't get you two to bury the hatchet, how will our species? It has to start somewhere."

Marianne smiled, as did Valdemar. "Liliane?" he began.

"Yes?" she answered.

"You're a good person."

Liliane blushed, though Valdemar couldn't tell if it was out of happiness or embarrassment. "Thanks, Valdy."

"Aww . . ." Iren said with an eminently *punchable* expression. "That is so cute."

"You shut up," Liliane said while glaring at him. "How about we unveil Valdy's new painting before I slap you?"

"Yes to both," Frigga said before winking at Valdemar. "I leave the honor of unveiling the masterpiece to the artist. I haven't even peeked at it yet."

Valdemar rose from his seat, held his breath, and pulled the velvet curtain.

His action was met with gasps as he unveiled *The Nocturne* to the world.

Finished last night with pigments and blood, the portrait showed a naked Frigga riding a giant dragon-bat with only a sapphire necklace for decoration. Her posture oozed eroticism, her ashen skin glistening thanks to the advanced light and shadow effects, her sly smile and gaze enough to condemn a man's soul to damnation. But though Frigga had asked for skulls and macabre sights as a background, Valdemar settled on something else as he finished his work in the dead of the night.

He had painted the world's surface.

Frigga's mount flew above the frozen wasteland that the Mask of the Nightwalker had shown Valdemar, with the Whitemoon's ghastly light shining upon the ruins of fallen human empires; the destructive planetoid's crater-eyes oversaw the dark elf below, as if she were the herald of the end times. Every crater, every star in the dark sky, had been painstakingly reconstituted to the smallest detail.

In a way, *The Nocturne* was probably one of Valdemar's best works short of the Painted Door. Though she had a rotten personality, Frigga was a lovely model who perfectly fit the macabre aesthetics of the surface world.

Valdemar glanced at his audience. Liliane's skin had turned scarlet and she looked about to faint. Iren examined the painted Frigga's curves with undisguised lust. Hermann examined the portrait's background with fascination. Marianne covered her mouth in embarrassment.

But it was Frigga's reaction that surprised Valdemar the most. He expected criticism if she found the work lacking, or self-congratulations upon seeing her own beauty if it pleased her.

"It's beautiful," the dokkar said with a weak voice, a single tear falling down her left cheek. She looked sincerely moved.

To his surprise, Valdemar didn't notice any hint of falseness in the dark elf; a first since he met her. She rose from her seat, her hand trailing against the paint. The portrait's lighting shifted as she did, the stars blinking in and out of existence, shadows moving between the ruins.

"You used pictomancy . . ." Hermann rasped. Indeed, Valdemar had merged his own blood with the painting to better represent the vision he saw through his mask.

"It's . . ." Liliane trailed off as she recovered from seeing her friend's naked form and paid attention to the rest of the painting. "Inspired."

"Haunting," Marianne added upon clearing her throat, her eyes wandering to the Whitemoon's terrible beauty. "It's like you went to the surface yourself."

If only she knew.

"By the Light, are you genuinely crying?" Iren asked Frigga in astonishment. "And here I thought you could only fake it."

"It is hard to move me, I will agree," Frigga said as she wiped away the tear running down her cheek. "But it happens."

"It is . . . surprising," Hermann agreed. "From a tasteless creature . . ."

"Your cubic drawings are trash, Hermann, and a child could do better," the dokkar replied while the troglodyte choked on his indignation. "But this? This is true beauty."

"It's a masterpiece, but if you show this painting in public, I don't give it two hours before it gets burned," Iren pointed out. "Then again, that's the goal, no?"

Frigga shook her head. "I won't show it."

Valdemar raised an eyebrow in her direction, after checking if Hermann intended to murder her first for insulting his artistic skills. Though the troglodyte would have Valdemar's sympathy if he tried, Liliane had managed to calm him down with gentle words. "I thought you wanted to cause a scandal?"

"I cannot." Frigga took a step back to better admire her painted copy and the cosmic darkness behind her. "The plebeians won't understand. This is true beauty, Valdemar, the kind only an elite few can appreciate."

"So you will keep it for yourself?" Liliane asked with a sigh of relief. "Good. It's beautiful, but it will scare people."

"Her nakedness . . . would make everyone run away," Hermann said with disdain.

"Aw, and here I wanted to see how people would react to our favored elf's naked glory," Iren complained. "Way to ruin my mood."

"There will be other opportunities," Frigga replied dismissively. "But this kind of work is something you change your mind for."

Valdemar was quite pleased with the result, especially since he didn't need more public attention with Shelley's activities.

Still, as his eyes wandered to the Whitemoon looking down on the world below . . . he wondered if he would have the opportunity to walk on the surface one day. Not see it through a mask, but actually observe the world above with his own two eyes.

Somehow, he had the feeling that many answers awaited him there.

Marianne had thought that they would travel to Sabaoth the old-fashioned way, but Lord Och had other ideas. The Dark Lord personally teleported them all the way from the Institute to his ally's palace, bending space more than four hundred kilometers.

Marianne didn't even know that mages could teleport so far. She thought that Lord Och could only do so in his Domain because he had altered it with magic, but such a display of sorcery made her rethink her hypothesis.

"Here we are," the lich declared as he lifted the veil of space and time and revealed their destination: a cyclopean dome of steel supported by soulstone Reliquary pillars. Enormous phantom projectors manifested hundreds of ghostly visions on the ceiling, each representing a different location across the empire and beyond, from Lord Och's fortress to Empress Aratra's palace. Metal statues of gigantic, clockwork humanoids stood watch over a central glass and steel elevator, the only exit Marianne noticed.

"There is no door?" she asked Lord Och.

"This place can only be accessed by teleportation," the lich declared as he stepped toward the elevator, his subordinates in tow. While Marianne had traveled light, bringing only her rapier and a new rifle to replace her old weapon, Valdemar carried a bag of sorcerous artifacts and the box containing his grandfather's portrait. "And it is only open to a select few. This teleportation line is available to me alone."

The fact that it led directly into the heart of Lord Bethor's fortress spoke volumes about the level of trust between the two archmages.

Marianne knew that Sabaoth's master had been one of Lord Och's apprentices and that the two kept a cordial relationship, unlike what happened with Lord Phaleg. Lord Bethor had since then become the empire's lead general and one of the most powerful magicians in the realm.

"Some say the most powerful," Lord Och said, having read Marianne's mind. The elevator, a complex device of glass windows held together by mechanical arms and cables, opened to let them in. "Though young Aratra and Lord Bethor never came to blows for fear of mutual annihilation, if they did . . ."

The elevator's door closed behind the group with a squeaky noise and it began its ascent.

"I would bet on my former apprentice."

Marianne shivered. She had seen a hint of Empress Aratra's power in the past, and to imagine anyone besting her in battle defied reason.

All of the Dark Lords had visited Empress Aratra at least once in Marianne's lifetime; all but Lord Bethor. They said he only ever left his Domain for the Dark Lords' secret gatherings or for war. Nothing else interested him.

"Is that why there are no guards? Because he doesn't need any?" Valdemar asked with a frown. "I sense blood everywhere, but no undead or living being besides us."

Blood?

Marianne closed her eyes as she focused on her psychic sight, and realized that her partner was right. She sensed blood in the walls around her, but diffused, like invisible veins coursing through the metal.

As the elevator continued its ascent beyond the fortress's confines, she received a glimpse of the truth. The glass windows showed her the outside world and the Domain of Sabaoth. The elevator ascended toward the tip of a titanic metal tower, bigger than any structure Marianne had ever seen. Lord Och's Institute and the plateau supporting it would have looked small if put side by side. The building occupied the center of a fortress-city of brass, steel, and obsidian belfries, of burning forges fueled by lava pits drawing heat from the very heart of the world. Volcanic hills vomited rivers of molten metal next to factories pumping alchemical fumes into the air, the smoke purified by trapped wind elementals. Armies of undead toiled on assembly lines overseen by armored knights.

"Do you see that?" Valdemar whispered, as he pointed at a red circle surrounding the metal tower.

Yes, she did.

Rivers of thick blood flowed in the tower's moat, before coursing through glass veins and pumps. The structure absorbed the fluid into itself, channeling it toward the tip.

"Whose blood is it?" Marianne asked, slightly disturbed. How many hundreds of thousands had it taken to fuel this river?

"All the people my former apprentice slew," Lord Och replied absent-mindedly. "Those whose bodies his soldiers managed to recover. Lord Bethor rarely leaves more than ash."

The elevator reached the peak of the tower, its gates opening into the Dark Lord's lair.

Marianne felt his terrible presence long before they reached that point. An invisible pressure had built up as they ascended, similar to the one that crushed her mind beneath Verney Castle; but where the black blood pit had been alluring, this boiling red pool promised only a swift death.

Marianne felt the texture of blood on her tongue, the feeling of doom looming over her. Valdemar sensed it, his fingers clenching as he carried his grandfather's portrait. They had reached the den of a terrible and fearsome creature. A droning noise echoed in Marianne's head, while her entire body struggled to stand still. Her survival instincts screamed at her subconscious, telling her to turn away, to turn back. She was a bat courting death by entering a dragon's lair.

Even the presence beneath Verney Castle hadn't felt so menacing, so . . . *deadly.*

Lord Och didn't care though. He stepped into the room, his subordinates slowly imitating him.

Lord Valar Bethor awaited them while floating above a pool of boiling blood. The Dark Lord of Sabaoth had no need for a throne room. His lair was instead a dome of glass housing a pool of blood wider than the Institute's hedge maze. Perhaps the entire tower had been created to channel it to this place. Only a small floor of metal around the elevator allowed the group to stand their feet.

Lord Bethor himself meditated in a lotus position. It was the first time Marianne saw him in the flesh; she had seen descriptions and statues of the man wearing his intimidating armor, but this time he wasn't wearing anything.

Not even skin.

The . . . thing before her looked humanoid but lacked skin of any sort. His surface was an ever-shifting ocean of dark and red blood. Small tendrils rose in random spots before collapsing back into the body. Marianne didn't hear any breathing coming from the figure.

For a second, she dared to glimpse at him with her psychic sight . . . only to be instantly blinded by a deadly crimson light. In it she sensed only cold fury and burning rage, so overwhelming that she had to cancel her ability before it could shatter her mind.

This man was a volcano. A burning power stirring in its deep slumber, ready to erupt at the first provocation. She glanced at Valdemar, only to find him gulping in dread and anxiety.

If this . . . *creature* found them wanting, they would never leave this room alive.

Only Lord Och remained quietly confident, even comfortable.

"Lord Bethor," the lich said with an emotional tone that Marianne had never heard him use before: fondness. "Forgive me for interrupting your meditation. I have brought you new students."

Lord Bethor opened his eyes and the tower trembled.

27

WITH A CARING HAND

Power. Valdemar had long wondered what made a Dark Lord who they were. Their immortality? Their ability to command vast armies? Their unrivaled magical knowledge? Their awe-inspiring spells? Now he knew.

As Lord Bethor opened his eyes, the aura that came from him dwarfed even Lord Och's at his most intimidating. The lich's defenses had been like a mist: mysterious, stealthy, and difficult to fight. Much like his body was a puppet controlled from his phylactery, Lord Och's magic was difficult to grasp and counter. When he had briefly experienced a glimpse of the lich's unrestrained might, Valdemar thought he had seen the pinnacle of Blood magic.

He had been mistaken.

As Valar Bethor opened his eyes and the tower shook from his awakening, Valdemar realized that he had never understood what true power was. Lord Bethor's defenses weren't a mist but a volcano ready to explode at the first provocation; his will was an earthquake. One could disperse mist in theory, at least for a time. But natural disasters could only be survived and suffered through.

If Valdemar were to be honest, he had only ever felt so intimidated in the Silent King's presence.

This sorcerer had reached such a level of power that he rivaled the Strangers themselves.

The sclera in Lord Bethor's eyes was as black as night, the irises a bloodred . . . and as they manifested, the very fabric of space rippled around the Dark Lord. Tiny cracks appeared in the air, opening and closing almost too fast for the human eye to notice. Crimson bolts of lightning flared up from the boiling pool beneath this absolute incarnation of strength, and Valdemar sensed his own blood echoing the phenomenon. His own bodily fluids wriggled beneath his skin, preparing to erupt out of his veins; whether to flee or fight, the summoner couldn't say.

Lord Bethor stood up as he emerged from his meditation. As his feet hit the boiling pool beneath him, the blood surged to cover him and crystalized. Crimson plate armor more intimidating than any Knight's covered him entirely, with a crown of spikes atop the helmet. Only his eyes peered through the visor.

He's stronger than his old master, Valdemar realized, utterly intimidated. The lich was wiser and more knowledgeable, but his former apprentice had eclipsed him in sheer magical firepower. Much like a volcano, Lord Bethor needed to sleep and meditate to keep his own power suppressed lest it destroy everything around him.

And he was *huge* too, just short of two meters and a half with his armor on. When the Dark Lord walked to the steel platform the others stood on, Valdemar and Marianne had long knelt in submission.

Only Lord Och remained on his feet. The lich and Lord Bethor faced one another, the latter two heads taller than his master.

"Lord Och," the giant said in a deep voice and with the respect of an old student greeting a favored teacher. "You visit me earlier than I expected."

"Time is a luxury for us, my old friend, but one that shouldn't be squandered. Considering the forces moving against us, I thought it wise not to waste any second of your time . . . or mine. I'm sure you will find these two new students quite promising."

Though Valdemar didn't dare raise his head, he sensed Lord Bethor's eyes looking down on him. "Do you need them alive?" the younger Dark Lord asked his elder.

"I would prefer alive," the lich said with a lighthearted chuckle, "but I can settle for undead."

Valdemar grit his teeth in frustration even though he had expected such an answer. He noticed Marianne clenching her fists at his side at Lord Och's jape.

"Good," Lord Bethor replied, his tone lacking any amusement whatsoever. "I shall return them to you, one way or the other."

"I would appreciate it. If they cannot survive you, they won't last against Blutgang either . . . but I know you shall know what to make of these two." Lord Och said. "After you are done with this trifling matter, you should visit my abode. I have new breakthroughs that will certainly interest you."

"I shall consider it."

"Then I leave you to teach these two the ways of our dark brotherhood." Lord Och happily bent to pat a silent Valdemar on the back. "Do not worry, apprentice. Lord Bethor teaches with a gentle, caring hand."

Valdemar doubted that.

The lich left without a word through the elevator, leaving his apprentice and Marianne alone with Lord Bethor in a room without exit.

For a long, agonizing moment, no one uttered a word. The only noise in the room came from the crimson bolts surging from the blood pool and the spatial cracks caused by Lord Bethor's mere presence. Valdemar glanced at Marianne, neither of them daring to stand up.

"Look at me," Lord Bethor ordered. "Both of you."

Valdemar and Marianne raised their heads to meet the Dark Lord's gaze.

"What is your name?" Lord Bethor asked Valdemar. "You who follow in my footsteps?"

The summoner cleared his throat. "Valdemar Verney, Lord—"

Snap.

A sharp pain erupted in Valdemar's left elbow, so strongly and gone so quickly that his mind barely registered it. Warm blood splashed his cheek and covered the metal ground beneath his feet. His left arm started to itch like that time the derro's lightning struck him. His fingers no longer answered his mental commands.

Because he had lost them.

Valdemar coughed, his breath trapped in his windpipe as he looked at his severed left arm wriggling on the ground among pieces of flesh and bones. Marianne's eyes had widened in shock, her skin turning pale.

"What is wrong?" Lord Bethor asked, his red eyes peering through his helmet. He hadn't even moved. "This is but an arm. Reattach it."

Valdemar hadn't even sensed his attack. The Dark Lord hadn't shattered his psychic defenses and magical protections; he had outright *ignored* them.

Realizing his life was on the line, the summoner gritted his teeth to ignore the pain and telekinetically commanded his arm to return to him . . . but his blood refused to obey him.

A sharp pain erupted in his left knee, his flesh and bones rupturing beneath his scholarly robes. This time, Valdemar let out a snarl of pure pain as he collapsed on his chest. Only a phantom sensation remained from his left leg.

"I shall cut one limb each minute," Lord Bethor warned with eerie serenity, "until I either sever them all or you succeed—"

Marianne's rapier lunged at the gap in the Dark Lord's visor.

Lord Bethor didn't even move, as Marianne crashed against the dome above the blood pool. The strength of the impact cracked the glass, while telekinetic force kept the swordswoman pinned against it. An invisible hand tightened around her neck and started choking her.

"Marianne!" Valdemar shouted, only for another psychic attack to sever his right leg and his words to turn into another snarl of pain.

"You should have struck before I even cut the first limb," Lord Bethor scolded Marianne with scorn. "If you had paid attention, you would have sensed my violent intent."

"I . . ." Marianne rasped through her constricted windpipe. "I wasn't sure if . . . I could even strike a Dark Lord . . ."

But Valar Bethor wouldn't hear any excuse. "A bodyguard's only duty is to keep their charge safe from threats, *any* threat. Even if it costs them their life. Even if it means fighting a Dark Lord. That your attack would have failed anyway can be forgiven; your failure to act immediately cannot."

He's insane, Valdemar realized in horror. *He's going to kill us both.*

Marianne grabbed the rifle secured at her belt and attempted to open fire on their assailant in a mad display of bravery. The Dark Lord scoffed, and the noblewoman's fingers released the weapon against her will.

Valdemar tried to think rationally. Could he manipulate his body fluids like ropes, to reattach his limbs? Should he fight back instead? Summon a monster to—

His right arm, the last limb he had left, exploded at the elbow in a burst of blood and bones. This time Valdemar bit his tongue rather than let out a sound.

"If you have time to plot my demise, you have more than enough to succeed," Lord Bethor said. "This is your last chance. The neck is next."

He couldn't defeat this monster.

Think, Valdemar, think . . . He instinctively turned his neck's skin to steel to protect himself, only to realize that not all of his abilities were restrained. *If I can manipulate my skin, maybe . . . the flesh too?* That was how biomancers reshaped bodies like clay.

Closing his eyes, Valdemar called upon his reserves of power. Instead of telekinetically commanding the blood in his severed arms, he focused on reshaping the flesh in his stumps. It was new and difficult, but he managed to create tendrils of veins and muscles. They erupted from his shattered left elbow and reconnected to his severed arm, bringing it back to his body. The summoner had his extended veins and muscles stitch back to his limb like a cloth.

Valdemar expected Lord Bethor to behead him anyway, but the Dark Lord didn't strike him. However, he didn't release Marianne. The noblewoman struggled so much to breathe that her face had turned almost blue. Her strength left her until she dropped her rapier on the metal platform, her precious weapon out of reach.

I've got to save her, Valdemar thought as he gritted his teeth and ignored the pain. More tendrils erupted from his other stumps, reattaching his limbs. It was shoddy work; some bone parts were missing and the summoner's knowledge of his own anatomy wasn't perfect. But though they appeared broken, his arms and legs had returned to him.

When Valdemar finally stitched back his last limb, Lord Bethor released Marianne. She fell on the platform, landing on the metal next to Valdemar as she desperately gasped for air.

"Good," the Dark Lord said.

A blood bullet had stopped within an inch of his helmet and now floated in midair. Valdemar's left index bled below the nail, the skin closing to cover the wound.

"What was that for?" Lord Bethor asked, somewhat amused.

"You deserved it," Valdemar replied coldly.

He hadn't expected to actually hit that maniac, but it was the thought that counted.

"I suppose I did. I admire your spirit, though not your recklessness." The Dark Lord turned the blood bullet to dust with a thought, before glancing at Valdemar's steely skin. "Why only cover the neck? I could have lied and hit another spot."

"A teacher ..." Valdemar gasped. He had reattached his limbs but they still hurt at the joints. "Told me that I should only cover my weak points to avoid exhausting my resources."

Valar Bethor snorted. "That is the logic of a weakling. Do only what you must to not exhaust yourself? You should instead go beyond expectations and push back your limits, until this armor becomes as easy to wear as a second skin."

Valdemar ignored the reproach before glancing at Marianne. Her face had regained color, though her voice was raspy. He put a hand on her shoulder to cast a healing spell, to help her recover faster. And as he used his magic, he realized that Marianne's psychic defenses were intact. The fact he could outright ignore shields and wards was the truly frightening part about Valar Bethor; even Lord Och needed to power through them first.

"You have much to learn," Lord Bethor said with contempt as he focused on Marianne. "Your spirit is crippled by regrets and hesitation. Your task as a bodyguard was clear, but you hesitated. Just as you failed to make a decision when your retainer needed you most, or how you cannot come to terms with your past."

"I ..." Marianne struggled to make words. "My duty is ... to serve the Dark Lords."

"It wasn't your duty that made you hesitate, but fear for your life. I could have been a cultist of the Strangers as well as a Dark Lord. Would you have let me kill him then? Where do your loyalties lie?" Lord Bethor glanced at her sword and rifle. "Your hesitation is reflected in your choice of weapons. There is nothing wrong with using tools, but you use them as crutches instead of force multipliers. You had many ways to escape my grasp. You could have used bone bullets, attacked with telekinetic force, or used the pool. Instead you relied on borrowed power rather than your own mastery of the Blood. How can you protect others if you can't even believe in yourself?"

Marianne looked down at the metal platform and didn't meet the archmage's gaze.

Lord Bethor didn't expect a response anyway and quickly glanced at Valdemar next. "As for you, you possess limitless potential ... but in your obsession to reach this plane of Earth, you failed to tap into it. You do not know your own body's limits, and worst of all, you fail to grasp the true nature of the Blood. You cannot even establish dominance over your summoned thralls."

"I would like to see you," Valdemar hissed through his teeth as he tried to use healing spells to regenerate the missing bones in his arms. "Tame a Gnawer . . ."

Lord Bethor took his remark as a personal challenge. The archmage waved his hand, and a small rift in space opened at his left. The tentacled shape of a Gnawer emerged from the crack, hissing in hunger.

He doesn't use a summoning circle? Valdemar thought as he watched on, astonished. *Impossible . . .*

Even more spectacularly, the Gnawer didn't attack anyone. These incarnations of hunger could barely be kept in check by wards and otherwise attacked everything in the vicinity. But the mass of tentacles before Valdemar coiled like a calm snake, waiting for orders. It looked . . . It looked tamed.

"If a dog disobeys, the fault lies in his master," Lord Bethor replied as he snapped his fingers, the Gnawer turning to dust instantly. "These creatures exist to serve us. But how can you hope to dominate them, when you haven't yet mastered your own flesh and mind? You have talent, Valdemar, but you have only scratched the surface of the summoning arts."

Valdemar's jaw clenched, but he said nothing.

Lord Bethor's tone softened, but only a little. "Thankfully, you both passed my test. Though you took your sweet time and should have opted for a better strategy, Marianne Reynard, you did attempt to fight a Dark Lord to protect your charge. This takes great bravery. As for you, Valdemar Verney, you did understand and complete my exercise within the allocated time . . . which is more than I can say for most of my would-be apprentices."

Valdemar glanced at the pool and suddenly wondered how much of the blood within belonged to people who failed to impress the Dark Lord.

"We shall begin with an aggressive training regimen to bring out the limitless potential I see dormant within you both," Lord Bethor said as tendrils of blood slithered out of his armored gauntlets. "By the end of it, you will either be counted among the empire's finest mages or its obituaries."

It wasn't even a threat, but a promise. If Valdemar and Marianne didn't improve, this Dark Lord would kill them and forget their existence. Unlike Och, he didn't care about their potential usefulness. A creature of his strength had no need for tools.

Lord Bethor's tendrils searched through Valdemar's possessions, examining his grandfather's packaged portrait and the journal, before seizing what interested them. The Mask of the Nightwalker.

"It's dangerous," Valdemar rasped.

"And yet you kept it for study . . . just as I kept mine, when the Nightwalker sent me a gift." The tendrils brought the mask to Lord Bethor's hand. "If you want to become a true summoner, you will make its power your own too."

Lord Bethor slapped the Mask of the Nightwalker against Valdemar's face without any warning. The summoner's skin turned cold as the artifact merged with it, transferring fresh air into his lungs.

"What you call your human form is an illusion, a prison," Lord Bethor explained. "The Blood allows one to reshape their body like clay, even transcend physicality. I have two legs and two arms only because I wish to, and my former master now exists as a possessing spirit. I shall teach you to reshape your body as you will, Valdemar Verney . . . but to be remade, you must be destroyed first."

The Dark Lord telekinetically lifted Valdemar above the blood pool. The summoner looked down at the substance as his own wounds fueled it, steam rising from this burning lake.

"A long fall awaits you," Lord Bethor explained. "This is the main artery of my tower, with the heart waiting at the bottom. The boiling blood will devour your skin and counter your regeneration; if you want to rise back to this room, you will have to heal using your ingenuity. But my tower will resist your attempts. To use its power, you must conquer it. You must understand the true nature of the Blood."

. . .

Shit, Lord Och was the *kind one*.

As he accepted his fate, Valdemar exchanged one glance with the horrified Marianne. "I have a question, Lord Bethor," the summoner said.

The archmage snorted. "Go on."

"Did this happen to you?" Valdemar asked sharply.

To his surprise, the summoner could have sworn he saw a flash of thoughtful sorrow pass in the Dark Lord's cold eyes. "Yes," Valar Bethor admitted with a grim voice, "but with dragonfire."

He released his magic and Valdemar fell into the boiling blood while Marianne could only watch.

The summoner attempted to control it telekinetically, only to be met with psychic resistance. The boiling substance pulled him down, devoured his robes, and ate away at his skin. Valdemar was brought back to his hospital bed in Astaphanos, suffering the exact same agony.

The world turned crimson and he sank.

Marianne woke up blind. Only darkness and a cold floor welcomed her when she emerged from unconsciousness. She felt sick, her throat still sore from Lord Bethor's strangling spell. She tried to rise and almost stumbled. Her gloved hand hit a wall to her left, one made of stone, from the texture.

Her hands instinctively reached for her sheathed rapier, only to find it gone, along with her firearm. Even the smaller blades hidden in her boots had vanished. She had only been left with the clothes on her back.

Even less than that, Marianne thought grimly as she touched her face. She sensed her eyes, open and yet useless. The noblewoman didn't know if she should be relieved that Lord Bethor only took her sight.

"Valdemar?" Marianne called. She didn't know how long she had been out; her memories were a blur. "Valdemar, are you here?"

Her words echoed around her, but she received no answer. Marianne was in some sort of metal tunnel from the sound. "Somebody?"

She attempted to use her psychic sight, but the darkness around her remained impenetrable. She sensed the warmth of artificial light on her skin coming from above, even if her magical senses were as crippled as her physical ones.

Had she been drugged with a potion? For what purpose?

"Your sight will be returned to you." Lord Bethor's voice startled Marianne. "Once you prove worthy of eyes."

Marianne tried to "look" in the Dark Lord's direction, only to realize his words came from everywhere at once. Maybe they only existed inside her mind, the mental whispers of an insane warlord invading her neurons.

This was worse than anything I expected, Marianne thought as she massaged her throat. "Is Valdemar . . . alright?"

"You can check for yourself once you get out of this maze."

Marianne gritted her teeth. She had to find Valdemar and get the hell out of here, Lord Och's orders be damned. The lich's former apprentice had clearly gone insane. "Bertrand . . ." she whispered, her throat hurting. "My retainer thought . . . that I should go to you to improve."

"You will," the Dark Lord's voice said without malice. "This may surprise you, Marianne Reynard, but I deeply respect people like you. You let go of love and wealth for the sake of your martial pride; this is admirable. Your only fault is that you cannot come to terms with the sacrifices you made along the way."

"Is this a lesson or a punishment?"

"I do not punish, I teach."

The noblewoman let out a sigh. Marianne had expected a harsh training regimen, but the Dark Lord had exceeded even her worst fears. She had heard rumors about his iron discipline, but this was a treatment she would have expected from the dokkars or the derros.

"I only give this training to warriors I expect great things from," the Dark Lord said.

Still, Marianne found it a little excessive.

"Your comfortable existence is exactly why you have stopped improving," Lord Bethor scolded her. "You have used your retainer, Lord Och's patronage, and your weapons as crutches. You let your thoughts fester like an open wound, obsessing over the past and constantly second-guessing yourself. You have shackled your beautiful spirit, and we will free you from these doubts as we strengthen your magic."

"How will blinding me teach me anything?" Marianne protested.

"Your sight, your hearing, your touch . . . *all* of your senses can be refined through the Blood and be used offensively. Touch will let you sense weak points in your foe's body. Your understanding of hearing will allow you to disturb others' ears. Smell and taste will tell you more than sight. I will teach you how to refine your senses to perfection one at a time. Then we will move on to more complex combat spells."

Fine. Marianne could see the logic, though she questioned the violence of the methods.

"Mankind is threatened on all sides," Lord Bethor replied. "Some of the foes you shall face in the future surpass you in power and cunning. A few may even match my strength. If you cannot survive these tests, you will not stand a chance against them . . . and death at my hands will be kinder fate than what awaits you should the forces behind the wererat prevail."

Marianne winced as she remembered Bertrand's mutation into a monster.

"Time is a luxury you cannot afford," the Dark Lord said before adding another difficulty. "I shall release a creature in this maze soon. It could be in ten minutes or an hour. It will hunt you down like a dog, and if it catches you . . . you will not die, but there will be pain."

Charming. Unlike Hagith, Lord Bethor was clearly fonder of the stick than the carrot.

"What must I do then?" Marianne asked as she walked, using a hand to steady herself against the wall. Maybe if she focused on her hearing, she could find her way. That was how bats locate objects in dark caverns, from what she understood. "Escape before it catches me?"

"You must find the exit using the spell I shall teach you. The creature only adds an additional motivation to learn more quickly." Lord Bethor marked a short pause. "If you listen well and prove as talented as my old master believes, you will escape unharmed. However, I must warn you that even my best soldiers get caught at least three times."

Marianne forced herself to smile defiantly.

"I will make it two or less," she said. "I am ready."

2 8

THE TREE OF LIFE

It took him hours to reach the bottom. Valdemar had long since stopped feeling pain by then, or anything else for that matter. The boiling blood had consumed his skin and left almost nothing but the flayed meat underneath.

Any other person would have perished from the experience, the flesh stripped from their bones. But even this charnel pit could only counterbalance Valdemar's regeneration. His body generated biomass faster than the boiling blood could erode it, but not fast enough to let him recover.

There was no denying his inhuman origins now.

The Mask of the Nightwalker had survived the descent as well, pumping fresh air into his lungs. Its icy surface contrasted with the searing heat of the bloody pit and its magical vision allowed Valdemar to see even in the deep darkness of Bethor's tower. In this case, blindness might have been a mercy.

The Dark Lord said that his lair's heart lay at the bottom and Valdemar thought he meant it figuratively. He didn't.

The summoner had landed on a pulsating, beating bed of meat. Countless bodies had merged together, their flesh intermixing into a vast field of arms, eyeless faces, and festering blisters. Bloated wound-pits inhaled the boiling blood only to pump it back into slimy arteries above. The vein through which Valdemar had fallen was only one of many.

All the corpses whose blood fueled the tower had fused in its core. Derros, dokkars, humans, troglodytes, warbeasts, surface monsters . . .

Lord Bethor did not discriminate. Valdemar even noticed the rotting skull of a colossal dragon peeking out of the structure, its bleaching bones half-sunk by fleshy tendrils. The gelatinous, quivering structure spanned as far as Valdemar's vision could see; maybe it ran underneath the entire Domain.

And if he couldn't escape, the summoner would become part of it.

At least nobody is looking, Valdemar thought as he observed the ceiling. Flesh and organic material covered the bloody arteries and walls of the tower, but none of them had eyes. Not even the gods would gaze into this dark hell, this deadly abyss.

Valdemar attempted to redirect the blood to lift himself back to the surface but he felt resistance. An opposing force pushed back against his will, denying his magic, denying his power, denying him. Valdemar thought that Bethor himself had stripped him of his magic, but the more he struggled, the more he doubted.

The *blood itself* refused to obey.

Without his magic, Valdemar attempted to swim back to the surface the old-fashioned way. His body was too weak from the descent and refused to move.

Maybe I should reshape my arms, Valdemar thought. His own body's resources were already strained countering the boiling of his flesh, so he turned to the festering heart for sustenance. *I could reattach my limbs. Maybe I could create more.*

Hands grabbed his flayed arms.

Valdemar looked on, horrified, as the eyeless faces of the abyss looked at him. Before he knew it, the heart of the tower started pulling him into itself, adding his flesh to the whole.

No, Valdemar panicked, trying to break free. But the more he struggled, the deeper the heart pulled him in.

"*We are one.*"

These words were not words. No mouth uttered them. They were just chaotic feelings that his empathic mind struggled to translate. The hateful flesh carried the malice of the dead.

Valdemar's true sight told him that the souls were long gone, but their grudges still infested their remains. Their lingering feelings had coalesced into a shapeless force; not a soul, but a haunt, a resentful will at the very heart of the world.

And now, it wanted Valdemar's flesh too.

Let me go, the summoner asked. When his plea went unanswered, he started giving orders with his will backed by magic. *Let me go, I said!*

But though Valdemar was skilled in the Blood, the collective's power dwarfed his own.

"*Your lord has no power here, red prince,*" the hateful flesh replied. "*Our king cast you down with us.*"

The hateful flesh existed in fear of the Dark Lord above. It hated and worshiped him in equal measure. Valar Bethor was a god and the corpses were his throne.

What was one more body buried beneath the foundations?

Time lost its meaning. Valdemar's face had joined the living tapestry at the tower's bottom, only his mask peeking out of the flesh. The word "body" meant nothing to him anymore. Without skin, all the flesh looked the same; the sinews, the veins, the nerves and the organs had interconnected with a thousand pathways. He had become a cog in a living machine.

And yet his mind endured.

Maybe it was the Mask of the Nightwalker that allowed Valdemar to keep his sanity. Something in it repelled the hateful flesh. Or maybe it would be a gradual process, his will eroded over the years until he surrendered his individuality.

It would never happen.

"*We are one,*" the flesh said.

Without me, Valdemar thought as he tried to focus. His mind pushed back the whispering cacophony.

Should he sleep and dream? Close his eyes and think of the well? Would his nightmare startle even this hateful flesh and make it recoil?

"*No connection here,*" the collective replied as it sensed his plan. "*No escape. Only walls.*"

Valdemar couldn't sleep. To dream meant to dive into the collective unconscious shared by all living things, but the tower acted as an impermeable skin of steel keeping his mind walled in.

This entire place worked similarly to his Painted Field; an enclosed realm separated from the outside world. A pocket realm, made of flesh rather than paint. Neither could he summon anything. Nothing could enter or escape this cage, not even calls or pleas. Like a bottle of wine, a lid kept everything inside.

A gatekeeper called Valar Bethor.

Though this abyss had many arteries, they all converged at one place at the summit. The Dark Lord heard Valdemar's attempts to call interdimensional outsiders to his side and cast his demands back into the abyss.

But . . . were all paths truly closed to the summoner?

Valdemar focused on the mask he wore, losing himself in the cold. This time, he didn't even need to sleep to dream of the surface. The boiling abyss of Bethor's tower vanished, swallowed by an even deeper darkness. A frozen wasteland of snow and flensing wind expanded before his eyes. The ruins of an elven city lay buried beneath a great glacier next to a frozen sea. The biting cold could turn steel brittle and chill the soul. The Whitemoon overlooked him from the night sky and answered his existence not with whispers, but with silence. Sometimes purple auroras flared in the heavens, only for the darkness to drown them as soon as they appeared.

In truth, Valdemar found the experience oddly comforting. The silence and mental separation from the hateful flesh eased the burden on his mind, allowing him to rest and recover mentally. The silence came as a relief.

Valdemar looked around himself but found the world smaller than in his first dream. He towered over frozen houses identical to those he saw in the Silent King's realm, although his steps produced no sound. The winds flowed around him as if he were part of the atmosphere itself, a living void.

He moved toward the frozen sea by no will of his own. His body, if it was even his own, walked by the will of another. Only when Valdemar reached the shore did he stop and kneel. His blackened, clawed hand swept snow aside, polished the ice underneath, and looked at his own reflection.

The creature that faced him wasn't a man or any entity native to Underland. Its shape vaguely reminded Valdemar of a gaunt humanoid, but with elongated legs, crooked horns, and too many arms for a man. He couldn't see the creature's skin within the darkness, though he noticed patches of white fur and black scales. A spiraling white crater marred its face, a cold volcano oozing mist rather than lava. Valdemar observed as the reflection opened its vertical maw, but he saw neither fangs nor throat, only the blackness between stars and icicles bent into the shape of tentacles.

The Nightwalker.

As Valdemar looked through the Stranger's eyes, so did it peer through the mask.

What are you? Valdemar thought. *What do you want?*

For a moment, he thought the ancient entity couldn't hear or understand him. That the mask only stopped at letting them share their sights.

But then the creature raised a clawed, crooked hand and pointed it at its reflection.

You? Valdemar thought, trying to understand the creature. *You are me?*

Another hand covered the creature's crater of an eye, but only half of it. A clawed finger pointed at the obscured side of its face, then back at the reflection.

Half? Half of me?

No. Not halves, but sides.

You are the me from another side? Valdemar tried to translate. The Nightwalker hadn't made a sound so far and appeared incapable of vocalization. *Which other side?*

The Nightwalker looked up, and Valdemar gazed at the Whitemoon's ghoulish visage. Only then did Valdemar realize the truth in all of its horrors.

The Whitemoon was more than a rogue moon. It was a Stranger with a powerful entity acting as its servant.

And since sides implied a conflict of some sort . . . Valdemar guessed he might have found the answer to an ancient question that bothered countless mages across history: why had the Whitemoon come to this world?

To wage war on another Stranger.

Maybe it had tried to freeze the world's surface in an attempt to slay the creature occupying Underland's tunnels, only to find it warmly hidden beneath the world's crust, out of reach from the cold and the alien horrors the rogue moon brought with it.

The Dark Lords knew the truth too; or at least Lord Och and Bethor certainly did. Had they covered it up to prevent a panic? To avoid revealing the existence of the eyes and their immense reach?

What does it have to do with me? Valdemar thought, knowing the Stranger would hear him.

The Nightwalker returned its focus to the frozen sea, before raising a hand and shattering the ice with a mighty blow. The Stranger gazed at its cracked reflection.

Break the ice?

Valdemar thought for a second that the creature meant it literally, before putting two and two together. The Dark Lords had set a barrier separating the surface from Underland below, allowing only a few explorers to pass through. Whitemoon cultists regularly attempted to break these wards and receive blessings from their alien masters above.

The Nightwalker wanted him to follow in their footsteps.

No, Valdemar replied, knowing better than to let this ancient horror descend into Underland. Monsters from the surface hungered for warm blood, and judging by its cultists' actions, this creature was no different.

And even if it was only interested in slaying the eyes, the Whitemoon hated life itself. It had caused the extinction of countless species and the survivors sheltering in Underland would suffer the same fate if it had its way.

Sensing his refusal, the Nightwalker raised its many hands at the skies. The freezing winds swirled above him, carrying snow and shards of ice. Purple auroras came to life above them and joined the storm, their lights bending into a dancing spiral that swallowed the skies. So terrible was the weather that the frozen city in the background trembled, the glacier collapsing from the sheer power of the battering winds.

It was a powerful spell if Valdemar had ever seen one.

But not one from the Blood.

It was a form of magic unlike any Valdemar had ever seen; not one that focused on manipulating life and death, but rather forces that were never alive in the first place. The wind, the cold, even cosmic radiation. He tried to understand how it worked, to analyze how the Nightwalker manipulated the elements, only for the Stranger to cancel his spell. The snow fell down to earth as the winds calmed themselves and the auroras died in the skies. The Nightwalker had given his audience a demonstration, but it asked for something in return for more.

Power.

The Nightwalker promised Valdemar magical secrets and power in exchange for his cooperation. It was a bribery attempt in all its crudeness. *Even so, what would I use this magic for in a world of the dead?* Valdemar asked rhetorically.

The Nightwalker once more covered half its face, a finger moving from one side to the other.

Switch sides? Was the Nightwalker offering to make Valdemar one of the alien creatures inhabiting the surface? To cast away his humanity—what little half he had inherited from his mother—and embrace the cold?

It might have been an appealing offer to a depraved cultist eager for power, but not to Valdemar. He didn't bother trying to deceive the Nightwalker either; if it could understand the summoner's thoughts, then lies wouldn't work.

Still, it cost nothing to be polite. Valdemar thanked the Nightwalker for the information it had shared, but firmly declined the offer. The summoner sensed no anger from the Stranger, nor did he receive threats. The creature simply looked at its cracked reflections without a word.

The creature was patient. Cold could turn even the hardest steel brittle with time and it was unchanging as ice. It would wait for Valdemar to change his mind.

The summoner closed his eyes and the connection with it, his mind returning to the bottom of Bethor's tower. He meditated on what he had learned and tried to make sense out of it.

There was a war going on, with mankind caught in the middle. The Blood was a connection, life; even the undead were half-alive. This "Cold" that the Nightwalker used relied on forces that were never alive in the first place. It reminded Valdemar of how elementals manipulated fire or wind. The Blood and the Cold were opposites.

But my tower will resist your attempts. To use its power, you must conquer it. You must understand the true nature of the Blood.

Lord Bethor said that Valdemar could only escape by figuring out this riddle. He thought he already knew what the Blood was, namely that it was an esoteric force of magic. But the existence of sorcery beyond the usual framework called that into question.

And if the Blood was truly linked to life and death, why couldn't Valdemar use it normally in this pit of flesh? Even if magic created sympathetic connections between individuals, the summoner should have been capable of tapping into his own body's reserves to cast spells just fine.

Unless . . . unless he had misunderstood his magic entirely? That no matter how strong he could become, he still needed to tap into an outside element to use the Blood at all? Something that the tower cut him off from? But what? What was missing?

Valdemar opened his eyes, his buried mask facing the fleshy walls.

The eyes were missing.

A black pool that transformed life into something else . . .

A primordial dream acting as a subset of a larger Stranger's reverie, protecting sentient life from the raw emotions of the Qlippoths . . .

Something that had existed long before mankind delved into Underland . . . from the very dawn of the world . . .

It's its *Blood,* Valdemar realized in horror. *The blood of our progenitor.*

Separation was an illusion. All life in Underland shared a single lineage; they were but pieces of something far larger than themselves.

"The cancer theory seems to be the likeliest explanation for the biological oddities we observed, Lord Och; mutant cells breaking off from the body, weakening it and causing a reaction."

It all made a grim kind of sense now.

But what was Valdemar's place in all of this? A tool to destroy the infection? A way to reincorporate it? Or an unforeseen mutation, a cosmic biological weapon?

You are the me from the other side.

These were questions for later. Valdemar would have all the time to ponder them once he escaped this hellhole.

Now that he understood the true nature of the Blood, the summoner considered the hateful flesh with new eyes. He had tried to control it the way a master brought a dog to heel, but you couldn't inspire fear and obedience in your own hands or feet. Either it was a part of you or it wasn't. His mistake was to see this heart of corpses as an outside element he had to bend to his will, instead of a separated part of himself that he had to reincorporate into the whole.

This time, Valdemar stopped struggling. The flesh welcomed him at first, welcoming him into the whole. Only when the summoner sprung the trap did it try to reject him, and by then it was too late.

This place was a cancer separated from the Blood outside, a mass of corrupted cells lumped together and cut off from the body outside by walls of steel. It would exist forever in isolation, growing with each piece it absorbed. You didn't sew a tumor into a healthy body, and so Valdemar didn't try.

Instead, his will became a virus. His nerves spread to the corpse-network trying to consume him and his blackened blood with it. Valdemar's consciousness infected the hateful flesh, and where strength had failed, subversion prevailed.

My consciousness isn't in my brain, Valdemar realized as eyes opened on the fleshy walls. Not those of his progenitor, but his own. *It's in every cell of my body.*

He was not a human, but the blood of a god incarnated into a man-shaped vessel. As long as a single part of him remained, his soul would remain anchored to this plane.

No wonder Lord Och advised him against leaving severed arms around. With time they would become mindless cancers of their own.

Valdemar could have probably infected and subverted the entire tower given time, but it would take more mental effort than he was willing to invest. It would change him too, and he might stop thinking of himself as human and become something else. Something like Valar Bethor or his "father."

So Valdemar stopped once he had assimilated enough flesh to rebuild a body of his own, albeit one larger and capable of carrying him back to the surface. His human self was buried in a three-meters-tall armor made of harvested corpses lumped together. A hundred hands worked as one to carry him upward through the artery leading back to the summit.

The boiling warmth of the blood around him eroded it slowly, until nothing but a husk remained once he saw the light above.

At long last, Valdemar's hands, his real hands, emerged from the boiling pool. Air hurt as his nerves reformed, veins pumping black blood regenerating through his arms. He lifted himself onto the metal platform as he cast away his borrowed flesh-suit, letting it fall back into the tower's artery. If anything, Valdemar felt like an amphibian crawling on land for the first time.

Lord Bethor was meditating in the middle of the pool, his armor gone and his eyes were closed. Valdemar didn't interrupt him. He instead rested on the steel platform, waiting for his native regeneration to kick back in and rebuild his skin.

The process took only minutes.

Once he had fully recovered, Valdemar removed the Mask of the Nightwalker and put it aside. He didn't care if he was naked. He was just happy to breathe true air again.

"Do you understand now?" Lord Bethor asked without opening his eyes. "What the Blood is?"

Valdemar sighed. "This is a body," he whispered, "and we are cancerous cells."

And the Dark Lord confirmed his theory. "All life native to Underland was born from the black blood your bodyguard saw, primordial slime that slowly evolved into humans, dokkars, dogs, and dragons over eons. We began to develop a consciousness separated from our godly progenitor, walling our minds off from its dreams and nightmares. I daresay our existence was a complete accident."

Valdemar blinked as a crack in space opened right above him and fresh mage robes fell through onto his lap. The summoner didn't even know teleportation could work with lifeless matter alone.

"Ialdabaoth," Lord Bethor said as Valdemar clothed himself. The word resonated in the summoner's mind like a dark promise, an ominous echo. "That is the name the Pleromians called our maker. It dreams, Valdemar. It mindlessly manifests the Qlippoths in its slumber, but though it often shows flashes of awareness, they never last. It is a sleepwalking god, almighty, unaware, unconscious."

"We only wield a piece of its power," Valdemar whispered, the clothes feeling comfortably warm compared to the boiling blood of the tower.

"Yes. Though our skills in magic vary from the strength of our souls and bodies, we all borrow a sliver of our maker's magic to a degree. It can affect even life from outside its lineage to a degree or call to other dimensions, as your meeting with the Silent King showed."

And it had attracted foes from the darkness of space.

"How do I fit in all of this?" Valdemar asked. "Why was I born?"

Unlike his teacher, Lord Bethor deigned to give a straightforward answer.

"You are a bridge," he said. "Not only between worlds, but also between our progenitor and mankind. Perhaps you were meant to unite us back with Ialdabaoth or to destroy us, the way we burn tumors. I do not know, and what the gods want does not matter. You are cursed with free will, Valdemar Verney, as we all are."

Valdemar wondered if he could infect other beings of flesh with a single mind. Maybe that was the purpose that the Verney cult intended for him, to serve as a weapon to return castaway parts into the whole.

If so, he wanted no part in it. Valdemar liked his free will and didn't want to take it away from anyone else.

No wonder the Primordial Dream reacts badly to me, the summoner thought with a grim form of amusement. He had a strong connection to it by virtue of his mixed parentage, but he was a subversive element inside a rebellious corner of the dreamlands. *I truly need to build a new Painted Field here.*

"Lord Bethor, why did you create that thing at the bottom?" Valdemar asked as he moved back to his feet. "What insight did you hope to gain?"

"That will be a discussion for another day," Lord Bethor said. Clearly, he wasn't one for idle chatter. "Now that you understand yourself and transcended the limits of a human form, we shall focus on body-modification and shapeshifting spells. We will also lay the groundwork for you to learn advanced summoning arts. You will become like a dragon, as competent in melee as at range. But first . . ."

"Yes?"

"You will get some rest. Tiring you out beyond what is necessary will only make you slower, and the first ritual I shall teach you cannot suffer a failure. It will influence your entire summoning career."

This time, Lord Bethor opened his eyes.

"It is time that you summon your familiar."

2 9

THE DEATH OF THE SENSES

The machine was right above her, stalking her, *hunting* her. Marianne could hear the *clinks* and *clanks* of its armor reverberating through the thin metal ceiling separating them. Though her gaze remained obscured by blindness, her mind visualized the creature from the sounds it made: a gaunt, two-meters-tall skeleton of steel, with syringes and needles for fingers and a metal mask for a face. She heard the gears and servos grinding in its elongated limbs and the biomechanical organs pumping nutrients into its artificial brain. Her Blood-enhanced nose smelled the scent of oil and rust that followed it everywhere. Her hand sensed the sound of the machine's feet traveling through the walls.

But the only taste in her mouth was that of her own fear.

Lord Bethor had guessed correctly. Pain was a great motivator to learn.

A drop of blood traveled down her cheek, but Marianne didn't dare to move. She was already holding her breath the best she could, in spite of the scars, the bruises, and the metal needle in her chest—a parting gift from her last encounter with the monster.

The noblewoman knew that running wouldn't save her. She had tried before, when the creature cornered her after Lord Bethor taught her how to use her hearing to walk straight and find her path. First she attempted to fight, only to discover that neither her fists nor bone bullets could get past the creature's iron shell; it didn't even have enough blood in its body for a telekinetic strike.

Marianne had tried to escape after realizing how outmatched she truly was. But the machine moved with superhuman speed. Even after she called on the Blood to strengthen her legs and lungs, it swiftly caught up to her. Its metal hand had grabbed her head, smashed it against a wall with enough force to break her nose, and carved a wound on the left side of her face; one deep enough to scratch the cheekbones.

It mauled Marianne the same way a cat would have played with a rat, tossing and kicking her around. And when it got bored after a full minute of that brutal treatment, it stabbed her in the chest with a metal needle right between the ribs. It hadn't struck any vital area, but it impaired her breathing and hurt whenever her muscles contracted. Marianne hadn't been able to remove it and doubted that anyone but a trained surgeon could.

Afterward, the machine had stopped beating her and fell inanimate for a few minutes. It gave Marianne a short window of time to put some space between them.

How long had she haunted this maze, unable to find an exit while pursued by that *thing*? Hours? Days? With only Lord Bethor's occasional advice to rely on, Marianne had long lost all sense of time.

She controlled her breathing and slowed her own heartbeat to a crawl. It wasn't a skill Lord Bethor taught her, but one that she developed on her own while trying to avoid the machine. Its hearing acuity was downright superhuman.

Marianne's efforts seemed to pay off, the machine walking along the tunnel above without any change in behavior.

Then the drop of blood fell from her face and onto the cold iron floor.

Marianne immediately heard the machine's servos grinding to a screeching halt, its metal head snapping down to look in her direction. Could its eyes see through the floors and ceilings? Marianne didn't think so but she felt its gaze all the same.

Think, think, she thought as the machine froze like a cat trying to hear a mouse's breathing. Marianne called upon the Blood, and though a ceiling of steel stood between her and her foe, her magic ignored it.

There was little to target though. The machine had no heart, only pumps; no veins, only cables. In a way, it was the perfect killer. It didn't need to feed or sleep, and it had no higher thoughts to distract it from its purpose. It had none of the usual frailties of a physical body, nor an opening to exploit.

But it still had a brain and synapses. And if it could hear Marianne, it must have had ears.

Desperation gave her new strength and allowed her to focus like never before, with even the pain in her cheeks and chest unable to distract her. Using her enhanced hearing in combination with the Blood's psychometric insight, she formed a biological map of the machine's nervous systems. She noticed the neurons linked to a biomechanical labyrinth of steel inside the creature's head: its inner ear.

The Blood couldn't alter metal nor the sound that entered this artificial organ . . . but it could alter the signals traveling to the brain. Marianne was no neuromancer or illusionist. She wouldn't be able to make an elaborate deception.

I just have to . . . slightly alter what it hears, Marianne thought as another drop of blood fell down from her face. *Same sound, different direction.*

She imagined the drop falling up rather than down, reaching the ceiling above the machine's head rather than the floor underneath its feet. She clung to this illusion so much that she started to hear it inside her own mind, the Blood echoing her lie. *Believe, believe . . .*

The drop fell onto the floor and the machine looked up.

This time, it didn't remain still. It crawled down on all fours, the joints in its limbs twisting until the creature looked more like a lizard than a humanoid form. It dashed at impressive speeds through the tunnels, but in the wrong direction. Believing Marianne to be above itself, the machine moved farther and farther away from her.

Once the machine was too far away to hear her—a distance she had learned through trial and error—Marianne allowed herself a breath of relief.

"Good," Lord Bethor's voice echoed in the corridors. "You have learned this spell well."

Marianne knew better than to answer. While the machine ignored the Dark Lord's words, it *always* picked up on her own.

Her teacher hadn't expected a back-and-forth anyway. "Illusion magic and telepathy are not so different," Lord Bethor explained. "In both cases, you must conceptualize the input that the individual must receive and send it to their brain through the Blood. Obviously, it is easier to trick a fellow human than a dragon, as these beasts use different senses than our own."

Which implied that the machine had been intentionally designed to be targeted by illusions.

"The more you can put yourself in your target's shoes, so to say, the better your illusions. To function, telepathy and mind-reading demand you understand the signals in the target's brain and the oscillations of the soul. Enhancing your senses is a necessary step toward mastering both arts."

When Marianne grew certain that the machine was many rooms away, she returned to exploring the maze. She gasped as her chest ached each time her muscles contracted to breathe, the metal needle embedding itself deeper and deeper into her flesh.

Turn left and go deeper, Marianne thought as she remembered her mental map of the maze. She had explored a good chunk of it, though each dead end made her paranoid. She always wondered if the machine would sneak up on her from behind, leaving her with no way out.

"This ability to gather information through the five senses and tuning it with the Blood can go beyond mapping a monster's innards," Lord Bethor continued to dispense his wisdom. "It can be used to learn the history of an object by studying its structure in depth. If you escape this maze, I expect you to refine this power. You will find it useful for your investigations."

If she escaped.

The Dark Lord's words said it all.

I mustn't lose heart, Marianne thought. *Despair is the death of the spirit.*

She *refused* to bleed and starve away in this tomb of metal with only a mindless machine for company. Marianne hadn't accepted death beneath Verney Castle and she wouldn't start now.

Her quest led her into a single corridor longer than all the others so far. Marianne considered changing her route, as it was too long for her to detect where it led. For all she knew, it might be a dead end, a trap.

But her Blood-enhanced senses detected a few things. The smell of blood. Hair on the floor. The distant sound of a thick liquid traveling through plumbing.

Corpses were dragged here, Marianne thought. *More than one.*

Lord Bethor had said that the machine caught the best of his students three times. Which meant the facility had been used by multiple people in the past; and considering the Dark Lord's methods, not everyone had made it through the process alive.

Which meant the corpses had to be disposed of. Lord Bethor didn't waste resources so Marianne doubted he would use an incinerator. In all likelihood, his failed student's remains would be repurposed into undead soldiers or their blood extracted to fuel his tower.

Maybe the corridor led to an exit. Maybe it led to a bloody pit. But it was a potential escape route all the same.

Marianne walked into the hallway with a steady rhythm. She had grown better about walking without her sight, relying on her inner ear to keep her balance. The echo of her footsteps bounced off the steel walls, giving her a crude vision of the room.

Marianne wondered how the world would look once she recovered her sight. Her eyes itched to the point she had to blink repeatedly to avoid tears. She thought Lord Bethor had taken her sight with a spell, but now she was convinced he had instead used an alchemical concoction. She had noticed foreign substances traveling through her eyes and blood, altering the frontal areas of her face.

She worried the blindness might become permanent if she didn't escape. Her enhanced senses could cover this handicap but sightlessness would cripple her swordsmanship. That was her greatest fear. To see all her efforts and sacrifices she made to become a warrior worthy of the Reynard legacy go to waste.

Is that what matters most to me? she thought. *Not to honor Jérôme or to protect Valdemar as I promised . . . but to be the best? When stripped of everything, is that all that remains inside me?*

Her questions went unanswered. Or rather, Marianne knew the answer within herself but she was afraid of vocalizing it. She didn't want to face the selfish desire inside her heart, the one that lurked beneath her words of remorse or her promises to help others.

And for now, it didn't matter. Questions would wait until after she secured her escape and survival. Lord Bethor had been right, doubts and hesitation didn't have their place in a dangerous situation. Her mind had to remain clear as freshwater.

After a few minutes, Marianne finally reached the corridor's end. As she worried, it led to a dead end . . . but not the kind she had feared. Her fingers slowly trailed on a reinforced door of steel so thick that artillery would struggle to bring it down. She knocked on it with her fingers, focusing as the noise traveled through it and echoed a wide space beyond. She had found the exit.

But it was *locked.*

"No," she whispered as her hands traveled along the door. She tried to find a handle to seize, a lock to pick, a hole, anything. But the exit was airtight and smooth as a mirror. "No . . ."

The door only opened from one side, and she was on the wrong one.

This had all been a trick.

"I must make my own exit," Marianne realized out loud. Could she break down the door? Could she reinforce her body enough to bend its steel? What other choice did she have?

Lord Bethor's voice echoed through the maze, but he neither confirmed nor denied her conclusion. Instead, he only harshened the test's difficulty.

"I will remove the fetters binding my warbeast," the Dark Lord declared. "Now it will hunt you to the full extent of its abilities. And if it catches you, it will kill you."

Now that Marianne had completed one part of the test, he moved the goalpost farther ahead.

The noblewoman held her breath as her enhanced ears picked up a clicking noise echoing through the maze. Was the machine trying to intimidate her with mechanical roars or cries? Somehow Marianne didn't think it was capable of scare tactics. Its mind was unclouded by emotions or distractions. If Lord Bethor had given it the order to kill Marianne, all its actions would serve this end.

But how would making noise help that creature locate its prey?

Bats, Marianne realized in horror. *Echolocation.*

The machine was sending noises across the tunnels and analyzed how it bounced back. Marianne tried to hold her breath and remain still, to no avail. Unlike when the machine tried to detect her by listening to the noise she made, it didn't matter what she did. Sounds bounced off her body and the creature registered a human-shaped item hiding in a tunnel.

The clicking noise turned into a strident cry and the machine started chasing her.

Marianne turned around and put some space between her and the exit. She knew that she would never get out of the corridor before the machine caught up to her location, but she couldn't afford to have her back against the wall.

Lord Bethor wanted a fight.

He would get it.

Marianne adopted a fighting stance even as she struggled against the pain in her chest and cheeks. Blood dripped on her lips as she reinforced her fists with a layer of bones. She wasn't as good with her hands as with her rapier, but she had to use the tools available.

Wait . . . Marianne thought as she "looked" at her right arm with her enhanced senses, examining the bone beneath the flesh. *I have a sword.*

Marianne clenched her teeth and struggled against the sheer pain in her arm, as she drew upon the Blood and her body's last reserves to grow a new bone. The sharp end of a blade erupted from her forearm, centimeter by centimeter. Blood and bone bullets caused much pain, but *nothing* like this.

"Fuck," she whispered, tears raining down her cheeks and mixing with her blood. "Fuck . . ."

By the time she managed to get a bone rapier out of her right arm, the machine had already entered the corridor. Marianne grabbed her weapon and prepared herself to fight for her life as blood poured out of her wounds.

The machine caught up to her in seconds while running on all fours. It moved as fast as Shelley, but unlike the unskilled wererat, it struck with lethal precision. The machine didn't shriek a threat or offer a warning. It simply rose on its two back legs and aimed for its target's chest with its claws.

The motion took less than a second, but to Marianne, it seemed to last forever. She heard the sound of the servos, sensed the vibrations in the air, and smelled the oil. Her mind gathered all these sensations into a perfect picture.

Marianne dodged by sidestepping to the left and struck back with her rapier.

Her bone blade was as strong as steel and her aim true, but the weapon bounced off the creature's armored chest. However, at the moment of contact, Marianne enhanced her sense of touch to analyze the vibrations. Her mind visualized the results and mapped out the internal workings of the creature. She saw the weaknesses in the joints and how the biomechanical organs all fit together.

It has a brain and spine, weak points, Marianne thought as the machine raised both of its arms and tried to find a hole in her defense. *I have to strike the joints in the neck and sever it.*

To allow the creature to turn its head, the builders made the neck flexible, fragile. One strike at the weakest point would do the deed.

Like a true duelist, Marianne waited for the machine to attack and leave itself open to retaliation. Its left hand twisted to attack from below, but as it advanced, the noblewoman noticed that its joints didn't move as they should.

A feint!

The true attack came from the right and aimed for her head. Metal needles lunged for Marianne's carotid with enough force to behead her. The machine had reached the same conclusion as she did and identified the neck as a weak spot.

Wagering everything in this one strike, Marianne let the monster's weapons approach as close as possible before dodging. The needles grazed her skin and hair without drawing blood, like a razor brushing against an invisible beard. Carried by its momentum, the machine moved a step forward just as Marianne's rapier lunged for its throat.

The blade struck true.

Guided by her complete awareness of the space around her, Marianne hit the machine in the weakest part of its gaunt neck. Her rapier hit the spine between the joints and went through it. The noblewoman let out a roar of sheer anger as she used the blade like a lever, wagering all her strength and weight in the motion. She felt the needle already inside her chest tear through her muscles and draw blood, but she powered through.

Her sword cracked along its blade, but the machine's neck broke first.

The head went flying like a bottle cap and bounced off the walls, while the decapitated body lost its balance. Marianne took a step back as it collapsed on the ground before her feet, her broken blade showered in oil and spinal fluid.

For a moment, the noblewoman could only breathe loudly, her body as tense as a cable. She almost expected the beast to rise back to its feet and strike her by surprise once again.

It stayed down.

And Marianne laughed.

All the stress accumulated in the last hour left her body, replaced with joyful ecstasy. A rush of endorphins traveled through her body, filling her with pleasure and the satisfaction of a perfect victory. She basked in her senses, and even the blood dripping from her chest, cheek, and arm felt as pleasurable as a warm shower.

"Do you understand, Marianne Reynard?" Lord Bethor's voice asked with a hint of satisfaction. "The lesson I meant to teach you?"

Marianne breathed heavily, before calming down enough to answer. "I was so distracted looking for an exit . . . that I failed to study my foe closely." If she had focused on fighting back instead of trying to escape the creature, she would have noticed the structural weakness earlier.

"Yes. The beast defeated you in your first encounter because it focused entirely on one task at a time. Its mind was unclouded by judgment or distractions. It decided the goal it would pursue, and when it did, it dedicated all its strength toward achieving it."

Though she couldn't see, Marianne turned her blind eyes to the beheaded machine. The head was alive, desperately trying to move to get at her. In spite of the damage it suffered, it *still* wanted to kill her. "You want me . . . to become *that?*"

"Of course not. Tools cannot learn and improve. In our ability to innovate and think, we humans are superior to animals, mindless golems, and auto-machines. I do not ask that you relinquish your intellect or self-awareness. Only that you focus them on what truly matters. A blade cannot cut left and right at once. You must direct all your energies in one direction if you hope to prevail."

Marianne chuckled, though she didn't even understand why herself. *I don't even have enough strength left for a healing spell,* she thought. "I broke your record."

"You did," Lord Bethor conceded. "You have passed this first round of training and your sight shall be returned to you. You may see small changes in your visual acuity."

Slowly, a veil was lifted from Marianne's eyes. She saw the lights above her head, the iron walls, the white metal carcass at her feet, and the black oil dripping from its wounds. *It's like that pool,* she thought as she remembered Verney Castle. *It's wrong . . .*

It was wrong.

Something was wrong.

She saw the ripples in the oil and the blond hair on the machine's claws. She saw the veins in the creature's biomechanical red eyes and the slight traces of rust around them. She saw the slight weaknesses in the ceiling, the tiny cracks in the steel.

"What . . ." Marianne looked at her bloodied hands and the tiny microscopic hairs growing out of them. She noticed the countless lines on her skin, every single tiny scar. Her mind started counting them all, her eyes unable to look away. "What is this?"

"You were fed a mix of the Elixir of True Sight and other alchemical components through your eyes," Lord Bethor explained. "It will heighten your visual acuity and reflexes to near-perfection."

Marianne saw the microscopic black spots in her blood—and the tiny eyes looking back at her inside them. *It's inside us,* Bertrand's words echoed in her head as the wound in her chest ached. She saw the colors of the eyes as droplets of blood fell on the floor, spreading the infection further.

"It's . . . it's too much . . ." Marianne closed her eyes, but what little light filtered through her eyelids still caused her pain as her mind processed all the colors making up the visual spectrum. She put her hands over them in an attempt to cast her gaze in complete darkness. "It's too much!"

She was seeing *everything* in perfect detail, all at once.

"Too many things . . ." Even her eyelids had eyes looking back at her. "I can't . . . I can't think . . ."

"Your struggle will not be to learn how to use your sight but to process the information," Lord Bethor said without any warmth. "Valdemar will take care of your wounds as you rest and figure it out. I will give you some time, and then we shall resume training."

Marianne let out a scream as her eyes itched so much that she struggled against the urge to tear them out.

By the time the door opened, her nails had sunk into her skin.

30

ONLY HUMAN

The bed was cold and Valdemar's fingers were warm. Marianne grunted as they stabbed into her back like daggers. Although he had used some kind of healing spell to lessen her pain, her enhanced sense of touch reduced its effectiveness.

"If you could please stop moving," Valdemar asked. While Marianne kept her eyes closed, she visualized him perfectly with her other senses. He had to kneel beside her bed to operate on her naked back, his teeth grinding as he tried to extract the machine's needle from her chest; it had gone so deep into her flesh that it was easier to remove from the back. Her shirt lay on the steel floor and close to the only door. "The more you strain your muscles, the harder it is for me to remove the needle."

"I'll try." Marianne breathed slowly as she did in the maze, trying to relax the best she could. But when Valdemar's fingers touched the needle, she had to bite her pillow to suppress the pain. The bandage on her facial wound started to itch, and the soulstone around her neck felt as if it burned against her skin.

Valar Bethor afforded his apprentices no more comfort than the smallest of his soldiers. He had given them a single room with bunk beds, a small desk, a shower, and toilets. The cell—Marianne couldn't call it anything else—barely reached nine square meters with a window too small for someone to jump through.

Valdemar had started redecorating it though. The few times Marianne had managed to open her eyes, she had seen expanding paintings on the walls representing moths, foxes, flowers, dunes, and alien land-scapes. This Painted Field would help Valdemar sleep, hopefully without summoning a phantom hamlet.

"I am going to remove the needle very slowly to avoid causing inter-nal damage," the summoner said. "I need you to exhale as I do it. Think of something pleasant and relaxing."

"Like what?" Marianne asked dryly. She didn't want to sound snappy, but she had had a rough day.

"I dunno, a warm hot bath? Reading a novel?" Valdemar hesitated. "Making love?"

Marianne couldn't help but turn her head and glare at him . . . before instantly closing her eyes as the visual stimuli overwhelmed her. She bur-ied her face in the pillow once more.

"Was the suggestion so ridiculous?" Valdemar asked with a sigh. "The first thing that comes to mind for me is painting, but I don't think you do that to relax."

I will think of the warm bath, Marianne thought while she tried to imagine warm water on her skin. Now that she thought of it, could she cast an illusion on herself? Trick her own mind to ignore the pain?

As it turned out, lying to oneself came more easily than deceiving a kill-ing machine. Marianne imagined herself in her family's manor bathroom, enjoying a warm bath with only flashes bringing her back to reality.

He's fusing his hand with my back, Marianne realized as she wavered between dream and reality. She had to bring down her own psychic defenses to prevent a backlash from the operation, but her enhanced senses gave her a detailed picture of Valdemar's activities. His hand had turned into roots digging between her bones and muscles, extracting the needle inch by inch.

As their flesh briefly became one through the medium of his hand, Marianne noticed the subtle abnormalities in his biology. Valdemar looked human, with human organs, but his blood moved seamlessly even without his heartbeat. The heart *helped*, but it wasn't *necessary*.

A grail, Marianne thought, *a god's blood in a human-shaped container.*

"One, two," Valdemar whispered, before swiftly extracting the needle. The sudden pain made Marianne grit her teeth and dispelled her own illusion. "Three."

His fingers magically knitted her flesh together, closing her wound. Marianne let out a breath of relief, made even better with no metal needle to impair her lungs. *It feels better than the warm bath,* she thought. "Thank you, Valdemar."

"It's longer than my index finger," the summoner said as he examined the needle. "I'm surprised you could even talk with something like this so close to your lungs."

"And I'm surprised you could survive in boiling blood without your skin."

"I'm sure I would have been appetizing once fried," Valdemar said, and Marianne couldn't help but chuckle. "I'll let you rest before we operate on your face."

"No," she said before clearing her throat. "Sorry, umm . . . if you are willing to, I would like to be done with it as soon as possible. If I'm not asking too much."

"As you wish. Give me a few minutes to clean my hands."

"Would that change anything?" Marianne asked as she grabbed her clothes and put her shirt back on. She sensed a slight change in Valdemar's blood pressure before he turned his head away. *How can he be embarrassed after painting Frigga naked?* Marianne wondered with amusement. Still, she appreciated his gentlemanly behavior.

"The needle and the blades that cut your face were infected with special bacteria," Valdemar explained as he put the needle on the desk. "They disrupt blood pressure and clotting. If you couldn't use the Blood, you would have probably become paralyzed or bled out."

"I . . . I didn't know," Marianne admitted, surprised and disappointed in herself. "I didn't notice any poison."

"You wouldn't have unless you had either access to biomancy spells or perfect awareness of your body," Valdemar replied as he moved to the shower room. "Your healing spells are passable, but not good enough to expunge that kind of infection."

Marianne sat on her bed, her back against the steel wall. "I was never good at healing magic," she admitted. Valdemar's remark had put her in a sorrowful mood. "When I was young, I thought it didn't matter. That I should instead improve my strength so much that I wouldn't need to heal in the first place."

"What changed your mind?" Valdemar asked over the sound of running water, washing his hands over a small sink.

"I saw someone I loved bleed out in front of me." The sight of Jérôme agonizing in a puddle of his own blood, life leaving his eyes as his slashed throat turned into a red fountain . . . Marianne would never forget it. "He looked at me. His eyes begged me for help. And all I did was panic."

Valdemar closed the water. Marianne wondered if he was looking at himself in the bathroom's mirror as he tried to find an answer.

"*He* was your fiancé, wasn't he?" he guessed.

"Yes," she admitted as Valdemar returned, kneeling in front of her. His left hand brushed against her facial bandage before slowly removing it. "I'm still not sure I could have saved him with my current spells."

"Don't do that," Valdemar said as he put her bandage aside and examined the scar. "Dwell on what could have been. It leads nowhere."

"I know." Valar Bethor thought the same. "Valdemar?"

"Yes?"

"Do you believe it is alright to make sacrifices for your dream?"

"Of course I do," Valdemar said as he cast a spell on her.

Marianne focused on his magic, and as she did, she realized he was expelling the machine's leftover bacteria from her wound. "Even if the sacrifice in question is someone else?"

"Depends if the goal is noble or not. If I had to kill one person to save ten with no third option in sight, I wouldn't hesitate." Valdemar paused for a moment. "You're not asking me, but yourself."

Marianne sighed. Should she tell him? She had only ever discussed this with Bertrand, but her friend and retainer wasn't here anymore.

"I told you before," Valdemar reminded her as his fingers touched her facial wound. The blade had cut to the bone, leaving it exposed. "You don't have to say it if you don't want to. Everyone is entitled to their private life."

"No, it's alright," she said while clearing her throat. "But . . . I would be thankful if you did not repeat what I'm about to tell you."

Instead of continuing with the surgery, Valdemar knelt and joined his hands. He didn't say a word and waited for Marianne to speak.

"I loved him. Jérôme. Even if our betrothal had been arranged." Unknown to their parents, they hadn't even waited for the wedding to consummate their relationship. "But there was one thing about him that I *hated*."

"That he wouldn't let you wield the rapier?"

The mere mention of her missing weapon made Marianne feel naked and incomplete. Lord Bethor hadn't returned it to her. He wouldn't give it back unless she learned to stop relying on it.

"He said he would let me borrow it behind closed doors," the noble-woman replied. "Jérôme . . . My father chose him because he was every-thing he had wanted in an heir. A dashing young man, well-loved, with a promising military career among the Knightly Orders ahead of him and a talent for swordsmanship. He was someone mindful of appearances . . . and he knew that my ancestor's rapier was the symbol of the Reynard family. That whoever carried it was its head."

Valdemar listened without a word and Marianne was thankful for that. It was easier for her to articulate her thoughts without interruptions.

"Even though we loved each other, the marriage between our families was a political alliance first and foremost," Marianne explained. "Jérôme was meant to inherit both my father's titles and his own estate. He was afraid that if he let me wield the rapier, then others wouldn't recognize him as the true new head of House Reynard. That it would weaken him politically."

Marianne sensed movement in the air around Valdemar's face. Using the Blood, she identified his expression as a sneer.

"I know," she said. "That's how I felt too. Eventually, we had an argu-ment and I demanded a duel to settle the rapier issue. I said I would give my all. We met in the gardens when everyone was asleep or occupied, with Bertrand as our only witness and referee."

Valdemar finally spoke. "You didn't warn anyone else?"

"No," Marianne replied. "Nobody would have sanctioned the duel, and most witnesses might have warned our families to prevent it. Even Bertrand wanted to speak up until Jérôme and I ordered him to remain quiet."

Valdemar didn't offer any condemnation. "How did the duel go?"

"I dominated him from start to finish." Jérôme had been good and gave his best, but he was never her equal in battle. "At one point . . . I saw an opening to disarm him. He tried to stop with his sword, but his parry accidentally drove my blade through his throat. As he fell on the ground with his neck bleeding, I realized he wasn't wearing his soul-stone. Because he trusted me."

She sensed Valdemar's body tense up, the paint on the walls rippling. *He's angry,* Marianne realized to her shock. *At me?* She tried to ignore the reaction as she continued her tale. "Bertrand was no expert healer, so he asked me to stay with Jérôme while he looked for help. By the time doc-tors arrived, he had already perished in my arms."

"It was an accident," Valdemar whispered while trying to comfort her, though Marianne still sensed an undercurrent of suppressed anger in his voice.

"The Empress ruled it that too, but my father told me in no uncertain terms that the noble families of Saklas wouldn't want to associate with the Reynards so long as I remained. I was . . ." Marianne cleared her throat. "I was so ashamed and guilt-ridden that I didn't even dare come to Jérôme's funeral. Bertrand . . . he felt guilty too. He never said it, but I know this is why he followed me into exile."

"You are blaming yourself for the wrong thing," Valdemar said firmly. "You didn't sacrifice your fiancé, you simply threw away the life you could have had with him. You didn't make the choice to slay him."

"Did I?" Marianne asked grimly. "I was happy to beat him, Valdemar. To give him bruises. When I struck him, I wondered if a part of me—"

"A *part* is not the *whole*, Marianne," Valdemar interrupted her harshly, to her surprise. She had never heard him use such a harsh, venomous tone, not even when he spoke of the inquisitors who arrested him. "Did you strike Jérôme with the intent to kill? Did you want to murder him when you raised your sword?"

"N-no," she blurted out. "Of course not."

"Then it's settled," Valdemar grunted. "Poisoning your husband to inherit his fortune is not the same thing as accidentally pushing him down the stairs in an argument. The result may be outwardly the same, but the context is wildly different. Intention matters as much as the expected result."

"Yet you're angry at me too," Marianne pointed out.

"I'm angry," the summoner admitted, "but not at *you.*"

Marianne froze, before tensing up. "Say it."

"You won't like it," he warned her.

"We agreed to tell the truth to each other," Marianne reminded him as she clenched her fists. "Say what's on your mind."

Valdemar took a long, deep breath before speaking. "It was beyond foolish to walk to a duel with a master swordswoman without a soulstone. As stupid as walking into a fire."

Marianne's nails sunk into her palms so deep, she worried they might draw blood. "Don't say that."

"Do you even know the cost of a soulstone?" Valdemar asked with a hint of envy. "Marianne, if I had been rich enough to buy one I would have carried it everywhere. Everyone in my family would have done the same, just like you're doing right now. This is a chaotic world and death visits as it wills. Your fiancé courted it."

"He *trusted* me," Marianne snapped back angrily. *Why am I raising my voice?* She thought, surprised by her own reaction. "Jérôme trusted me and died for it."

"What does trust have anything to do with it?" Valdemar marked a short pause. "Did you wear your soulstone during the duel?"

Marianne gritted her teeth.

"You did," Valdemar stated. "Because you knew there was a chance Jérôme *could* win, even if you were better than he ever was. Because you respected his abilities."

"You imply he didn't respect mine?"

"That's how it comes across to me. Duels are restricted for a reason, Marianne. Walking into one without any protection, even if it's a supposedly friendly one . . ." Valdemar shook his head. "That doesn't sound like trust to me. More like *arrogance*."

"I bested him in practice," Marianne hissed, her tone cold as ice. "He knew I was better."

"Then why didn't he carry the soulstone?"

"Because he thought I wouldn't have hurt him!" By now, she was shouting.

"So he thought you would go easy on him even though you were ready to throw your marriage away for the prize?" Valdemar snorted. "Did he truly know you?"

Marianne recoiled as if slapped.

"Marianne, we *barely* know each other and I can tell you always give your all in a fight," Valdemar argued. "Enough to attack a *Dark Lord*. Jérôme must have been willfully blind to think you would pull back your punches . . . or truly conceited."

Marianne tried to keep her calm and failed. "You know nothing."

"I've never been in love with a woman, so I can't say about what Jérôme felt . . . but I loved my grandfather enough to defend Earth's existence even in the face of mockery and criticism. Why wouldn't he bear the burden of shame and let you bear that sword?"

"His political career—"

"Exactly," he interrupted her. "Because he cared more about his *public image* than *you*."

Marianne opened her eyes.

The visual stimuli caused her pain, but it didn't overwhelm her. She could have been pierced with needles everywhere and her glare would have remained unwavering.

Valdemar stood before her, with his human face twisted into worry, his human eyes full of concern, and her blood dripping from his fingers.

"Why are you looking at me like that?" Marianne asked with anger, restraining herself from slapping him. She couldn't stand pity.

"Because you are trying to see things that weren't there," Valdemar replied with a sigh. "Like I did. Nostalgia blinds us to the bad parts of the past."

"Is that what this is about?" Marianne asked as she glanced at the covered portrait in a corner of the room. "You're projecting your disappointment with your grandfather on me."

This time, it was Valdemar's turn to wince. He lowered his head and looked at the floor with bitterness. Marianne instantly regretted her words but didn't find the strength to say so out loud. She closed her eyes, a tense silence settled between her roommate and her.

"Maybe," he admitted. "Probably. But that doesn't make what I say untrue."

Marianne gritted her teeth but didn't answer.

The noblewoman should have brushed his words aside like Captain Léopold's . . . but she couldn't get them out of her head, to her surprise. *Did I truly misunderstand everything?* she thought. *Jérôme can't have . . . he respected me.*

Marianne thought back of all her moments with her fiancé, trying to look for any hint of contempt behind the smile, searching for any hidden meaning behind his words when they discussed with other nobles. She knew he was always eager to boast about his skills in battle, about how only his future wife could make him sweat. Marianne thought he had been boasting for the both of them, but had it been a subtle mockery instead?

It had been years since that duel, and she had been young and lovestruck beforehand. Had she glossed over Jérôme's flaws? Idealized him? Maybe Marianne was the one who didn't know him at all.

She was mulling over her own memories when she noticed Valdemar was speaking out loud.

"If I had spent all the time researching summoning and Earth on biomancy instead, maybe I could have healed my mother from her mental illness," he said with surprising gravitas. "I could have created a soulstone by studying necromancy or stolen one. That's how I tortured myself after she died: by thinking of the roads I hadn't taken."

Now it was Marianne's turn to listen. He had given her that courtesy, she would return it.

"After a while . . ." Valdemar sighed. "Hard as it sounds, I realized that I put my dream above my mother's well-being. I loved her, but I wanted to show everyone the sun even more. I regret I couldn't save her *and* continue my research, but I made my choice. Just as you chose to duel Jérôme even knowing the possible consequences, because you prized your warrior's pride more than marital bliss."

"You still want to reach that place?" Marianne asked, trying to clear her own thoughts. "Even knowing your grandfather might have deceived you."

Valdemar nodded slowly. "Yes. Even if the dreamer wasn't perfect, the dream is worth following. Because no matter what my grandfather raised me for, our people still deserve better than this tomb of stone and flesh."

His next words were heavy with determination.

"We deserve better than *the eyes*."

Only then did Marianne realize that they had stopped looking back.

Even when she closed her eyes before, they had been there in the darkness, peering through the blood vessels in her eyelids. But they had vanished. When did they vanish?

Since Valdemar touched my cheek, she realized. She thought he had only expelled the machine's bacteria . . . but he had instead removed the eyes *inside* her eyes.

To make her feel better.

Marianne's anger vanished, like waste cleared by water. "I need to think," the noblewoman said, unsure how to react.

She heard Valdemar's nod, his head moving through the air. His hand touched her cheek while his magic fixed her bones and knitted her flesh and skin together.

"Is this your first time operating on someone?" Marianne asked, trying to change the subject to something lighter. "I could tell you were uncomfortable during the surgery."

"I raised and restored corpses as undead for clients," Valdemar said, before clearing his throat. "Operating on a living subject is a harder task, but I think I'm good at it. I find biomancy surprisingly easy to grasp."

Like almost all fields of the Blood, Marianne thought. She couldn't help but feel slightly jealous of him, even though she knew it was irrational. He needed an entire magical apparatus to even sleep normally.

By the end, Marianne touched her own unblemished skin. Her festering wound had closed without even leaving a scar.

"You know," Valdemar said as he rose to his feet, "I would like to paint you one day. You have a very beautiful face."

"I'm not sure how I should take that remark," Marianne said with a thin smile. "But it would be with pleasure."

"Take it however you want, you are quite graceful," Valdemar replied with a shrug. "Are your eyes—"

"I'm getting better." She could take a look for a few seconds before all the visual information overwhelmed her. Before she couldn't even open her eyes. "You look normal."

She heard him freeze in place. "What do you mean?"

"My eyes see everything now, but you look the same as you always did," she explained. "Human."

"I see," Valdemar said when he meant *thanks.* Marianne didn't need enhanced senses to notice his palpable relief. "You know, I'm supposed to summon a familiar tomorrow. From what I read, the creature reflects the summoner."

Marianne could read between the lines. *He's afraid the familiar will take more after his father's side of the family.* "I'm sure it will be a good friend and creature," she tried to reassure him. "If intention matters as much as action, then surely nurture counts as much as nature."

"I hope so." Valdemar let out a sigh before raising his hand, paint spreading to cover the window outside. "We better go to sleep. Lord Bethor is going to come wake us up in six hours."

"Alright," Marianne said, exhausted herself from both the operations and her own tests. She lay on her bed and covered herself with a bedsheet. "Good night."

"Good night," he replied before climbing on the bunk bed above her own.

A few minutes later, when Valdemar was snoring lightly, Marianne opened her eyes. She gazed at the darkness of the room and the painted forms dancing on the walls, at the blood coursing through the alien landscapes. Then she looked up at the bed above her.

She hoped that Valdemar had better dreams than her own.

31

UNFAMILIAR

He dreamed of rats that night. They crawled in a grotesque pit dug in black oily stone, squeaking and gnawing on the flesh of the innocent. Hundreds of sharp teeth sank into the bones of unbelievers, breaking it down to feast on the marrow. Their bloodshot red eyes saw movement in the darkness, their claws unable to let them climb the pit's smooth walls and escape it.

A batlike monster enjoyed a feast of its own at the pit's edge, drinking the blood of a human maiden it had caught by surprise. Its fangs had torn apart her neck and shattered her skull, but it wouldn't let a single drop escape its ravenous thirst. Once the beast had reduced its prey to a dry husk of skin, it tossed it in the pit and let the rats feed on the leftovers.

The underground temple was as large as a cathedral. Once it had been the chest and innards of a giant creature whose bones and flesh had turned to stone. Riblike pillars held the ceiling in place as cultists prayed before a central black monolith covered in eyes and grasping maws.

His altar.

His eyes observed his congregation. Fifty of them were in attendance, but he heard many more praise his name. Most were humans, but not all; lycans walked among them, whether they bore the rat plague or the wolf one. Their minds were fragile, wavering between the meandering illusion of humanity and the animal instinct. Even a few dark elves were in attendance, while a wererat apostle led the sermon.

Lepers desperate for release. Dregs of society, left to rot in the gutters with no one to care for them. Jaded aristocrats searching for forbidden pleasures only a god could offer. Old men wishing for new youth, and young girls asking for love. When they wore their red robes and pallid masks, they all looked the same.

No matter where they came from, they were of but one flesh.

They had heard his call—and *listened*.

"Ialdabaoth!" they chanted. "Our progenitor, Ialdabaoth! Father of All!"

They prayed for many things. For power, for love, for pleasure. For release from the pain, the illnesses, and the ravages of age. For immortality and eternal youth. For rapture.

For *more*.

As his apostle's plague spread among the downtrodden and his handmaiden's dreams tempted the minds of the elites, more asked to join the brotherhood. Followers of false idols abandoned their faith to turn to the true god. His power grew with each new piece of rebellious flesh returning to his embrace.

His mother watched the proceeding from a dark dais. She was younger and more beautiful than ever, her white skin unblemished, her raven hair as lustrous as the deepest darkness. Her eyes had turned bloodred, gazing down on the congregation with the cold curiosity of an alien, soulless thing. All the worshipers desired her fiercely, but none dared to approach her. She existed as an object of desire, a forbidden fruit: tempting, but forever beyond reach.

The time to feed was at hand.

"Who shall offer his life to the Master of Masters?" the rat apostle asked. "Who shall prove their faith?"

Many whispered, but none obeyed the command. They were new. Tempted, but not loyal yet. The chosen had taught them fear and desire, but not faith.

At last, a man stepped forward, revealing the fur and the tumors beneath his red hood, the animal's face beneath his mask. He had lost his teeth and his skin had been wrinkled by time, homelessness, and alcohol. Mankind had cast him out long before the apostle's plague took root in him and his life had been forfeited to lung disease.

"Take me," the man rasped, his hands trembling. "Save me. Please . . ."

"Do you submit to the knife?" The rat apostle asked, revealing a sacrificial athame hidden beneath his robes. "Only the faithful will be rewarded."

But the man submitted all the same. His faith was born out of despair and loneliness; this man had nothing left to lose but his life. The mutant knelt before the altar and let the apostle do his work.

The faithful's screams filled the temple, as the knife peeled the skin off the sacrifice's flesh.

Other cultists trembled and recoiled at the temple, though his mother continued to watch with unblinking eyes. Fear filled their weak hearts and some glanced at the bat beast; only fear of retaliation prevented them from running away. Others watched on with curiosity and fascination.

Skins were prisons. They split individuals from the whole, denying him the brotherhood of the united flesh. The skin let minds build barriers from the darkness of *his* dreams and allowed the soul to lie to itself. It allowed the rebellious flesh to imagine a future away from *him*.

At long last, when the sacrifice had shed his skin like its clothes, the altar deemed him worthy. One of its mouths opened wide, a black tongue slithering between sharp fangs. The flayed sacrifice offered no resistance as the organ coiled around his waist and pulled him down the maw's gullet. The altar swallowed him whole while the rat apostle took the skin for future use.

He felt the sacrifice inside him, gnawed and chewed by his altar. The man's flesh joined with his own, returning from which it came. And as this willing soul embraced his authority, his magic started to reshape him. His soul surrendered its shell of humanity and welcomed the eldritch kinship.

After a minute of gnawing and chewing, the altar spat out the reborn sacrifice.

Gone was the twisted, sickly mutant that came in. A naked man stood before the altar, tall, strong, healthy, and vigorous. His muscles were stronger than steel, his skin a smooth and perfect disguise. His body radiated power and sexual magnetism. His hands could shatter stone and no weapon could claim his life.

The cultists watched, their fear replaced with veneration, lust, and desire. Before them stood the pinnacle of mankind, the ideal man. The sacrifice had walked into the altar a piece of worthless lead and walked out made of priceless gold.

"Worthy!" the rat apostle shouted in ecstatic delight, his words echoed by the congregation. "Worthy!"

His mother was pleased as she watched. The flock's fears were gone, replaced with hope and ambition. Their faith had been strengthened. All of them would lie, and steal, and kill to join the worthy. For the promise of power and immortality. And in due time, all would forswear their souls and flesh.

They were themselves, but they were also him.

They were masks for him to wear, husks through which his will manifested.

A god with a thousand faces and a million limbs.

"You will never grow old," his mother said as she descended from the dais to congratulate the faithful. The cultists all fell silent to hear her prophetic words. "You will be young forever. Your seed will take root in any soil, and no woman will resist you. Death will never claim your soul, so long as your faith remains true."

"Thank you," the sacrifice said as he touched his perfect skin with his fingers. "This feels . . . better than *anything*."

His mother smiled. It looked perfect and genuine, yet it was anything but. In truth, she looked down on these creatures so easily led astray. They entertained her, like sheep greeting their shepherd before walking into the slaughterhouse.

She was a higher being, a handmaiden of the Nahemoths, and among the greatest of the Qlippoths. Her god had willed her into existence for a mission, and she would fulfill it. No matter how many lives she had to take.

She glanced at her flock of sacrificial lambs. "All of you can become the best version of yourselves through the will of Ialdabaoth," his mother said. "All of you can be reborn, if you swear loyalty to the Red Grail and the Holy Blood who are one!"

"I swear!" an old man said while raising his hand, eager to escape the icy breath of death.

"I swear!" a nobleman joined in, lusting for the forbidden knowledge and power no money could buy.

"I swear!" a lovestruck woman declared, desiring the beauty that would catch her crush's eyes.

All swore one after the other, to his mother's pleasure.

"Go forth and spread the word!" she commanded them. "Shepherd the faithful into our flock and subjugate the unbelievers! Cast down the false idols of the Dark Lords and their thralls! Exterminate the gray dwarves who would deny our father's will! Only by proving your faith shall you join the worthy and the Promised Land!"

Her electric words filled her flock's hearts as she waved her hand. Space bent around the cultists, letting them slip from the temple and back into the world outside. "Go kill in his name," his mother ordered the sacrifice. "Stalk the night and teach them fear. Show them that as long as they hold the prince away from us, their subjects will pay the price. Let our enemies howl in despair, for we have returned."

"As you wish," the sacrifice said with a smile, his teeth pointed like a great beast's fangs. The former human relished the task; society had rejected him, and now he had the power to strike back. Vengeance always tasted better when sweetened with blood.

His mother teleported the sacrifice away, remaining alone in the temple with the rat apostle. Her pet bat came to her, submitting to her will.

"Their faith is weak," the rat apostle rasped with contempt, his athame still covered in blood. "Good Shelley doesn't trust them. They do not *understand* yet."

"They will serve all the same," his mother replied while scratching her vampire pet's head. "But I agree that you alone were faithful without expecting anything in return. As a reward for your devotion, I shall grant your wish."

Good Shelley licked his lips. "How many more skins?"

"Twenty more at least, with the right age and sex. Women will help sew it, but they cannot contain the male essence. Once it is done, I shall guide it back from the beyond . . . and the mortals shall know fear."

"Good Shelley has awaited this day for years, Milady," the rat apostle rasped. "It shall be done. The good Shelley lives to serve."

"I know." His mother smiled and looked at the altar. "See how devoted he is, my prince? All that we do in your name?"

His countless eyes blinked.

"I know you are watching," the *thing* disguising itself as his mother said with soft lips. "I cannot stop you. This world is your birthright."

"He is watching us?" Shelley cackled in delight and knelt. "Good Shelley begs for forgiveness, my lord! He thought you were dead, dead like Crétail!"

Crétail?

"Come to me," the woman whispered, as softly as a lover. "I am here. I was made for you, to guide you, to serve you. To lead you to your glorious destiny. I am your handmaiden, your slave. Come to me. I will show you true pleasure."

He felt her words echoing in his mind like twisted temptation. The sensation filled him with a mix of horrid lust and horrible revulsion. How did this *thing* dare to use his mother's face and offer him such a thing?

"The Dark Lords are deceiving you, my prince," the creature whispered, her red eyes haunting as they peered into his own. "They will use you for their own selfish gain and then they shall discard you. Don't you want to know who is at the well's bottom? He is in great pain, my prince."

He closed his eyes, and Valdemar woke up gasping for air.

"Valdemar?" Marianne asked from the bed below his own. "Valdemar, what is going on?"

The summoner didn't answer immediately. Instead, his eyes fixated on the painted ceiling above his head. Once it showed pictures of moths and the Silent King's realm. Now the surface had changed, representing the twisted temple of the flesh and its terrible congregation.

His mother stood at the center of it all, looking back at him.

"They are rebuilding their cult?" Lord Bethor asked, his eyes peering through his armor's helmet.

Valdemar nodded as he finished drawing the summoning circle on the ground with his own blood. It was his most complex one yet, combining hexagrams, alchemical symbols, ancient runes, and multiple other symbols forming elaborate patterns. If anything, Valdemar was thankful for the ritual. He needed something to take his mind off the dream.

Due to the risks involved with summoning familiars, Lord Bethor had elected to run the ritual in an isolated chamber in his tower's bowels . . . though Valdemar wouldn't go as far as to call it a room. It was a cube of steel with only one door for exit.

This man allows himself no pleasure, the summoner thought as he observed Valar Bethor. He had yet to see any kind of decoration in the tower that didn't serve a functional purpose.

Marianne kept her arms crossed, her back against a wall. She had barely spoken since she had noticed the transformed Bertrand among the painted congregation.

"What I don't get is why I dreamed at all," Valdemar said as he finished the circle. He thought his Painted Field would prevent it. "It was even worse than the well."

"The Painted Field works as an artificial dreamscape," Valar Bethor pointed out. "A dreamscape protects you from intrusions from the Primordial Dream and the Outer Darkness. However, I suspect that by mentally closing yourself to these two realms, your power sought release through another medium."

"The Blood," Valdemar guessed as he looked at his own hand.

No matter how hard he tried, he couldn't escape his bloodline.

"Yes," Lord Bethor said. "We have no reason to trust the Lilith's words, but if she is speaking the truth, then she cannot prevent you from observing them. This could prove invaluable to gathering information on their activities."

"A Lilith?" Marianne asked with a frown. "I read about them in the Bestiary."

"They're the handmaidens of the Nahemoths and the second strongest Qlippoths," Valdemar explained while clenching his fists in rage. "They embody lust, especially the perverse and the taboo kinds; but unlike other Qlippoths they don't have a stable form. Instead, they possess living vessels, devour the soul until only a husk remains, and then spread madness and destruction."

Marianne took the information and quickly put two and two together, biting her lips. "The lab," she whispered. "That cloud thing that emerged from the black wound and attacked me . . ."

"She was trying to possess you." Valdemar gritted his teeth in rage. "And when she failed, the Lilith settled on an easier vessel."

That disgusting creature had jumped into one of his mother's clones, despoiling her flesh and taking it as a host. She had then teleported to Astaphanos to haunt him, only to retreat and avoid exposing herself. She must have contacted Shelley afterward, masterminding the wererat plague and turning her attention to recruiting new cultists. With her powers, it would have been child's play to find vulnerable, ambitious people and entice them with promises.

Though the thought of attacking his mother's image filled him with revulsion, Valdemar knew what he had to do when they crossed paths. He couldn't let that foul monster make a mockery of his mother.

And the vile way she had tried to tempt him . . . the thought still left a disgusting taste in his mouth. *I'll kill her,* Valdemar promised with a heart full of anger. *I'll add her to the cohort of the dead.*

Dead like Crétail.

Shelley's words still haunted Valdemar, alongside what the Lilith had said. *He is suffering?* the summoner thought. *Nahemoths don't have a gender. It makes no sense.*

Had the cultists been trying to confuse him and tempt him with knowledge? Or maybe Marianne's gut was correct and this "Crétail" word mattered more than it seemed.

"I still don't get how they can teleport," Valdemar admitted. "Liliths have multiple abilities, but bending space isn't one of them."

"I think I can guess how," Marianne said softly, catching Valdemar's gaze. "It's the same way Lord Och moves around. He soaked his fortress with his blood and teleports by using it as an anchor. Since Ialdabaoth's body covers all of Underland and his messenger leads the cult—"

"They can access any tunnel that we Dark Lords didn't ward with powerful magic," Valar Bethor finished. "Clever."

Valdemar frowned. "You do not sound surprised, Lord Bethor."

"This was one of the theories I entertained when plague cases started appearing in areas under my purview without triggering the Earthmouths' alarms." The Dark Lord immediately thought about a war plan. "We need to destroy this Lilith. Once the rat and his mistress are gone, the rest will follow. They are lost weaklings led astray by empty promises, damned souls that won't do anything without a strong master to whip them into action."

"Do you think you could locate their temple?" Marianne asked Valdemar, though she was clearly unsure of herself. "I . . . this would be risky, but . . ."

"But it might be the only way to find Bertrand," Valdemar finished her sentence, causing Marianne to look away. "It's alright. I promised I would help."

"I shall be present next time you sleep," Lord Bethor declared. "By combining our powers, we shall coax out the Blood's secrets. *After* you summon your familiar."

Valdemar couldn't help but chuckle. This man was relentless.

Marianne protested though. "Lord Bethor, shouldn't we focus on the dream connection instead? If they can look back into him the same way he can observe them . . ."

"They cannot," Lord Bethor replied dryly. "Or else they would have already contacted their 'prince' long ago. A wise slave does not see the world through their master's eyes."

Marianne didn't look convinced, but she knew better than to argue with the Dark Lord further.

Focusing on the task at hand, Valdemar touched the circle with his bloody hands and chanted the words of power. "Oh, planes of power," he recited the formulas. "I beseech you, listen to my call!"

As the circle brightened and the Blood called to the planes beyond Underland, Valdemar remembered his discussion with Valar Bethor about familiars.

A familiar is a living conduit between its summoner and the planes, the Dark Lord had explained to him. *By binding yourself to one, you will bypass the need of a summoning circle. However, familiars are attuned to specific dimensions and entities. Some will even refuse to summon creatures whose nature they abhor.*

Do you have one, Lord Bethor? Valdemar had asked, having seen him summon a Gnawer without a circle.

Yes . . . but pray you never meet it.

"I call thee, my other half!" Valdemar shouted as space started to bend inside the circle. "Cross the veil and join me! I offer thee my blood if you would share my life until all is dust!"

"What is he calling?" Marianne asked, slightly anxious as crimson lightning erupted from the circle and illuminated the room. "An animal? A demon? An elemental?"

"This ritual calls the creature best suited for the summoner's nature," Lord Bethor replied. "Fools try to use catalysts to call a specific familiar, but true mages should only rely on their own power."

"What if he summons a Qlippoth or something hostile to humans?"

Valdemar had asked himself the same question. Besides the difficulty in summoning one, the reason why familiars were uncommon was that they *weren't* under the caster's control. Sometimes they even actively resisted the bonding process, with many summoners having perished at the fangs and claws of their "partners."

"I will kill it," the Dark Lord replied dismissively, "and he shall try again. It will tear out a part of his soul each time, but eventually he will summon a good match."

Even so, from what Valdemar had understood, summoning the familiar was only half the work. Afterward, the sorcerer would have to attune his soul to it and strengthen the bond between them. A process that could take days, months, or *years*.

Thankfully, the summoning spell wouldn't take so long.

I'm sensing it, Valdemar thought as he looked into the circle. The veil between the planes grew thinner, images crossing through the boundaries between universes. Pictures of endless waters beneath dark skies formed in his mind, alongside the twisted geometries of abyssal cities. *A dark ocean . . .*

Something swam in the waters on the other side, sensing his call and answering it. A telepathic presence contacted Valdemar's mind, cold and alien. The summoner felt invisible, squamous tentacles brush against his brain as they tried to figure out how it worked. Whatever the creature's nature, it had clearly never encountered humans before.

Valdemar didn't detect any hostility in the mental contact, only childish curiosity and playfulness. *I'm here,* he thought as space rippled inside the circle. *Just a tiny bit closer and I will show you a whole new world.*

His familiar happily accepted and broke past the veil.

Space shattered for a brief second, and a creature the size of a human baby stumbled through. It disrupted the summoning circle as it rolled on the ground, the magic in the air dissipating in a bright flash of red light.

Valdemar locked eyes with his familiar's. All six of them.

Is this my other half? Valdemar thought as the creature looked up at him with curiosity. He had never seen such a strange chimera. The alien entity was vaguely humanoid, but with blue-green skin and the head of a squid. Its tentacles moved around independently as they touched the steel ground, while two batlike purple wings flapped in its back. The creature had two large black eyes around the same place as humans and four more on the sides of its head. It was clearly a baby of some sort, with short, underdeveloped limbs and four webbed fingers.

It was . . .

It was quite cute.

"Lord Bethor?" Marianne asked with a chuckle. She clearly found the familiar as strangely adorable as Valdemar himself. "What kind of creature is this?"

But the Dark Lord squinted behind his helmet, his tone wary. "I do not know."

Neither did Valdemar. The creature didn't resemble any Qlippoth or outsider that the summoner was aware of. Perhaps it came from the elemental plane of water? Or a dimension close to it?

The Dark Lord's cold response instantly put Marianne on her guard, but Valdemar simply looked at his familiar with curiosity. The beast tried to stand on its tiny legs before touching its summoner with its tentacles. They were cold and salty to the touch, but they wriggled in happiness when Valdemar scratched the creature on the cheeks. *Pretty friendly for an alien entity,* the summoner thought with amusement.

"Ct . . ." The creature started to make noise with its strange voice. It sounded like a human speaking underwater. "Hu . . . lhu . . ."

"You can talk?" Valdemar asked with a frown, ignoring the wary gazes Lord Bethor and Marianne sent him. "What's your name?"

Whether because it had learned the human tongue through their brief mental contact or something else, the creature seemed to understand his words and gave an answer.

"Ktulul!" the creature said while waving its tiny hands. "Ktulhu! Tulu!"

Was that its name? Ktulu? Though it might be wearing a disguise of some kind or grow into an abomination, Valdemar found it hard to keep his guard up in the familiar's presence. It radiated that aura humans felt in the presence of babies and that inspired protective urges.

If the creature was a reflection of himself, then Valdemar had to hope it was good inside. For both of their sake.

"Ktulu," the summoner said as he grabbed his familiar and cradled him like a child. The creature was no heavier than a cat and just as affectionate. "I will call you Ktulu."

Valdemar wondered how it would look once all grown-up though.

ABOUT THE AUTHOR

Maxime J. Durand, also known as Void Herald, is a wizard from the magical land of France who ceased studying law to write stories about dragon adventurers, time travelers with depression, and magicians trying to cure death (and life, too). Now, he can't stop.

Podium
DISCOVER
STORIES UNBOUND
PodiumAudio.com